W9-BYF-717

**Please check all items for damages
before leaving the Library.
Thereafter you will be held
responsible for all injuries
to items beyond reasonable wear.**

Helen M. Plum Memorial Library

Lombard, Illinois

A daily fine will be charged for
overdue materials.

THE WORLD OF QUEST

VOLUME TWO

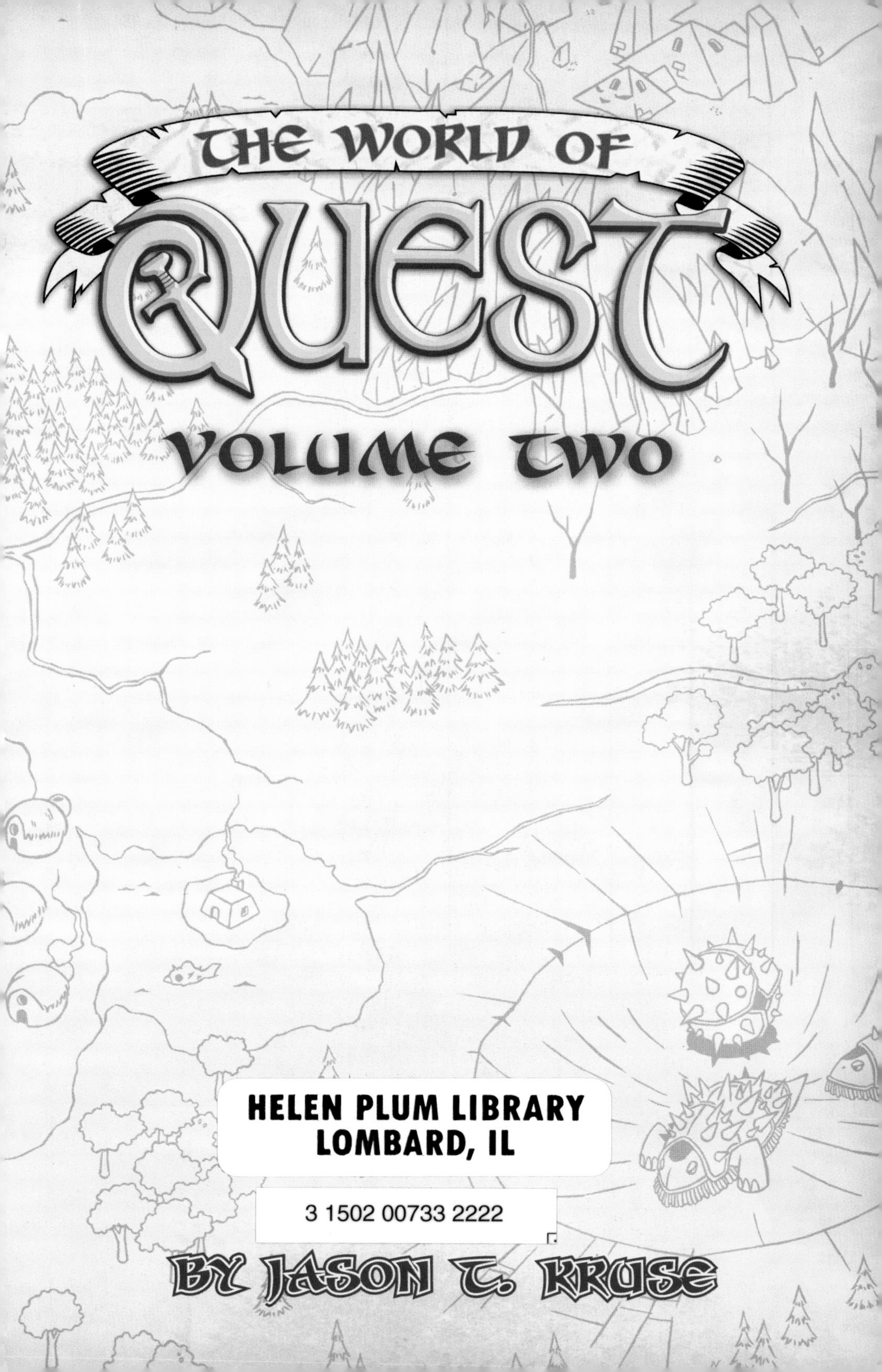

BY JASON T. KRUSE

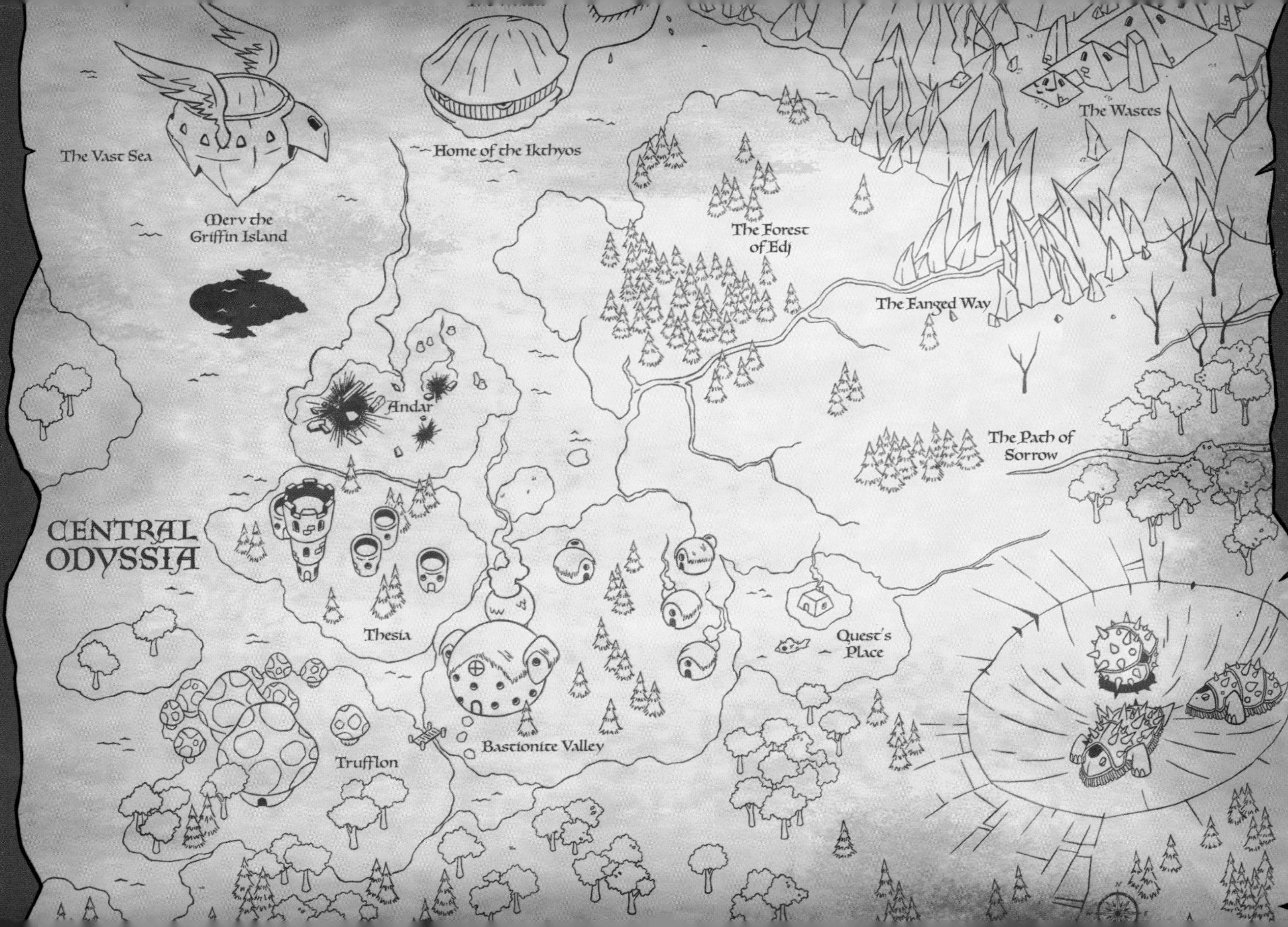

CENTRAL ODYSSIA
The Vast Sea
Merv the Griffin Island
Home of the Ikthyos
The Wastes
The Forest of Edj
The Fanged Way
Andar
The Path of Sorrow
Thesia
Quest's Place
Bastionite Valley
Trufflon

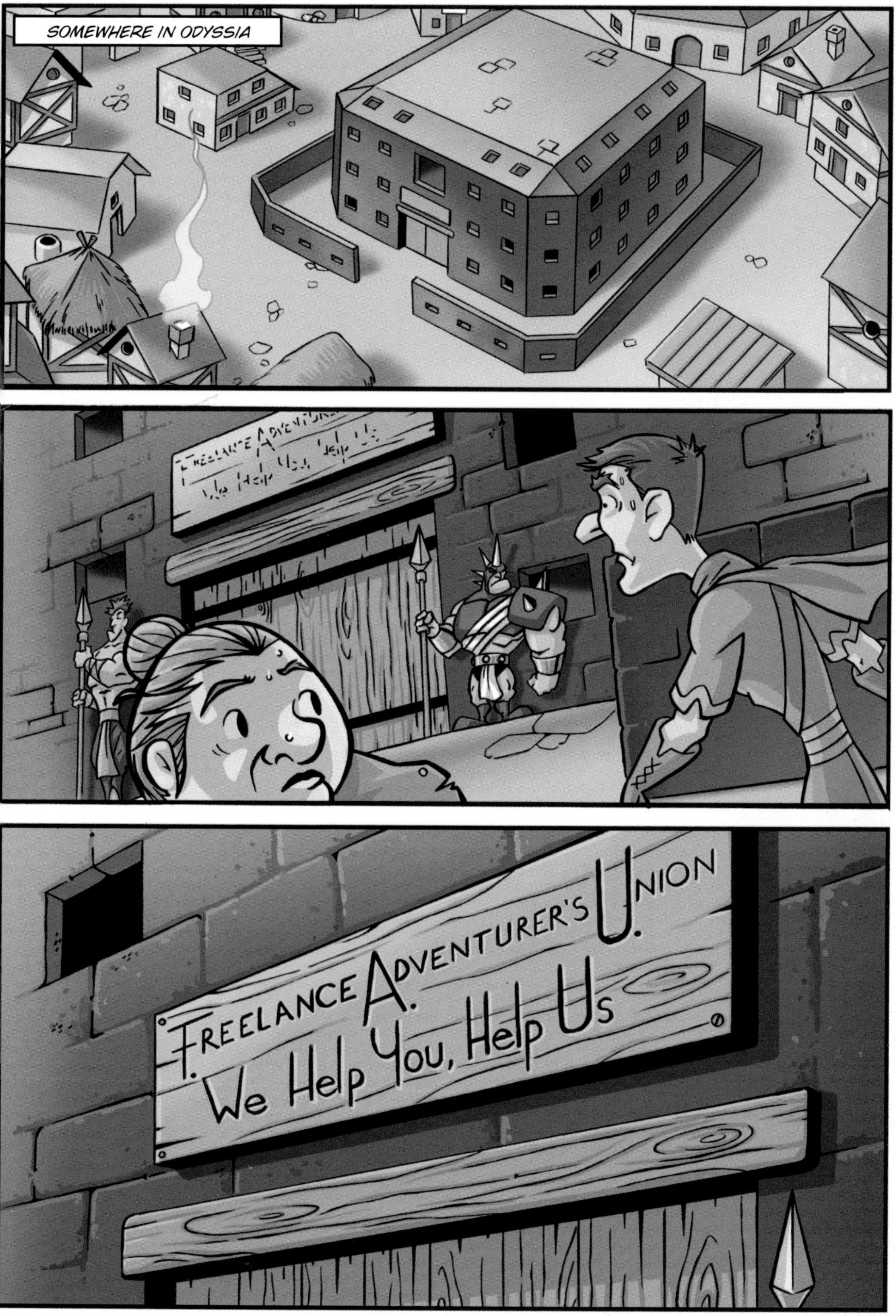
SOMEWHERE IN ODYSSIA
FREELANCE ADVENTURER'S UNION
F. A. U.
We Help You, Help Us

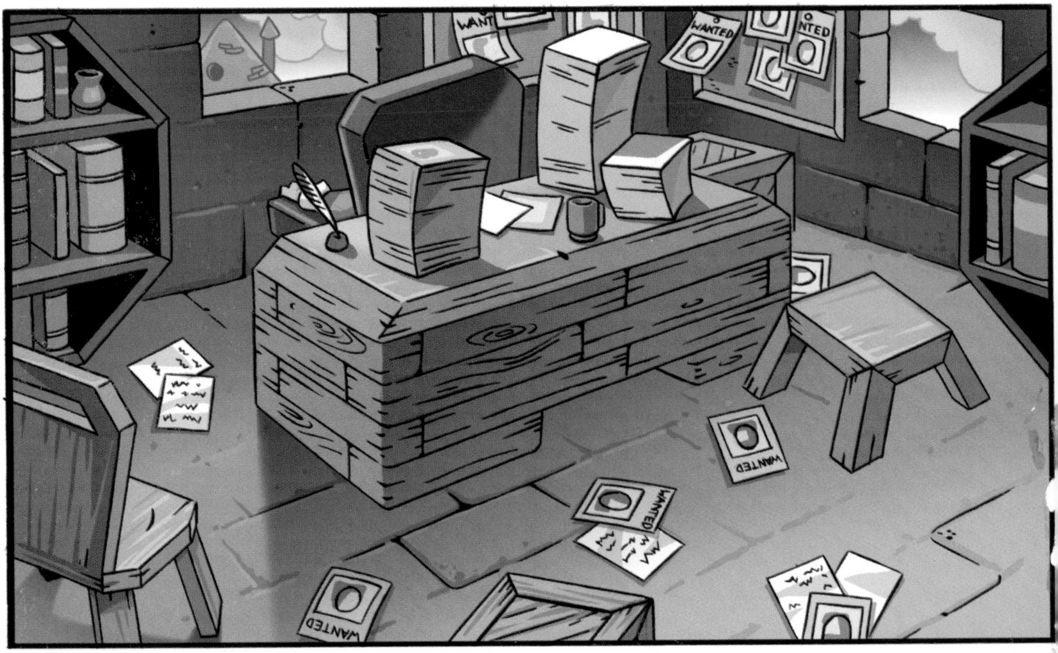
WANTED
WANTED
WANTED
WANTED
WANTED

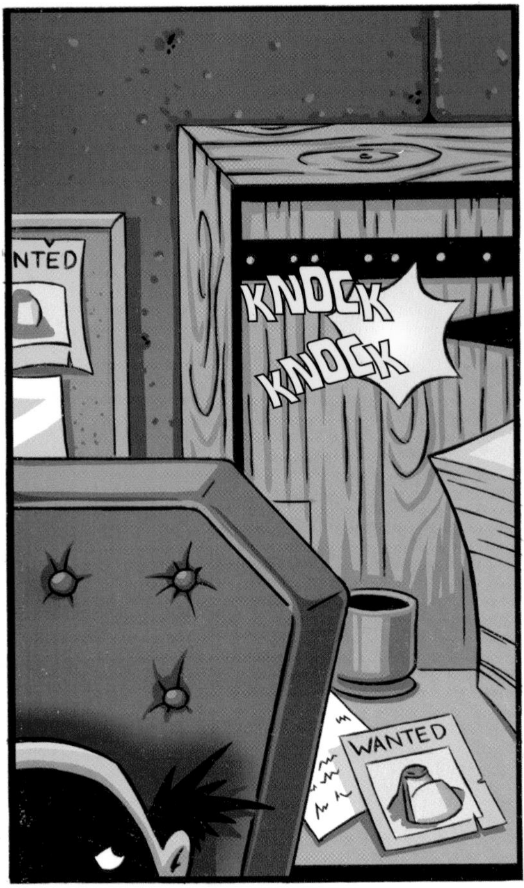
NTED
KNOCK
KNOCK
WANTED

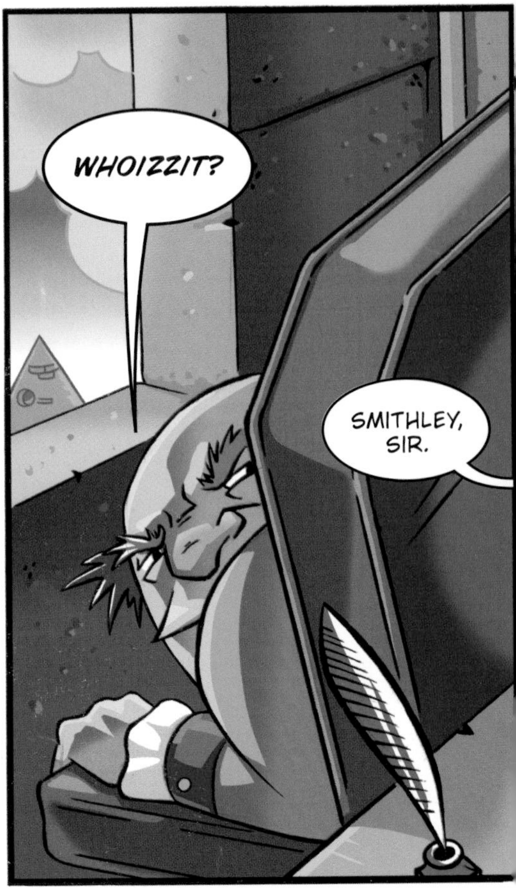
WHOIZZIT?
SMITHLEY, SIR.

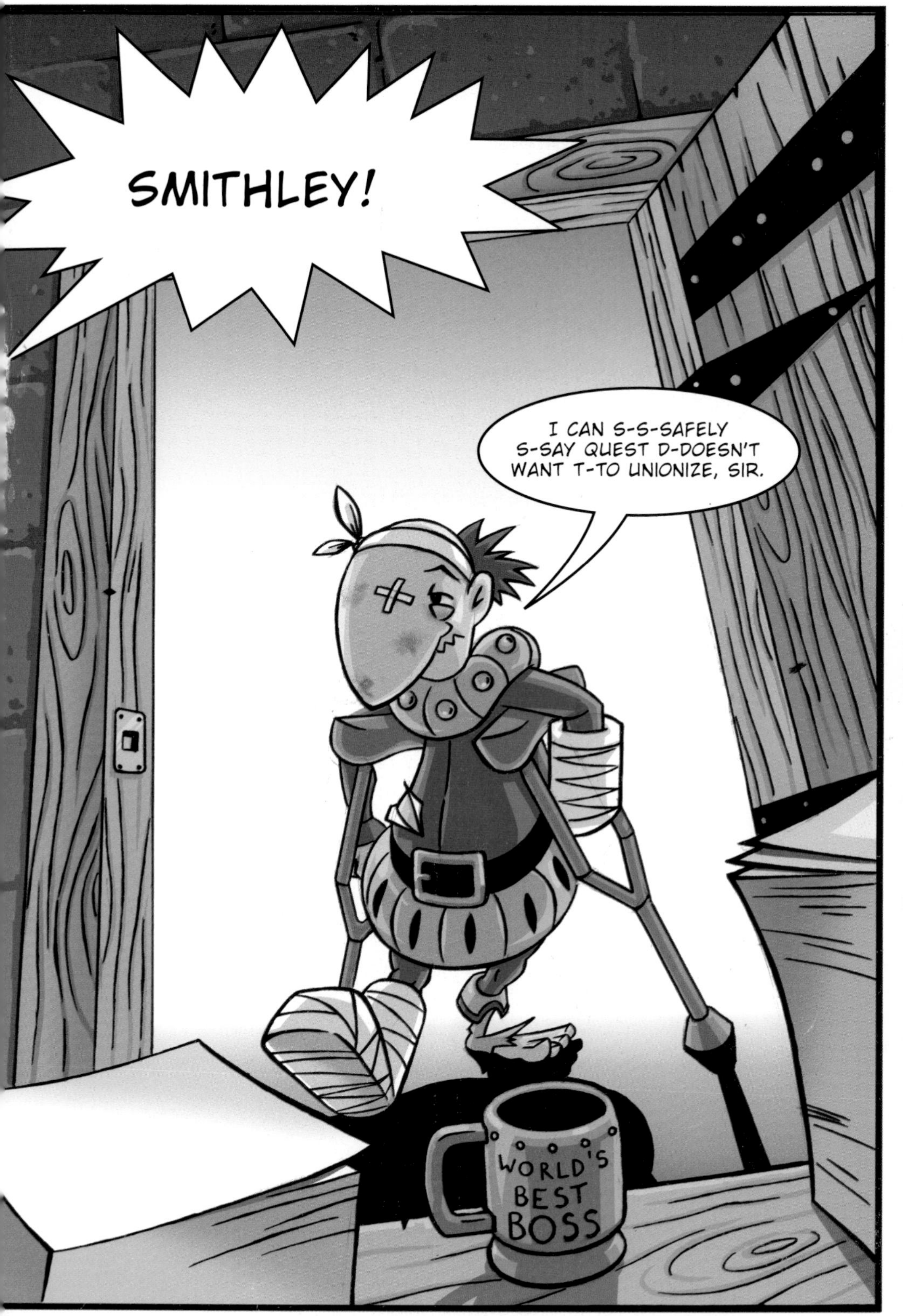
SMITHLEY!
I CAN S-S-SAFELY S-SAY QUEST D-DOESN'T WANT T-TO UNIONIZE, SIR.
WORLD'S BEST BOSS

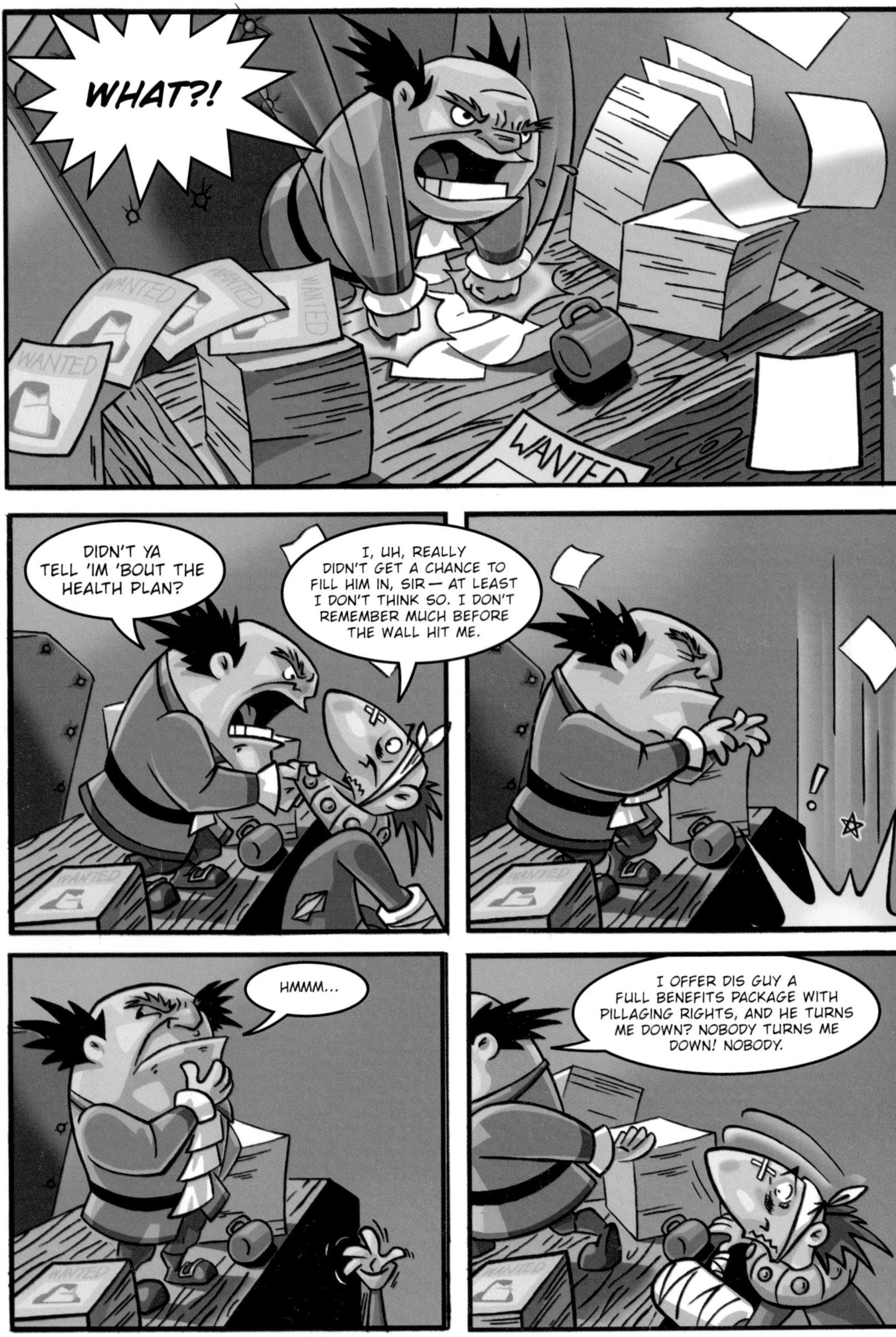
WHAT?!
DIDN'T YA TELL 'IM 'BOUT THE HEALTH PLAN?
I, UH, REALLY DIDN'T GET A CHANCE TO FILL HIM IN, SIR— AT LEAST I DON'T THINK SO. I DON'T REMEMBER MUCH BEFORE THE WALL HIT ME.
WANTED
HMMM...
I OFFER DIS GUY A FULL BENEFITS PACKAGE WITH PILLAGING RIGHTS, AND HE TURNS ME DOWN? NOBODY TURNS ME DOWN! NOBODY.

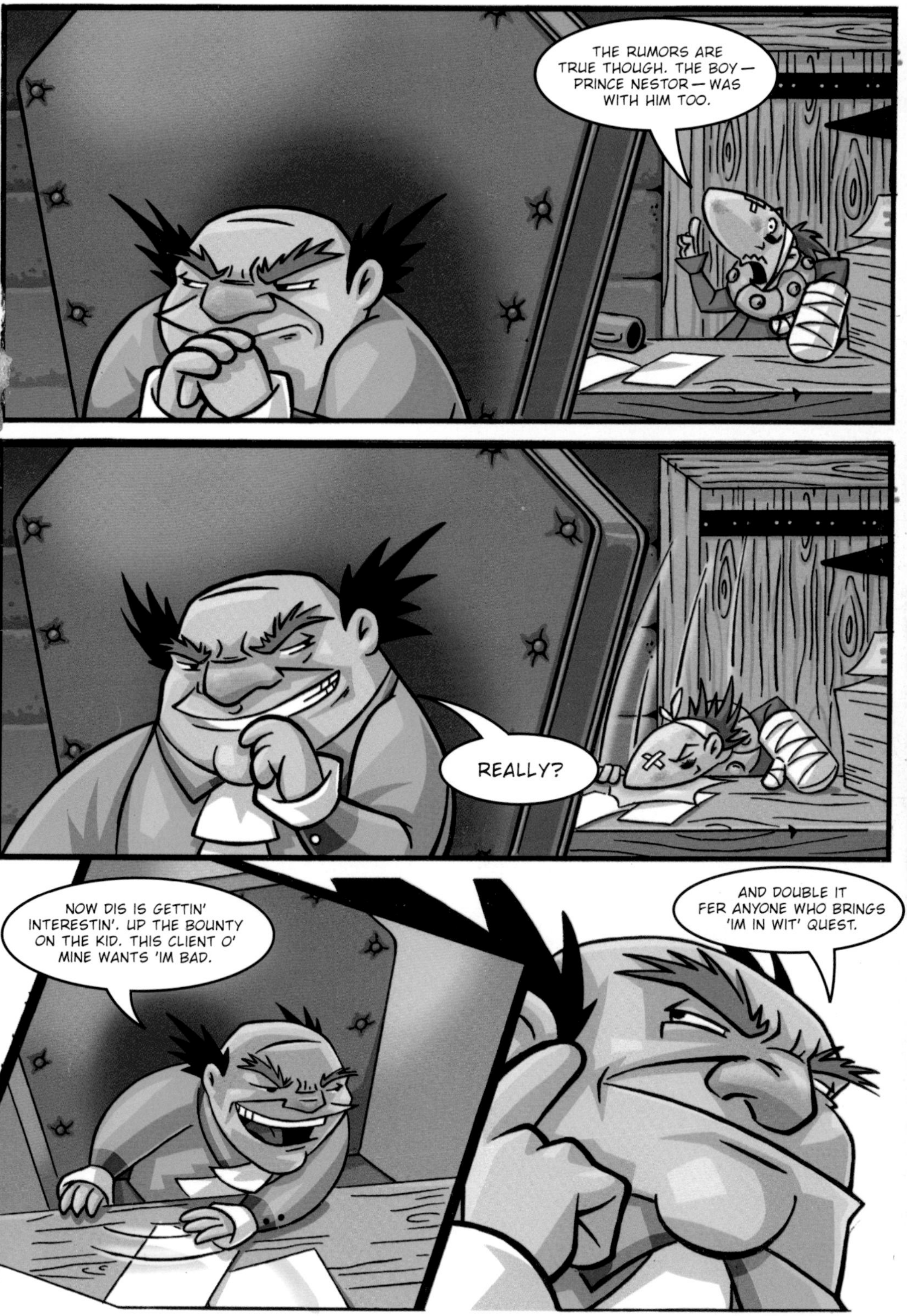
THE RUMORS ARE TRUE THOUGH. THE BOY— PRINCE NESTOR—WAS WITH HIM TOO.
REALLY?
NOW DIS IS GETTIN' INTERESTIN'. UP THE BOUNTY ON THE KID. THIS CLIENT O' MINE WANTS 'IM BAD.
AND DOUBLE IT FER ANYONE WHO BRINGS 'IM IN WIT' QUEST.

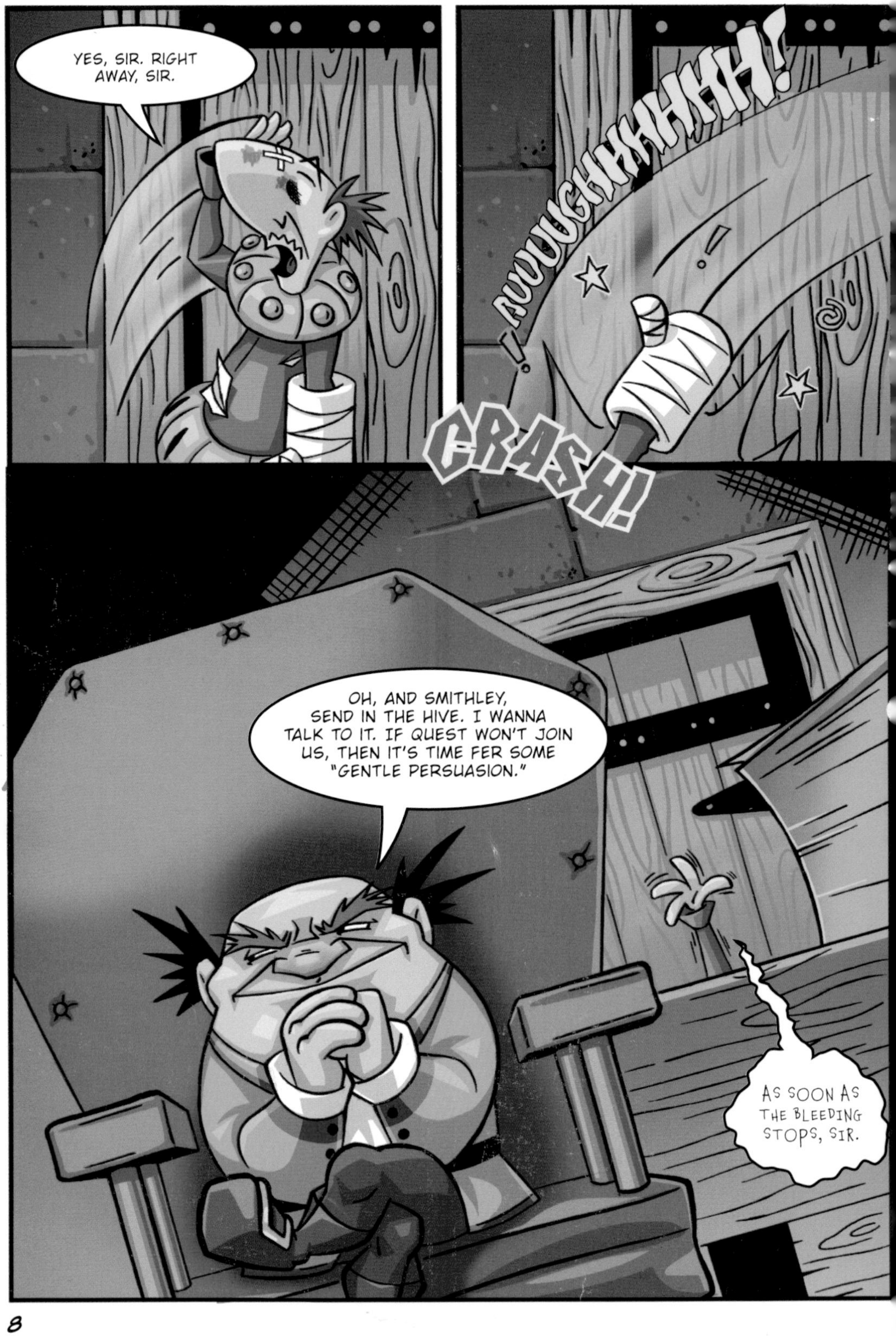
YES, SIR. RIGHT AWAY, SIR.
AUUUGHHHHHHH!
CRASH!
OH, AND SMITHLEY, SEND IN THE HIVE. I WANNA TALK TO IT. IF QUEST WON'T JOIN US, THEN IT'S TIME FER SOME "GENTLE PERSUASION."
AS SOON AS THE BLEEDING STOPS, SIR.

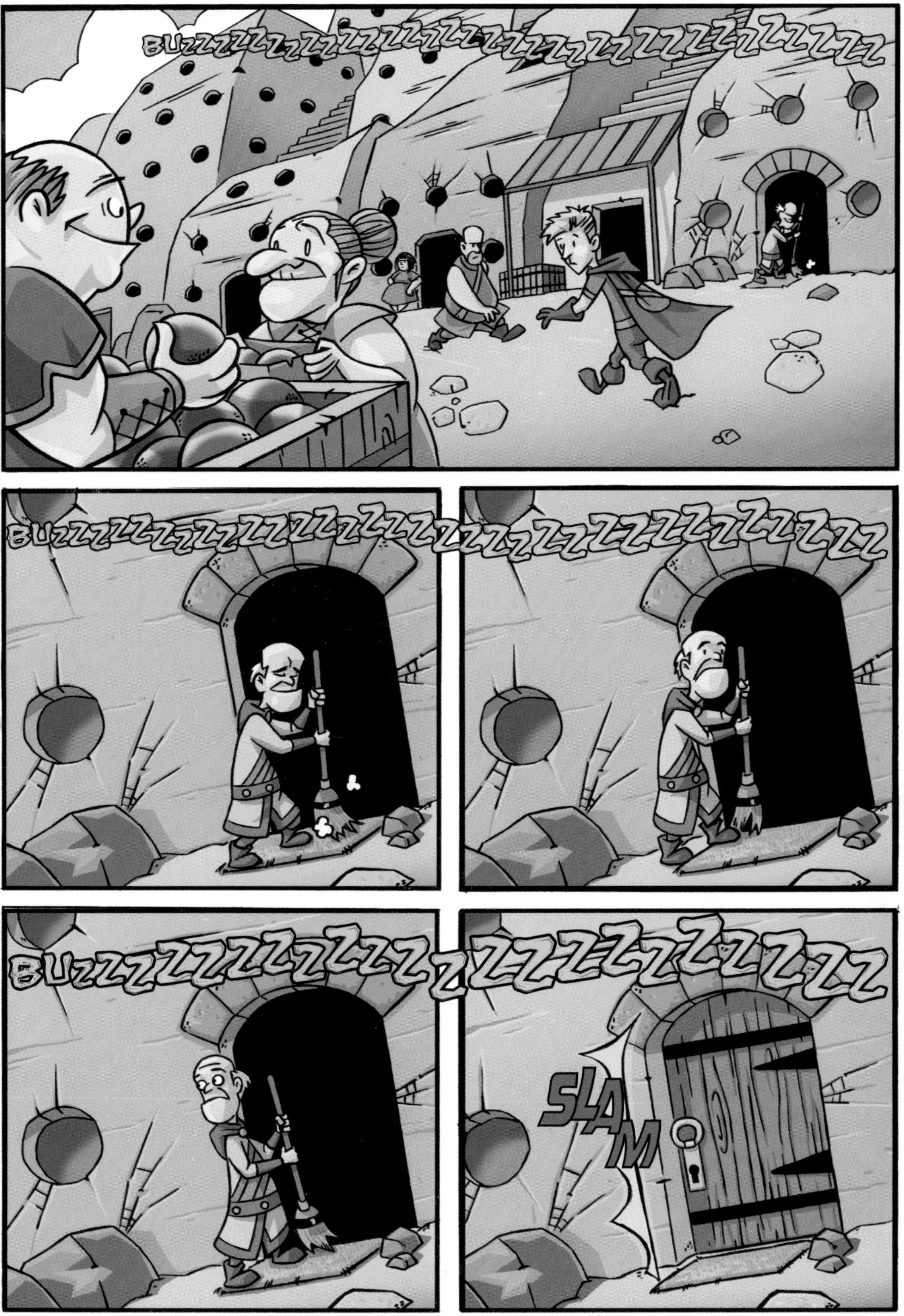
BUZZZZZZZZZZZZZZZZZZZZZZZZZZZZZZZZZZZ
BUZZZZZZZZZZZZZZZZZZZZZZZZZZZZZZZZZZZZZ
BUZZZZZZZZZZZZZZZZZZZZZZZZZ
SLAM

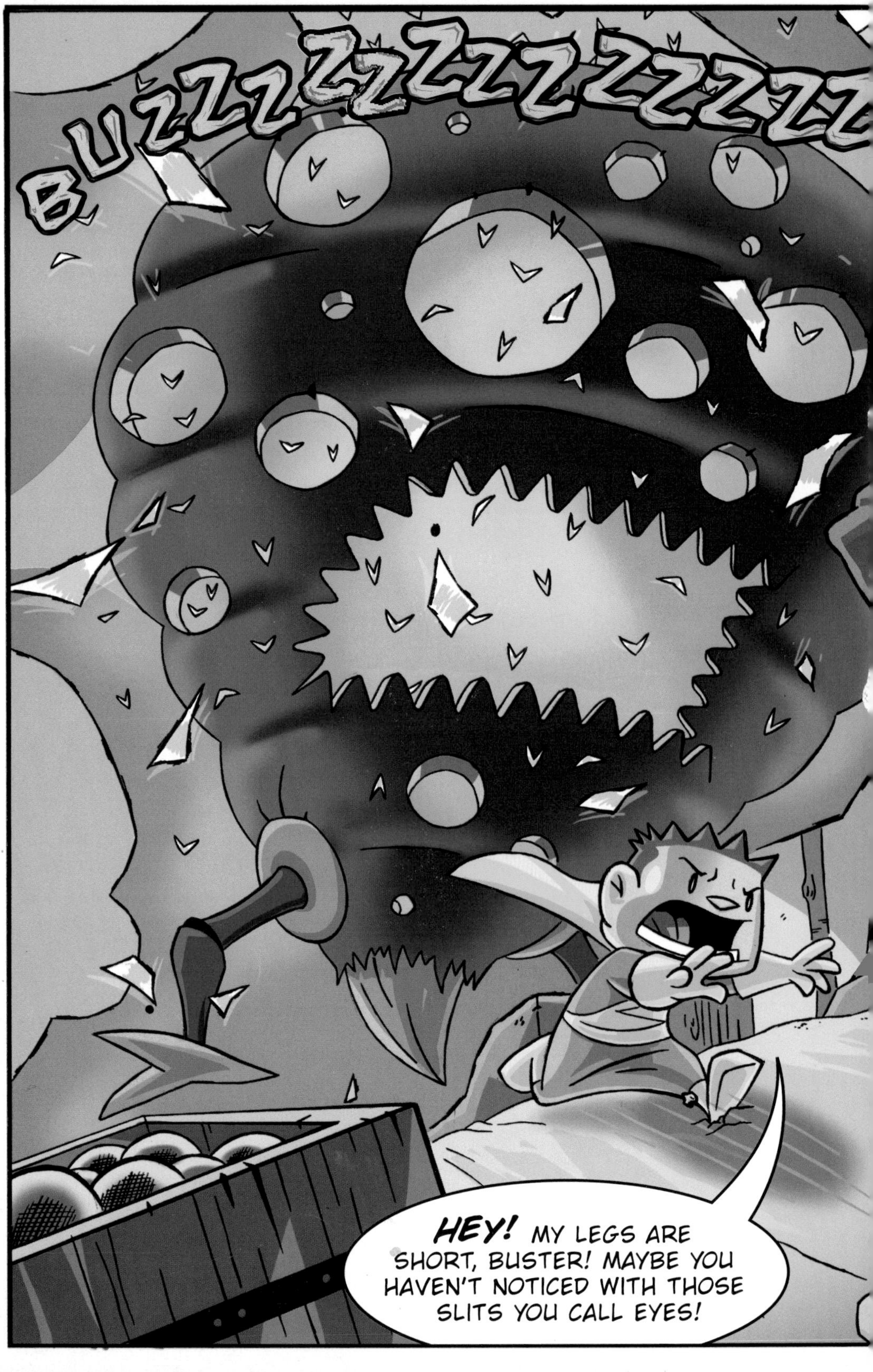
BUZZZZZZZZZZZZZ
HEY! MY LEGS ARE SHORT, BUSTER! MAYBE YOU HAVEN'T NOTICED WITH THOSE SLITS YOU CALL EYES!

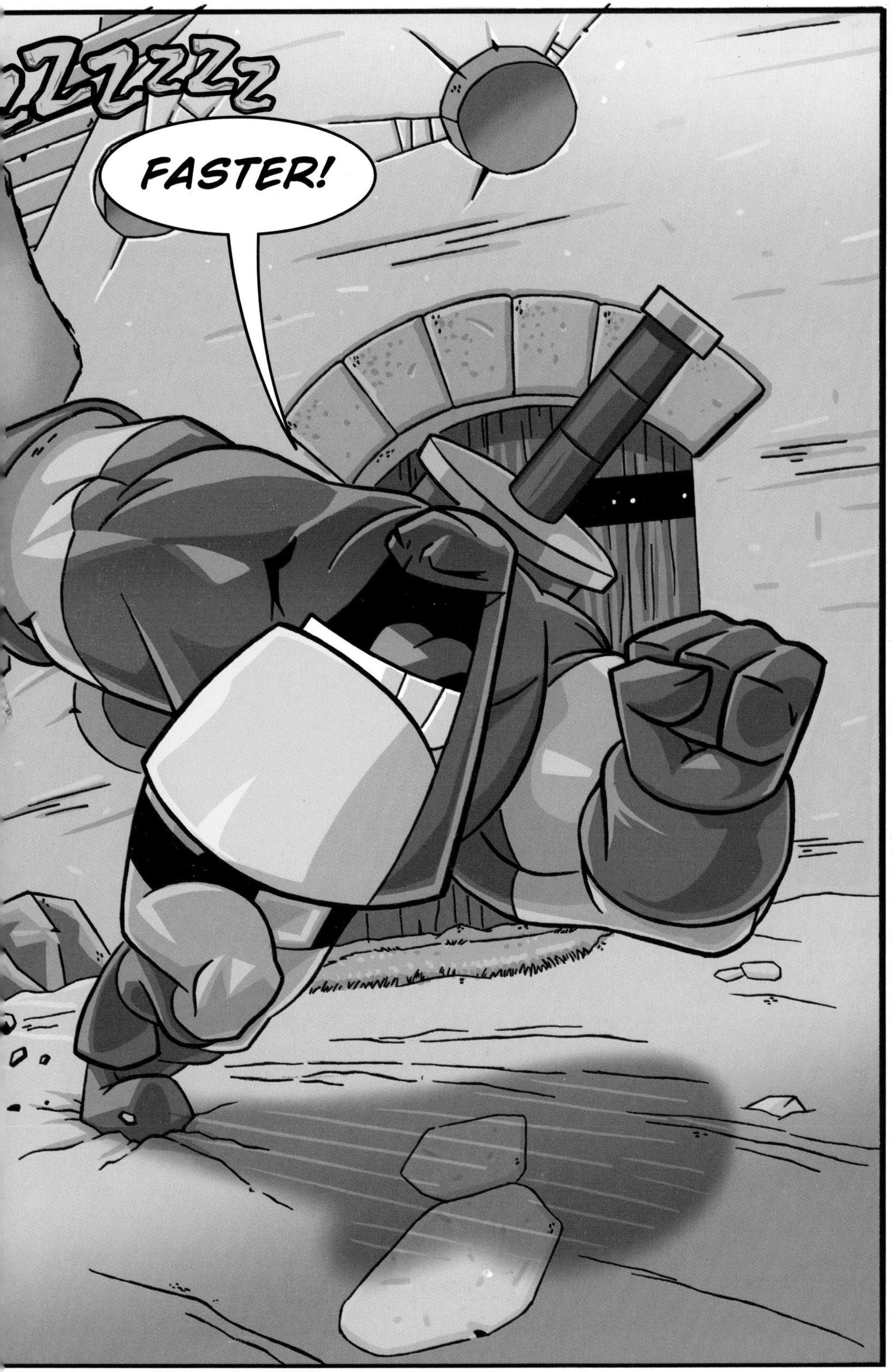
ZZZZZZz
FASTER!

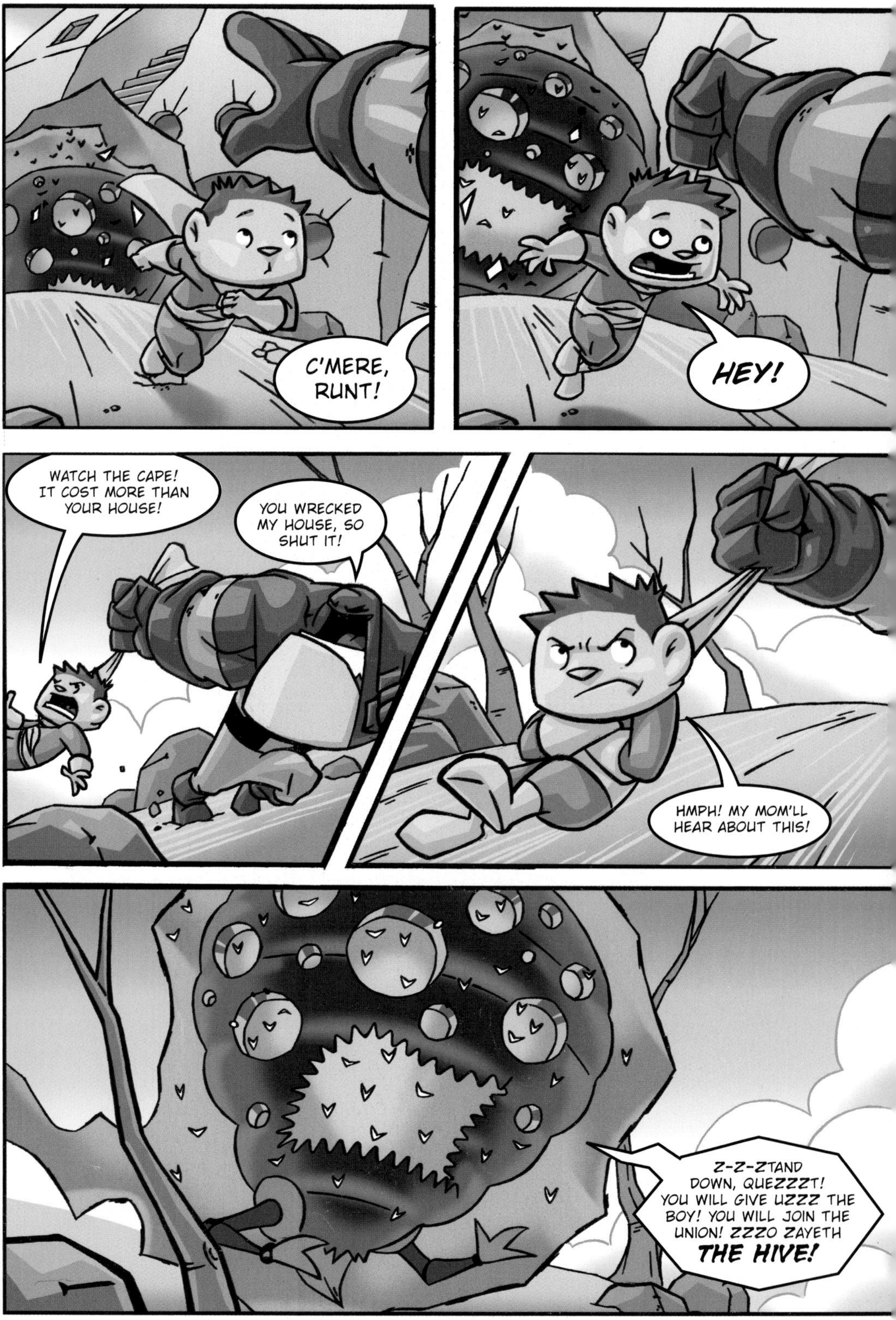
C'MERE, RUNT!
HEY!
WATCH THE CAPE! IT COST MORE THAN YOUR HOUSE!
YOU WRECKED MY HOUSE, SO SHUT IT!
HMPH! MY MOM'LL HEAR ABOUT THIS!
Z-Z-ZTAND DOWN, QUEZZZT! YOU WILL GIVE UZZZ THE BOY! YOU WILL JOIN THE UNION! ZZZO ZAYETH THE HIVE!

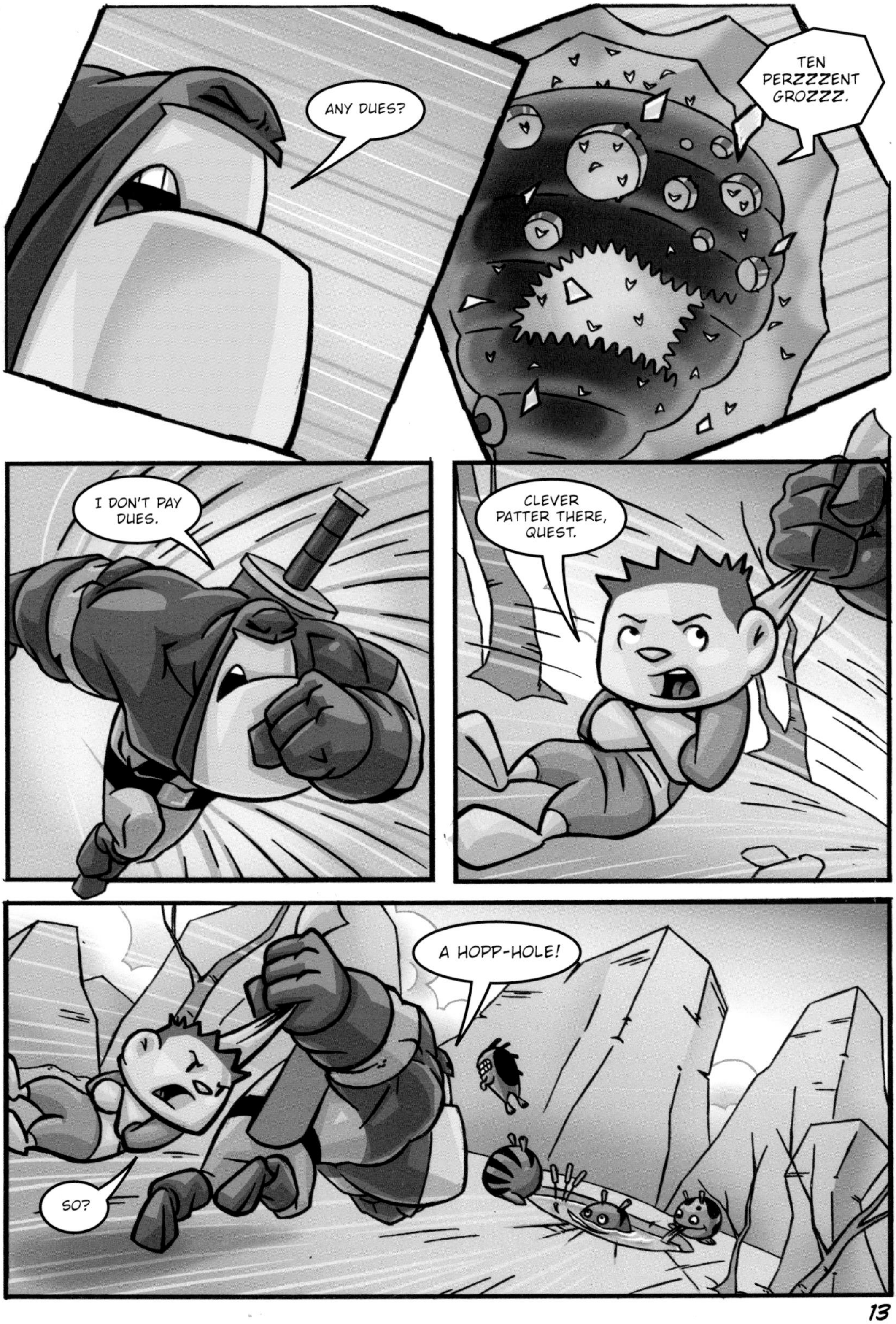
ANY DUES?
TEN PERZZZENT GROZZZ.
I DON'T PAY DUES.
CLEVER PATTER THERE, QUEST.
A HOPP-HOLE!
SO?

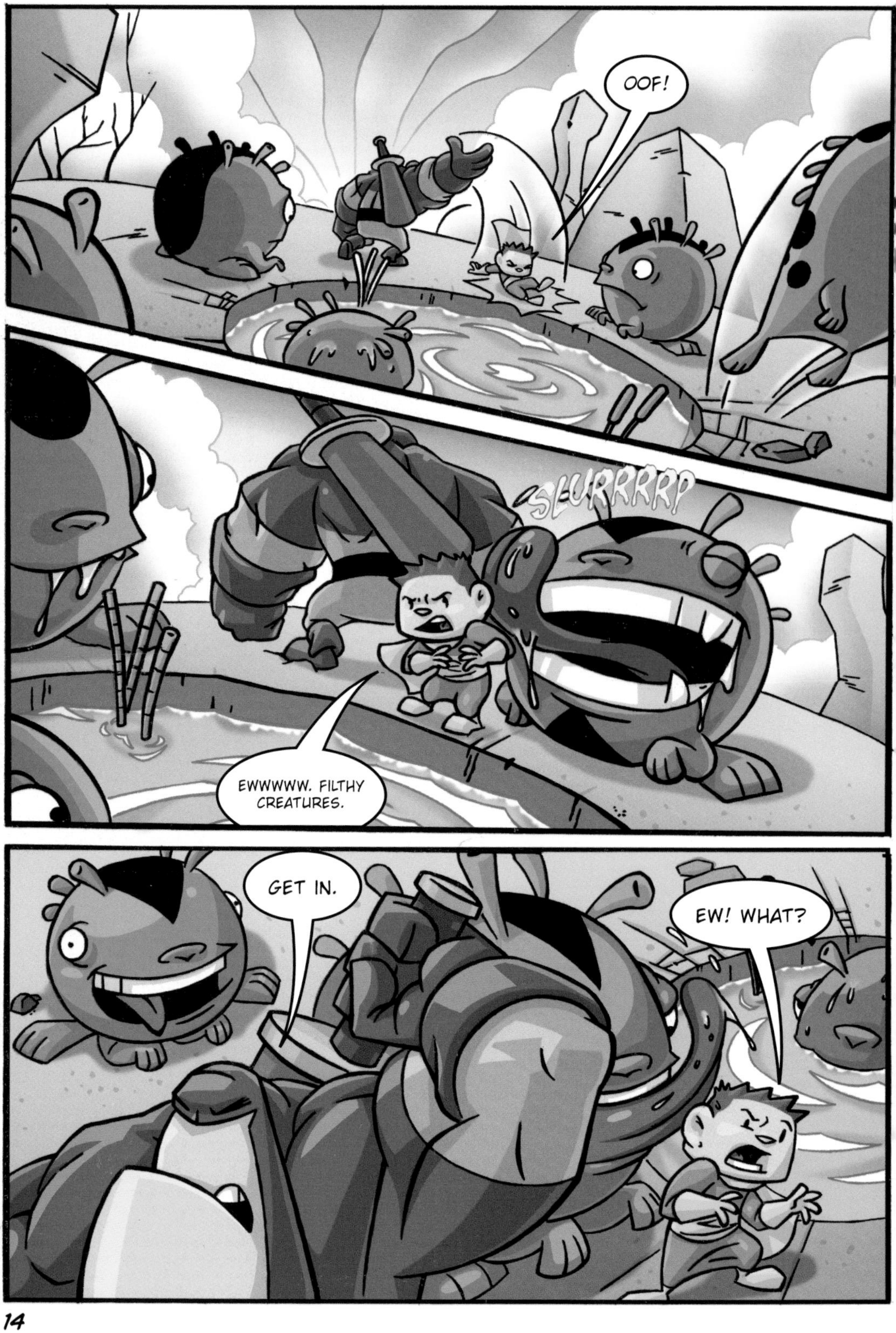
OOF!
SLURRRRP!
EWWWWW. FILTHY CREATURES.
GET IN.
EW! WHAT?

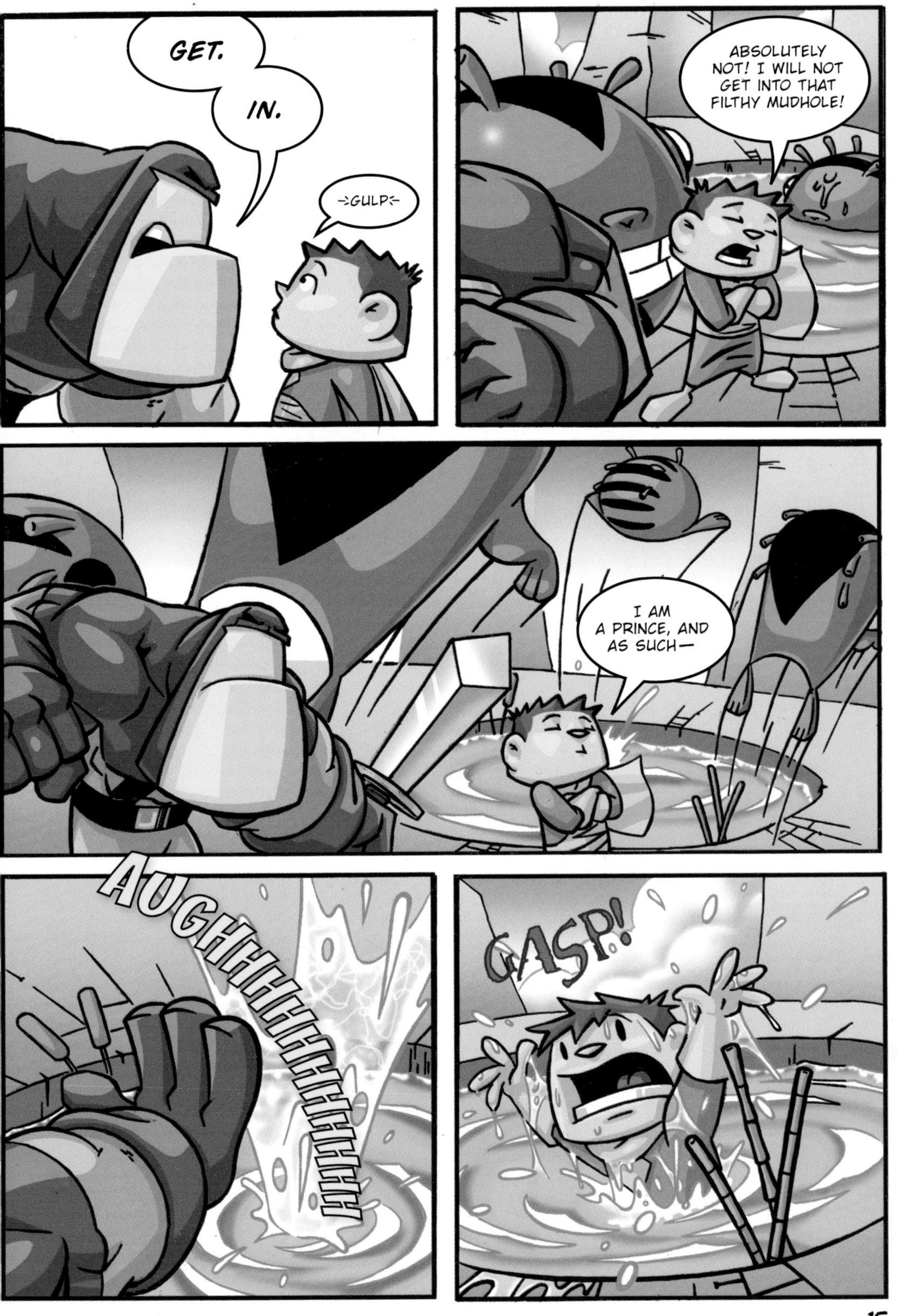
GET.
IN.
-GULP-
ABSOLUTELY NOT! I WILL NOT GET INTO THAT FILTHY MUDHOLE!
I AM A PRINCE, AND AS SUCH—
AUGHHHHHHHHHHHH!
GASP!

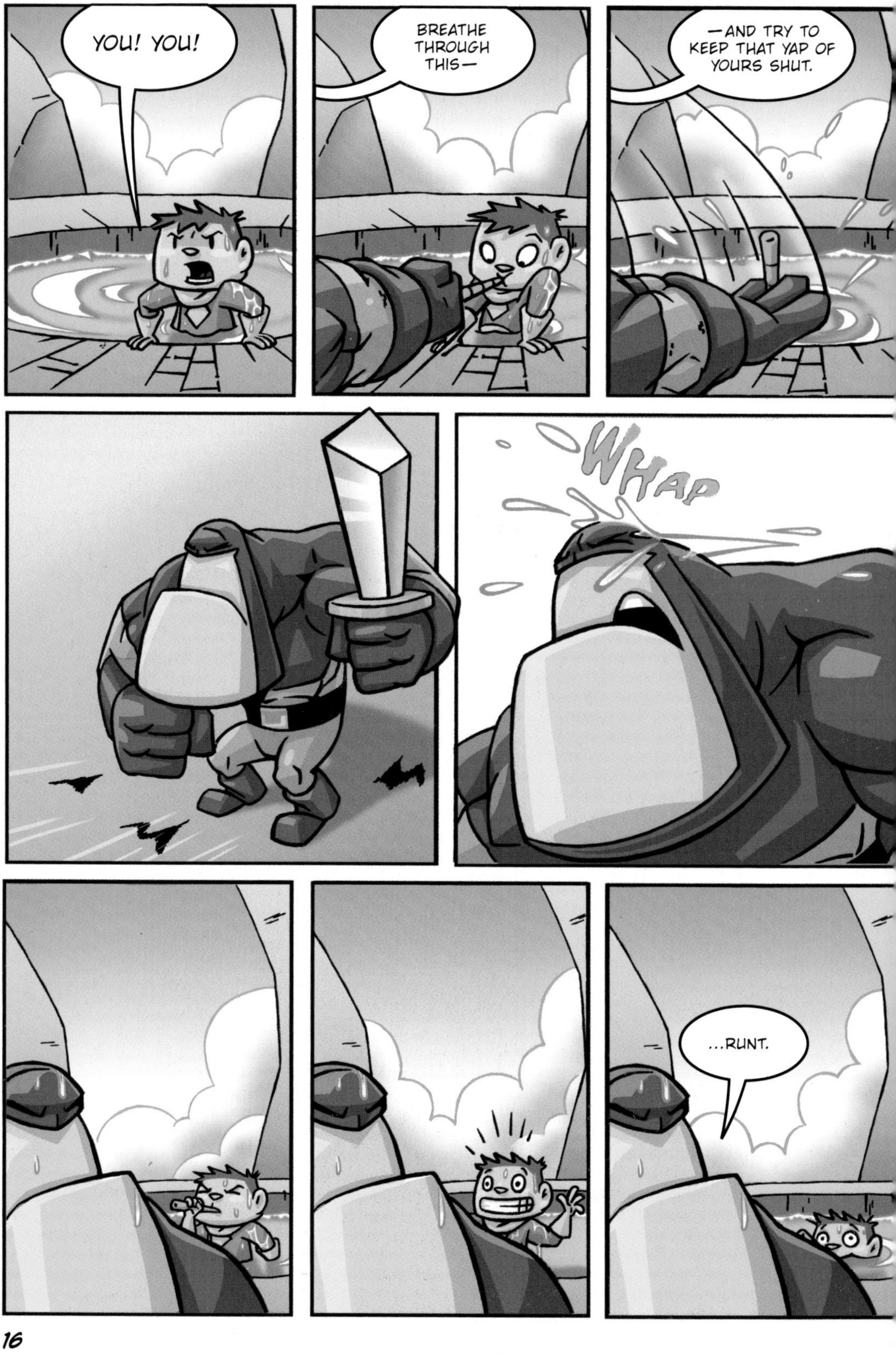
YOU! YOU!
BREATHE THROUGH THIS—
—AND TRY TO KEEP THAT YAP OF YOURS SHUT.
WHAP
...RUNT.

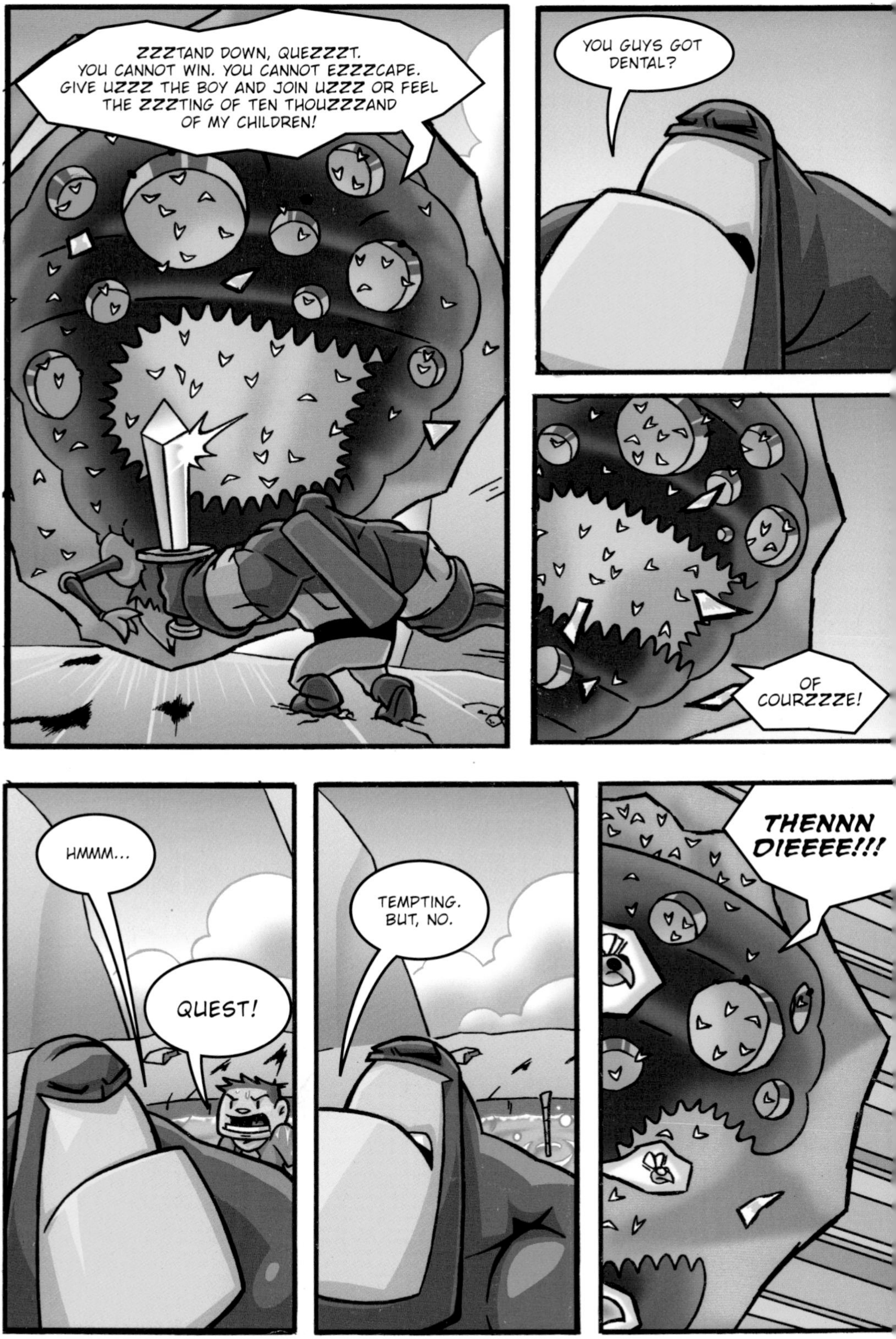
ZZZTAND DOWN, QUEZZZT. YOU CANNOT WIN. YOU CANNOT EZZZCAPE. GIVE UZZZ THE BOY AND JOIN UZZZ OR FEEL THE ZZZTING OF TEN THOUZZZAND OF MY CHILDREN!
YOU GUYS GOT DENTAL?
OF COURZZZE!
HMMM...
QUEST!
TEMPTING. BUT, NO.
THENNN DIEEEE!!!

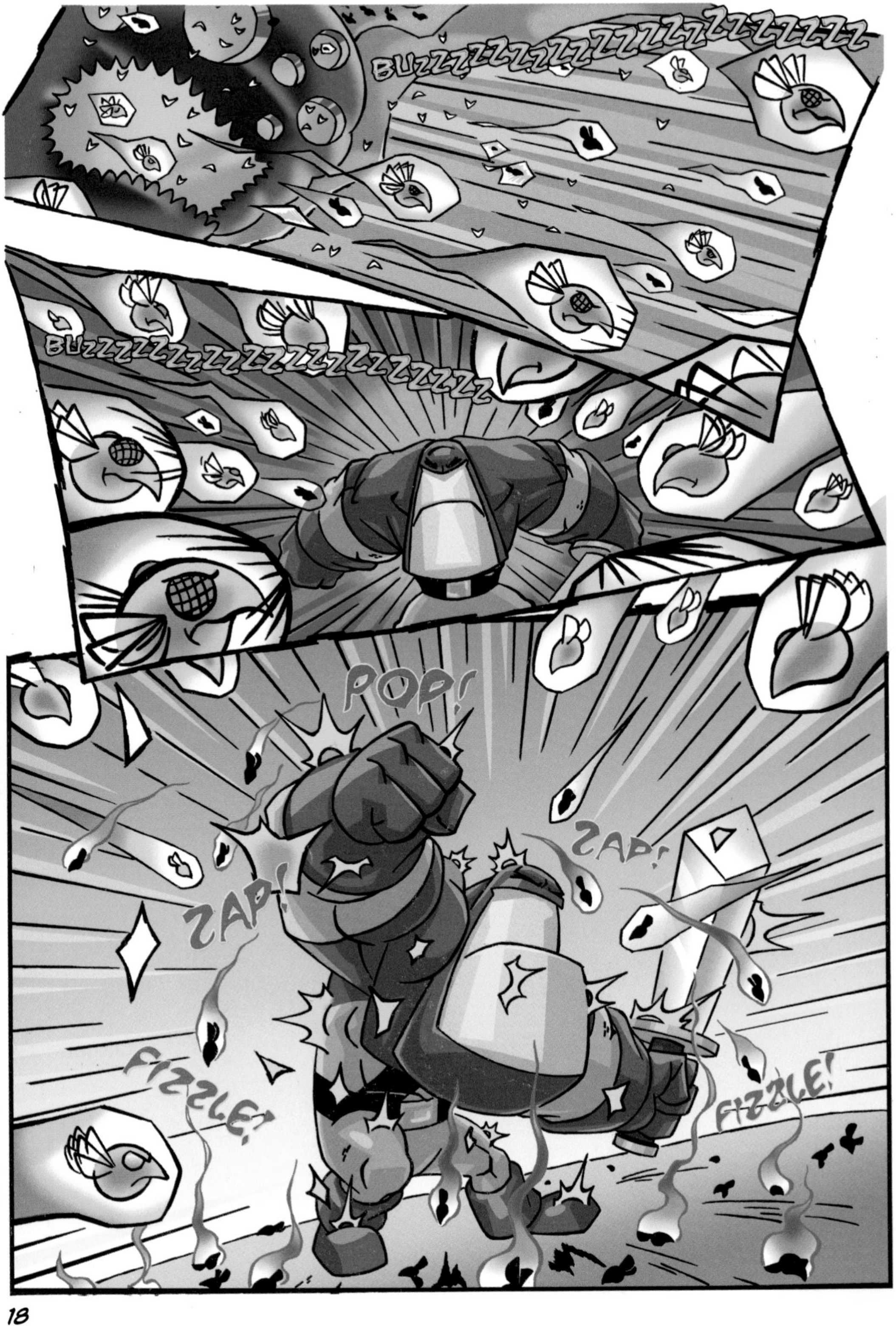
BUZZZZZZZZZZZZZZZZZZZZZZZZ
BUZZZZZZZZZZZZZZZZZZZZZZZ
POP!
ZAP!
ZAP!
FIZZLE!
FIZZLE!

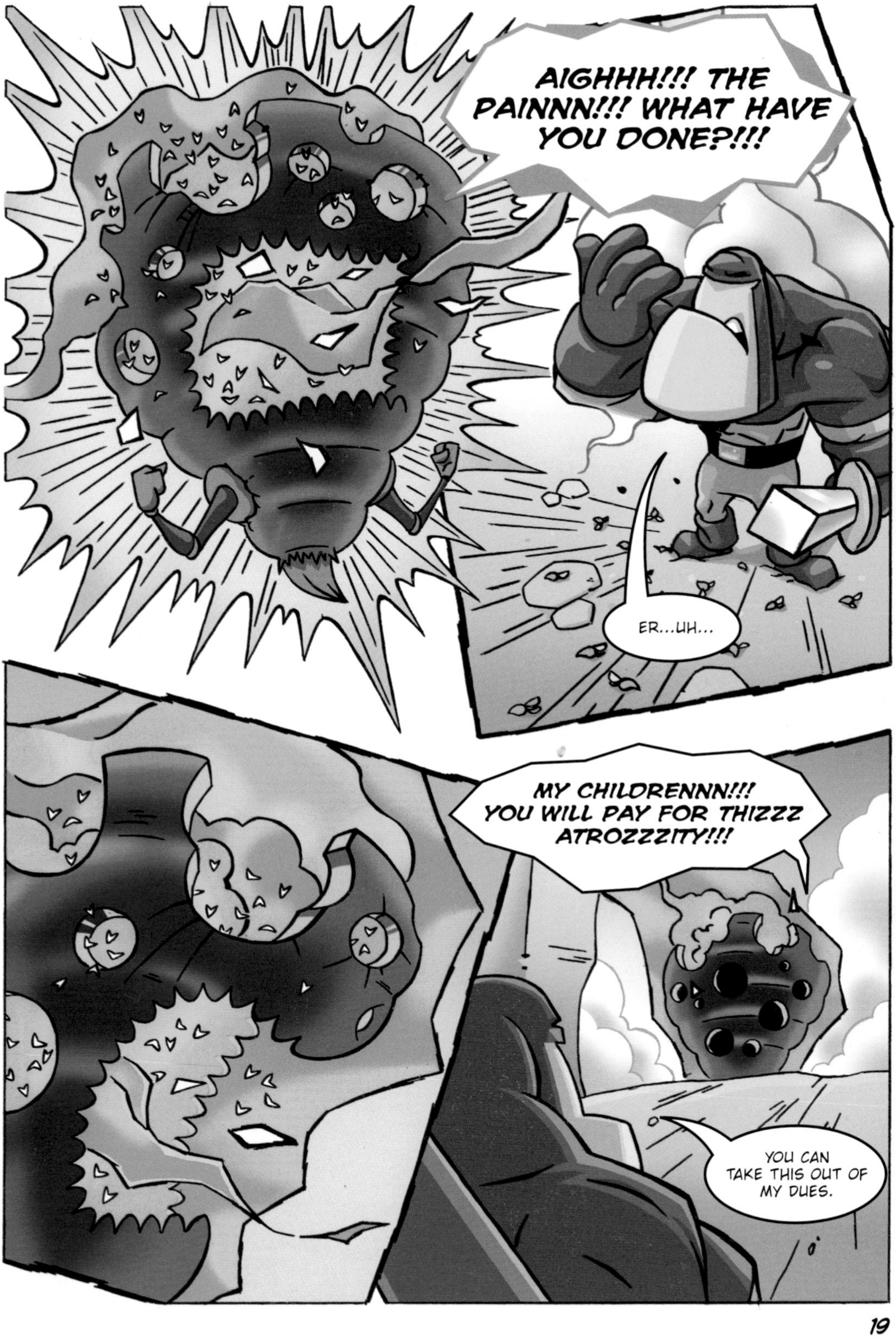
AIGHHH!!! THE PAINNN!!! WHAT HAVE YOU DONE?!!!
ER...UH...
MY CHILDRENNN!!! YOU WILL PAY FOR THIZZZ ATROZZZITY!!!
YOU CAN TAKE THIS OUT OF MY DUES.

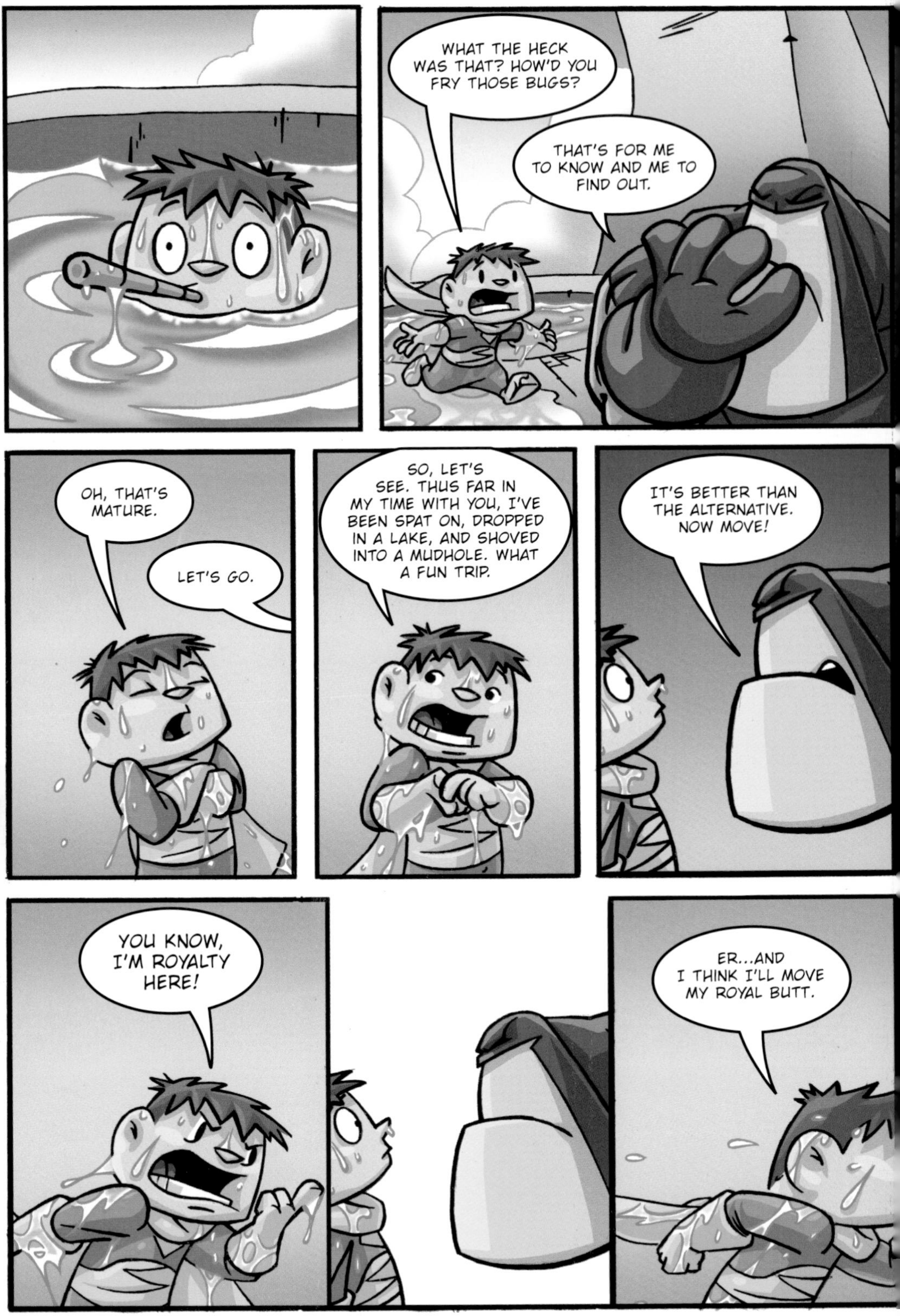
WHAT THE HECK WAS THAT? HOW'D YOU FRY THOSE BUGS?
THAT'S FOR ME TO KNOW AND ME TO FIND OUT.
OH, THAT'S MATURE.
LET'S GO.
SO, LET'S SEE. THUS FAR IN MY TIME WITH YOU, I'VE BEEN SPAT ON, DROPPED IN A LAKE, AND SHOVED INTO A MUDHOLE. WHAT A FUN TRIP.
IT'S BETTER THAN THE ALTERNATIVE. NOW MOVE!
YOU KNOW, I'M ROYALTY HERE!
ER...AND I THINK I'LL MOVE MY ROYAL BUTT.

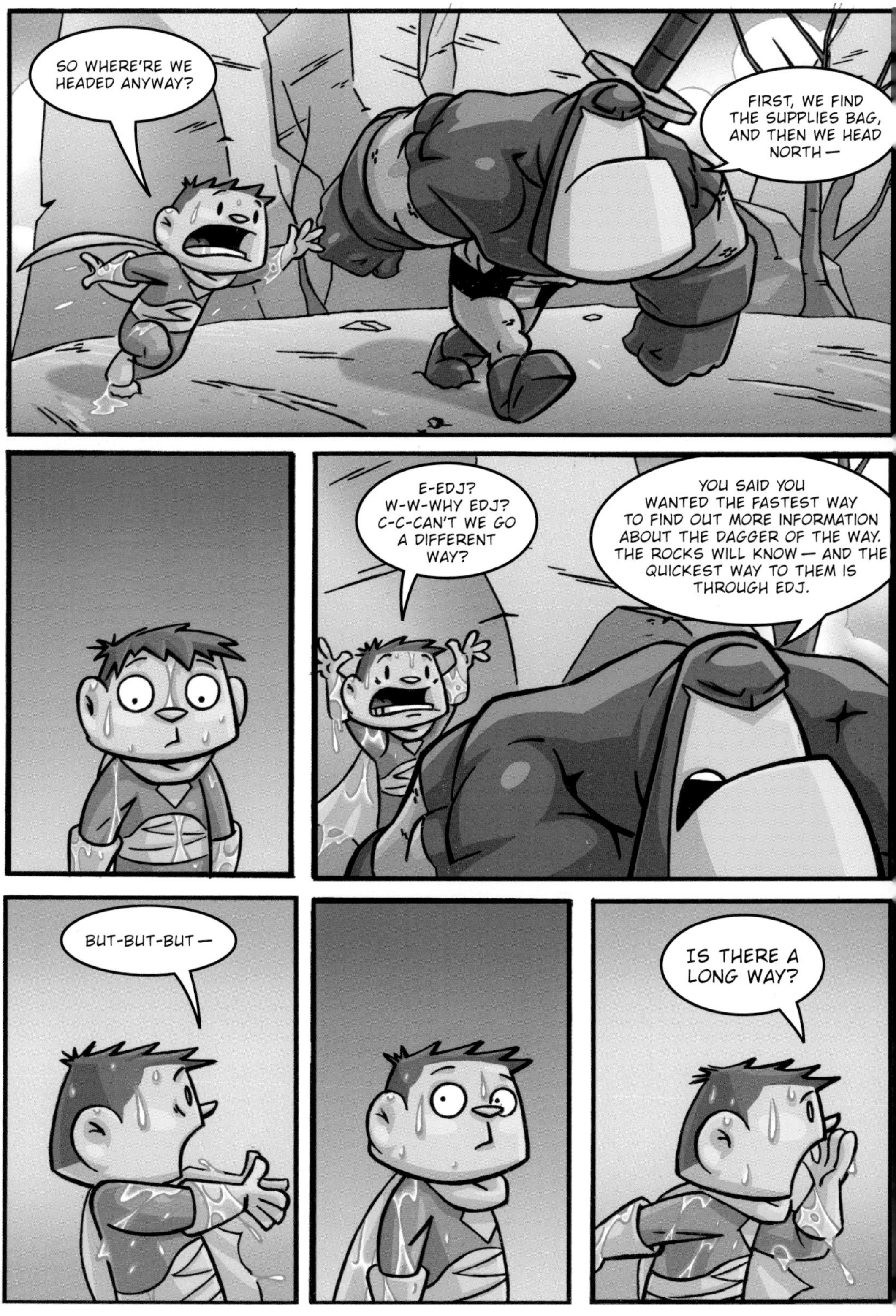
SO WHERE'RE WE HEADED ANYWAY?
FIRST, WE FIND THE SUPPLIES BAG, AND THEN WE HEAD NORTH —
E-EDJ? W-W-WHY EDJ? C-C-CAN'T WE GO A DIFFERENT WAY?
YOU SAID YOU WANTED THE FASTEST WAY TO FIND OUT MORE INFORMATION ABOUT THE DAGGER OF THE WAY. THE ROCKS WILL KNOW — AND THE QUICKEST WAY TO THEM IS THROUGH EDJ.
BUT-BUT-BUT —
IS THERE A LONG WAY?

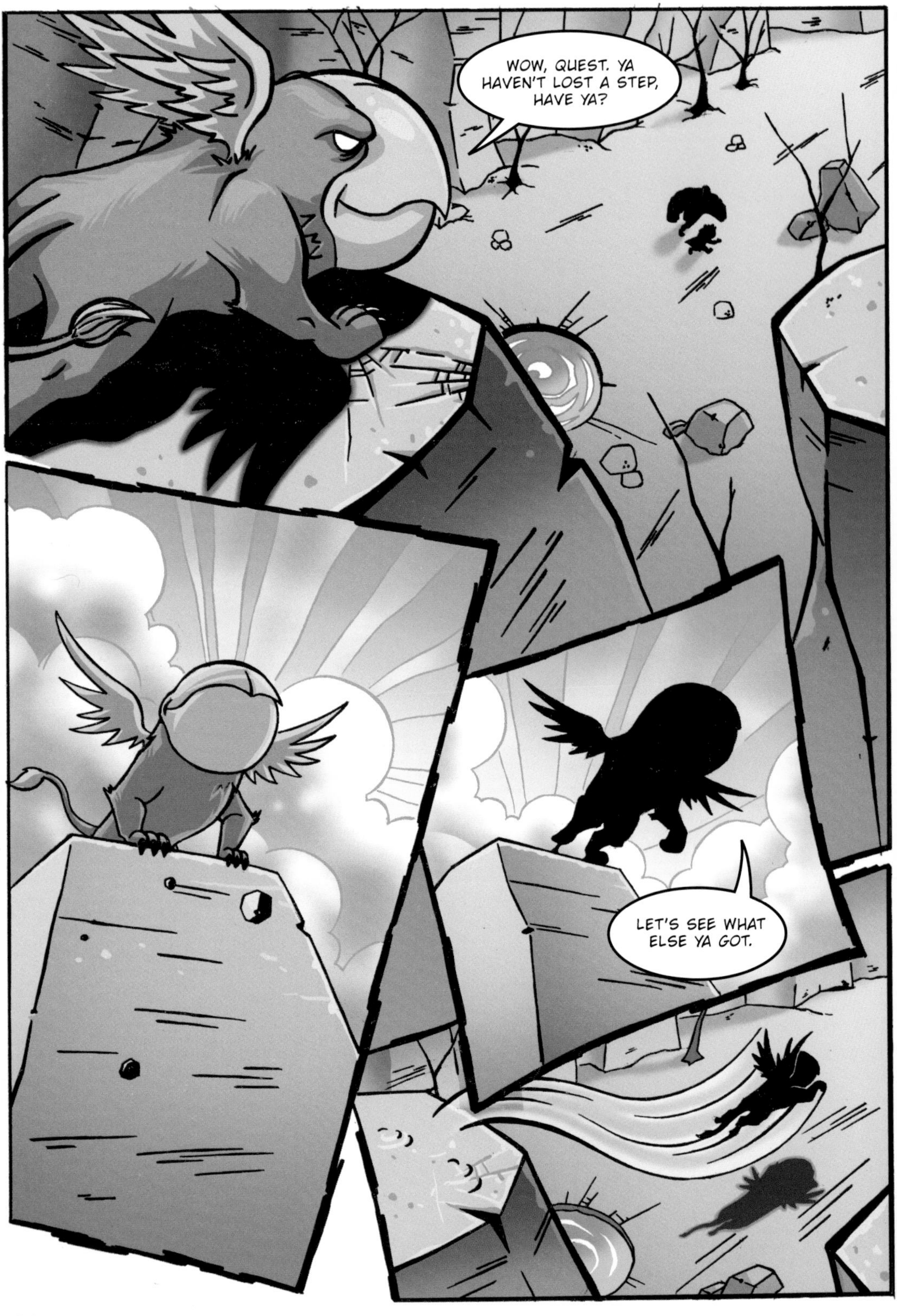
WOW, QUEST. YA HAVEN'T LOST A STEP, HAVE YA?
LET'S SEE WHAT ELSE YA GOT.

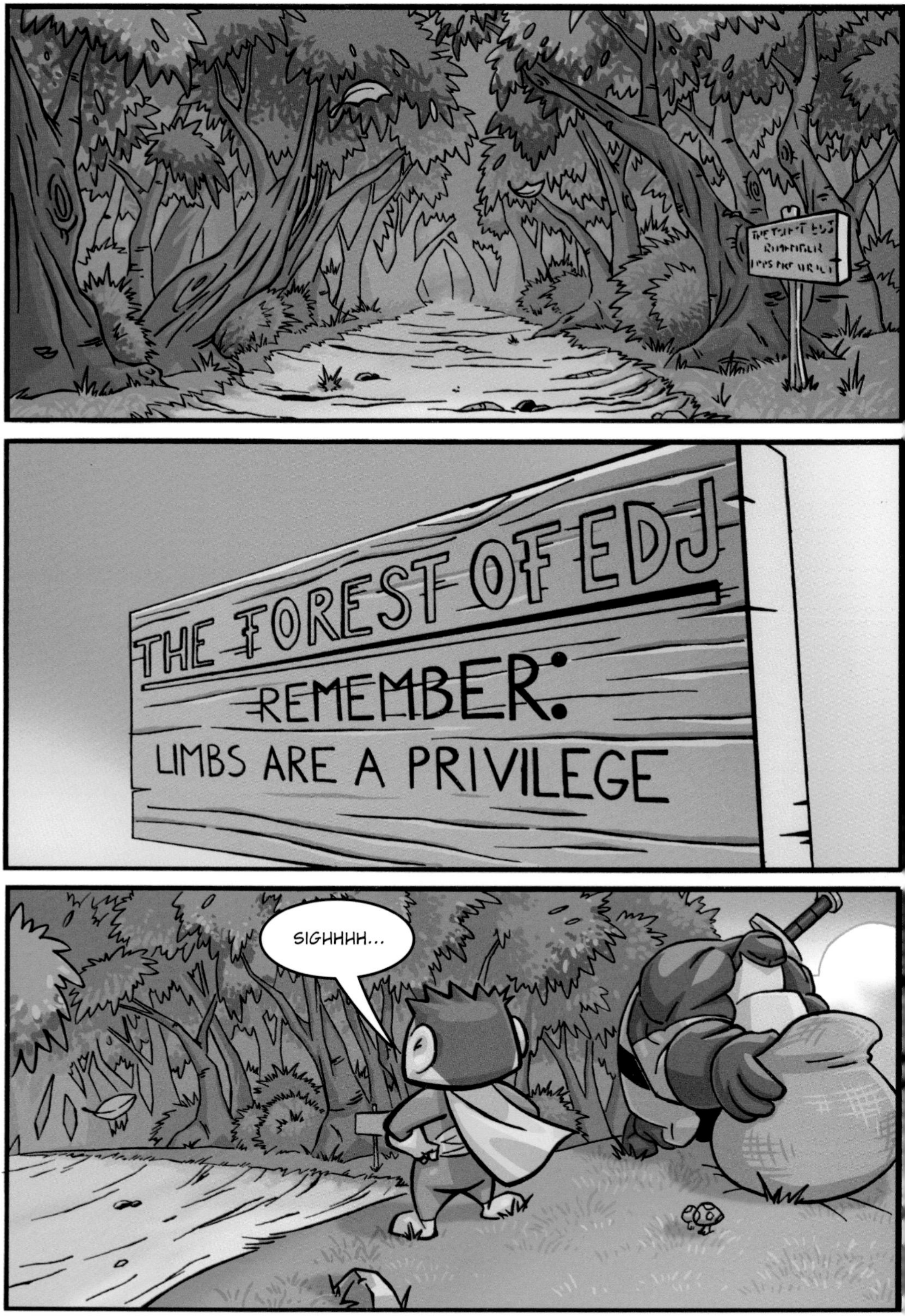
THE FOREST OF EDJ
REMEMBER:
LIMBS ARE A PRIVILEGE
SIGHHHH...

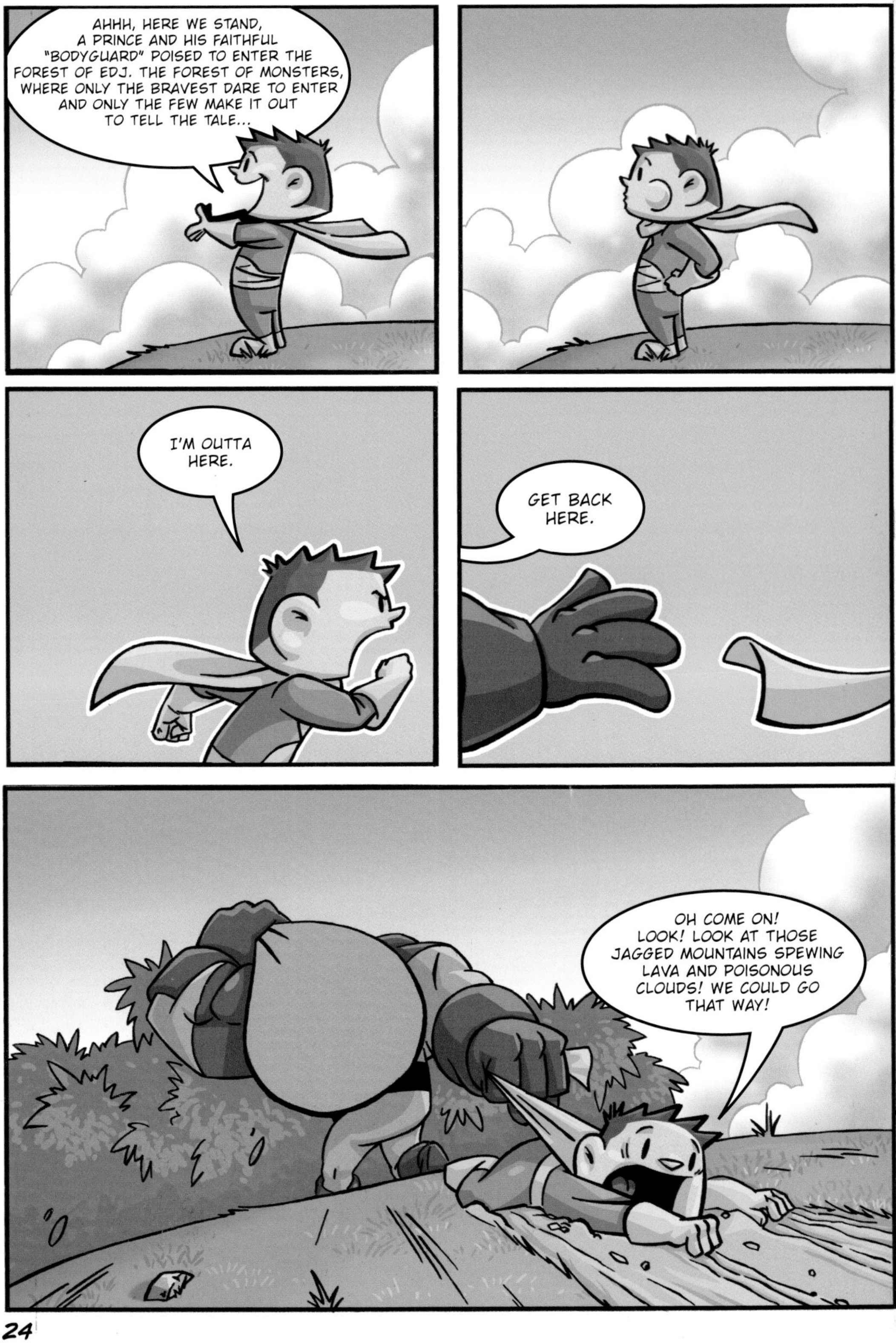
AHHH, HERE WE STAND, A PRINCE AND HIS FAITHFUL "BODYGUARD" POISED TO ENTER THE FOREST OF EDJ. THE FOREST OF MONSTERS, WHERE ONLY THE BRAVEST DARE TO ENTER AND ONLY THE FEW MAKE IT OUT TO TELL THE TALE...
I'M OUTTA HERE.
GET BACK HERE.
OH COME ON! LOOK! LOOK AT THOSE JAGGED MOUNTAINS SPEWING LAVA AND POISONOUS CLOUDS! WE COULD GO THAT WAY!

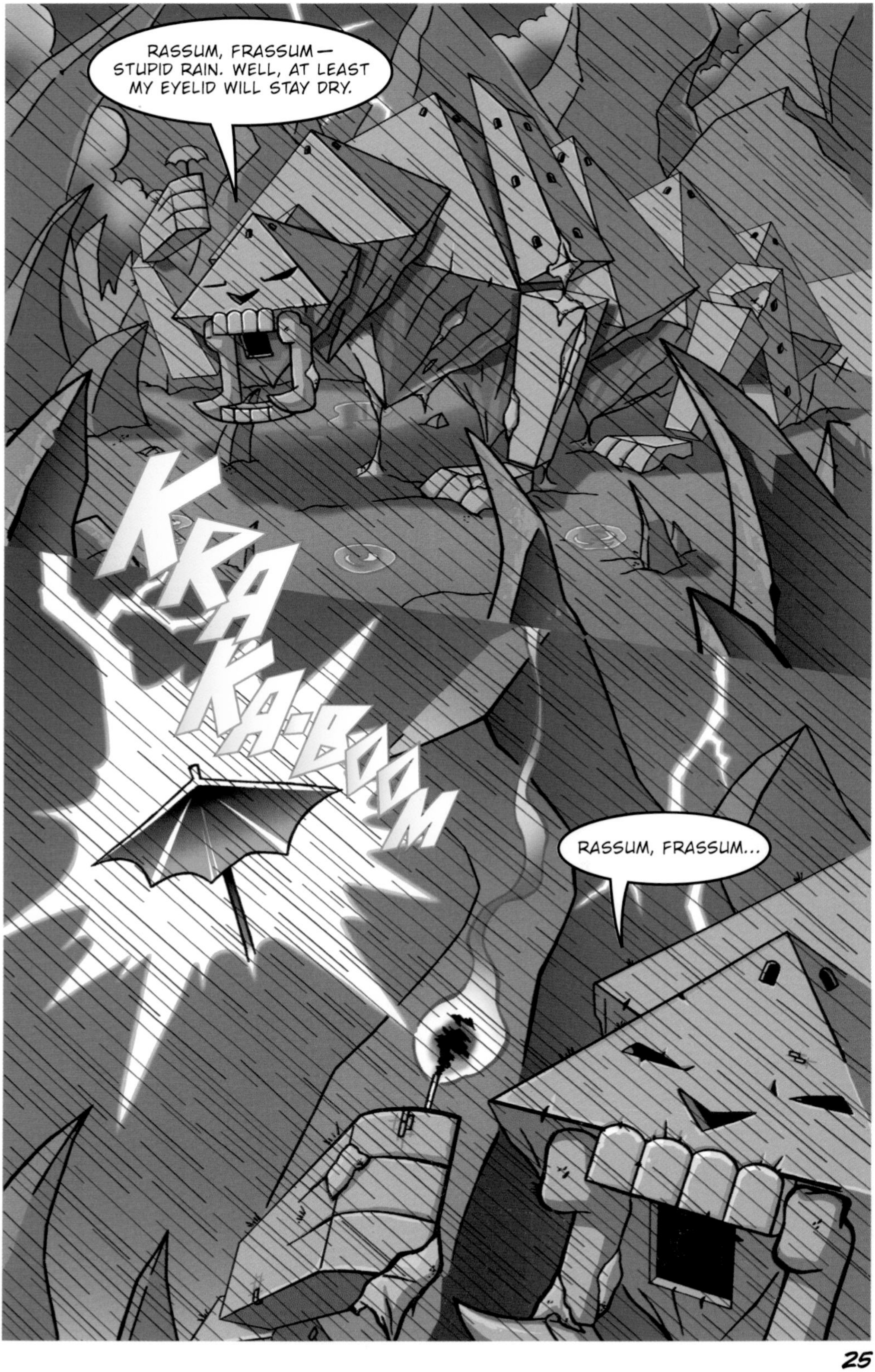
RASSUM, FRASSUM—
STUPID RAIN. WELL, AT LEAST
MY EYELID WILL STAY DRY.
KRA-KA-KA-BOOM
RASSUM, FRASSUM...

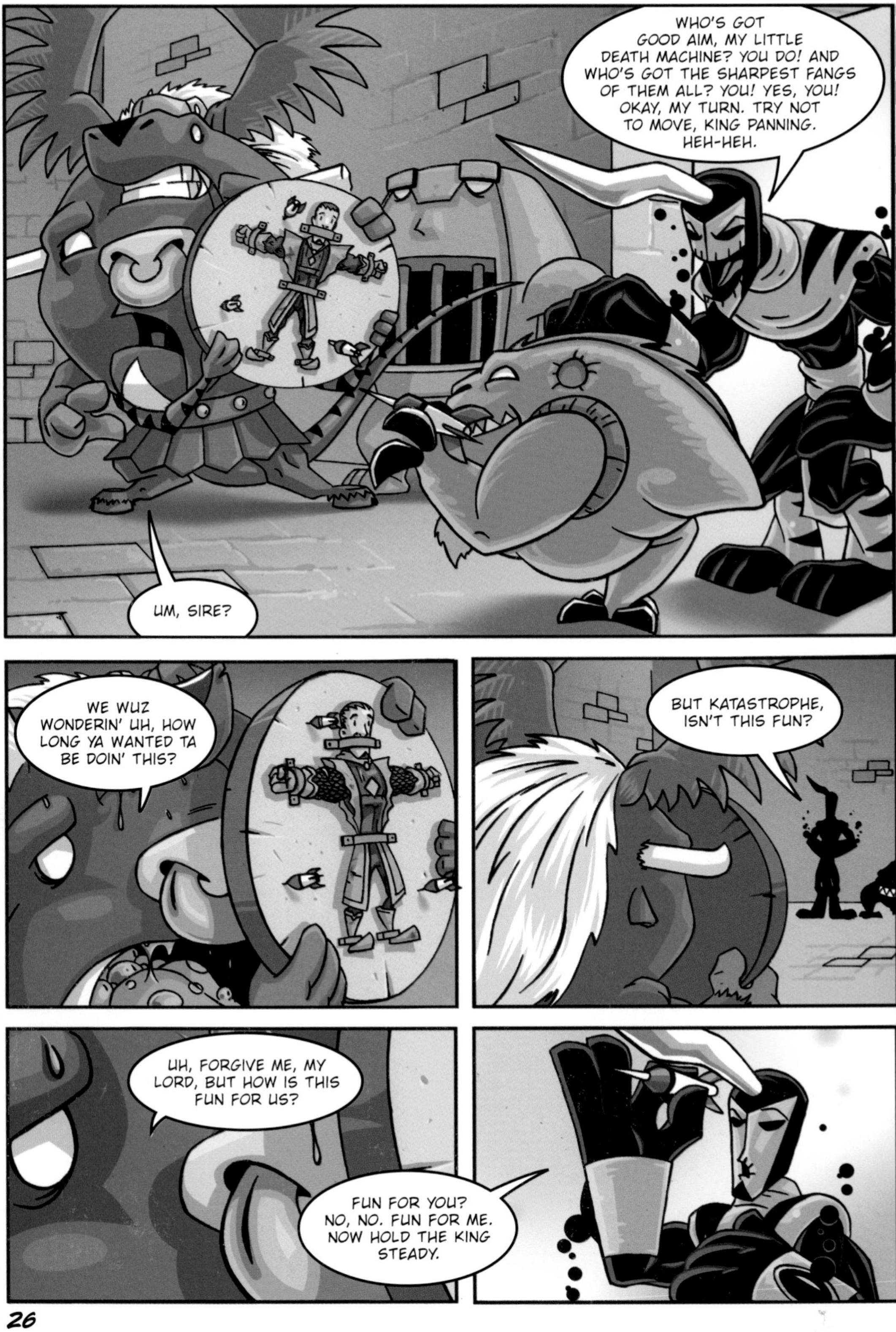
WHO'S GOT GOOD AIM, MY LITTLE DEATH MACHINE? YOU DO! AND WHO'S GOT THE SHARPEST FANGS OF THEM ALL? YOU! YES, YOU! OKAY, MY TURN. TRY NOT TO MOVE, KING PANNING. HEH-HEH.
UM, SIRE?
WE WUZ WONDERIN' UH, HOW LONG YA WANTED TA BE DOIN' THIS?
BUT KATASTROPHE, ISN'T THIS FUN?
UH, FORGIVE ME, MY LORD, BUT HOW IS THIS FUN FOR US?
FUN FOR YOU? NO, NO. FUN FOR ME. NOW HOLD THE KING STEADY.

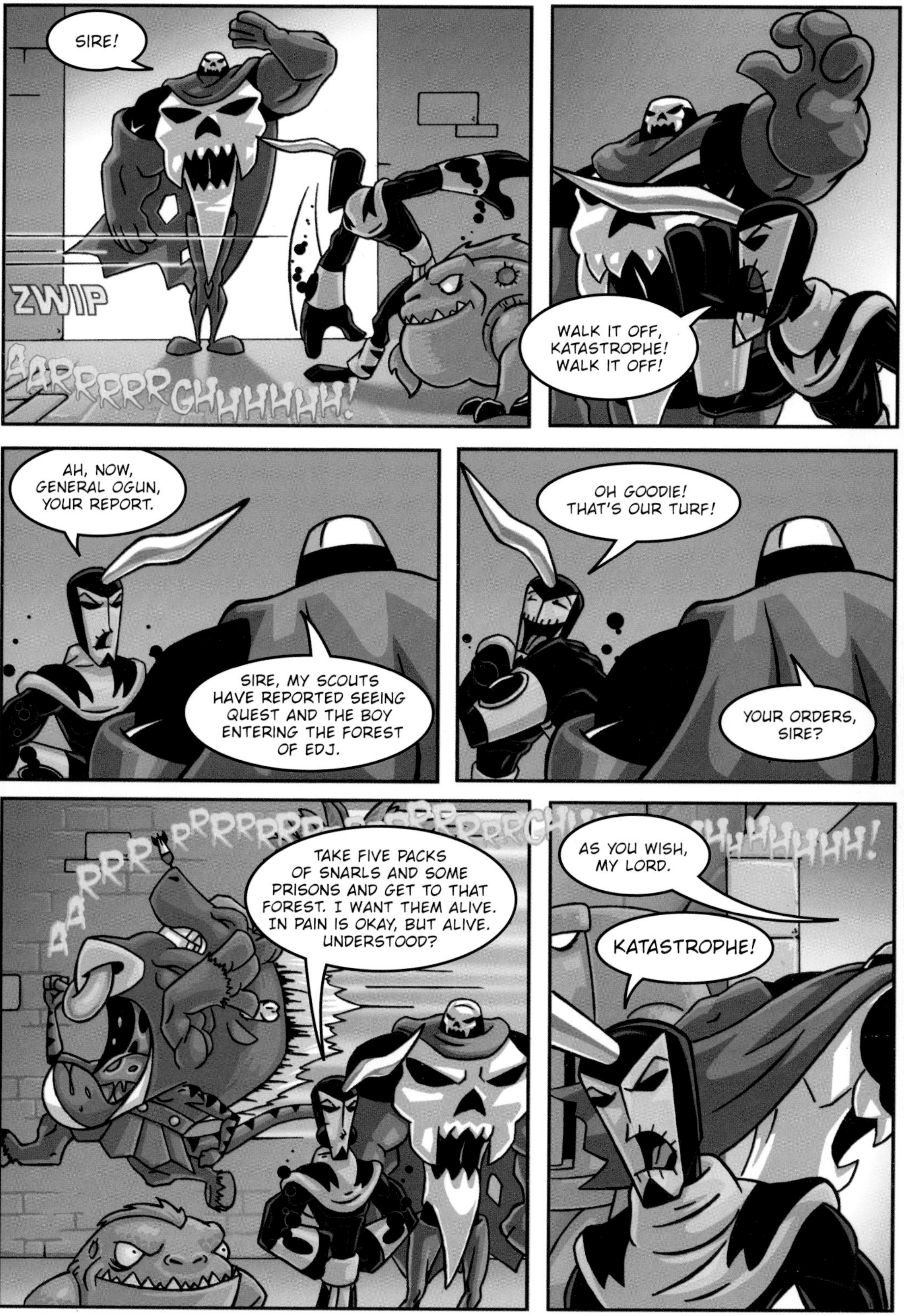
SIRE!
ZWIP
AARRRRRGHHHHHH!
WALK IT OFF, KATASTROPHE! WALK IT OFF!
AH, NOW, GENERAL OGUN, YOUR REPORT.
SIRE, MY SCOUTS HAVE REPORTED SEEING QUEST AND THE BOY ENTERING THE FOREST OF EDJ.
OH GOODIE! THAT'S OUR TURF!
YOUR ORDERS, SIRE?
TAKE FIVE PACKS OF SNARLS AND SOME PRISONS AND GET TO THAT FOREST. I WANT THEM ALIVE. IN PAIN IS OKAY, BUT ALIVE. UNDERSTOOD?
AS YOU WISH, MY LORD.
KATASTROPHE!

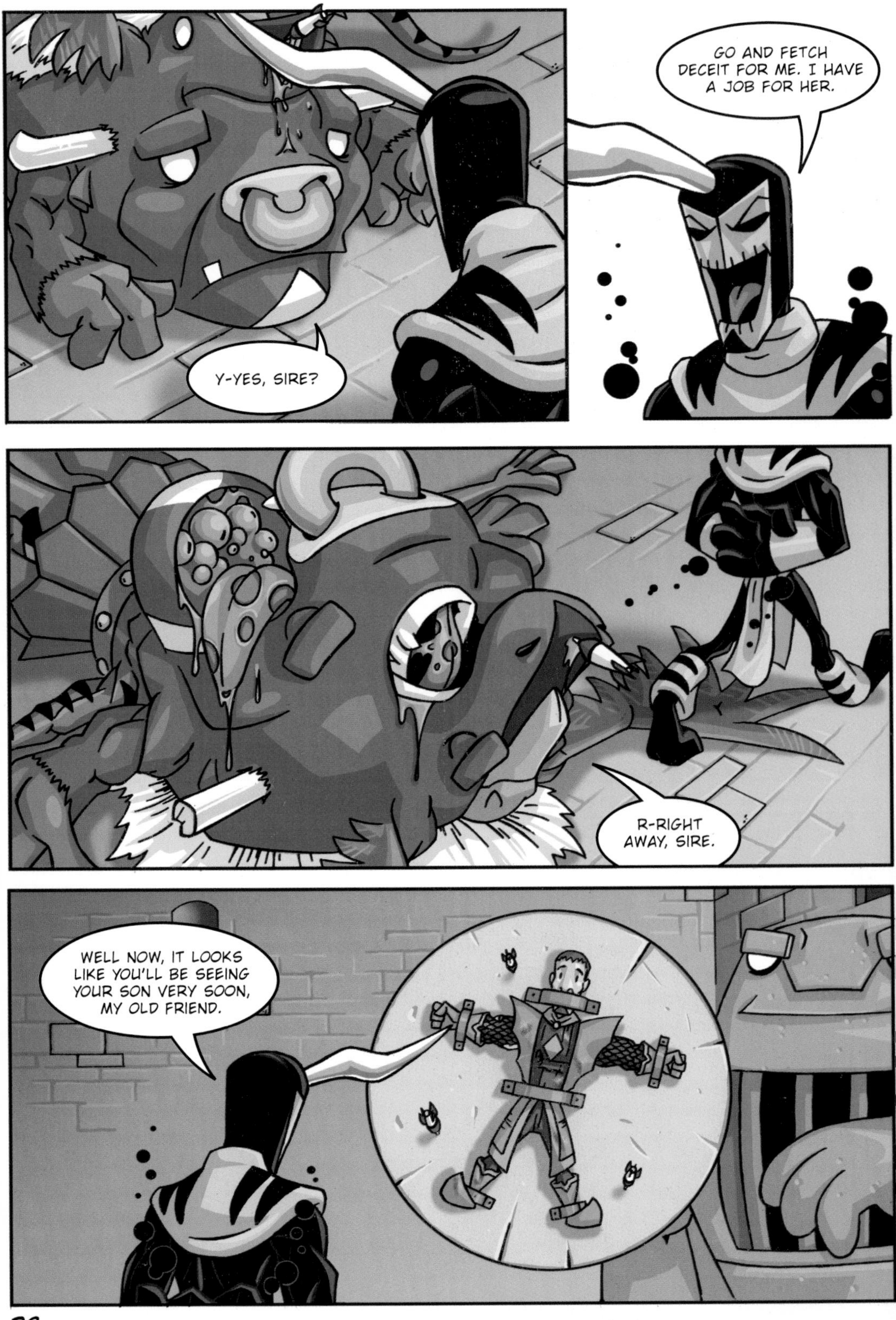
GO AND FETCH DECEIT FOR ME. I HAVE A JOB FOR HER.
Y-YES, SIRE?
R-RIGHT AWAY, SIRE.
WELL NOW, IT LOOKS LIKE YOU'LL BE SEEING YOUR SON VERY SOON, MY OLD FRIEND.

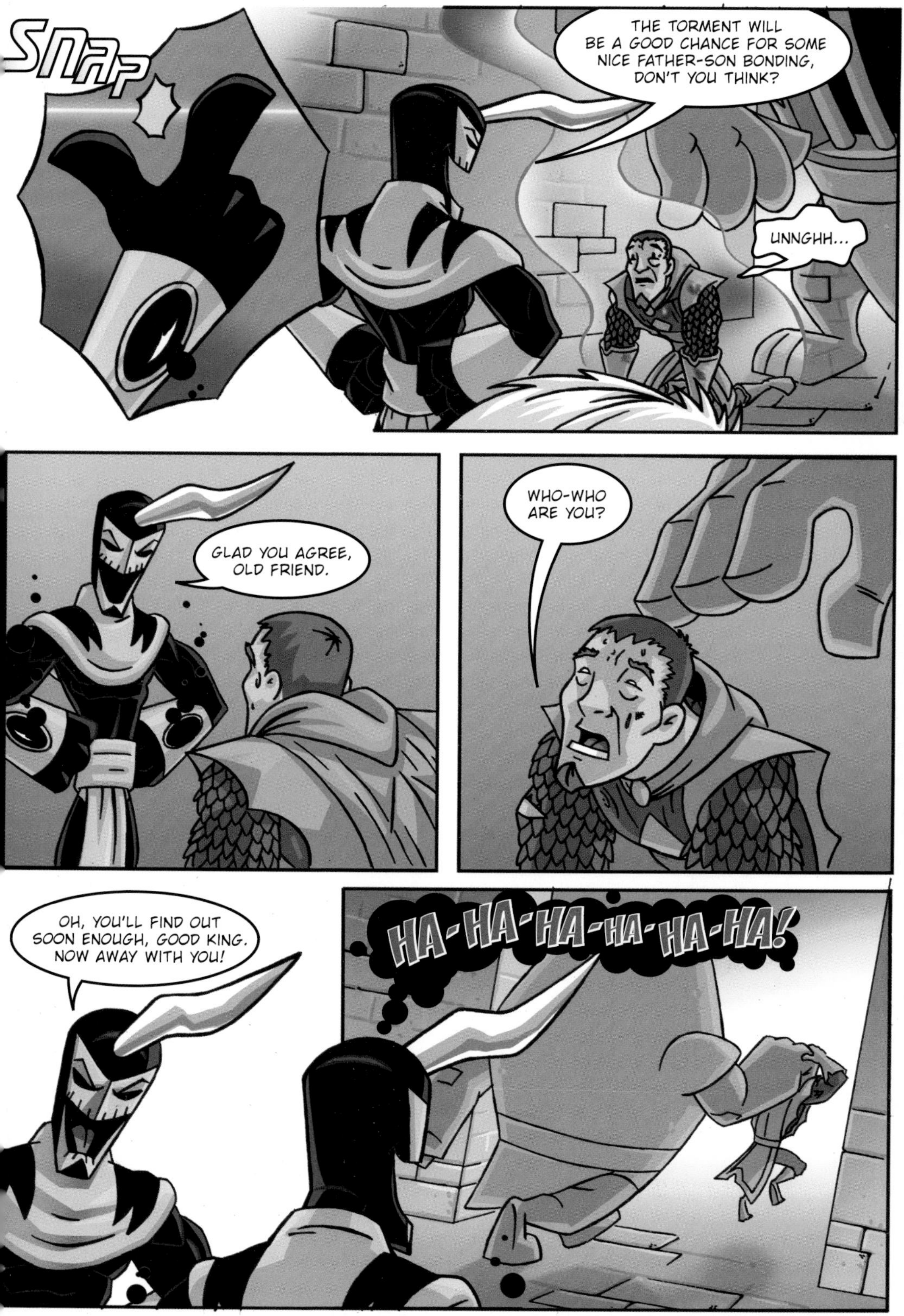
SNAP
THE TORMENT WILL BE A GOOD CHANCE FOR SOME NICE FATHER-SON BONDING, DON'T YOU THINK?
UNNGHH...
GLAD YOU AGREE, OLD FRIEND.
WHO-WHO ARE YOU?
OH, YOU'LL FIND OUT SOON ENOUGH, GOOD KING. NOW AWAY WITH YOU!
HA-HA-HA-HA-HA-HA!

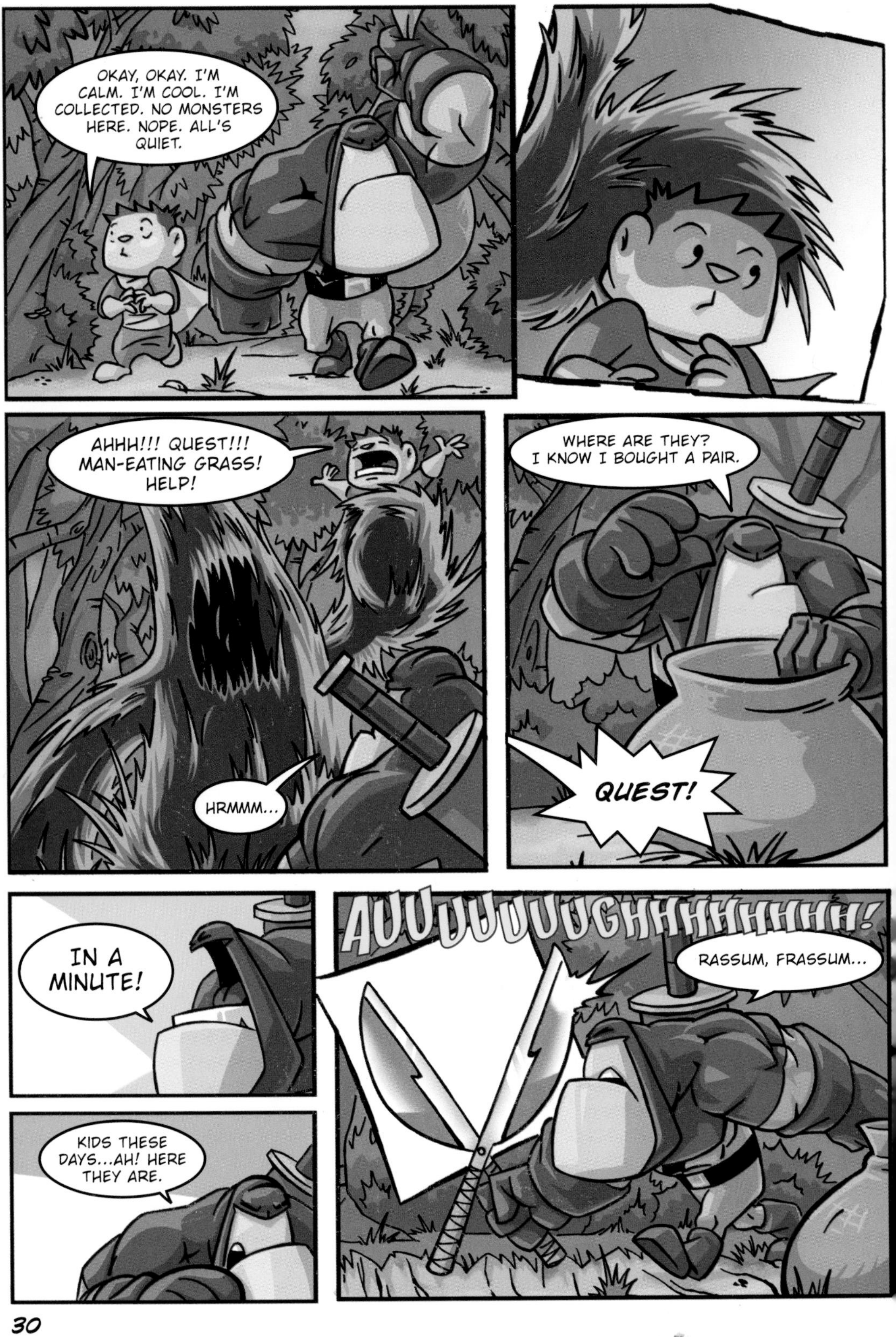
OKAY, OKAY. I'M CALM. I'M COOL. I'M COLLECTED. NO MONSTERS HERE. NOPE. ALL'S QUIET.
AHHH!!! QUEST!!! MAN-EATING GRASS! HELP!
HRMMM...
WHERE ARE THEY? I KNOW I BOUGHT A PAIR.
QUEST!
IN A MINUTE!
KIDS THESE DAYS...AH! HERE THEY ARE.
AUUUUUUUGHHHHHHHHH!
RASSUM, FRASSUM...

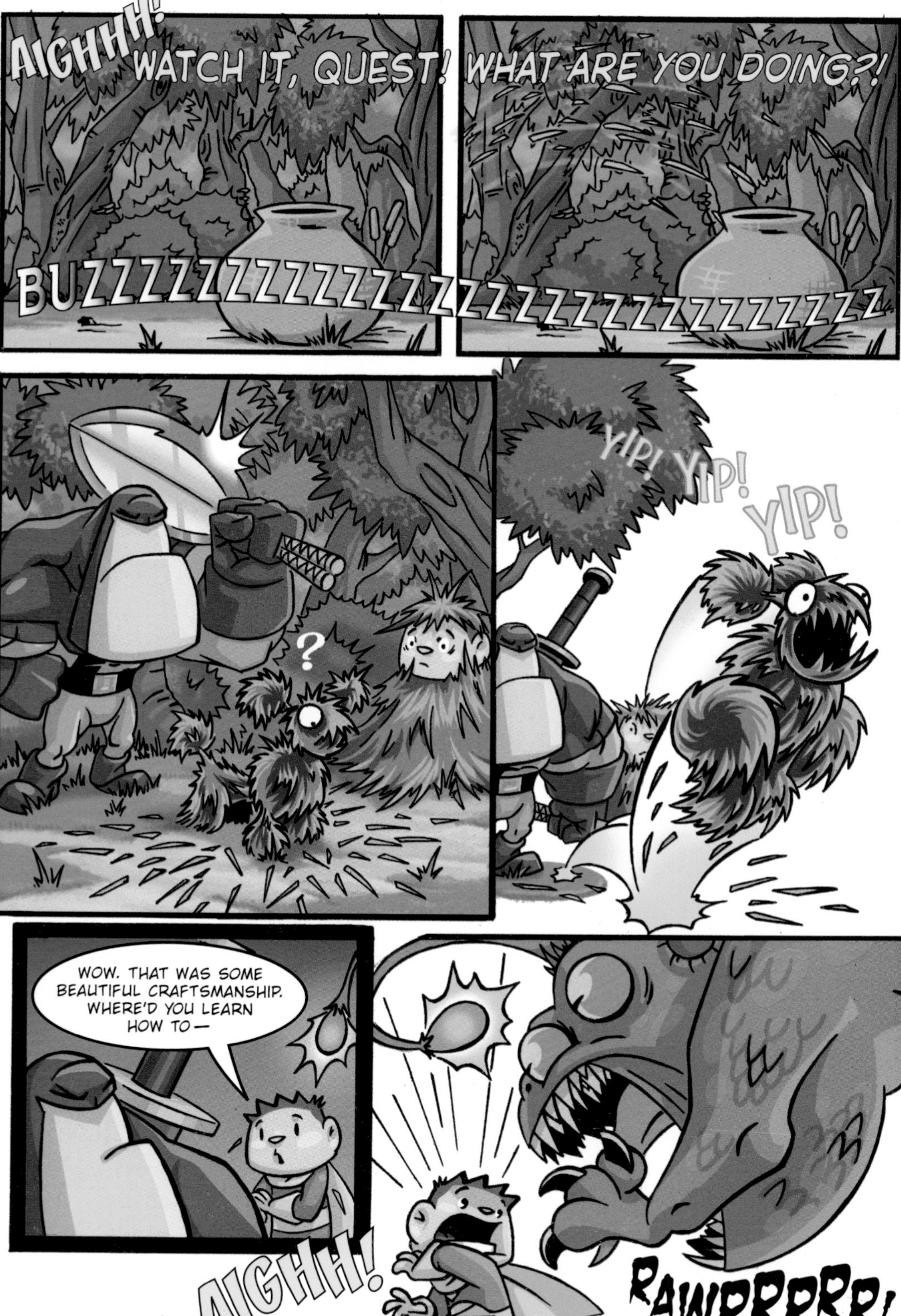
AIGHHH!
WATCH IT, QUEST!
WHAT ARE YOU DOING?!
BUZZZZZZZZZZZZZZZZZZZZZZZZZZZZZZZZZ
?
YIP! YIP! YIP!
WOW. THAT WAS SOME BEAUTIFUL CRAFTSMANSHIP. WHERE'D YOU LEARN HOW TO—
AIGHH!
RAWRRRRR!

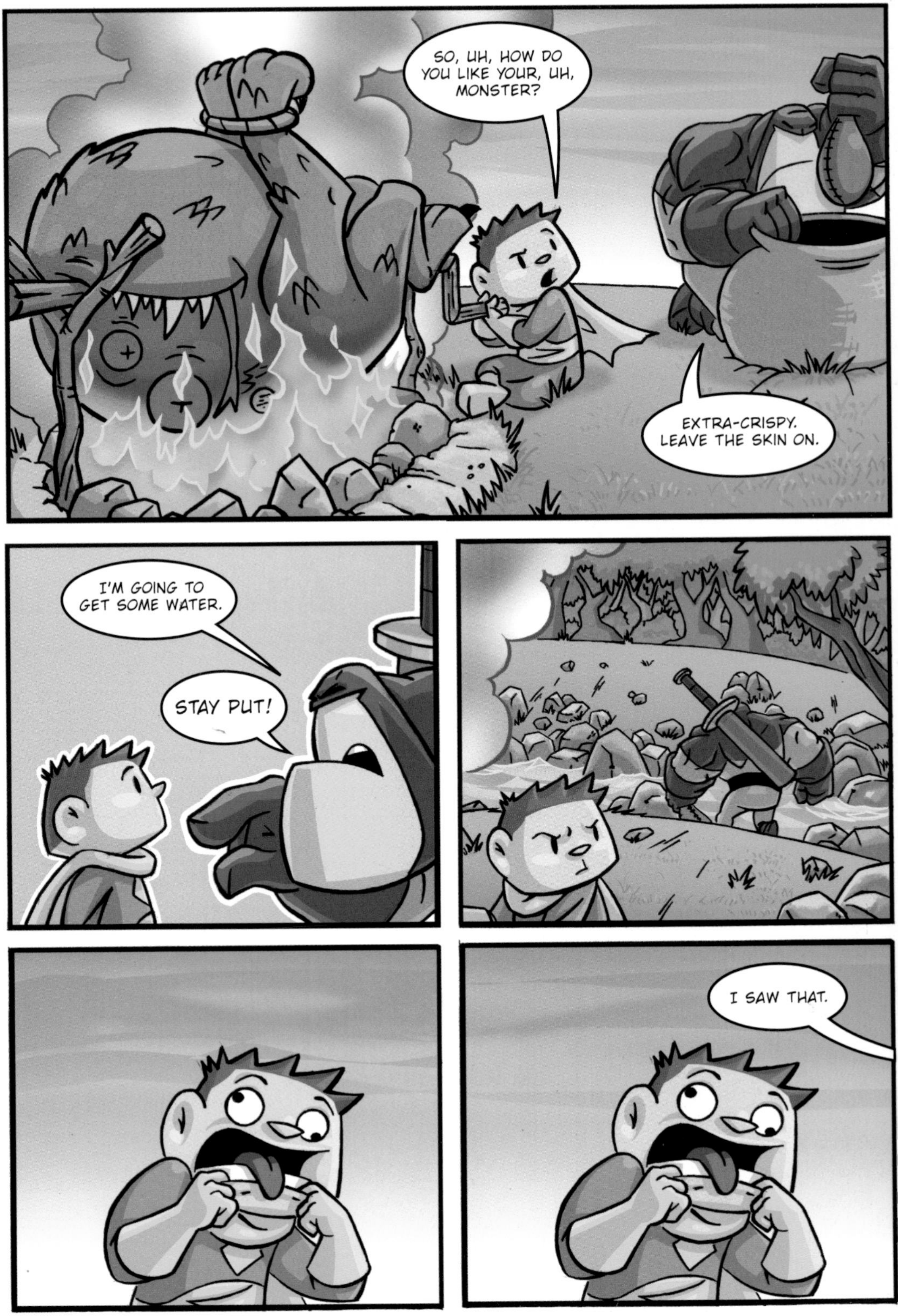
SO, UH, HOW DO YOU LIKE YOUR, UH, MONSTER?
EXTRA-CRISPY. LEAVE THE SKIN ON.
I'M GOING TO GET SOME WATER.
STAY PUT!
I SAW THAT.

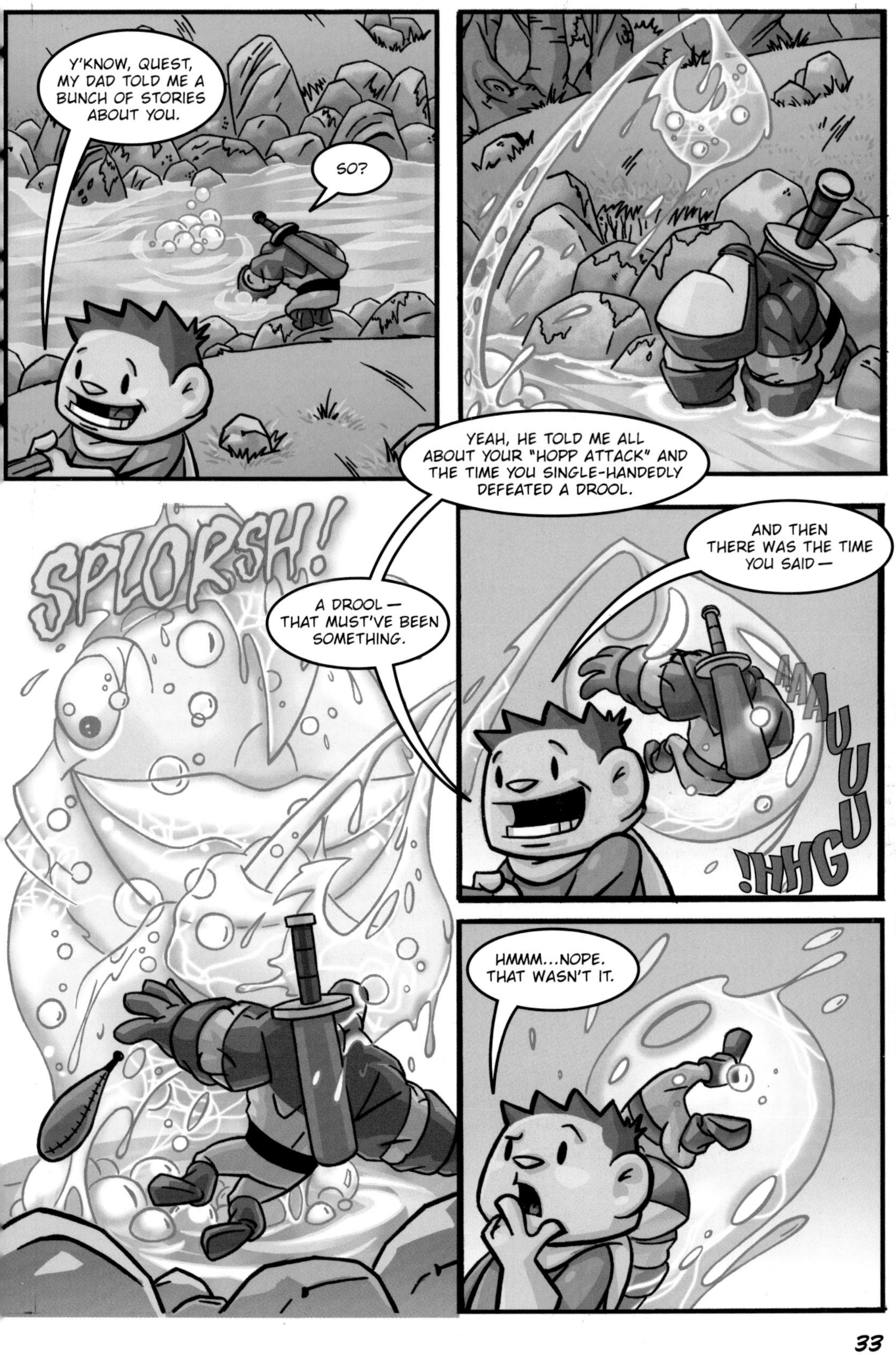
Y'KNOW, QUEST, MY DAD TOLD ME A BUNCH OF STORIES ABOUT YOU.
SO?
YEAH, HE TOLD ME ALL ABOUT YOUR "HOPP ATTACK" AND THE TIME YOU SINGLE-HANDEDLY DEFEATED A DROOL.
SPLORSH!
A DROOL — THAT MUST'VE BEEN SOMETHING.
AND THEN THERE WAS THE TIME YOU SAID —
AAAUUUGHH!
HMMM...NOPE. THAT WASN'T IT.

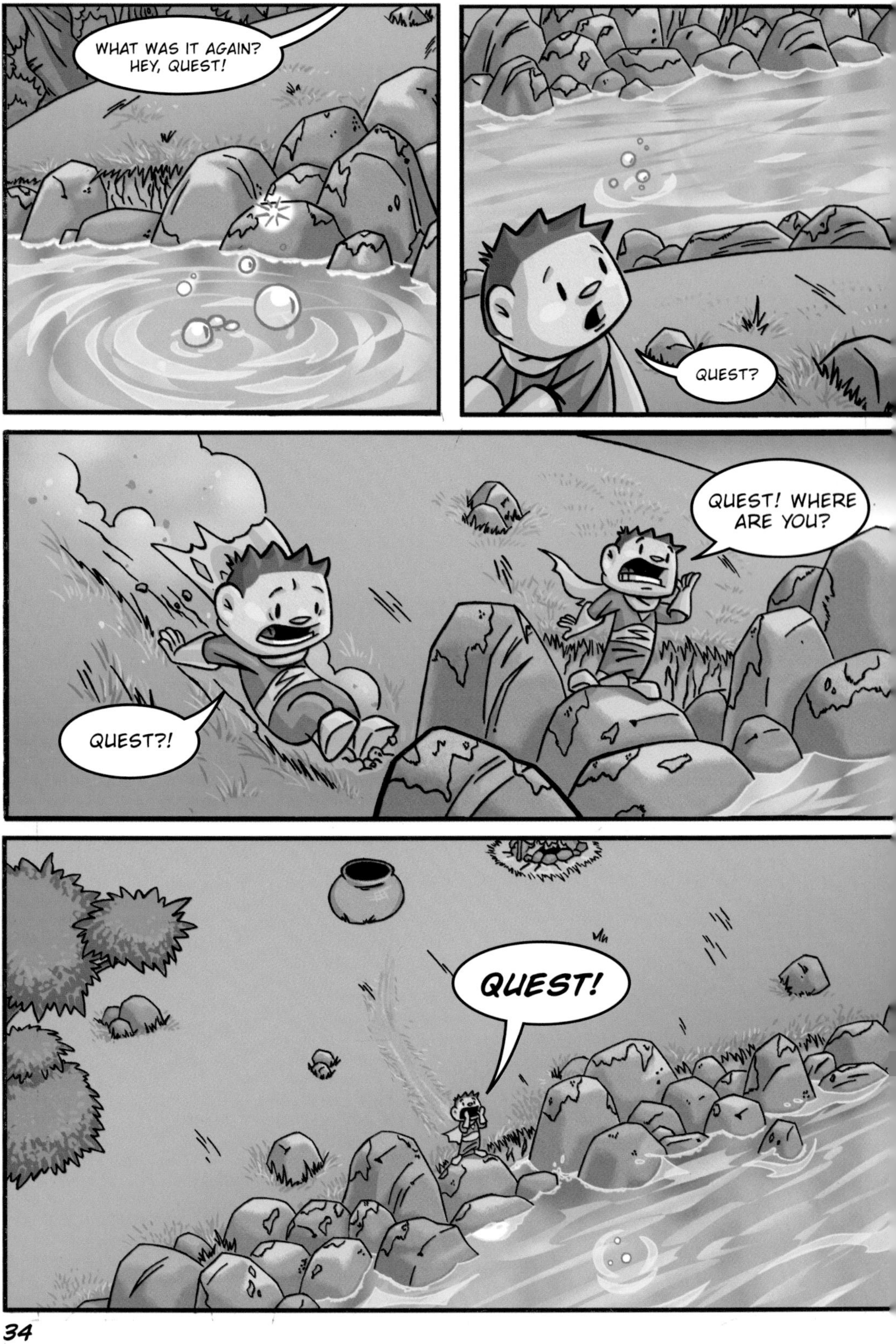
WHAT WAS IT AGAIN? HEY, QUEST!
QUEST?
QUEST?!
QUEST! WHERE ARE YOU?
QUEST!

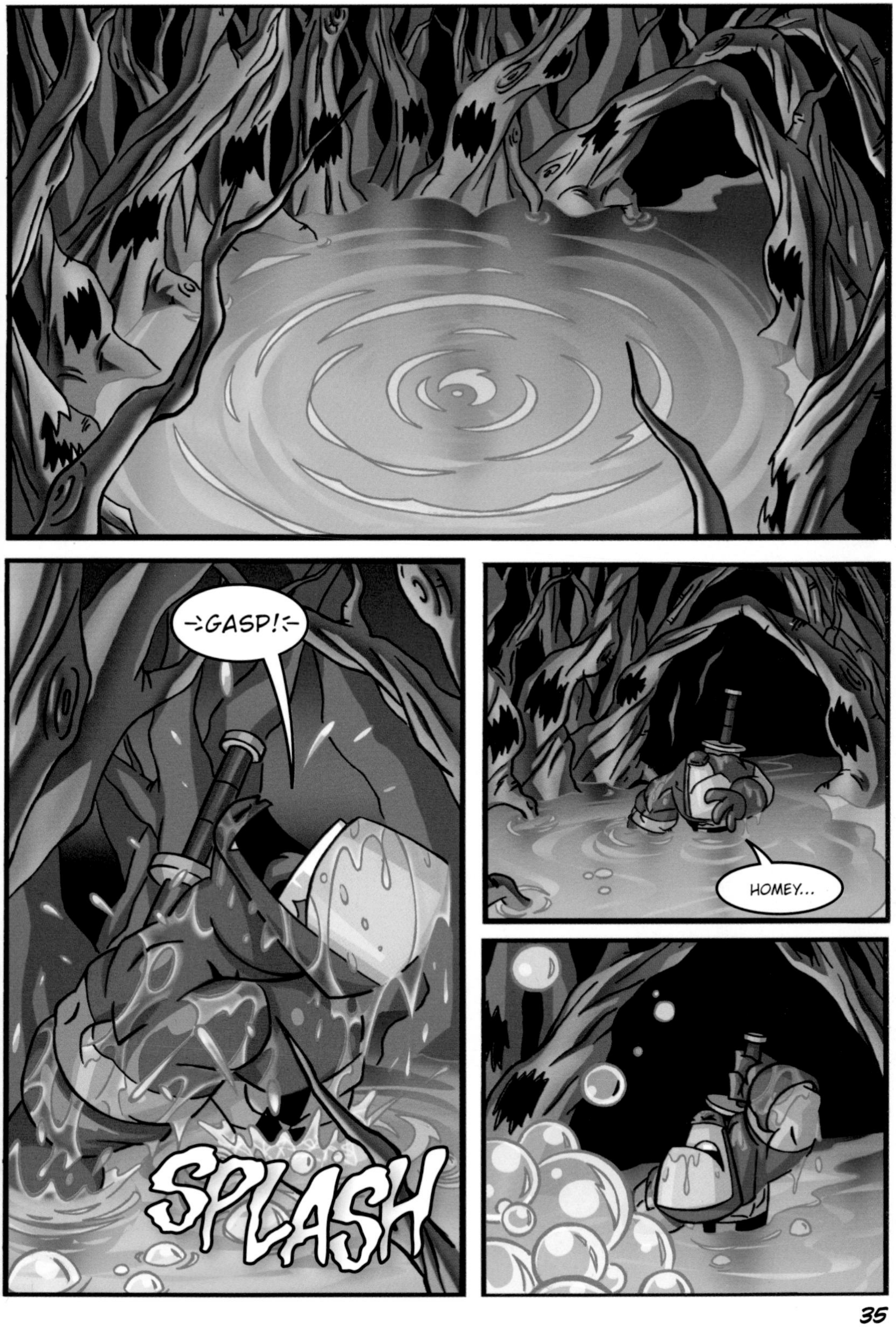

-GASP!-
SPLASH
HOMEY...

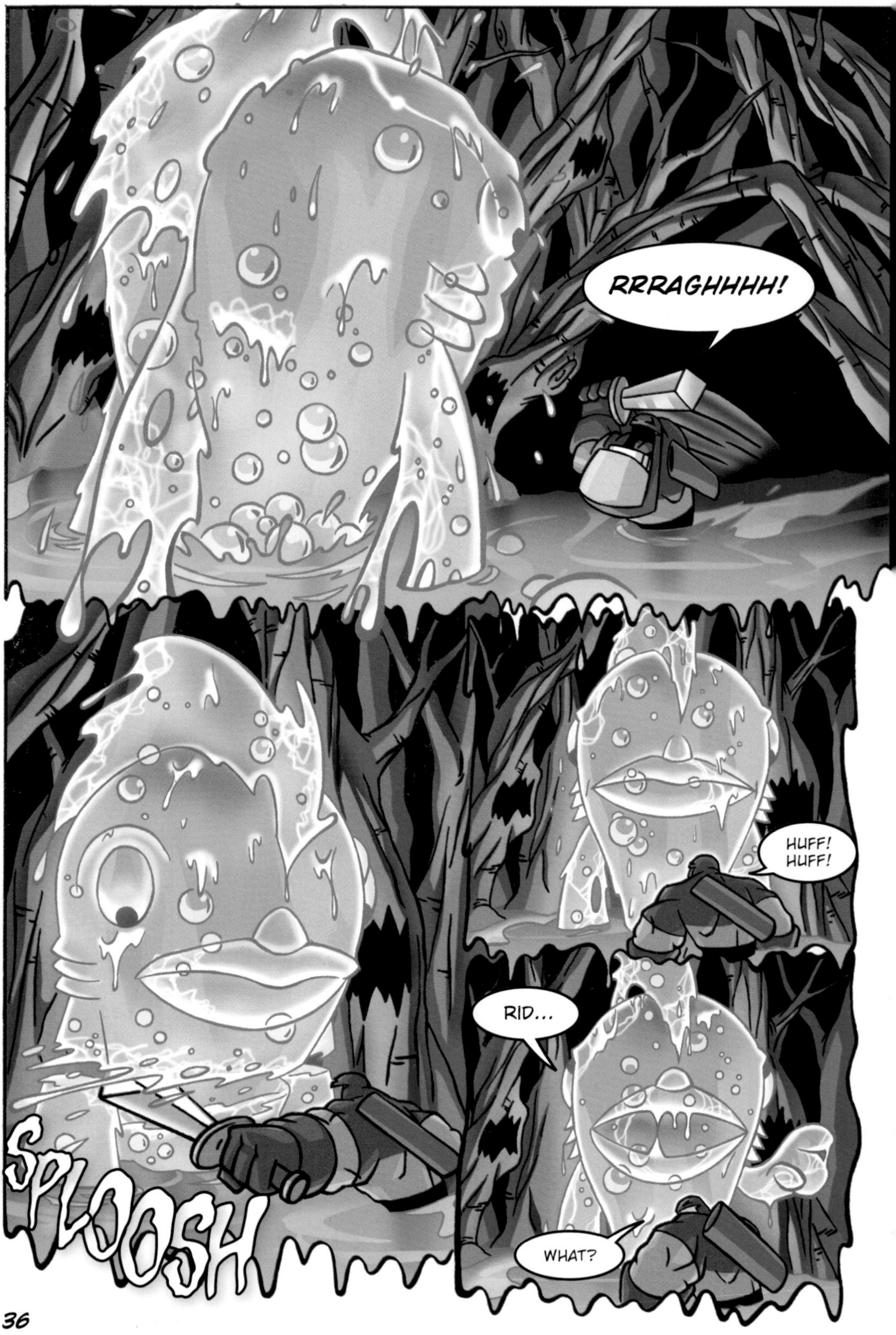
RRRAGHHHH!
SPLOOSH
HUFF! HUFF!
RID...
WHAT?

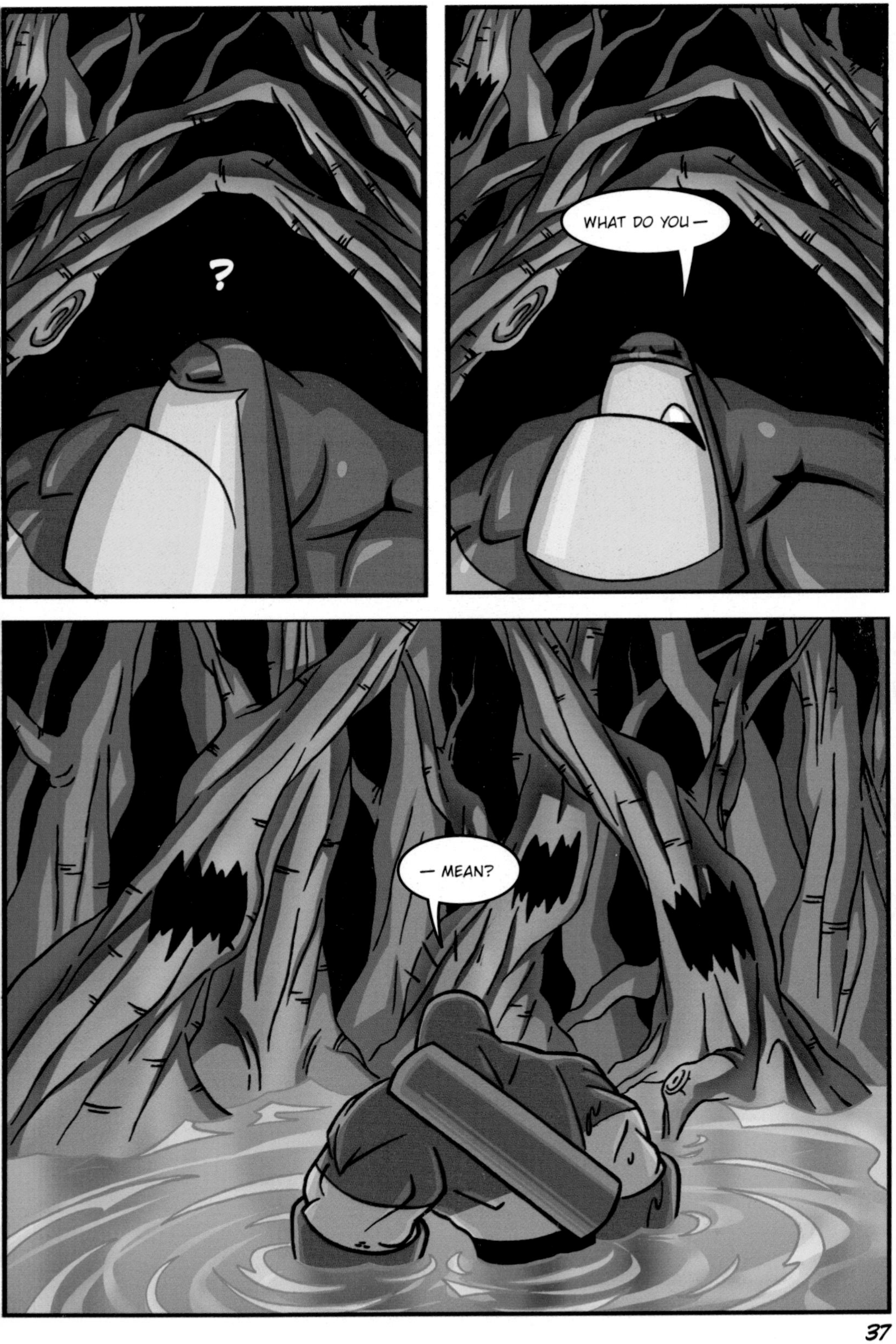
?
WHAT DO YOU—
— MEAN?

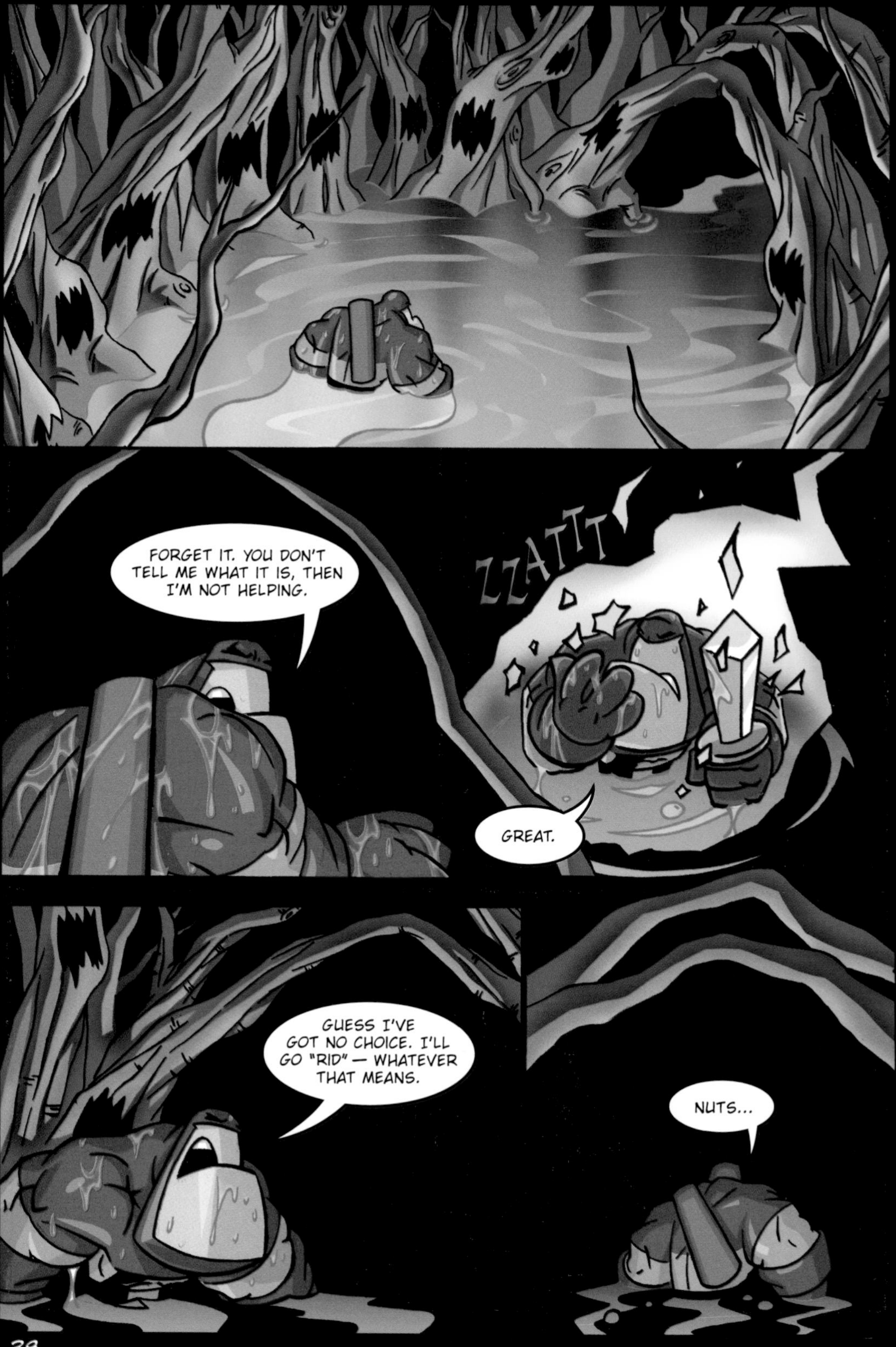
FORGET IT. YOU DON'T TELL ME WHAT IT IS, THEN I'M NOT HELPING.
ZZATTT
GREAT.
GUESS I'VE GOT NO CHOICE. I'LL GO "RID" — WHATEVER THAT MEANS.
NUTS...

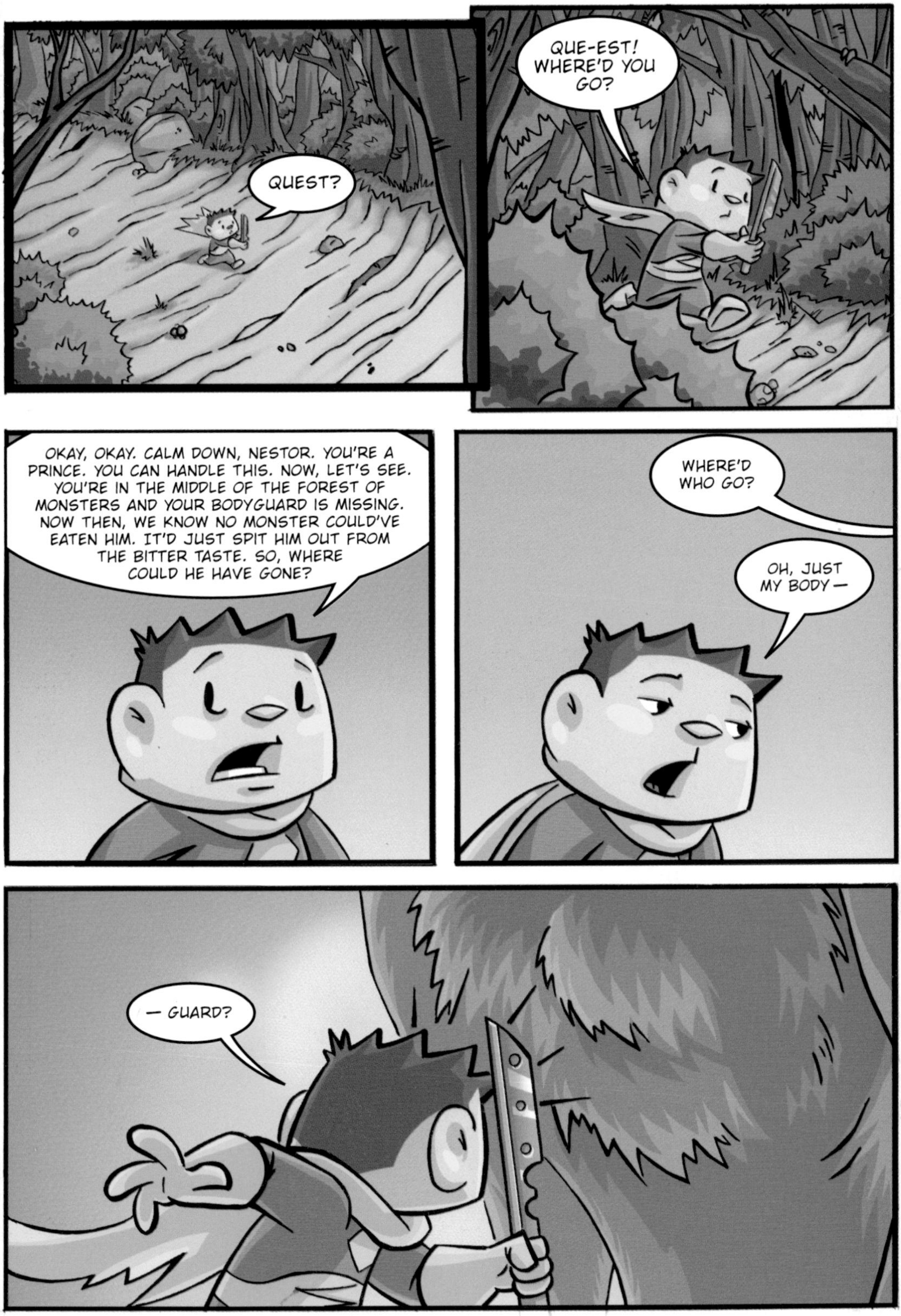
QUEST?
QUE-EST! WHERE'D YOU GO?
OKAY, OKAY. CALM DOWN, NESTOR. YOU'RE A PRINCE. YOU CAN HANDLE THIS. NOW, LET'S SEE. YOU'RE IN THE MIDDLE OF THE FOREST OF MONSTERS AND YOUR BODYGUARD IS MISSING. NOW THEN, WE KNOW NO MONSTER COULD'VE EATEN HIM. IT'D JUST SPIT HIM OUT FROM THE BITTER TASTE. SO, WHERE COULD HE HAVE GONE?
WHERE'D WHO GO?
OH, JUST MY BODY—
—GUARD?

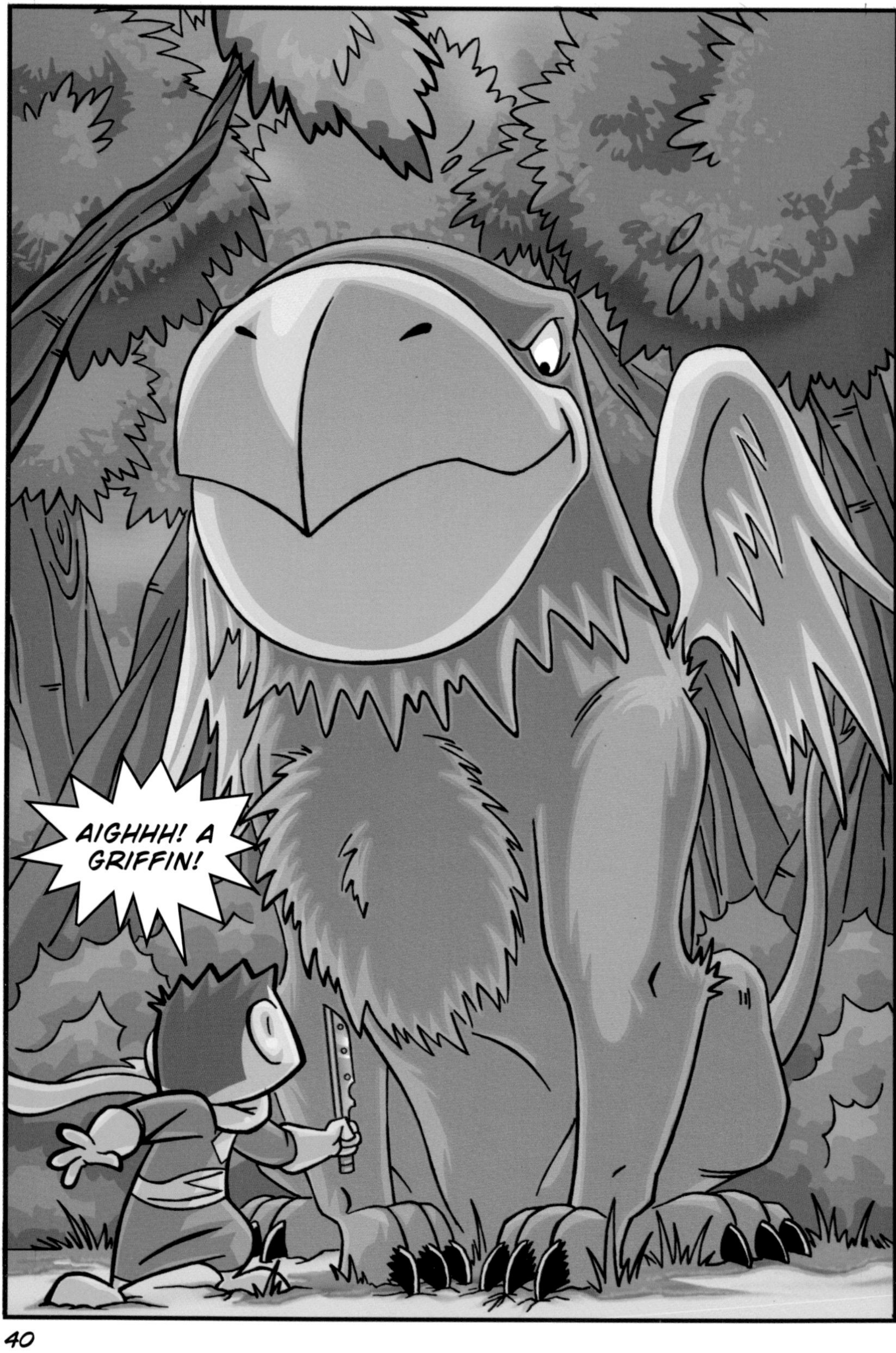
AIGHHH! A GRIFFIN!

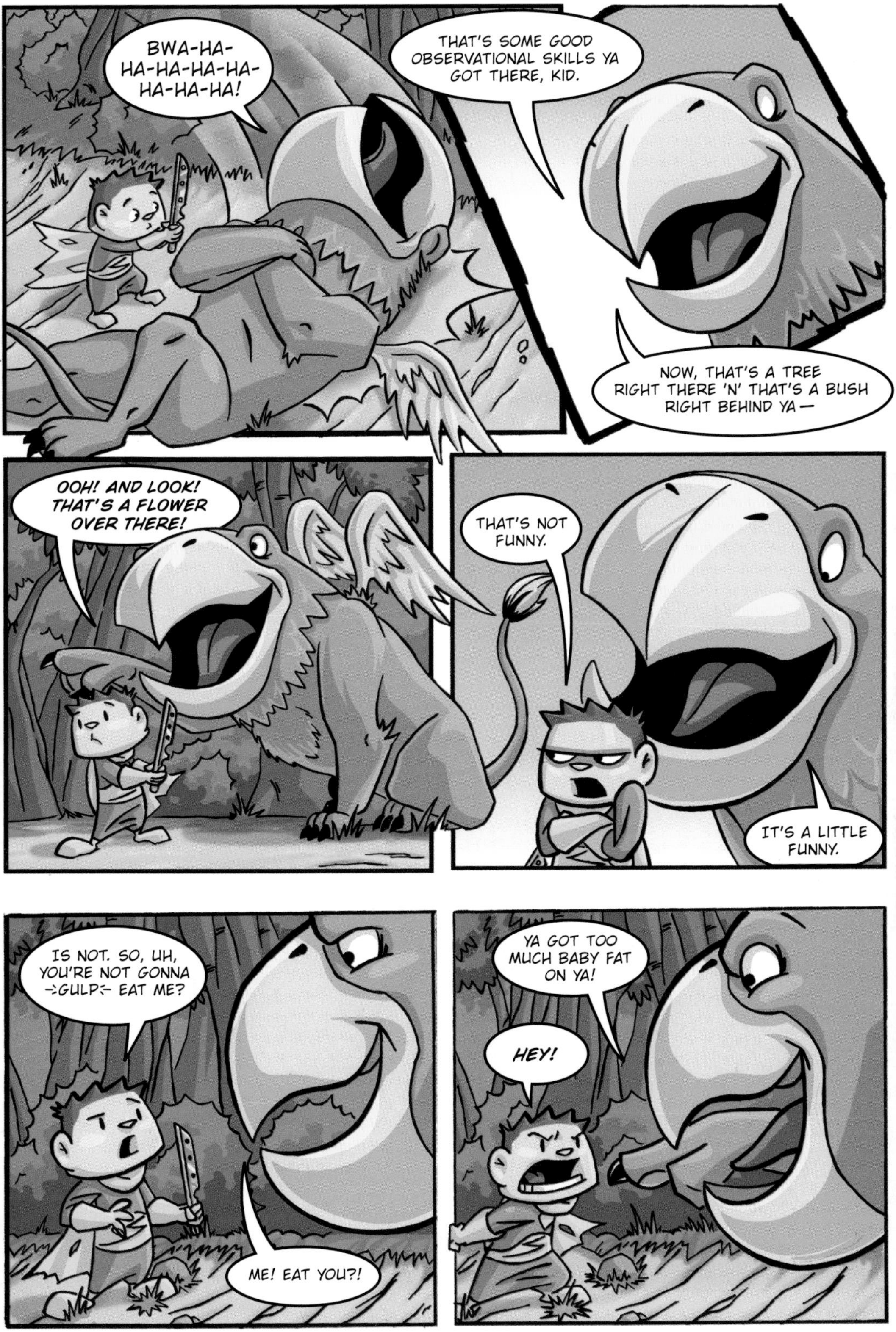
BWA-HA-HA-HA-HA-HA-HA-HA-HA!
THAT'S SOME GOOD OBSERVATIONAL SKILLS YA GOT THERE, KID.
NOW, THAT'S A TREE RIGHT THERE 'N' THAT'S A BUSH RIGHT BEHIND YA—
OOH! AND LOOK! THAT'S A FLOWER OVER THERE!
THAT'S NOT FUNNY.
IT'S A LITTLE FUNNY.
IS NOT. SO, UH, YOU'RE NOT GONNA -GULP- EAT ME?
ME! EAT YOU?!
YA GOT TOO MUCH BABY FAT ON YA!
HEY!

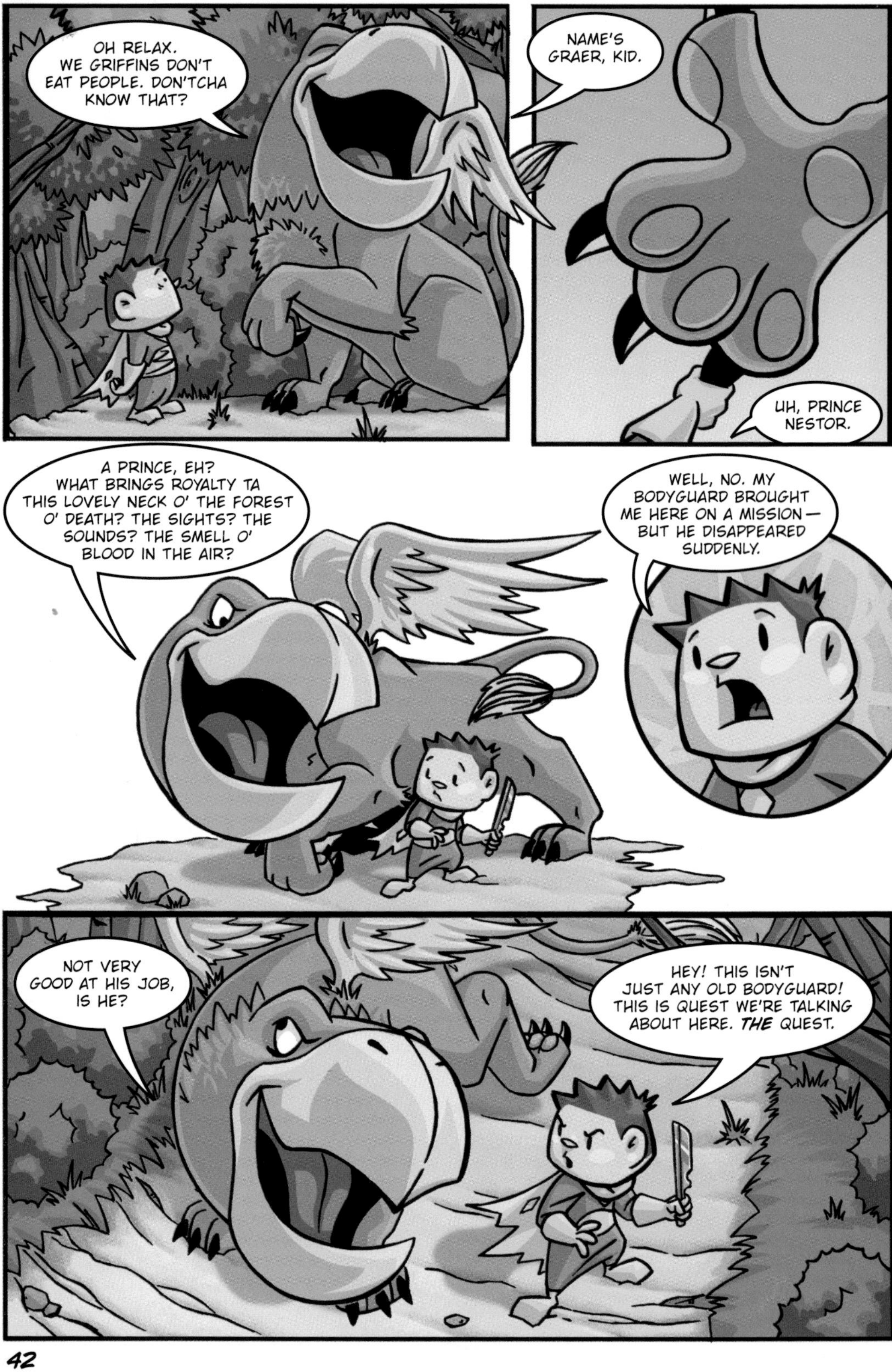
OH RELAX. WE GRIFFINS DON'T EAT PEOPLE. DON'TCHA KNOW THAT?
NAME'S GRAER, KID.
UH, PRINCE NESTOR.
A PRINCE, EH? WHAT BRINGS ROYALTY TA THIS LOVELY NECK O' THE FOREST O' DEATH? THE SIGHTS? THE SOUNDS? THE SMELL O' BLOOD IN THE AIR?
WELL, NO. MY BODYGUARD BROUGHT ME HERE ON A MISSION— BUT HE DISAPPEARED SUDDENLY.
NOT VERY GOOD AT HIS JOB, IS HE?
HEY! THIS ISN'T JUST ANY OLD BODYGUARD! THIS IS QUEST WE'RE TALKING ABOUT HERE. *THE* QUEST.

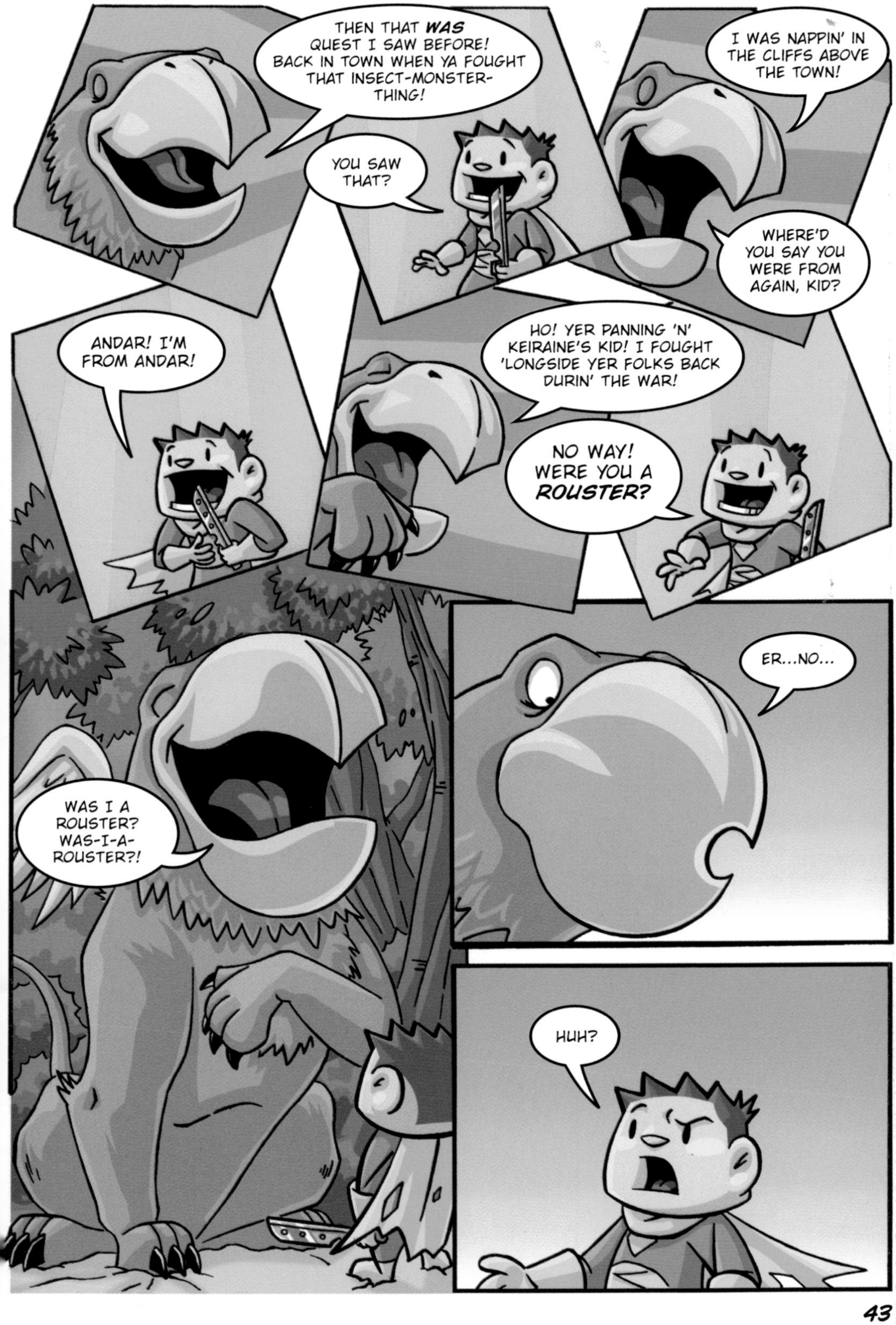
THEN THAT ***WAS*** QUEST I SAW BEFORE! BACK IN TOWN WHEN YA FOUGHT THAT INSECT-MONSTER-THING!
YOU SAW THAT?
I WAS NAPPIN' IN THE CLIFFS ABOVE THE TOWN!
WHERE'D YOU SAY YOU WERE FROM AGAIN, KID?
ANDAR! I'M FROM ANDAR!
HO! YER PANNING 'N' KEIRAINE'S KID! I FOUGHT 'LONGSIDE YER FOLKS BACK DURIN' THE WAR!
NO WAY! WERE YOU A ***ROUSTER?***
WAS I A ROUSTER? WAS-I-A-ROUSTER?!
ER...NO...
HUH?

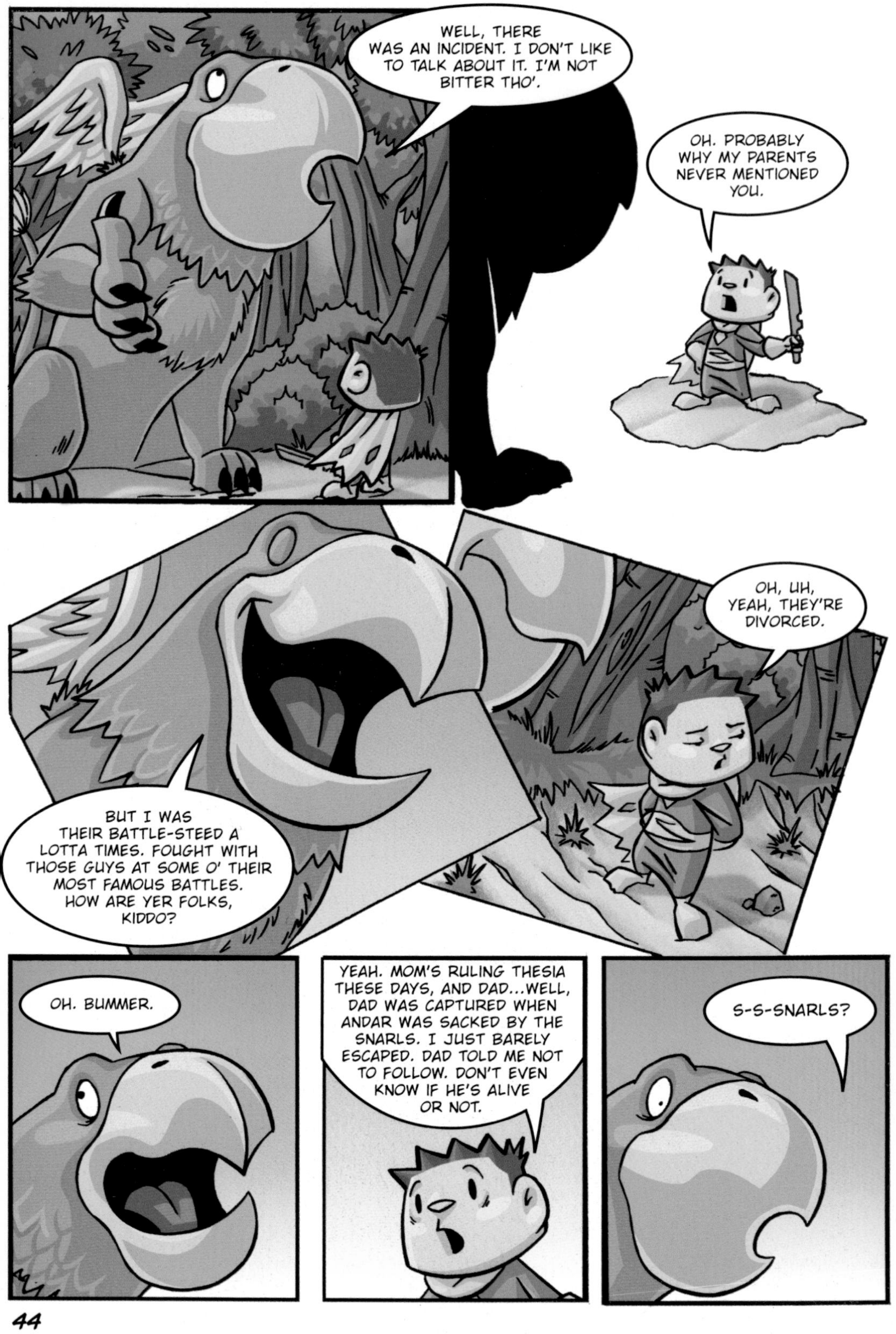
WELL, THERE WAS AN INCIDENT. I DON'T LIKE TO TALK ABOUT IT. I'M NOT BITTER THO'.
OH. PROBABLY WHY MY PARENTS NEVER MENTIONED YOU.
BUT I WAS THEIR BATTLE-STEED A LOTTA TIMES. FOUGHT WITH THOSE GUYS AT SOME O' THEIR MOST FAMOUS BATTLES. HOW ARE YER FOLKS, KIDDO?
OH, UH, YEAH, THEY'RE DIVORCED.
OH. BUMMER.
YEAH. MOM'S RULING THESIA THESE DAYS, AND DAD...WELL, DAD WAS CAPTURED WHEN ANDAR WAS SACKED BY THE SNARLS. I JUST BARELY ESCAPED. DAD TOLD ME NOT TO FOLLOW. DON'T EVEN KNOW IF HE'S ALIVE OR NOT.
S-S-SNARLS?

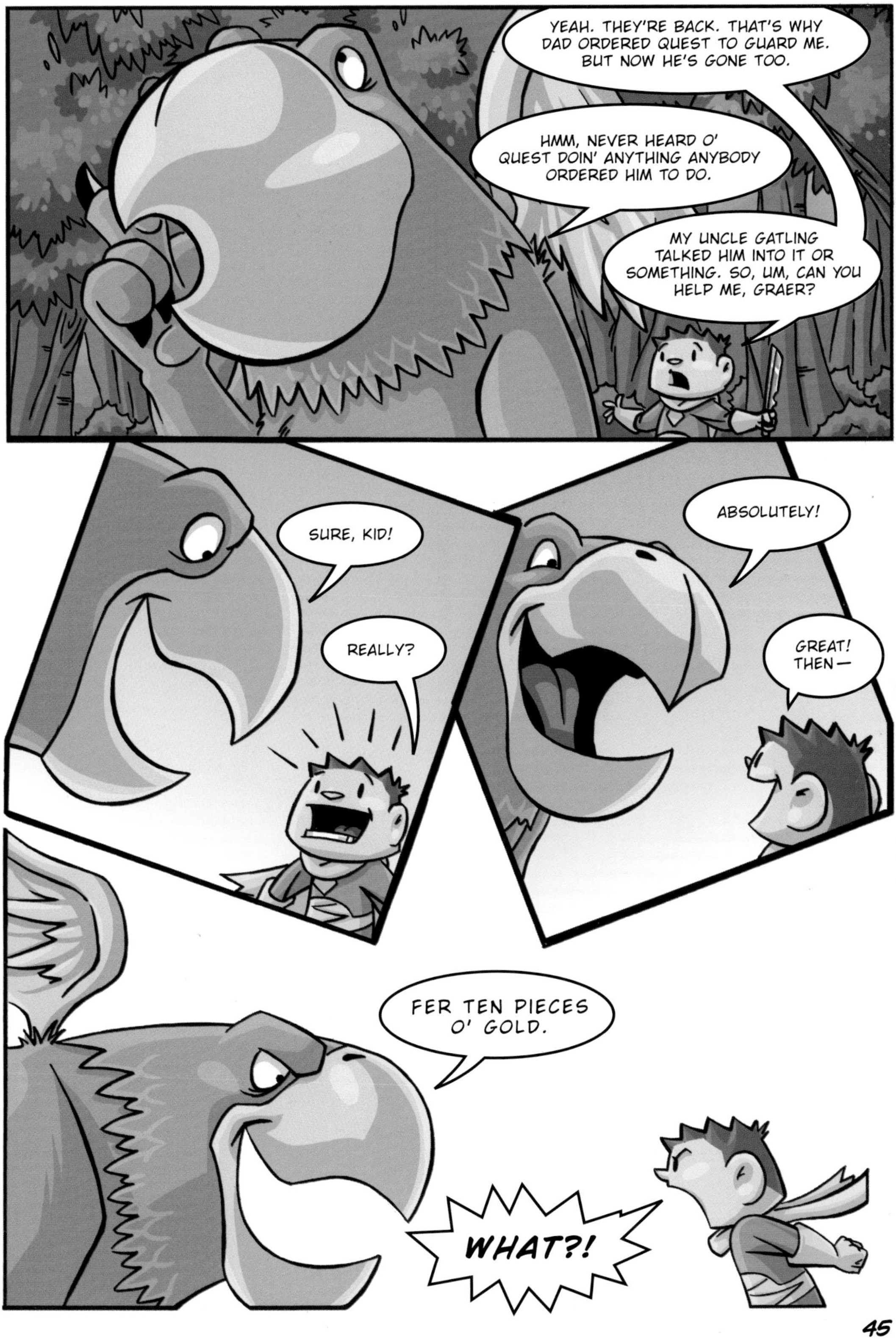
YEAH. THEY'RE BACK. THAT'S WHY DAD ORDERED QUEST TO GUARD ME. BUT NOW HE'S GONE TOO.
HMM, NEVER HEARD O' QUEST DOIN' ANYTHING ANYBODY ORDERED HIM TO DO.
MY UNCLE GATLING TALKED HIM INTO IT OR SOMETHING. SO, UM, CAN YOU HELP ME, GRAER?
SURE, KID!
REALLY?
ABSOLUTELY!
GREAT! THEN—
FER TEN PIECES O' GOLD.
WHAT?!

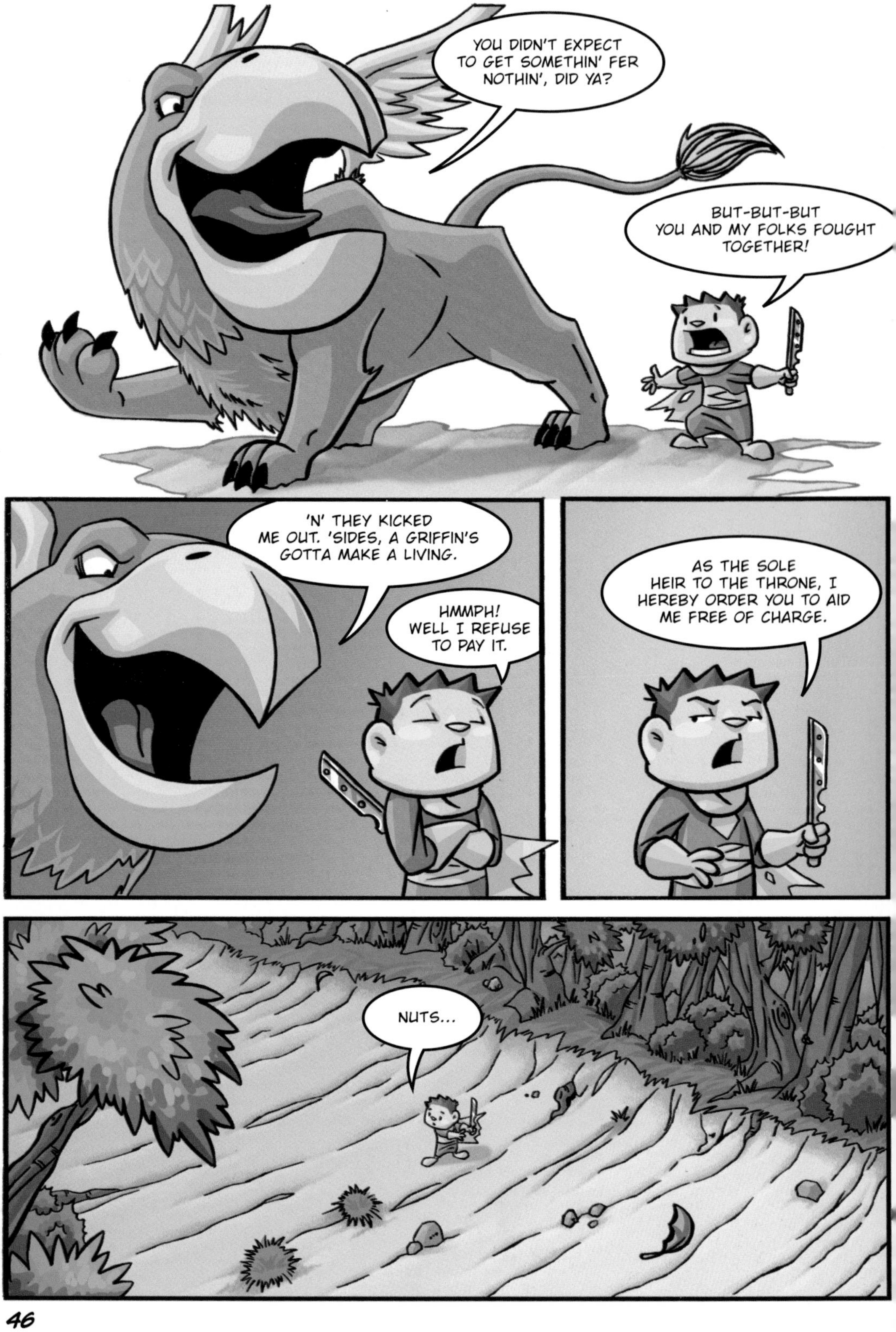
YOU DIDN'T EXPECT TO GET SOMETHIN' FER NOTHIN', DID YA?
BUT-BUT-BUT YOU AND MY FOLKS FOUGHT TOGETHER!
'N' THEY KICKED ME OUT. 'SIDES, A GRIFFIN'S GOTTA MAKE A LIVING.
HMMPH! WELL I REFUSE TO PAY IT.
AS THE SOLE HEIR TO THE THRONE, I HEREBY ORDER YOU TO AID ME FREE OF CHARGE.
NUTS...

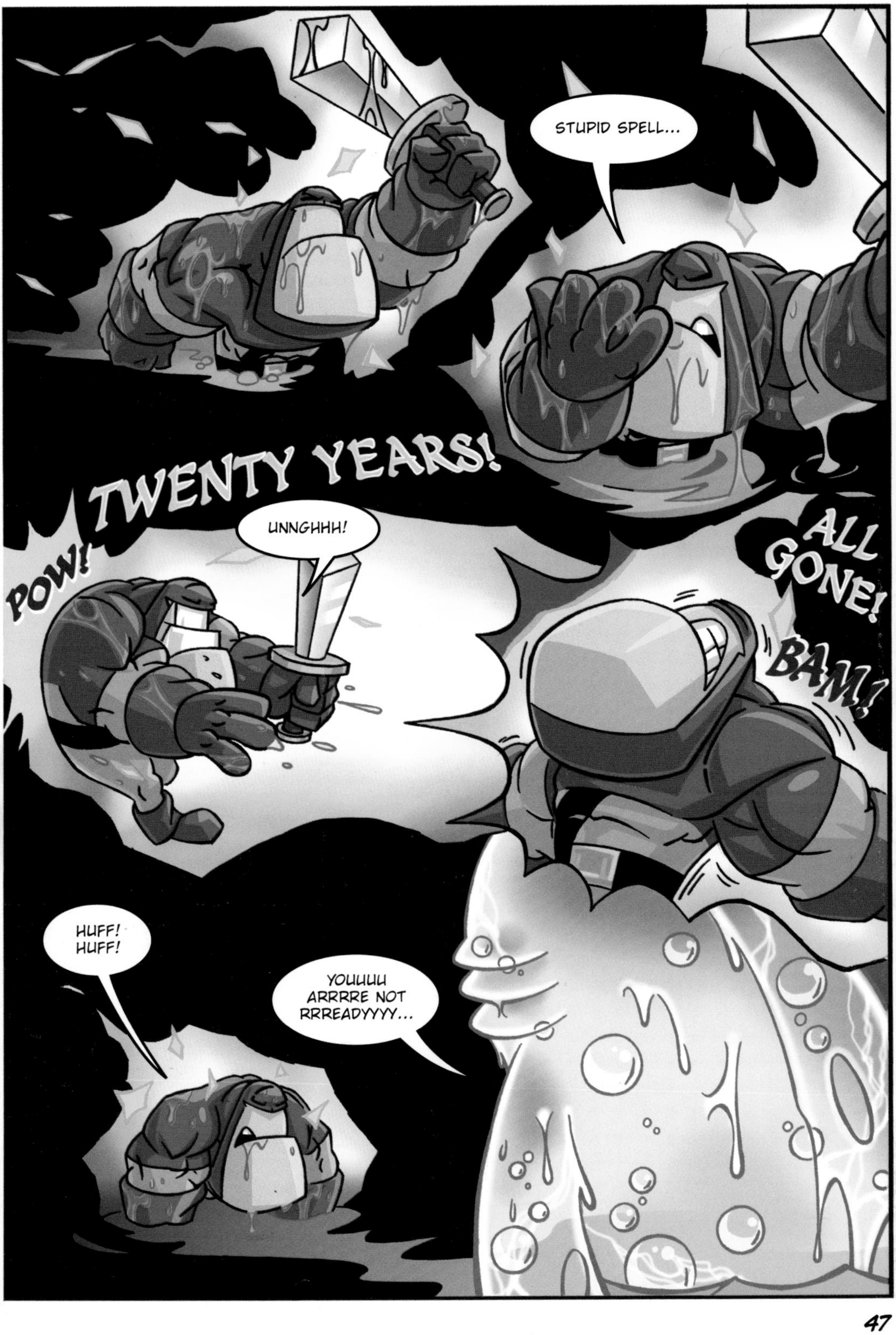
STUPID SPELL...
TWENTY YEARS!
POW!
UNNGHHH!
ALL GONE!
BAM!
HUFF! HUFF!
YOUUUU ARRRRE NOT RRREADYYYY...

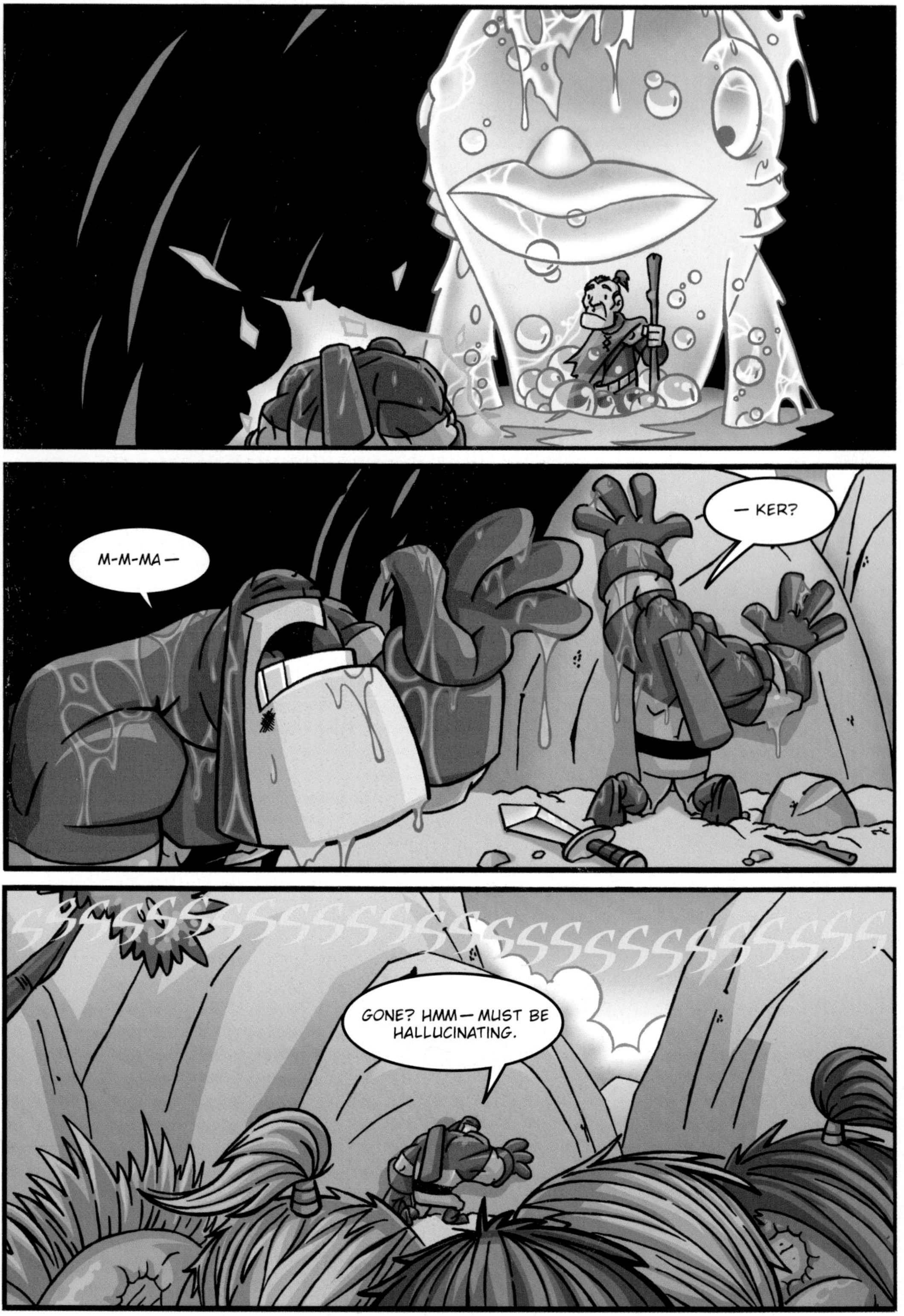
M-M-MA—
— KER?
GONE? HMM— MUST BE HALLUCINATING.

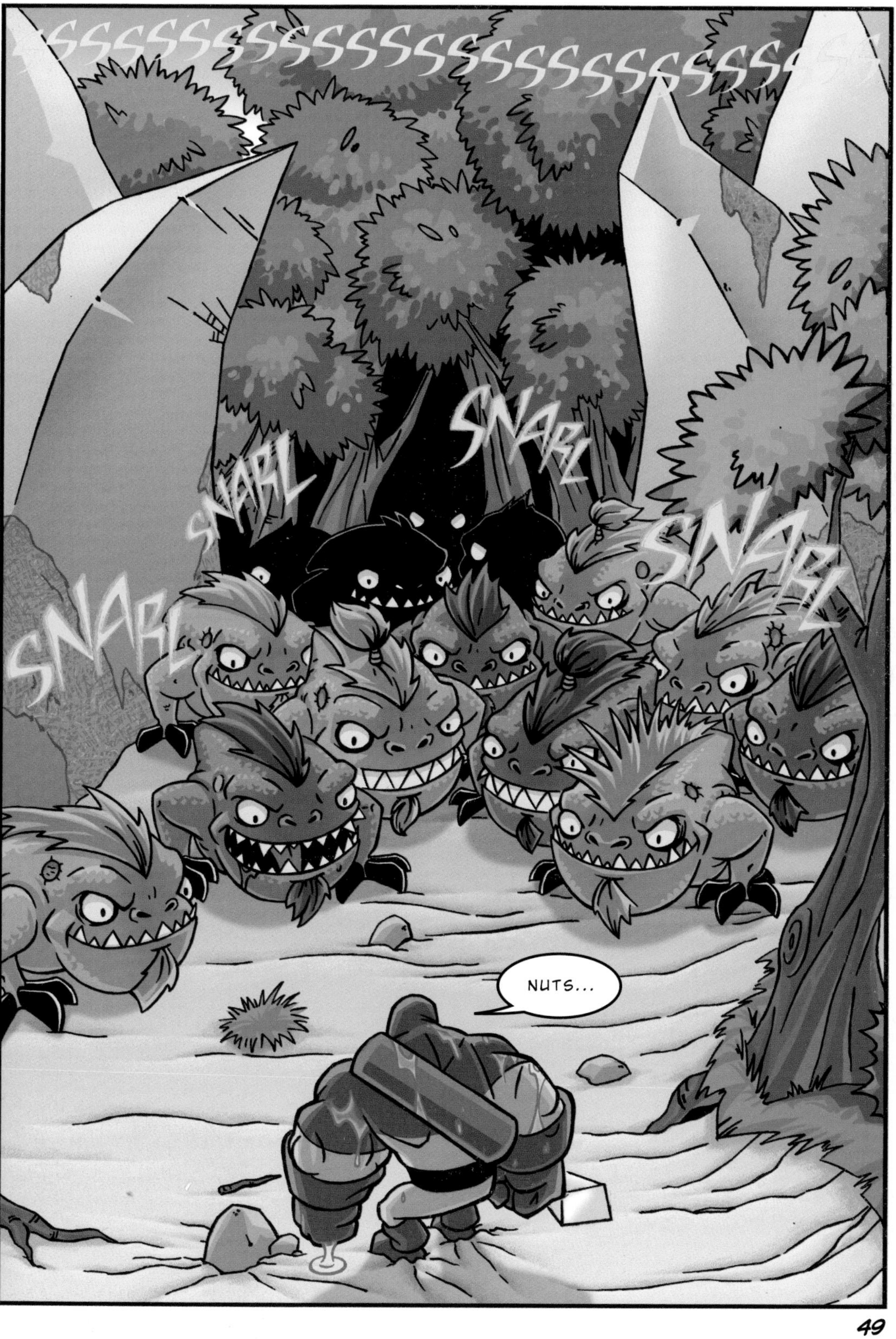
SSSSSSSSSSSSSSSSSSSSSSSS
SNARL
SNARL
SNARL
SNARL
NUTS...

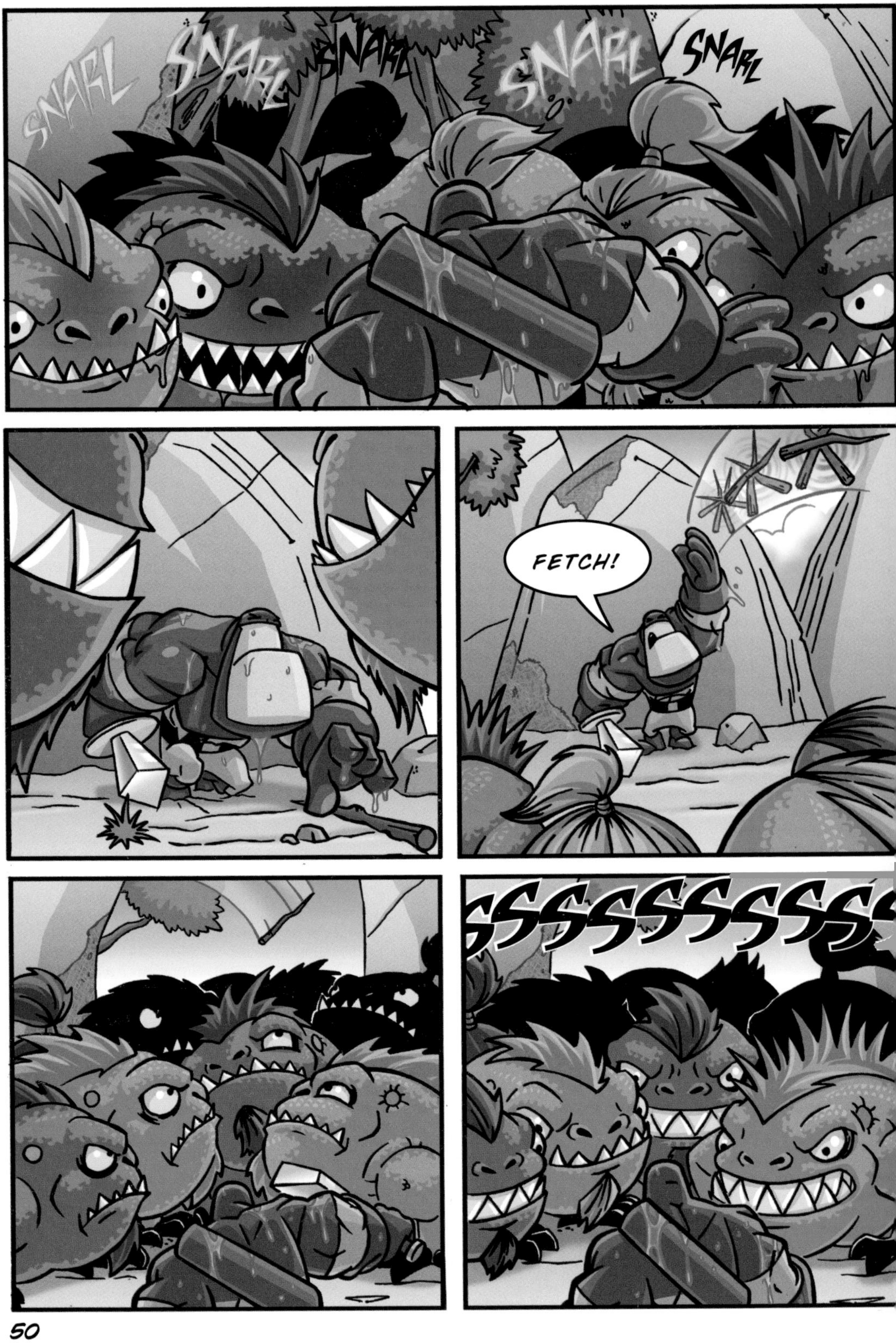
SNARL
SNARL
SNARL
SNARL
SNARL
FETCH!
SSSSSSSSSS

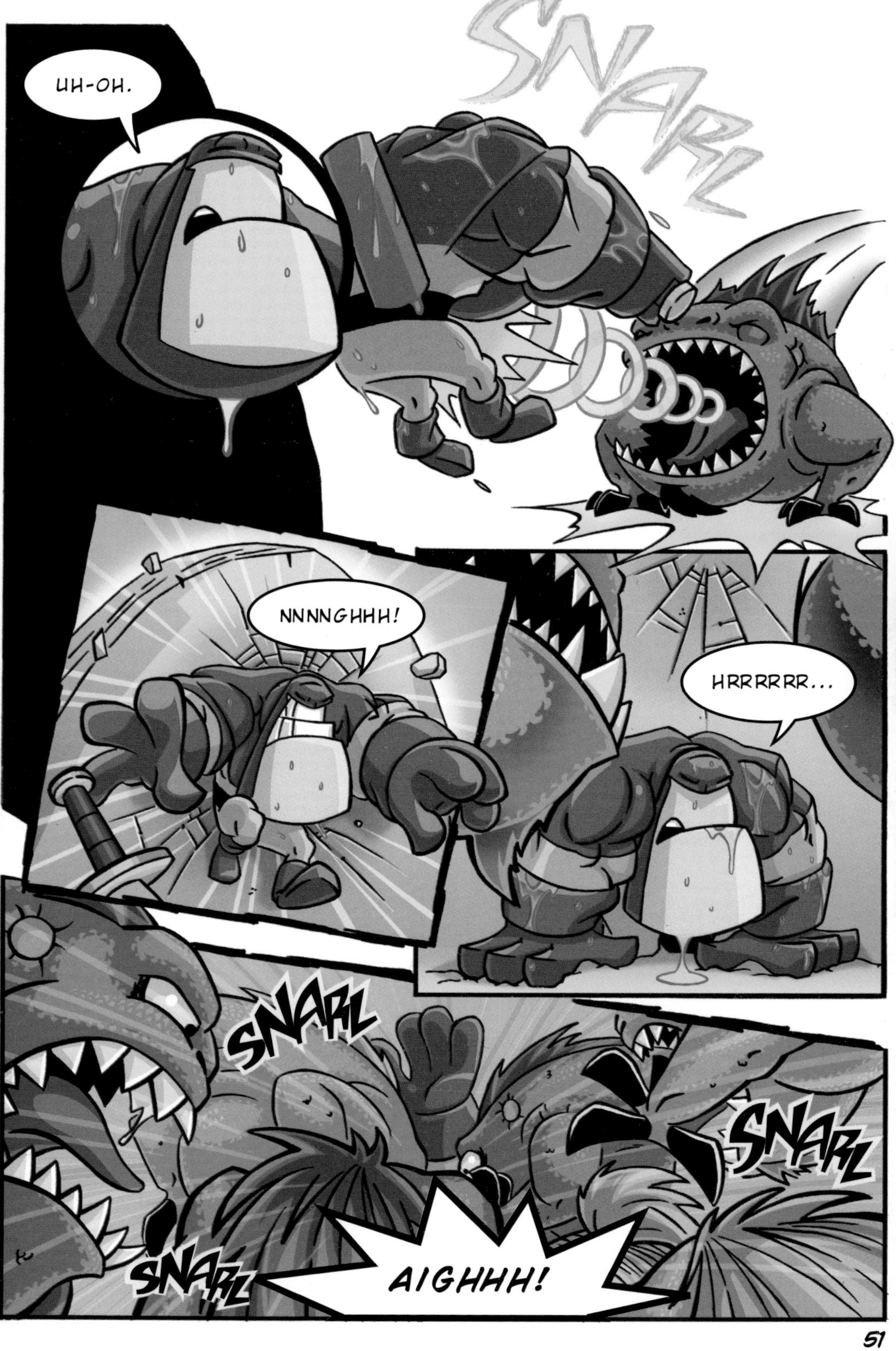
SNARL
UH-OH.
NNNNGHHH!
HRRRRRR...
SNARL
SNARL
SNARL
AIGHHH!

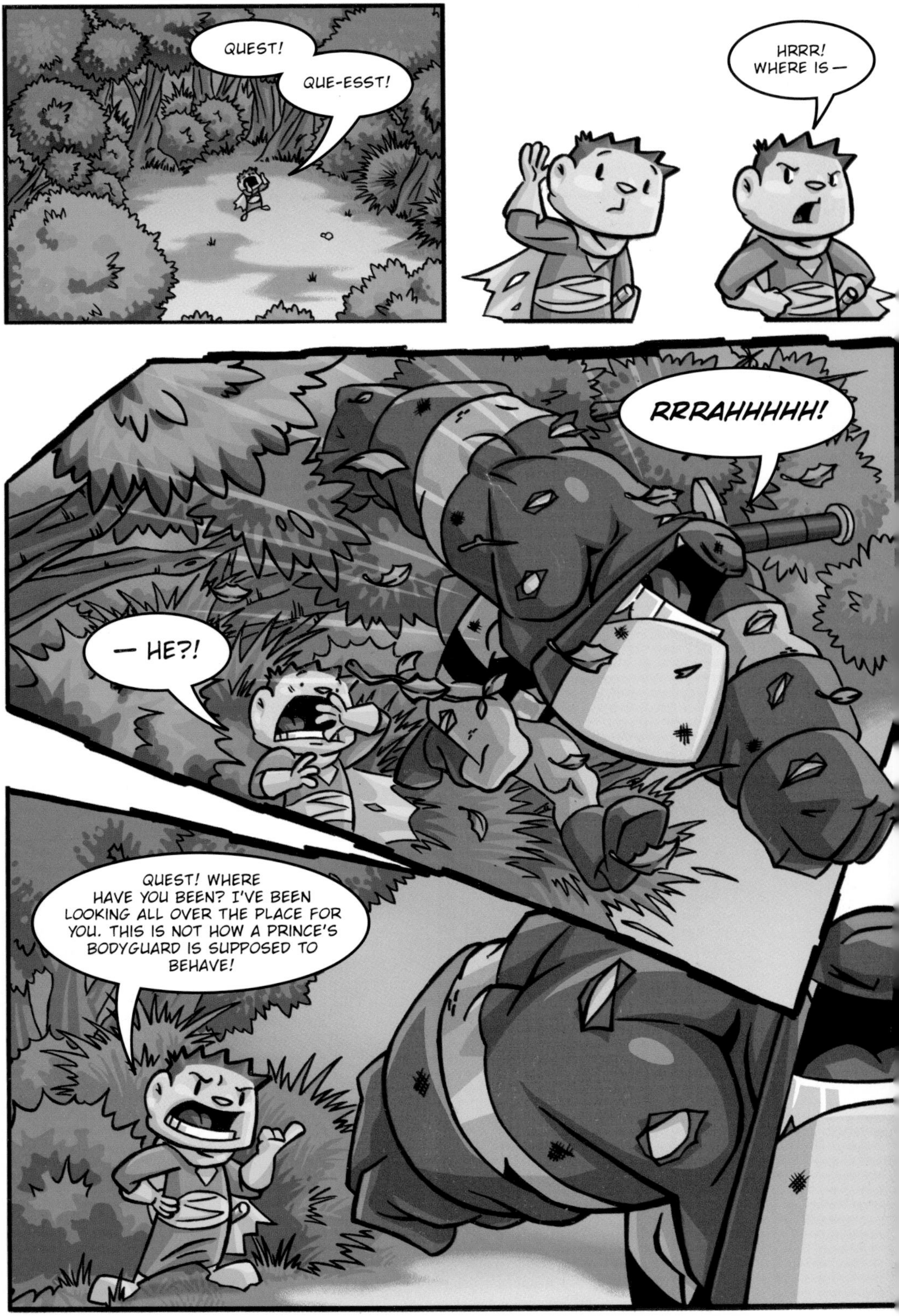
QUEST!
QUE-ESST!
HRRR! WHERE IS —
RRRAHHHHH!
— HE?!
QUEST! WHERE HAVE YOU BEEN? I'VE BEEN LOOKING ALL OVER THE PLACE FOR YOU. THIS IS NOT HOW A PRINCE'S BODYGUARD IS SUPPOSED TO BEHAVE!

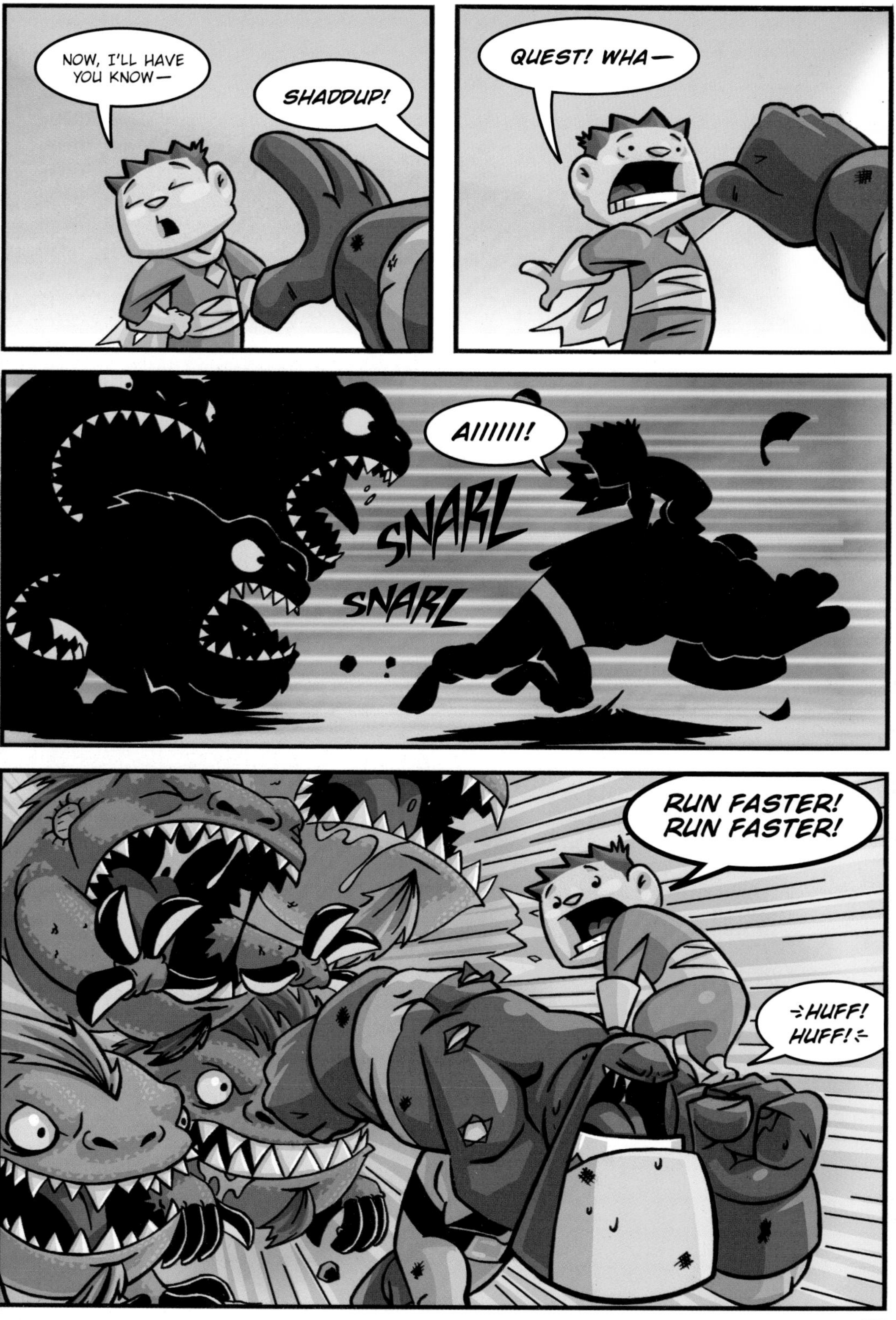
NOW, I'LL HAVE YOU KNOW—
SHADDUP!
QUEST! WHA—
AIIIIII!
SNARL
SNARL
RUN FASTER! RUN FASTER!
HUFF! HUFF!

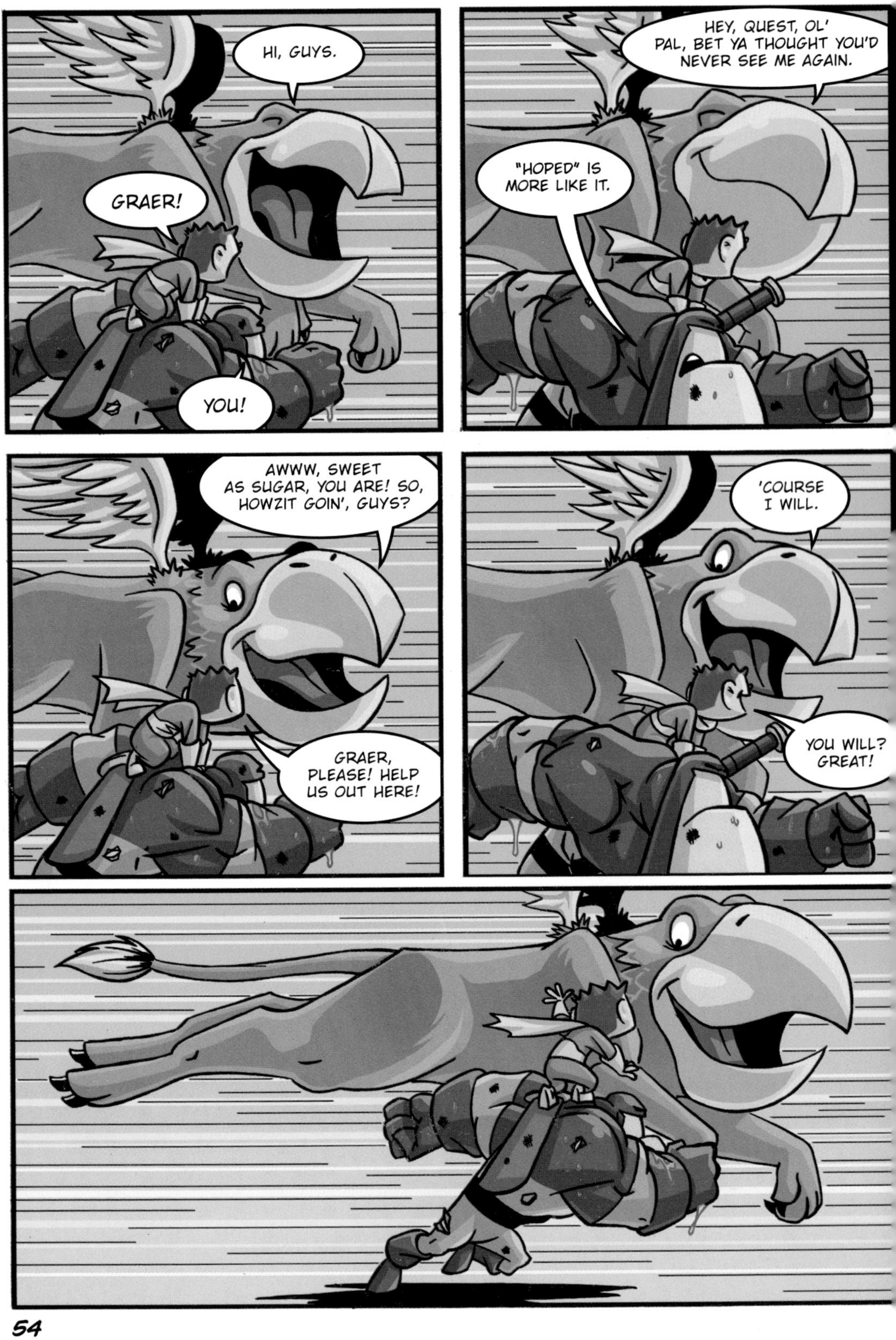
HI, GUYS.
GRAER!
YOU!
HEY, QUEST, OL' PAL, BET YA THOUGHT YOU'D NEVER SEE ME AGAIN.
"HOPED" IS MORE LIKE IT.
AWWW, SWEET AS SUGAR, YOU ARE! SO, HOWZIT GOIN', GUYS?
GRAER, PLEASE! HELP US OUT HERE!
'COURSE I WILL.
YOU WILL? GREAT!

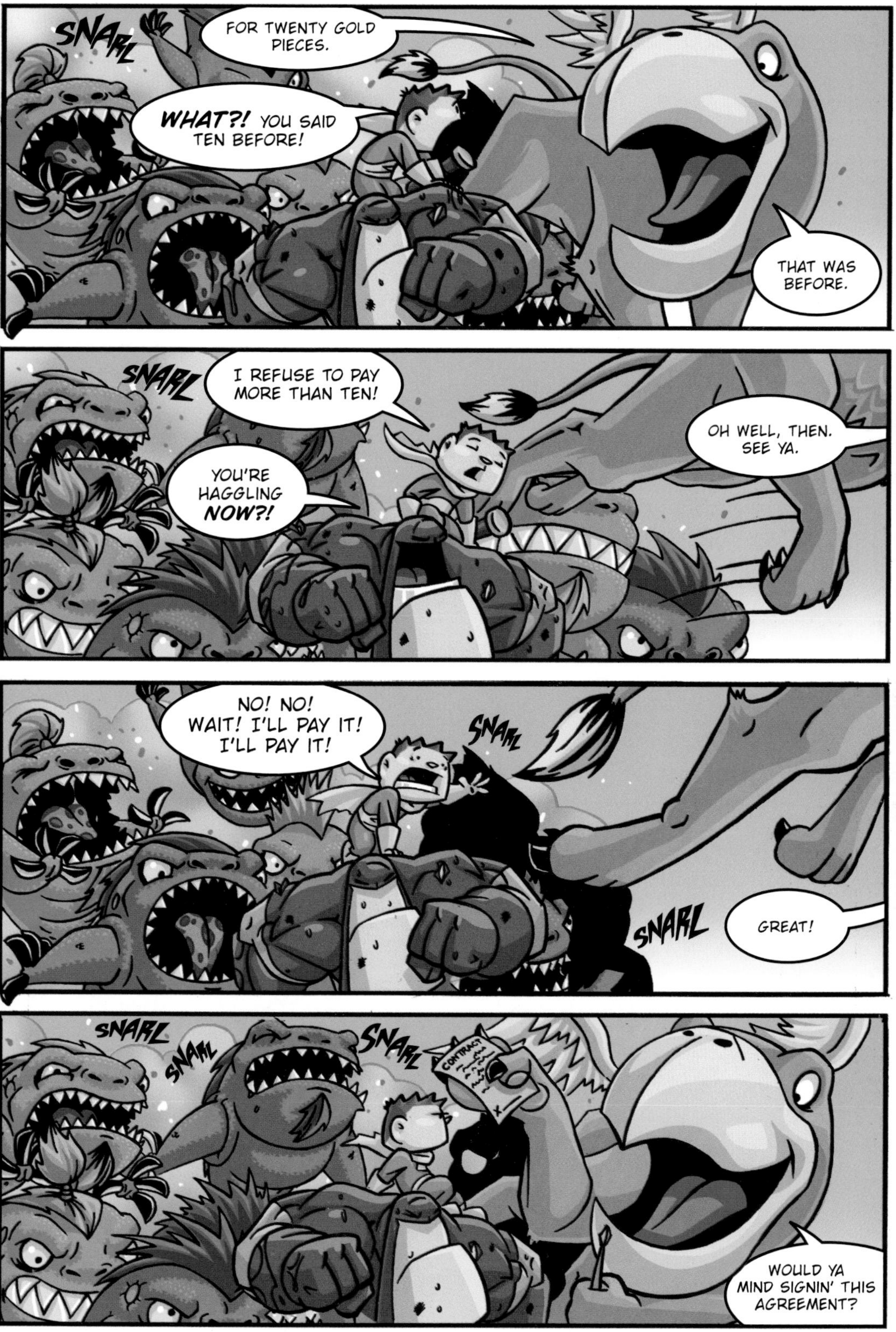
SNARL
FOR TWENTY GOLD PIECES.
WHAT?! YOU SAID TEN BEFORE!
THAT WAS BEFORE.
SNARL
I REFUSE TO PAY MORE THAN TEN!
YOU'RE HAGGLING NOW?!
OH WELL, THEN. SEE YA.
NO! NO! WAIT! I'LL PAY IT! I'LL PAY IT!
SNARL
SNARL
GREAT!
SNARL
SNARL
SNARL
CONTRACT
WOULD YA MIND SIGNIN' THIS AGREEMENT?

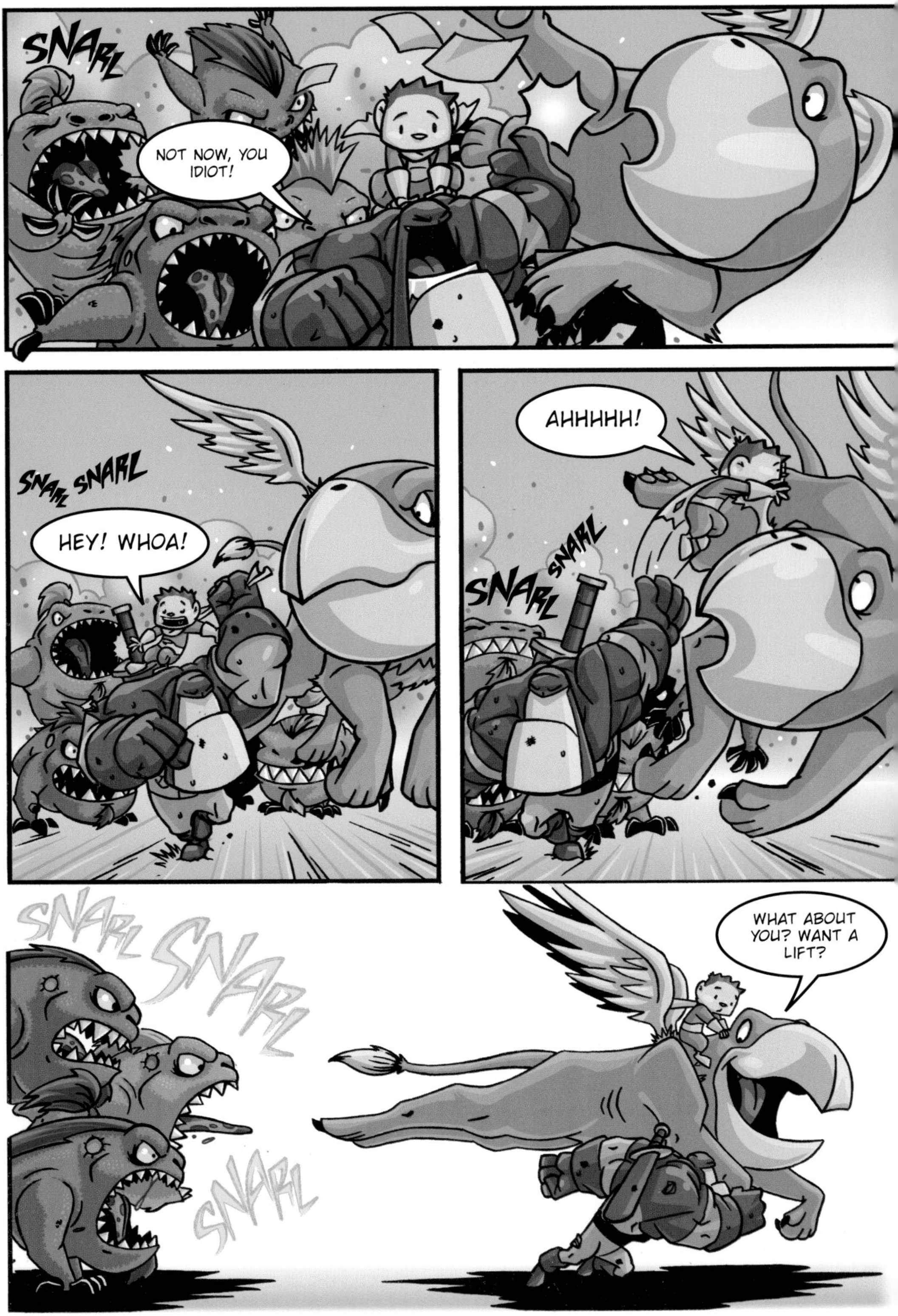
SNARL
NOT NOW, YOU IDIOT!
SNARL SNARL
HEY! WHOA!
AHHHHH!
SNARL SNARL
SNARL SNARL
WHAT ABOUT YOU? WANT A LIFT?
SNARL

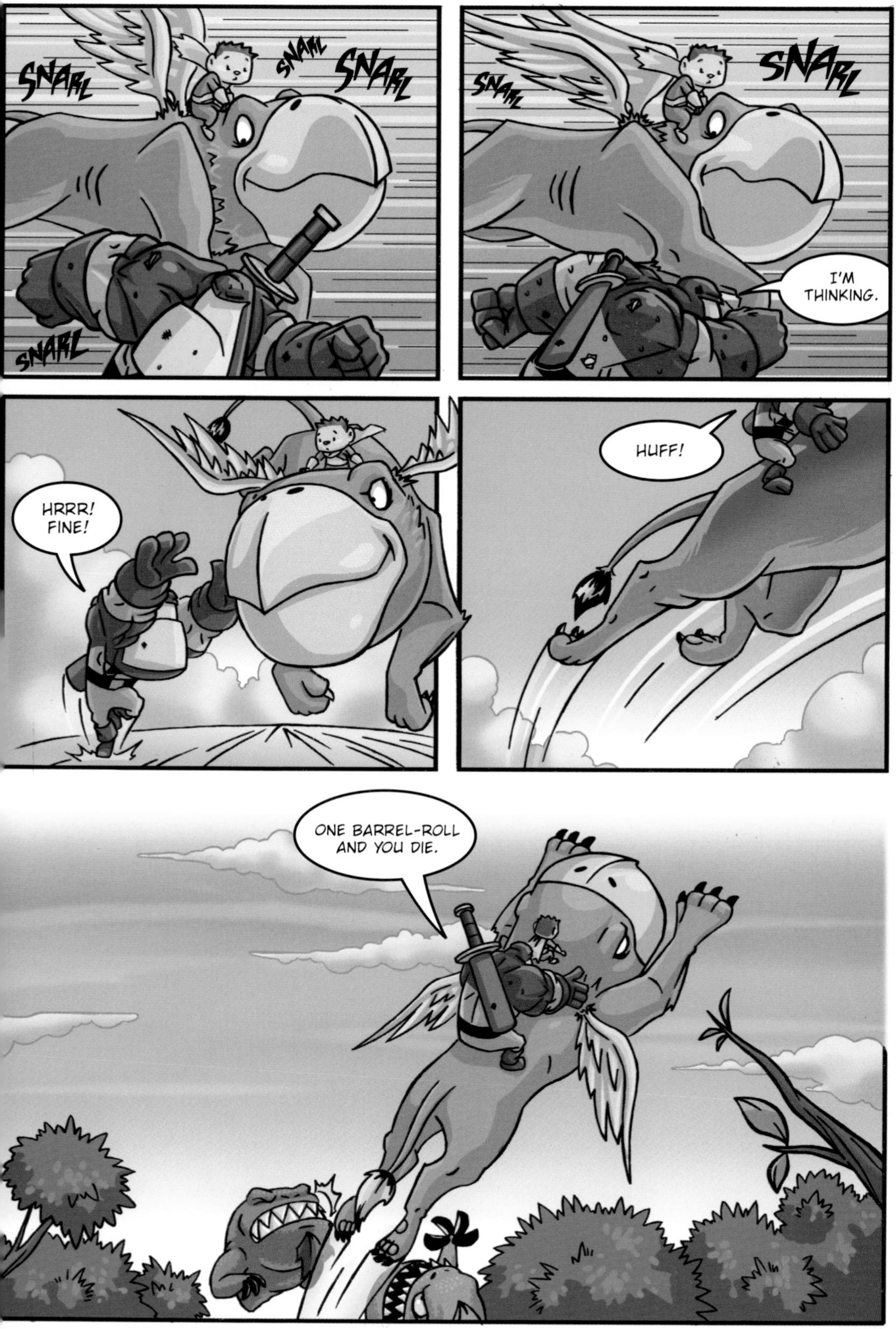
SNARL
SNARL
SNARL
SNARL
SNARL
SNARL
I'M THINKING.
HRRR! FINE!
HUFF!
ONE BARREL-ROLL AND YOU DIE.

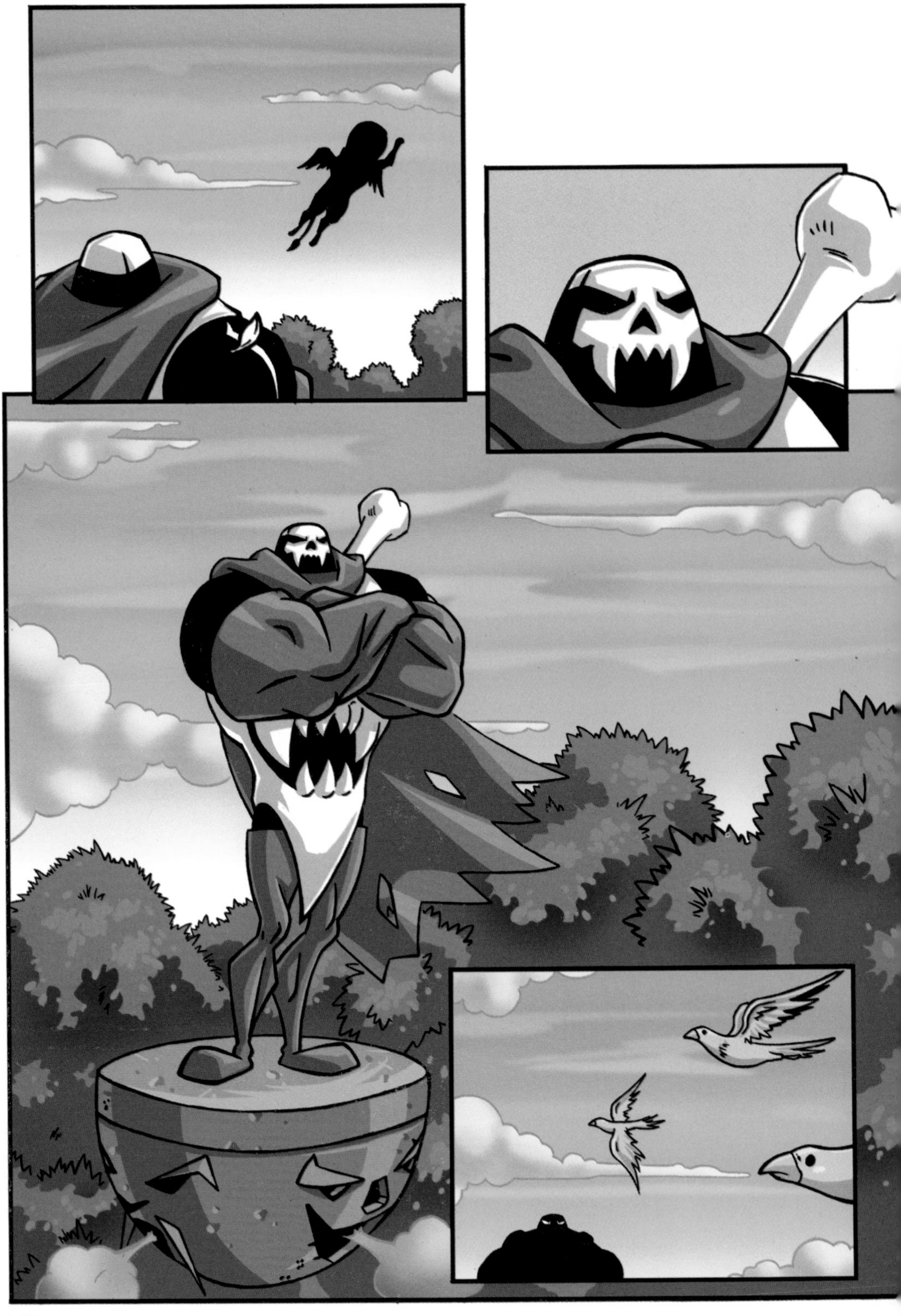

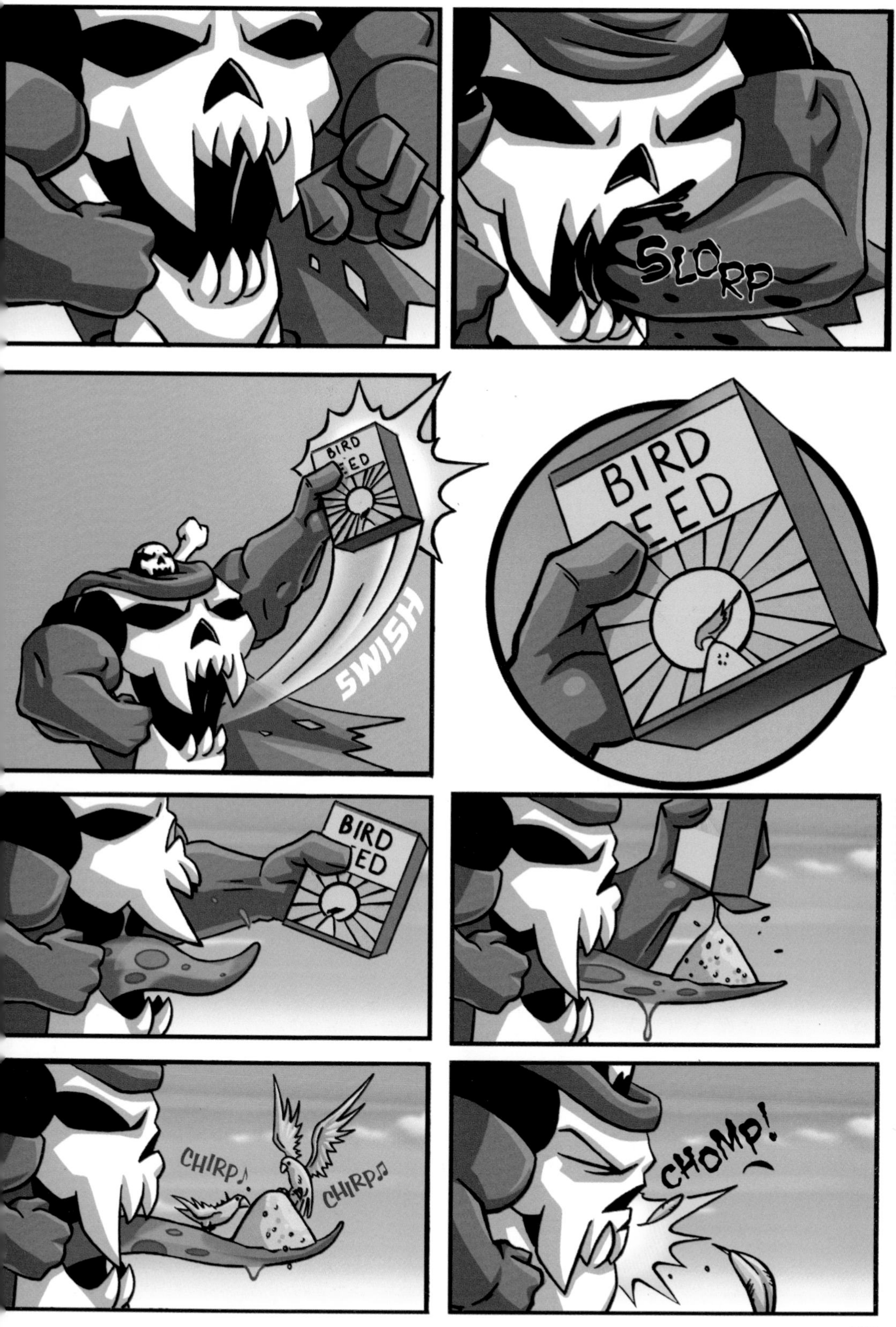
SLORP
BIRD
EED
SWISH
BIRD
EED
BIRD
ED
CHIRP♪
CHIRP♫
CHOMP!

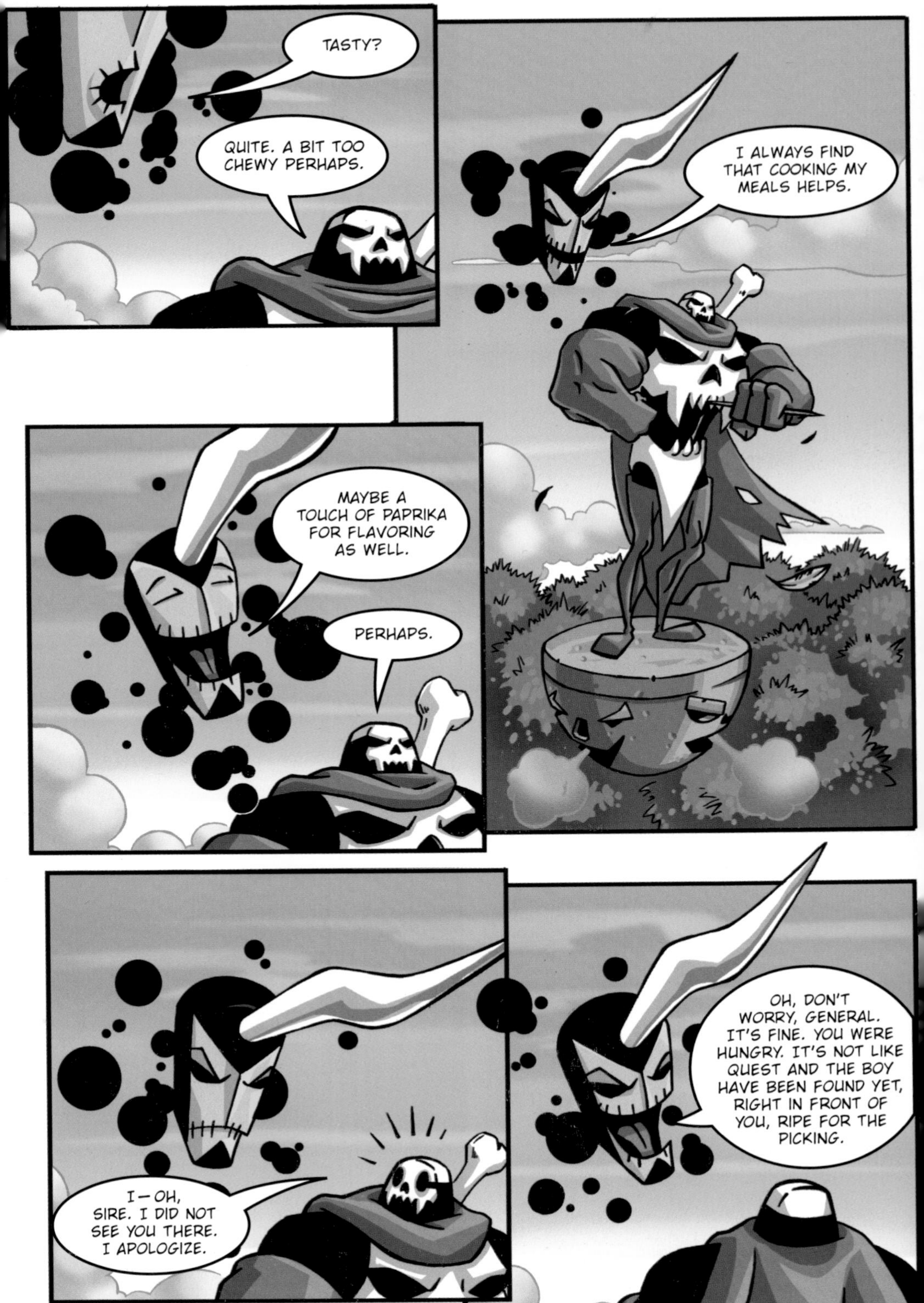
TASTY?
QUITE. A BIT TOO CHEWY PERHAPS.
I ALWAYS FIND THAT COOKING MY MEALS HELPS.
MAYBE A TOUCH OF PAPRIKA FOR FLAVORING AS WELL.
PERHAPS.
I—OH, SIRE. I DID NOT SEE YOU THERE. I APOLOGIZE.
OH, DON'T WORRY, GENERAL. IT'S FINE. YOU WERE HUNGRY. IT'S NOT LIKE QUEST AND THE BOY HAVE BEEN FOUND YET, RIGHT IN FRONT OF YOU, RIPE FOR THE PICKING.

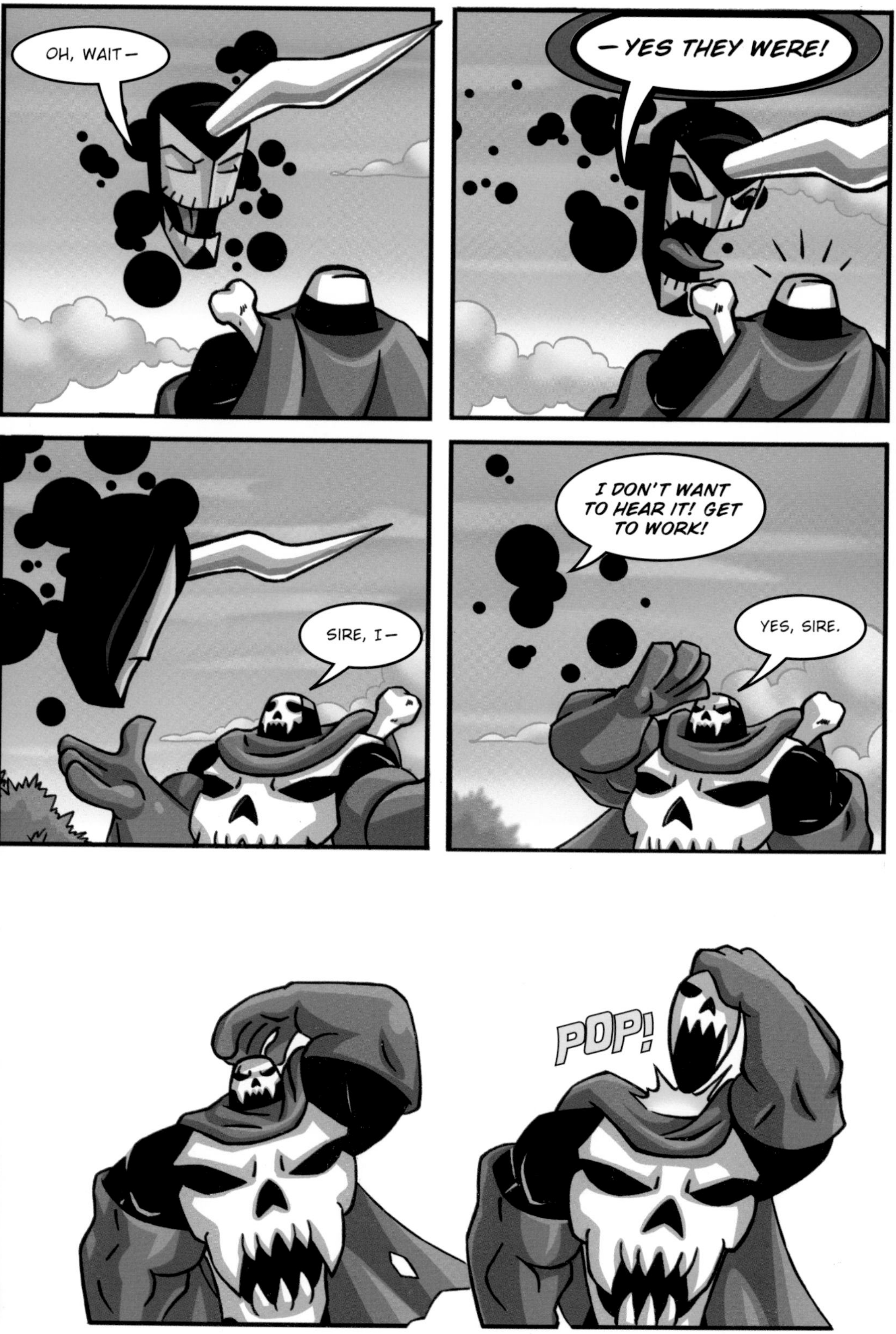
OH, WAIT—
—YES THEY WERE!
SIRE, I—
I DON'T WANT TO HEAR IT! GET TO WORK!
YES, SIRE.
POP!

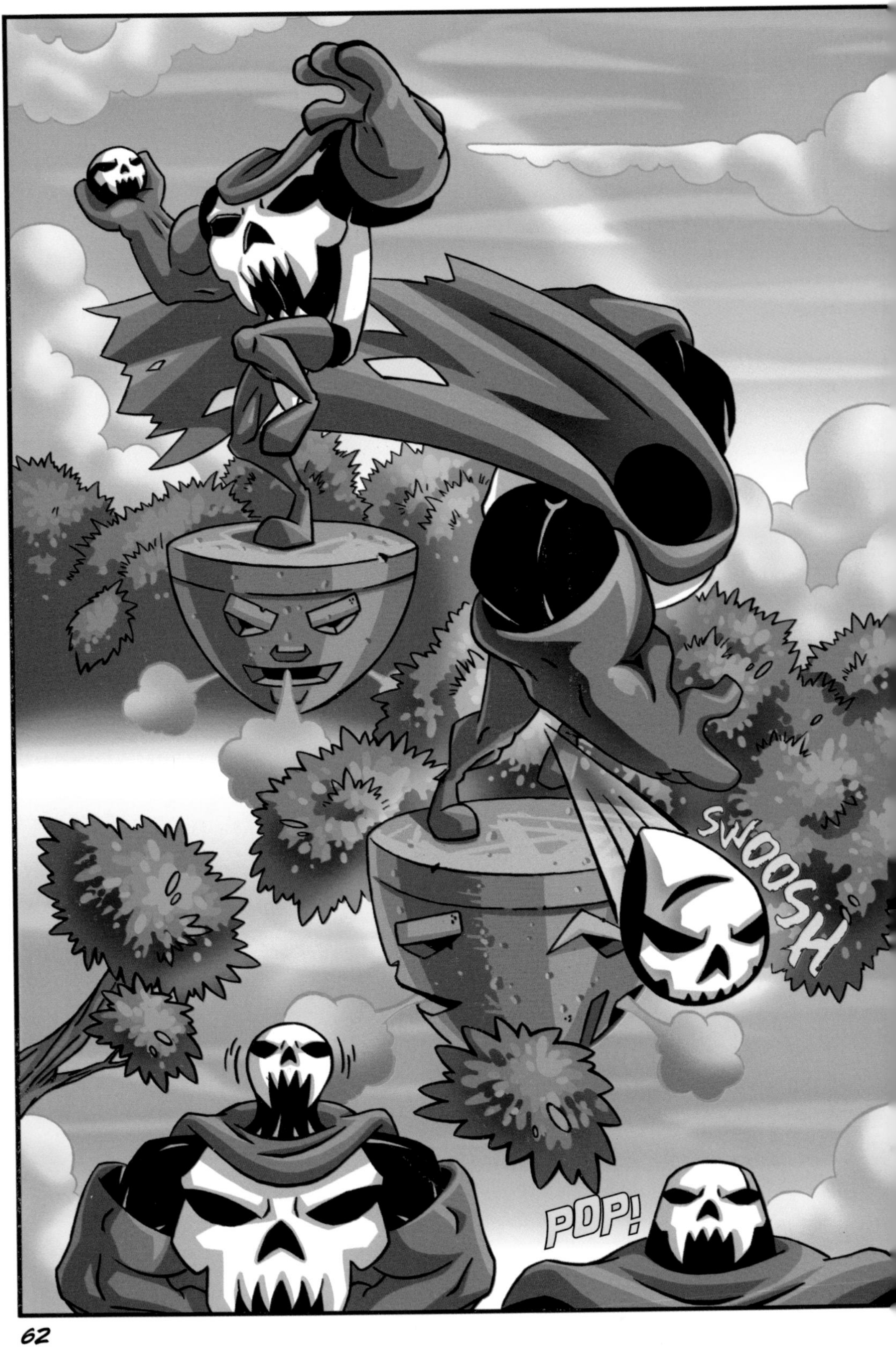
SWOOSH
POP!

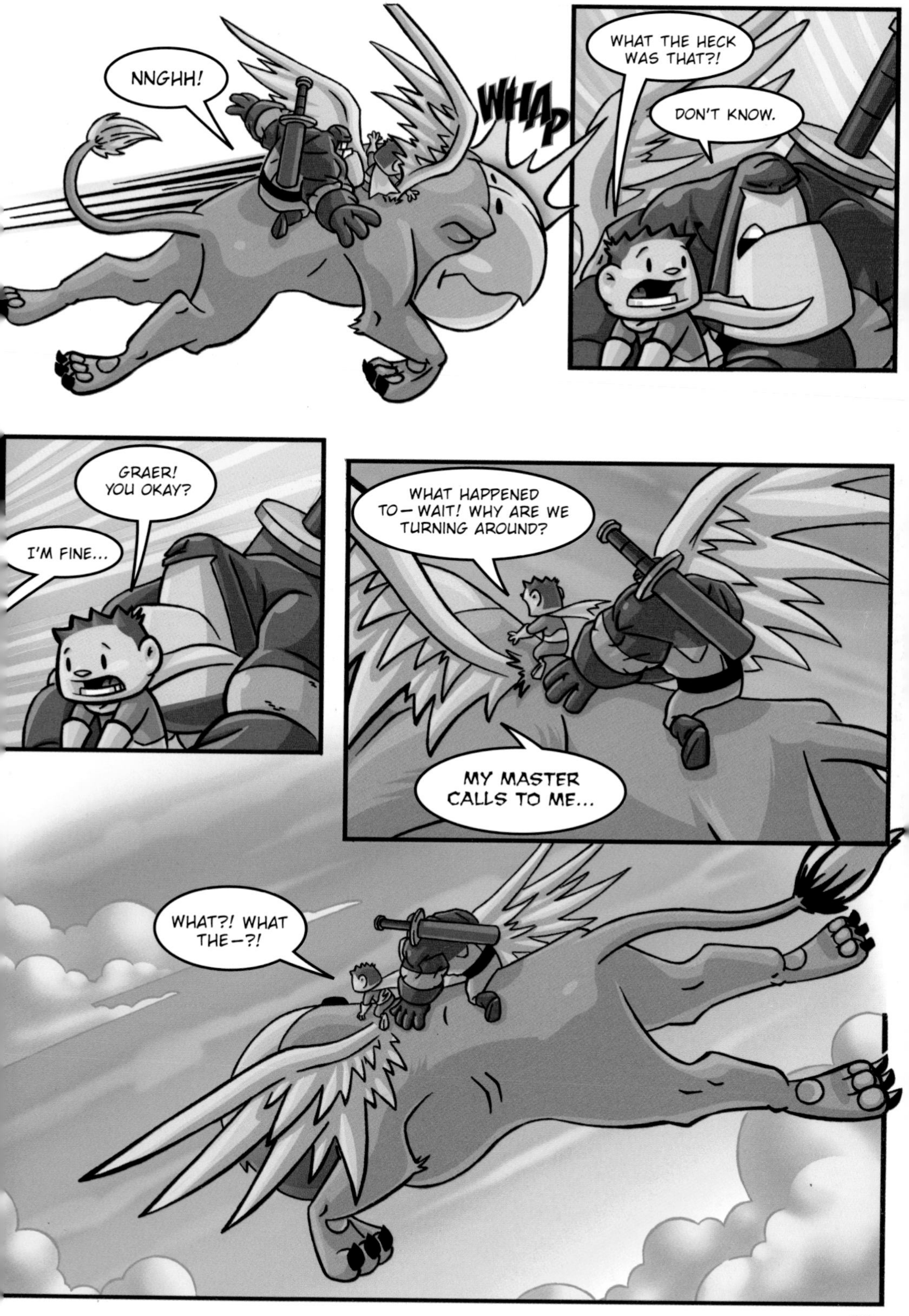
NNGHH!
WHAP
WHAT THE HECK WAS THAT?!
DON'T KNOW.
GRAER! YOU OKAY?
I'M FINE...
WHAT HAPPENED TO—WAIT! WHY ARE WE TURNING AROUND?
MY MASTER CALLS TO ME...
WHAT?! WHAT THE—?!

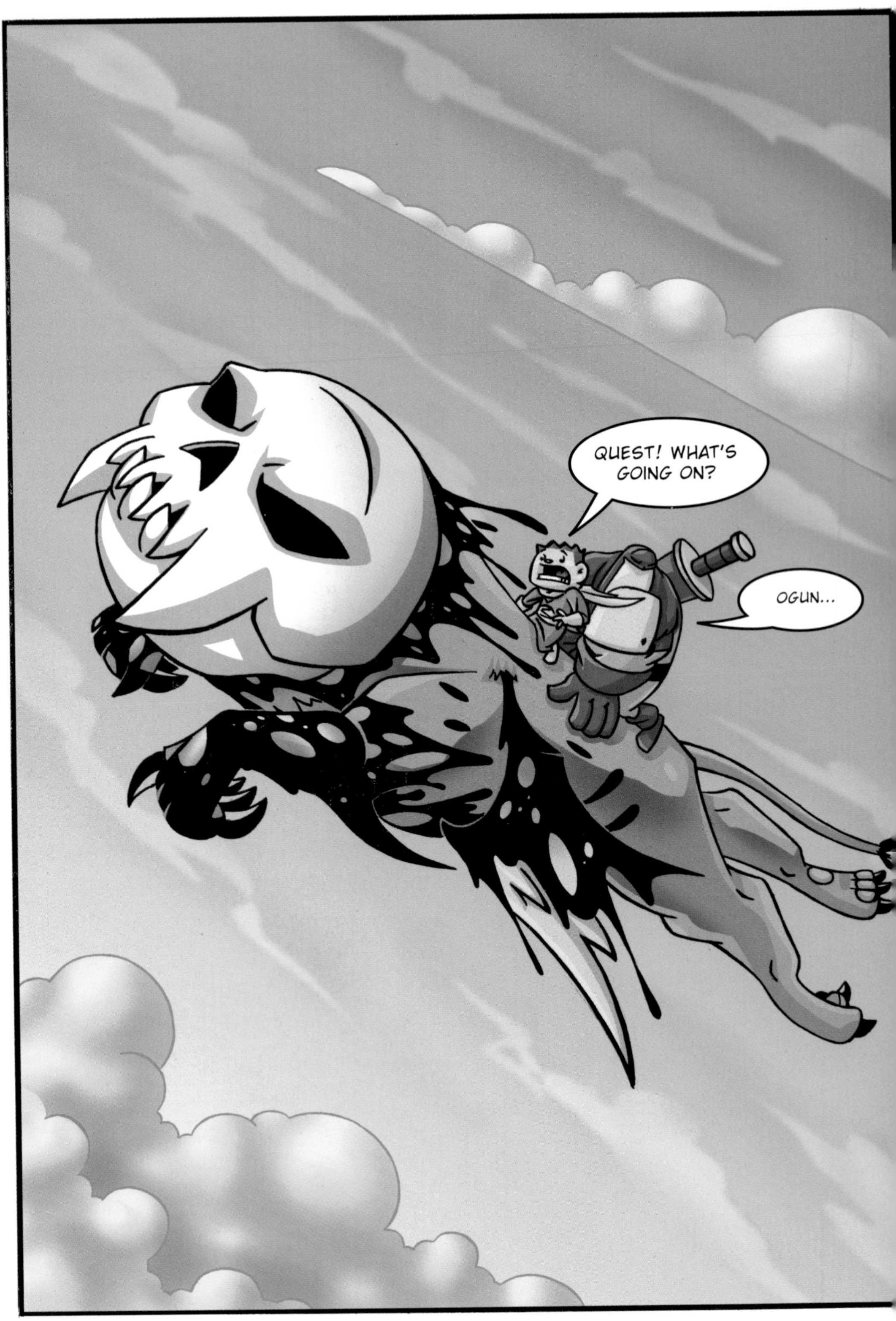
QUEST! WHAT'S GOING ON?
OGUN...

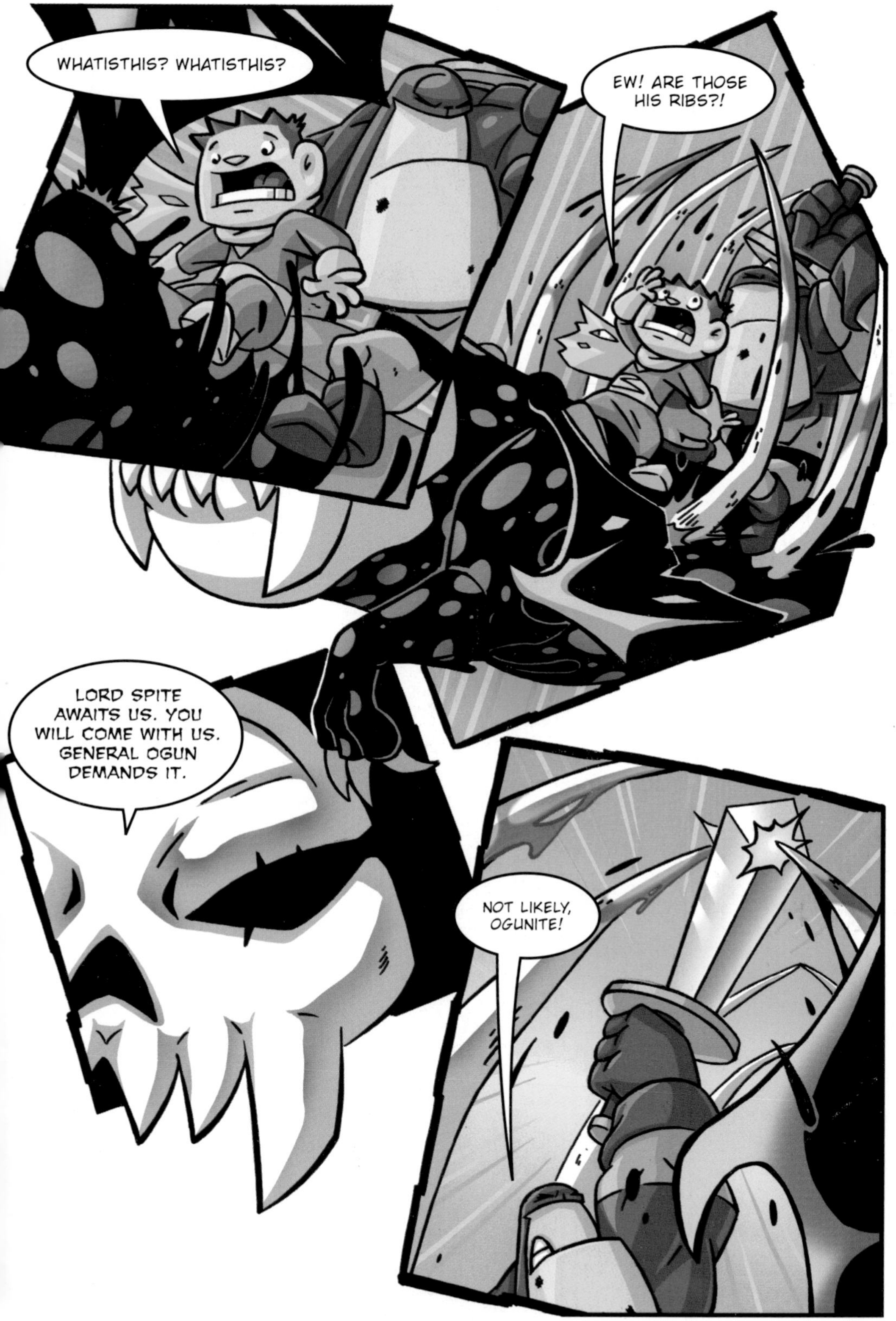
WHATISTHIS? WHATISTHIS?
EW! ARE THOSE HIS RIBS?!
LORD SPITE AWAITS US. YOU WILL COME WITH US. GENERAL OGUN DEMANDS IT.
NOT LIKELY, OGUNITE!

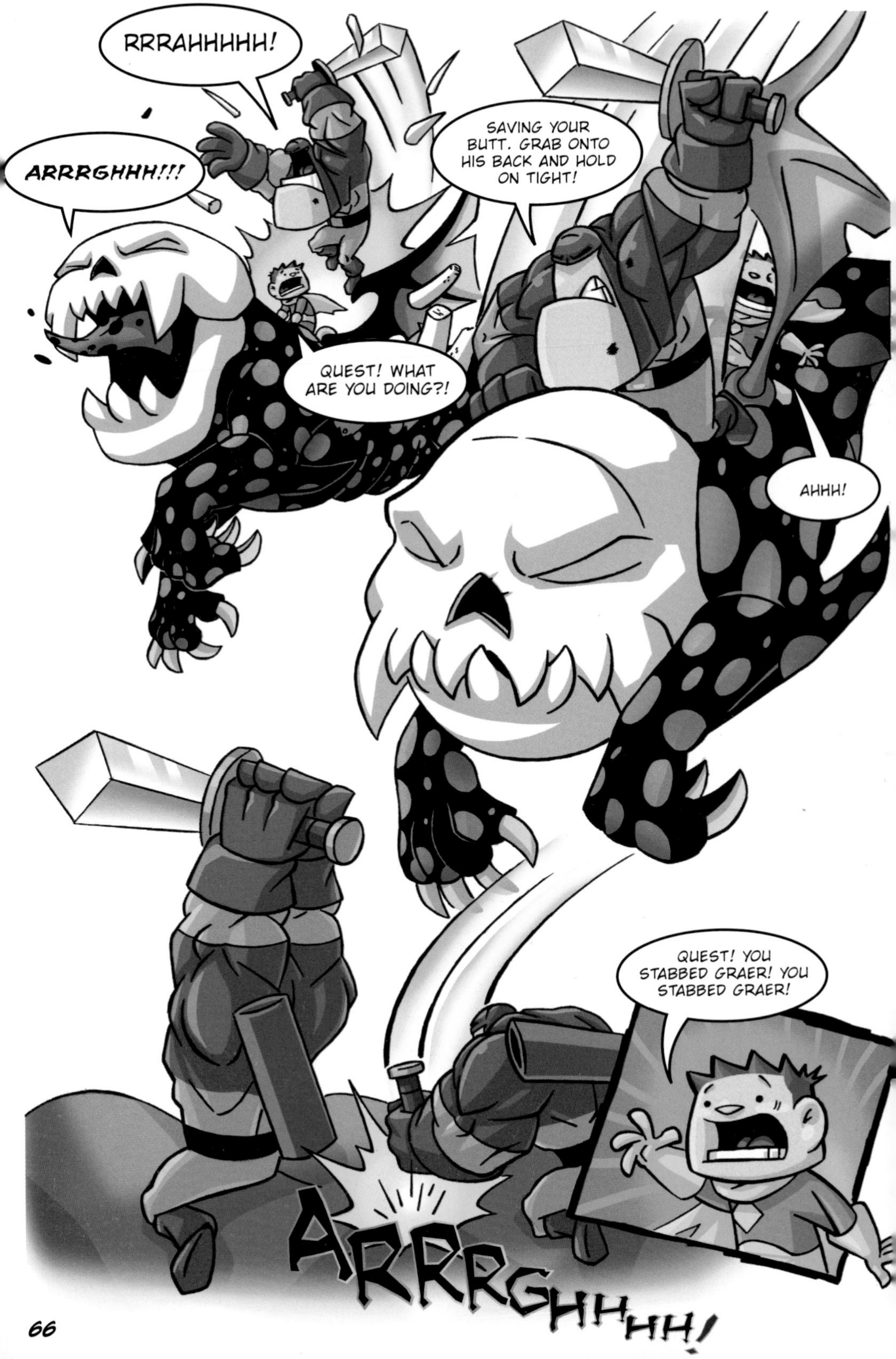
RRRAHHHHH!
ARRRGHHH!!!
SAVING YOUR BUTT. GRAB ONTO HIS BACK AND HOLD ON TIGHT!
QUEST! WHAT ARE YOU DOING?!
AHHH!
QUEST! YOU STABBED GRAER! YOU STABBED GRAER!
ARRRGHHHHH!

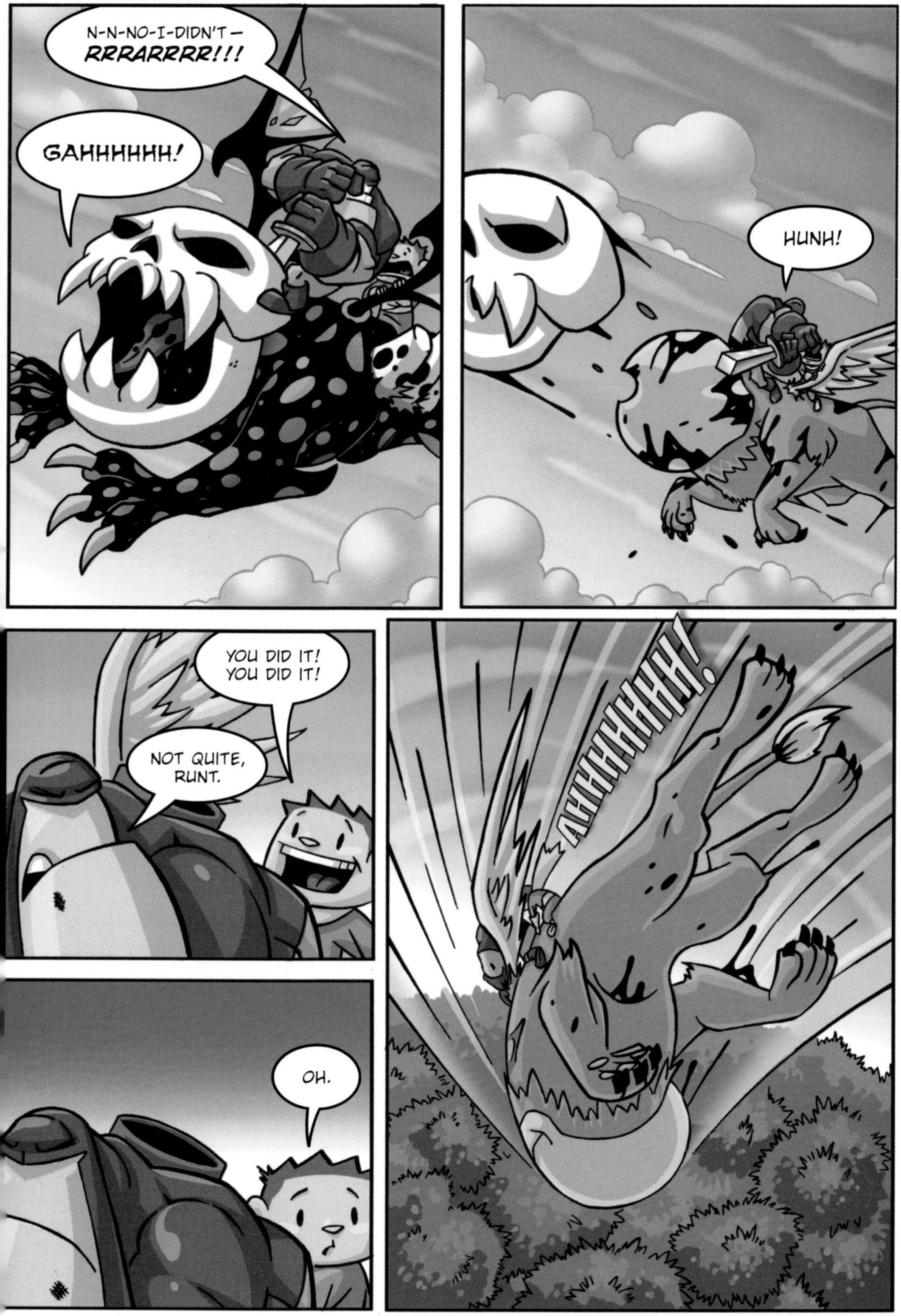

N-N-NO-I-DIDN'T—
RRRARRRR!!!
GAHHHHHH!
HUNH!
YOU DID IT! YOU DID IT!
NOT QUITE, RUNT.
OH.
AHHHHHHH!

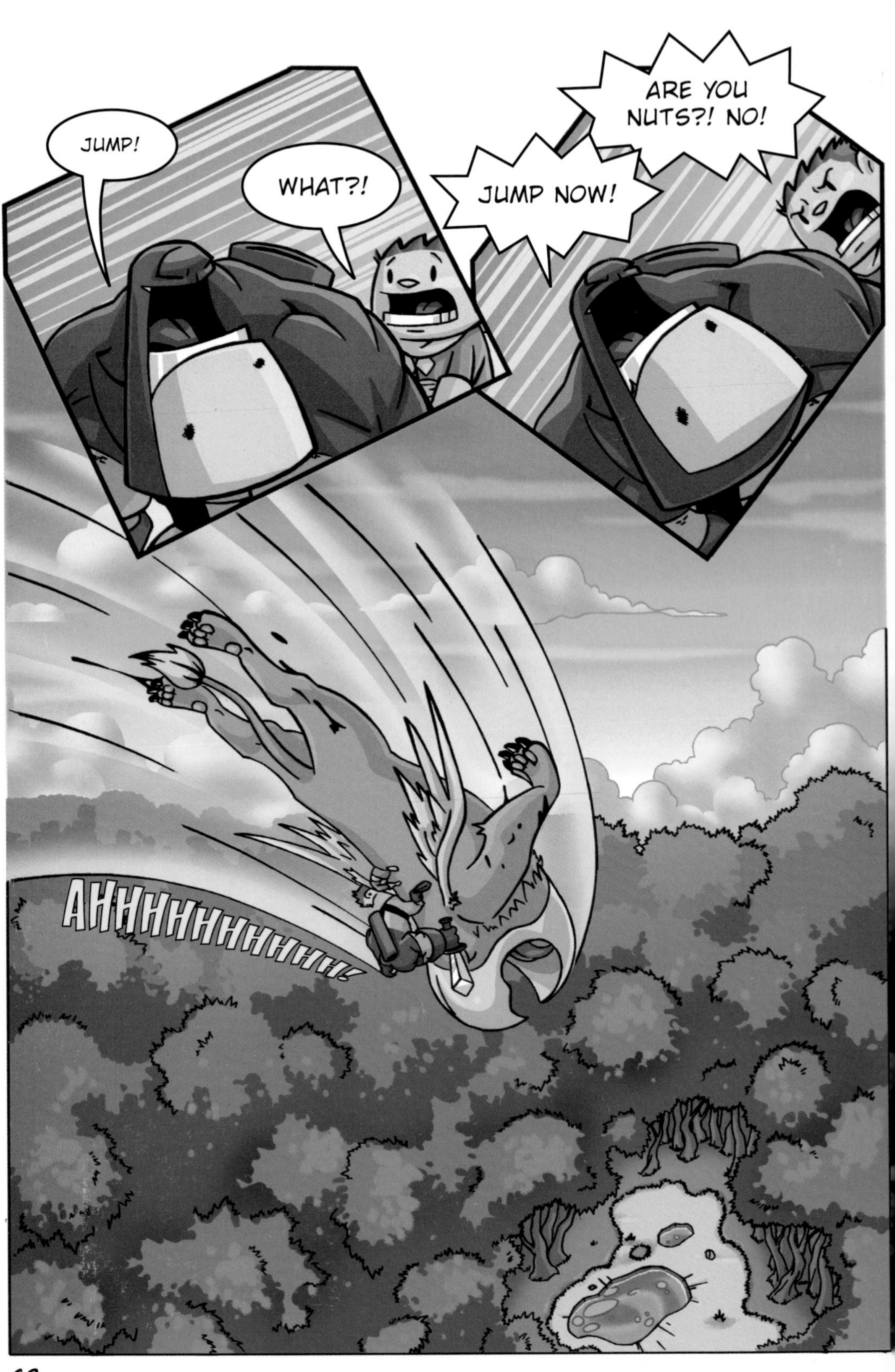
JUMP!
WHAT?!
JUMP NOW!
ARE YOU NUTS?! NO!
AHHHHHHHHHHHHH!

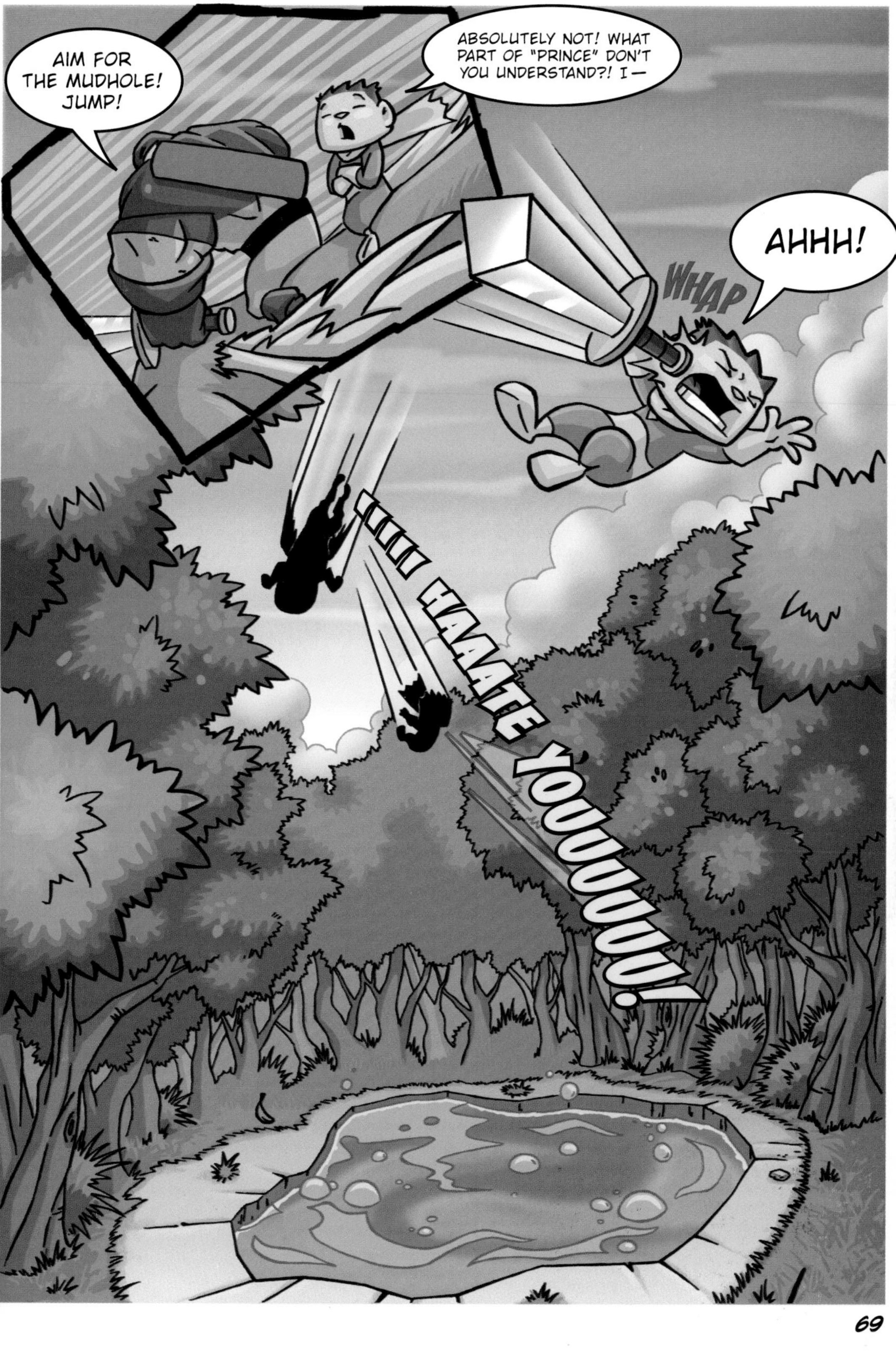
AIM FOR THE MUDHOLE! JUMP!
ABSOLUTELY NOT! WHAT PART OF "PRINCE" DON'T YOU UNDERSTAND?! I—
WHAP
AHHH!
IIII HAAATE YOUUUUUUU!

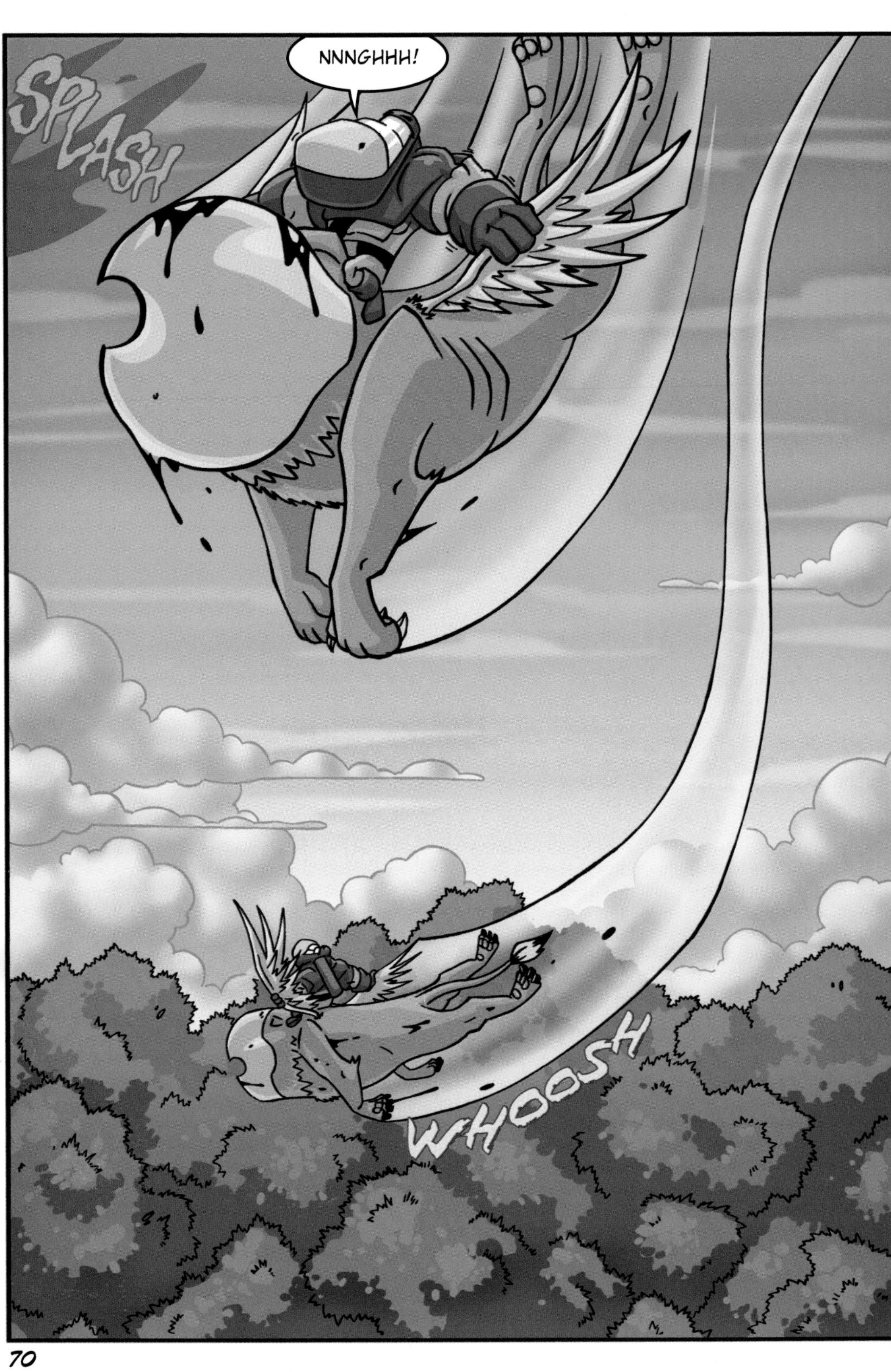
SPLASH
NNNGHHH!
WHOOSH

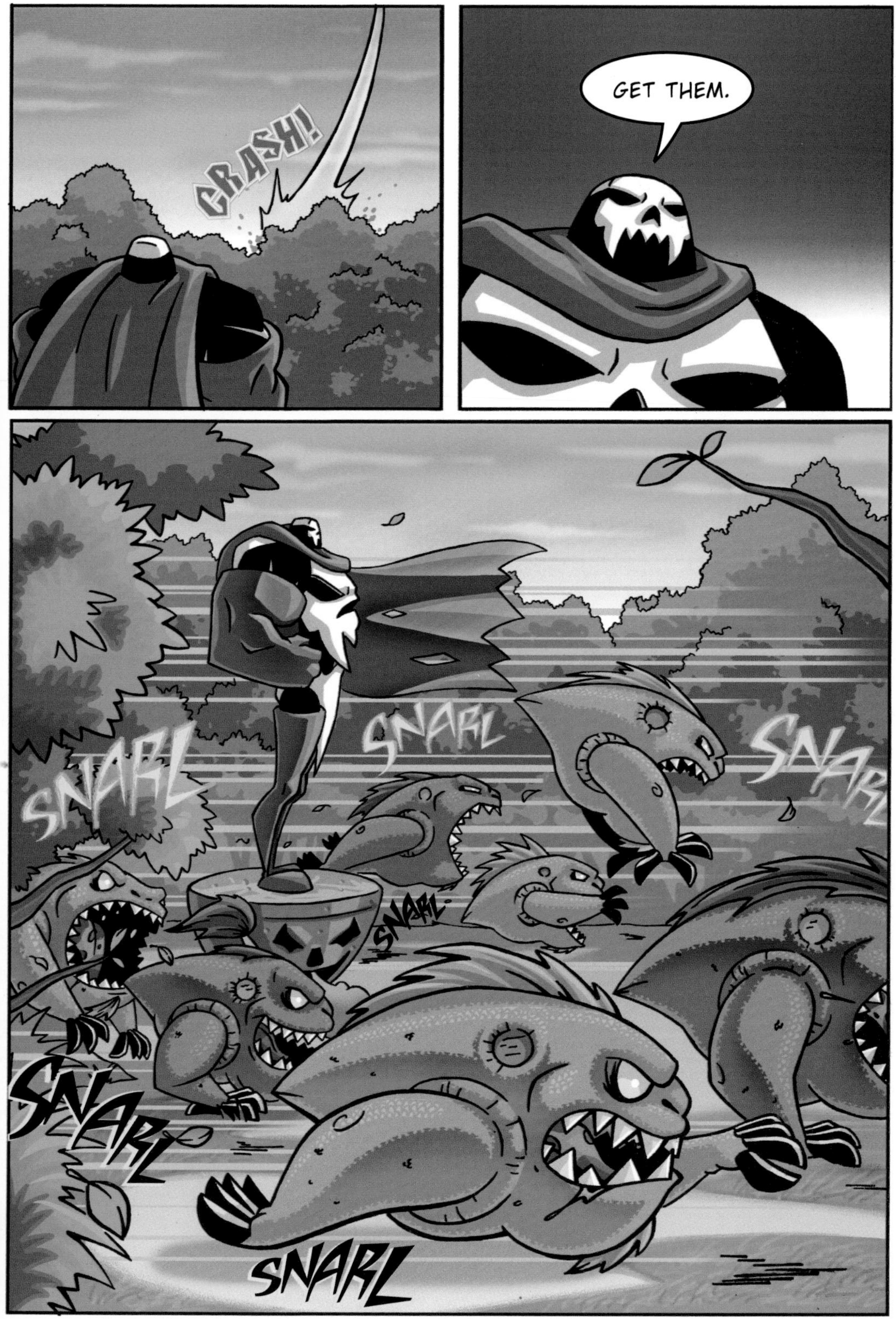
CRASH!
GET THEM.
SNARL
SNARL
SNARL
SNARL
SNARL
SNARL

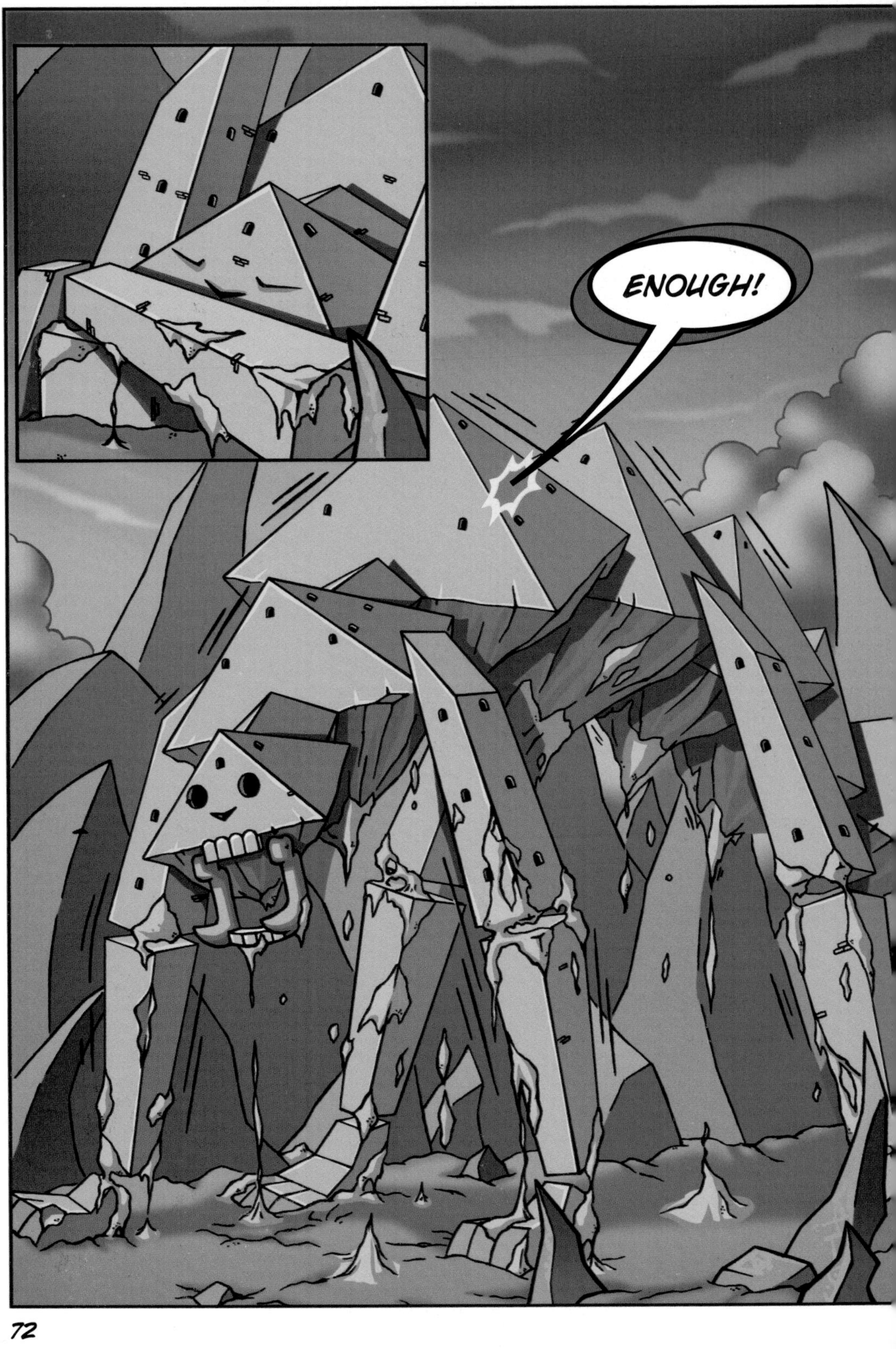
ENOUGH!

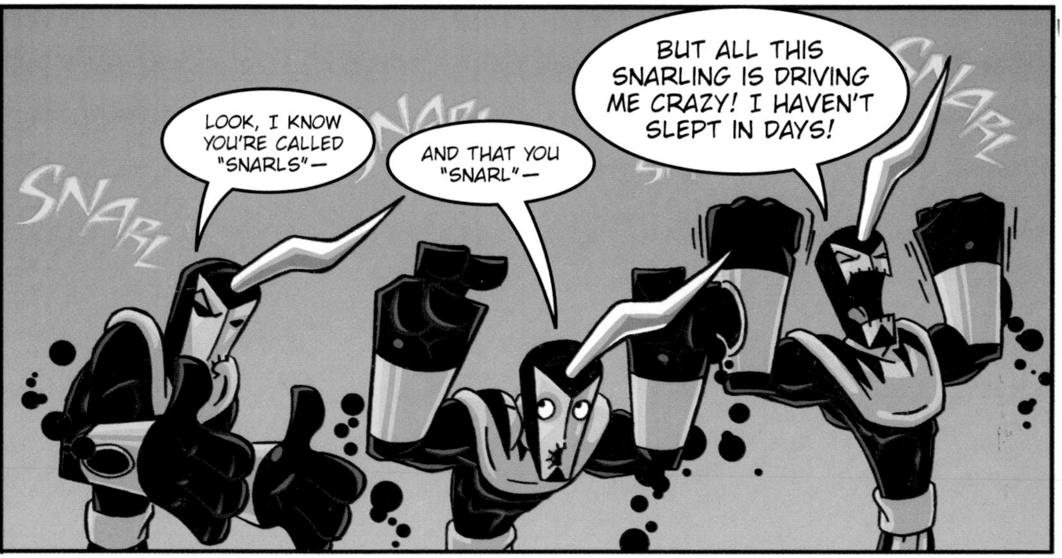
SNARL
LOOK, I KNOW YOU'RE CALLED "SNARLS"—
AND THAT YOU "SNARL"—
BUT ALL THIS SNARLING IS DRIVING ME CRAZY! I HAVEN'T SLEPT IN DAYS!
SNARL

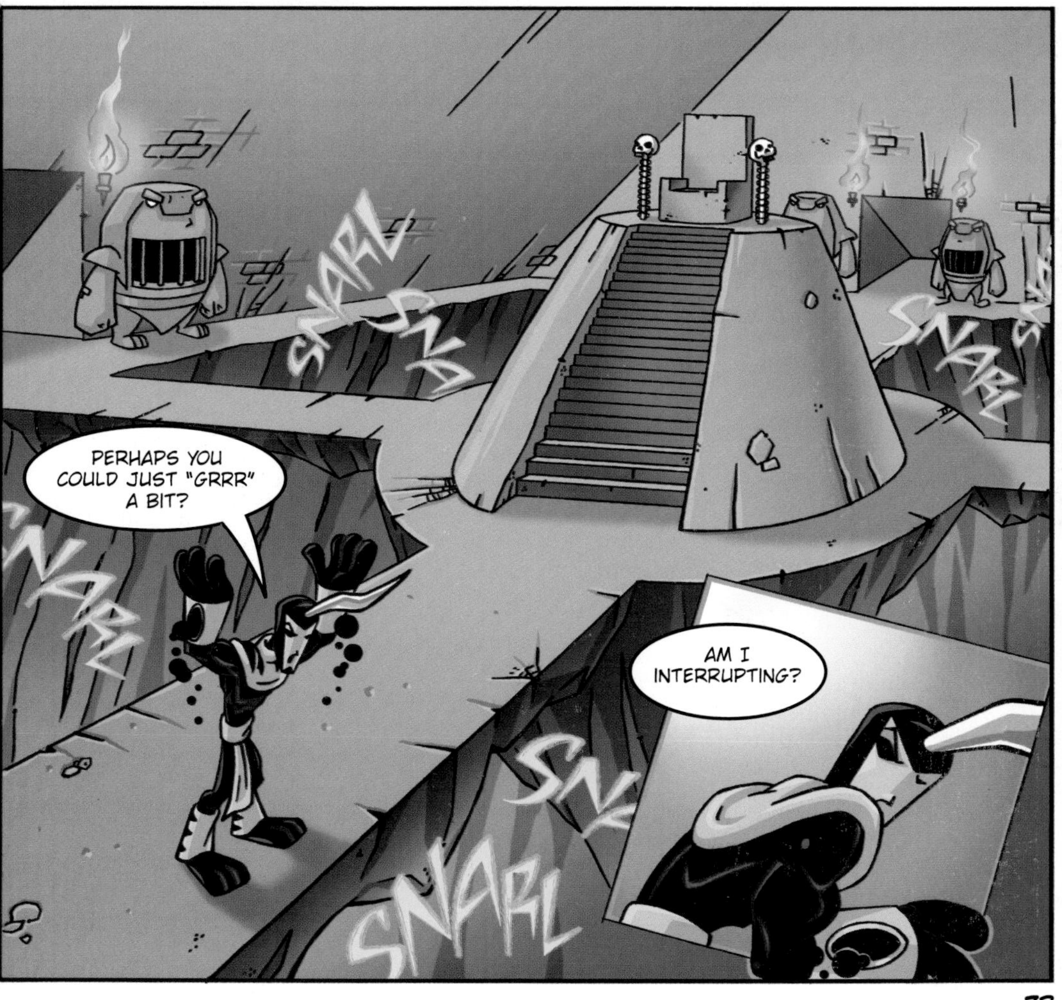
SNARL
SNA
SNARL
PERHAPS YOU COULD JUST "GRRR" A BIT?
SNARL
AM I INTERRUPTING?
SNA
SNARL

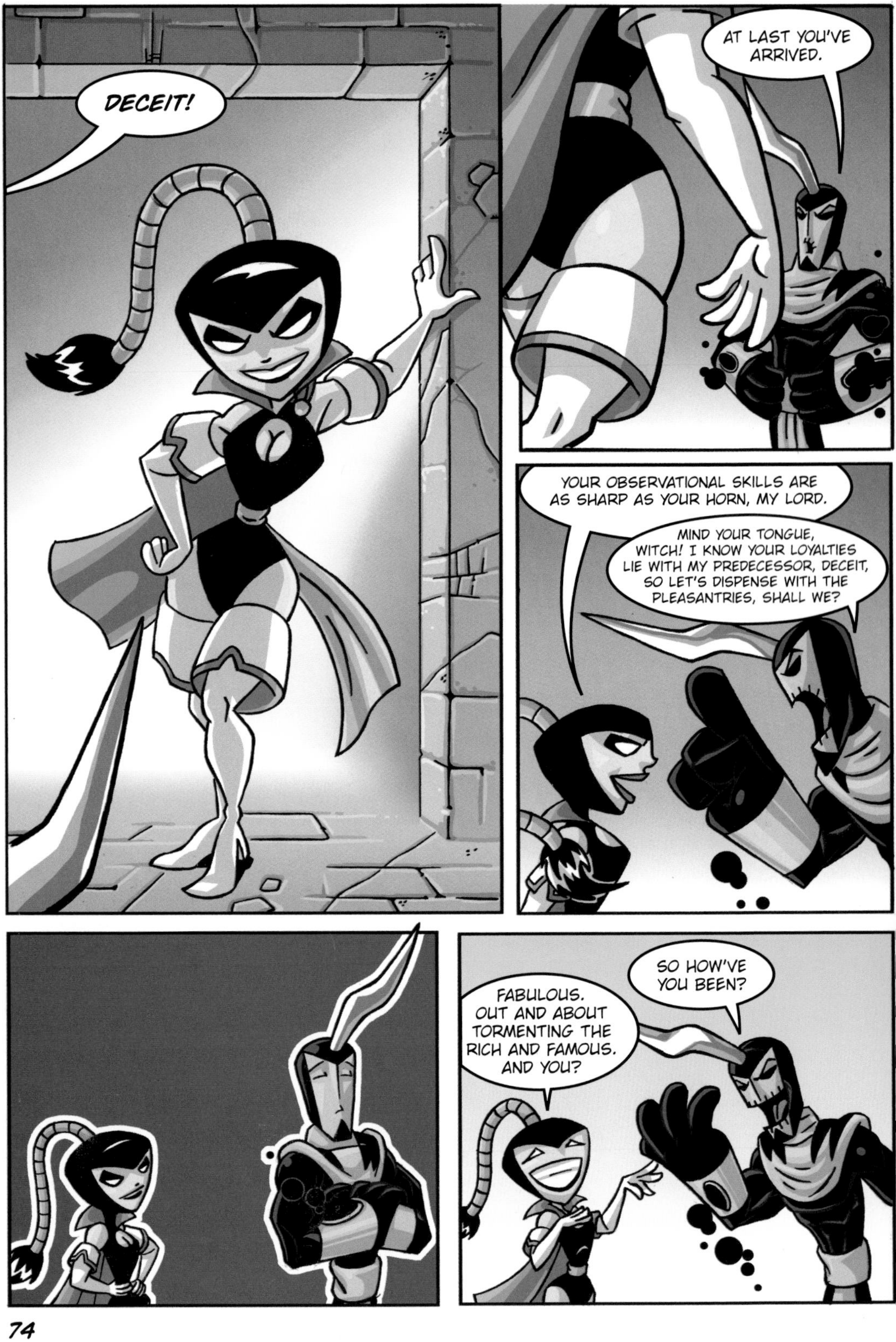
DECEIT!
AT LAST YOU'VE ARRIVED.
YOUR OBSERVATIONAL SKILLS ARE AS SHARP AS YOUR HORN, MY LORD.
MIND YOUR TONGUE, WITCH! I KNOW YOUR LOYALTIES LIE WITH MY PREDECESSOR, DECEIT, SO LET'S DISPENSE WITH THE PLEASANTRIES, SHALL WE?
SO HOW'VE YOU BEEN?
FABULOUS. OUT AND ABOUT TORMENTING THE RICH AND FAMOUS. AND YOU?

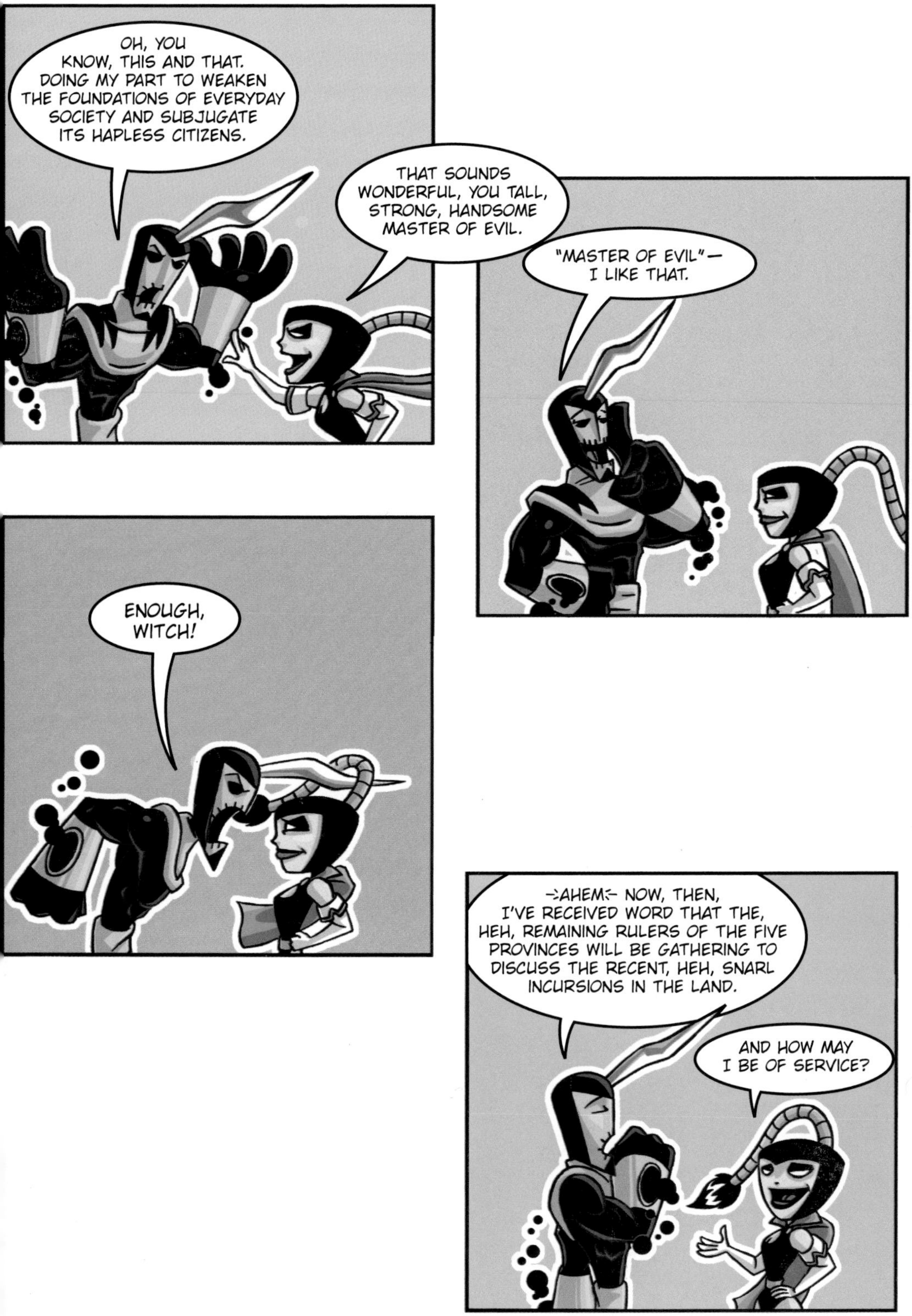
OH, YOU KNOW, THIS AND THAT. DOING MY PART TO WEAKEN THE FOUNDATIONS OF EVERYDAY SOCIETY AND SUBJUGATE ITS HAPLESS CITIZENS.
THAT SOUNDS WONDERFUL, YOU TALL, STRONG, HANDSOME MASTER OF EVIL.
"MASTER OF EVIL"— I LIKE THAT.
ENOUGH, WITCH!
-AHEM- NOW, THEN, I'VE RECEIVED WORD THAT THE, HEH, REMAINING RULERS OF THE FIVE PROVINCES WILL BE GATHERING TO DISCUSS THE RECENT, HEH, SNARL INCURSIONS IN THE LAND.
AND HOW MAY I BE OF SERVICE?

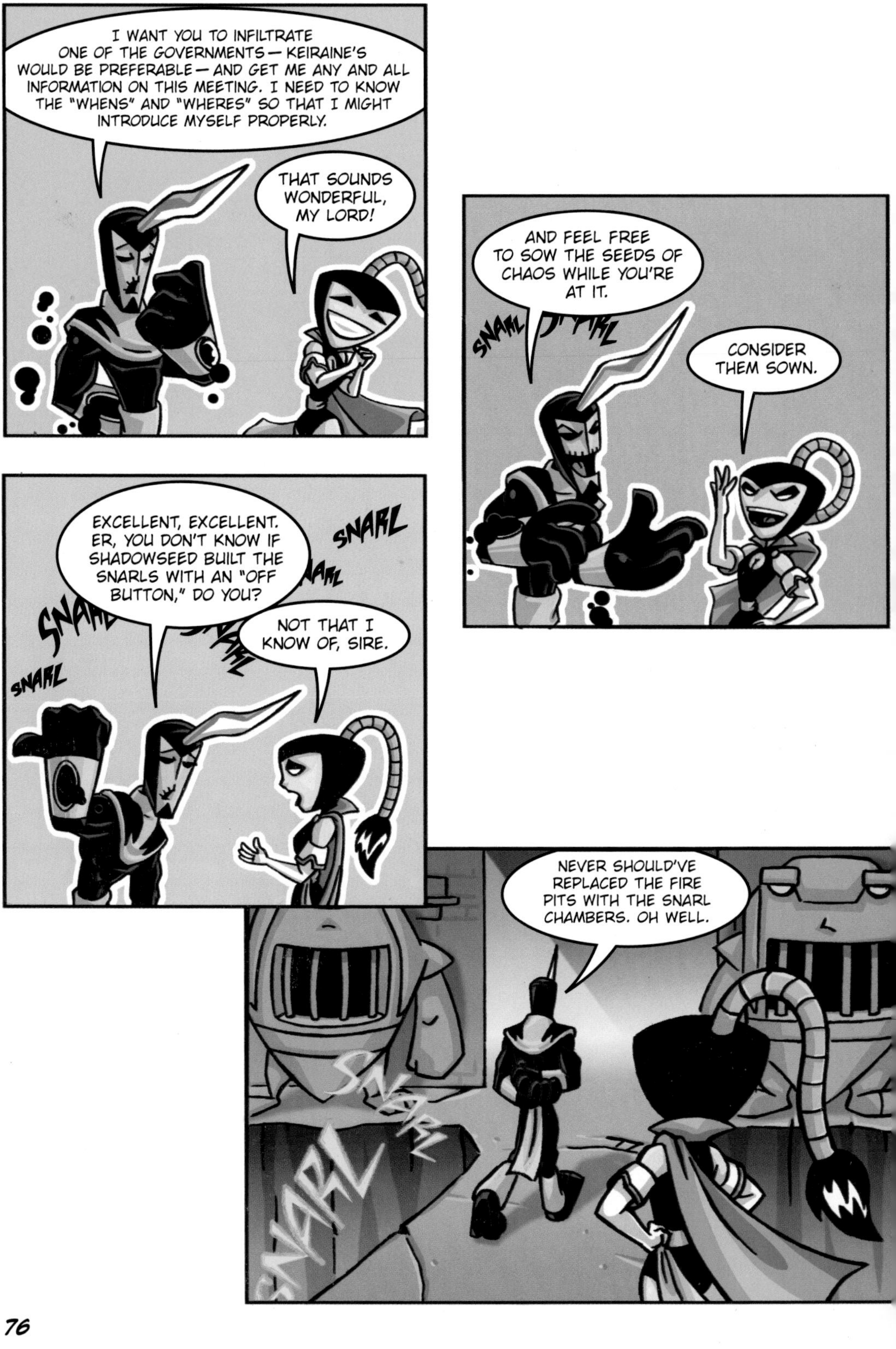
I WANT YOU TO INFILTRATE ONE OF THE GOVERNMENTS — KEIRAINE'S WOULD BE PREFERABLE — AND GET ME ANY AND ALL INFORMATION ON THIS MEETING. I NEED TO KNOW THE "WHENS" AND "WHERES" SO THAT I MIGHT INTRODUCE MYSELF PROPERLY.
THAT SOUNDS WONDERFUL, MY LORD!
AND FEEL FREE TO SOW THE SEEDS OF CHAOS WHILE YOU'RE AT IT.
SNARL
CONSIDER THEM SOWN.
EXCELLENT, EXCELLENT. ER, YOU DON'T KNOW IF SHADOWSEED BUILT THE SNARLS WITH AN "OFF BUTTON," DO YOU?
SNARL
SNARL
SNARL
NOT THAT I KNOW OF, SIRE.
NEVER SHOULD'VE REPLACED THE FIRE PITS WITH THE SNARL CHAMBERS. OH WELL.
SNARL
SNARL

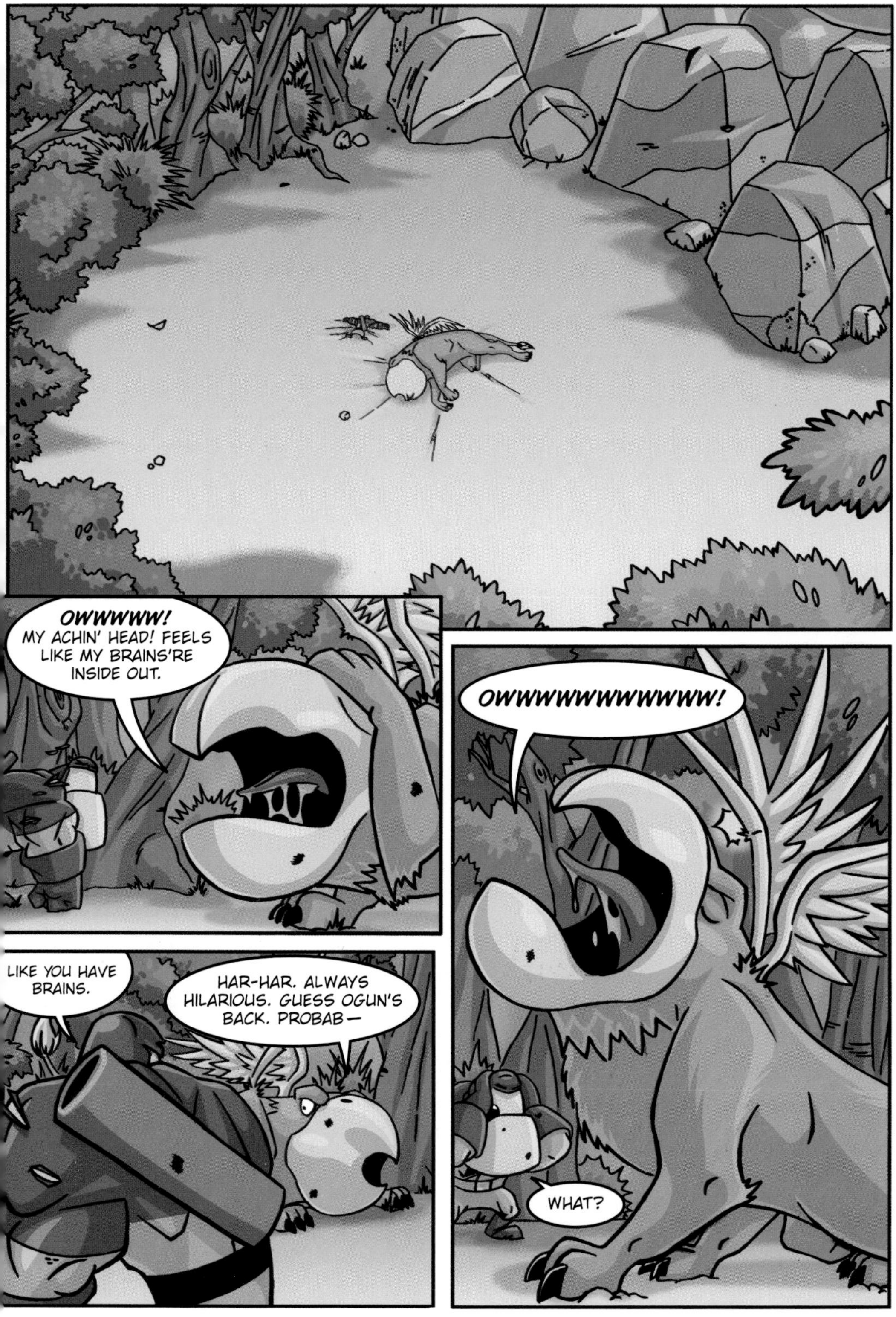
OWWWWW!
MY ACHIN' HEAD! FEELS LIKE MY BRAINS'RE INSIDE OUT.
OWWWWWWWWWWW!
LIKE YOU HAVE BRAINS.
HAR-HAR. ALWAYS HILARIOUS. GUESS OGUN'S BACK. PROBAB—
WHAT?

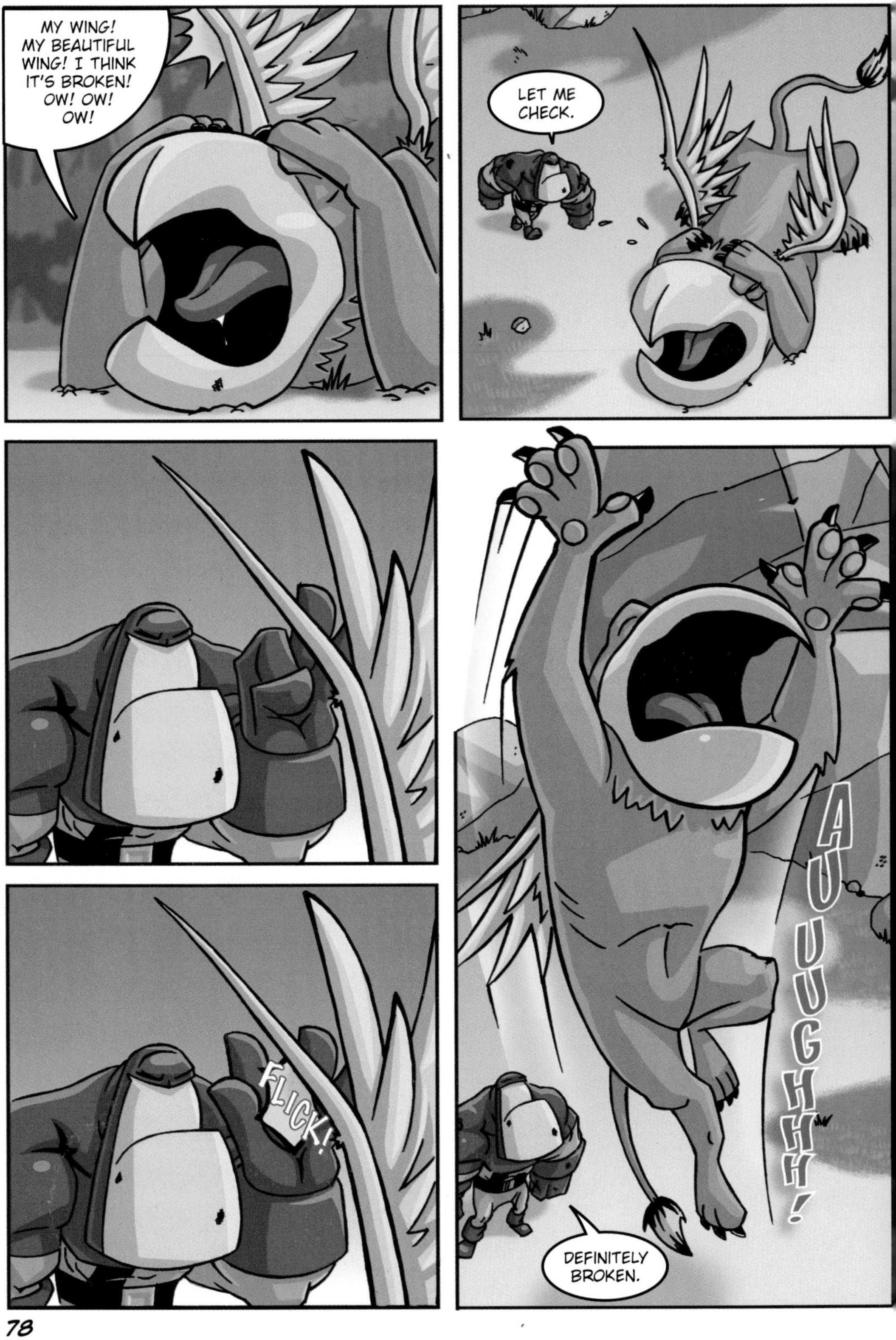
MY WING! MY BEAUTIFUL WING! I THINK IT'S BROKEN! OW! OW! OW!
LET ME CHECK.
FLICK!
AUUUUGHHHH!
DEFINITELY BROKEN.

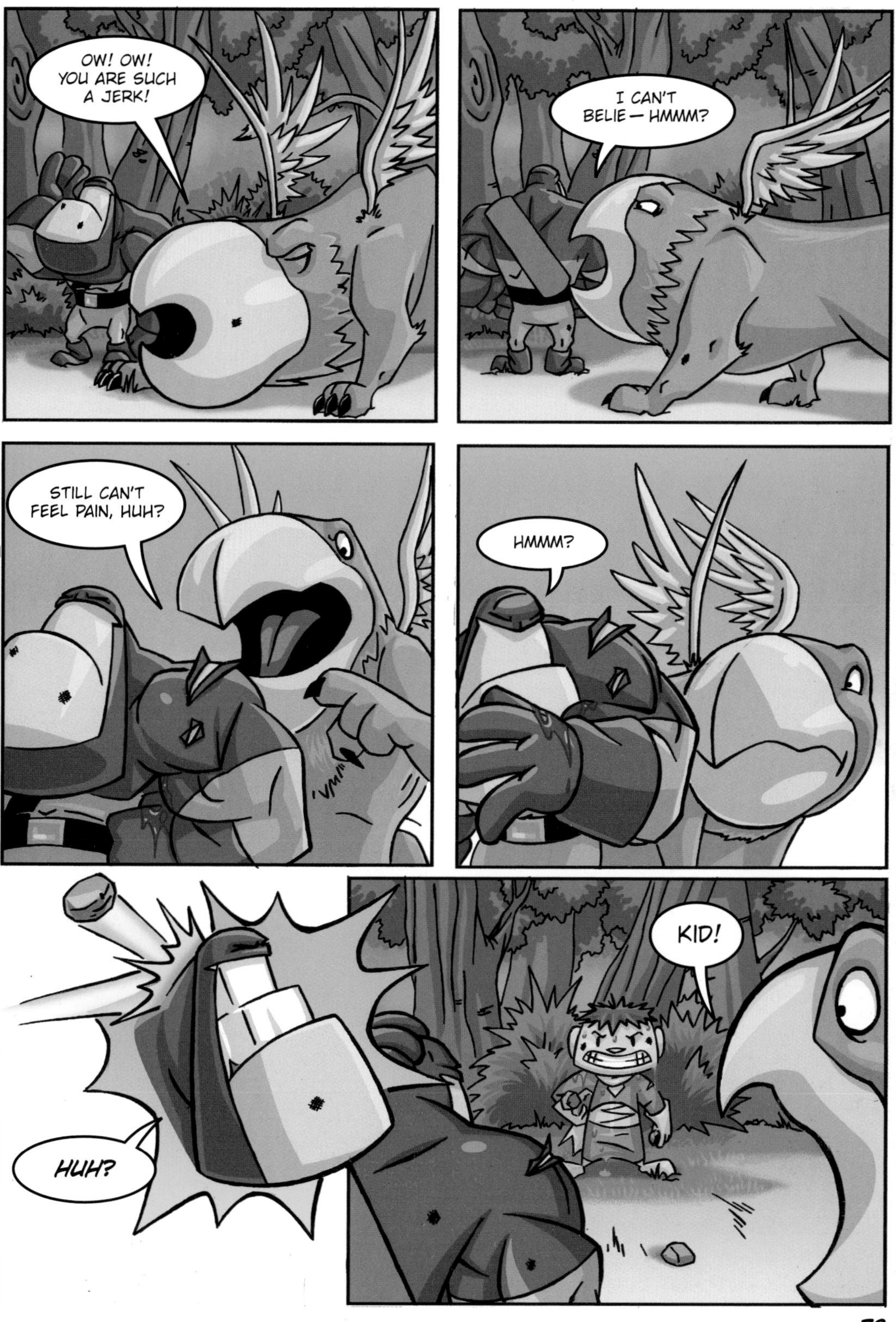
OW! OW! YOU ARE SUCH A JERK!
I CAN'T BELIE — HMMM?
STILL CAN'T FEEL PAIN, HUH?
HMMM?
KID!
HUH?

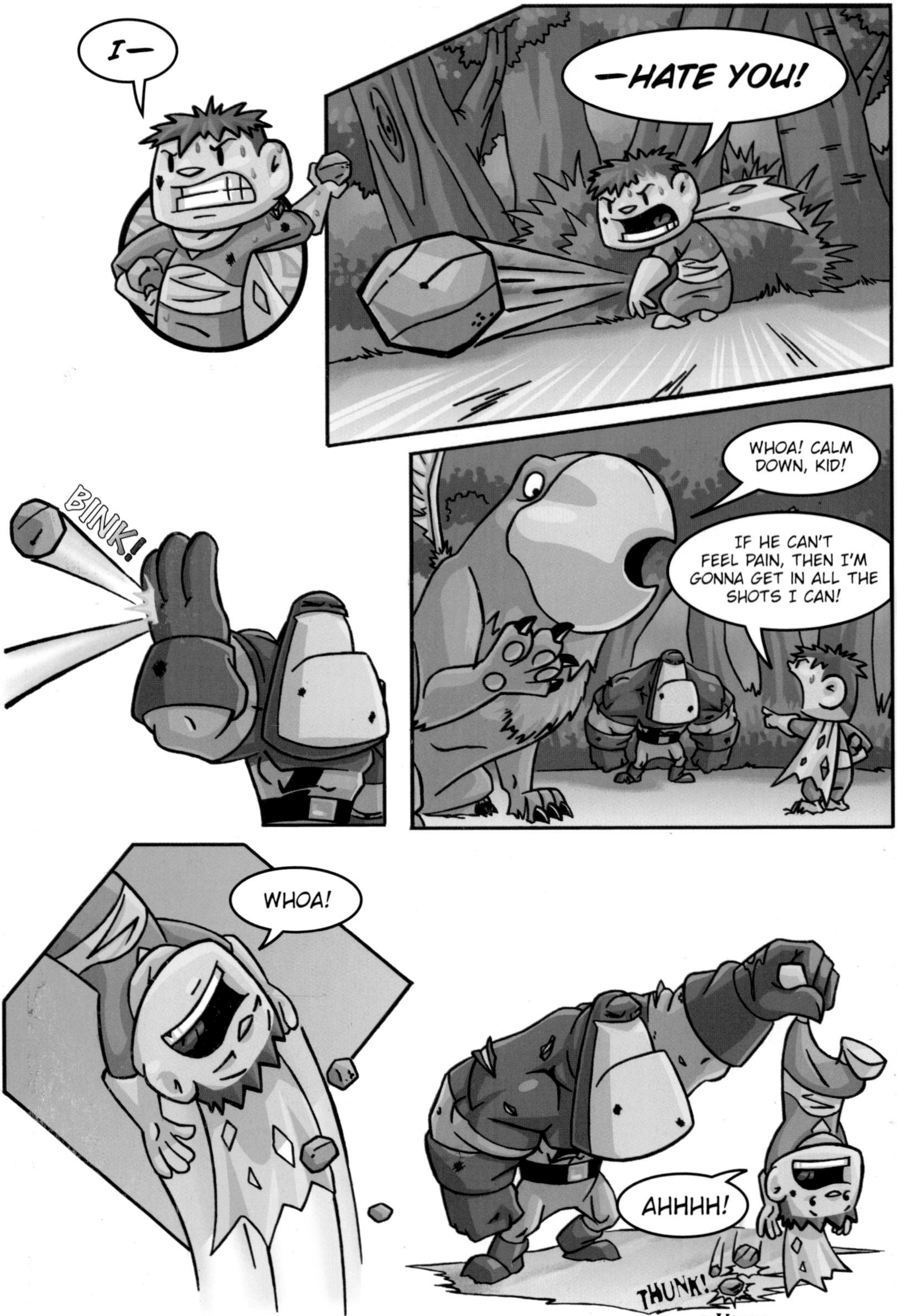

I—
—HATE YOU!
BINK!
WHOA! CALM DOWN, KID!
IF HE CAN'T FEEL PAIN, THEN I'M GONNA GET IN ALL THE SHOTS I CAN!
WHOA!
AHHHH!
THUNK!
THUNK!

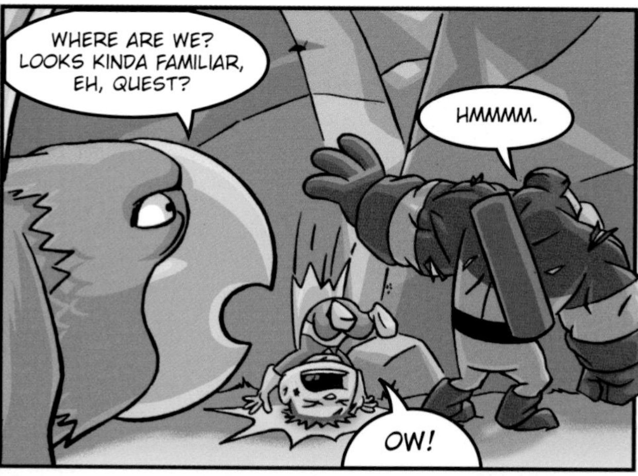
WHERE ARE WE? LOOKS KINDA FAMILIAR, EH, QUEST?
HMMMM.
OW!
LOOKS LIKE—

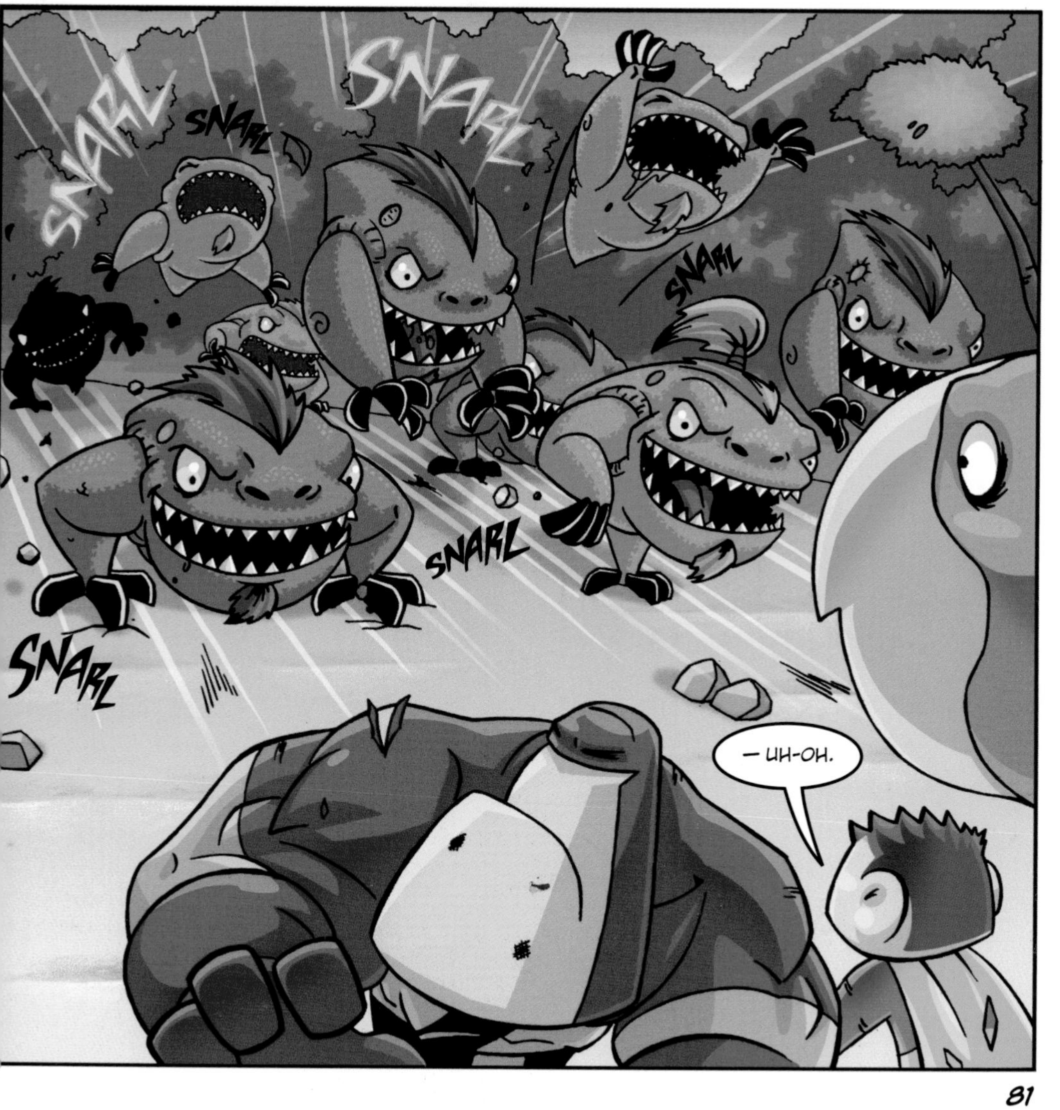
SNARL
SNARL
SNARL
SNARL
SNARL
SNARL
SNARL
—UH-OH.

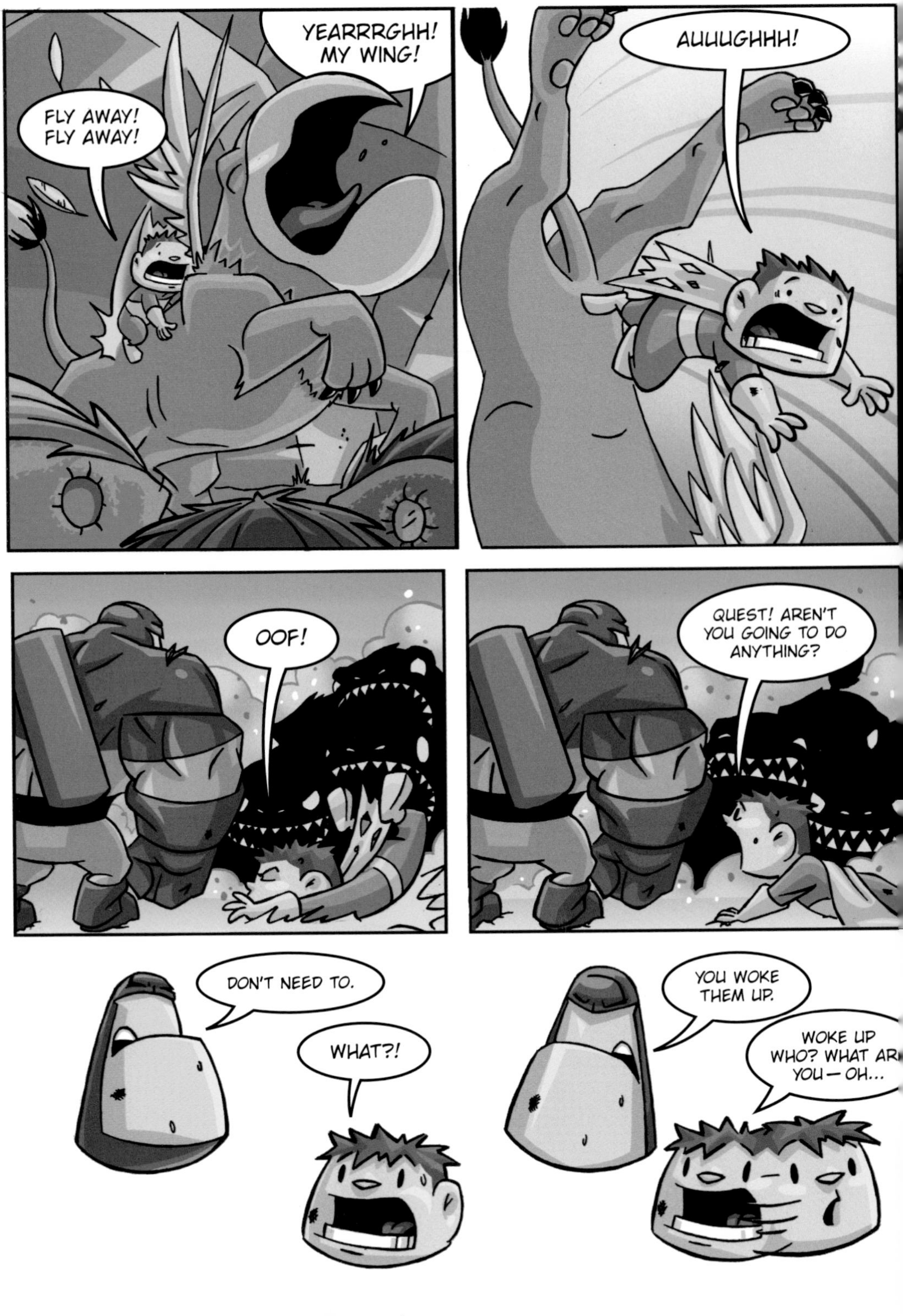
YEARRRGHH! MY WING!
FLY AWAY! FLY AWAY!
AUUUGHHH!
OOF!
QUEST! AREN'T YOU GOING TO DO ANYTHING?
DON'T NEED TO.
WHAT?!
YOU WOKE THEM UP.
WOKE UP WHO? WHAT AR
YOU—OH...

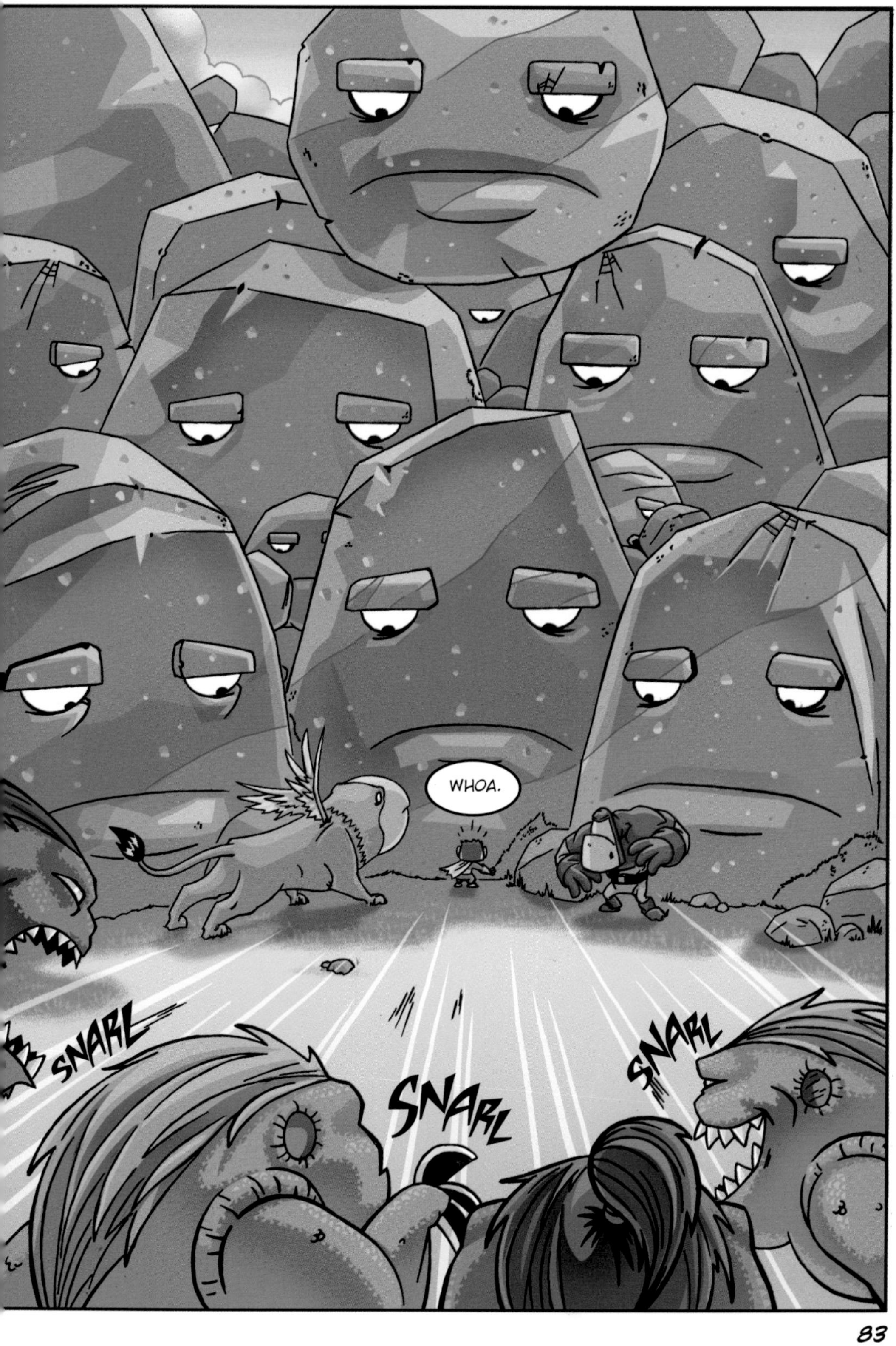
WHOA.
SNARL
SNARL
SNARL

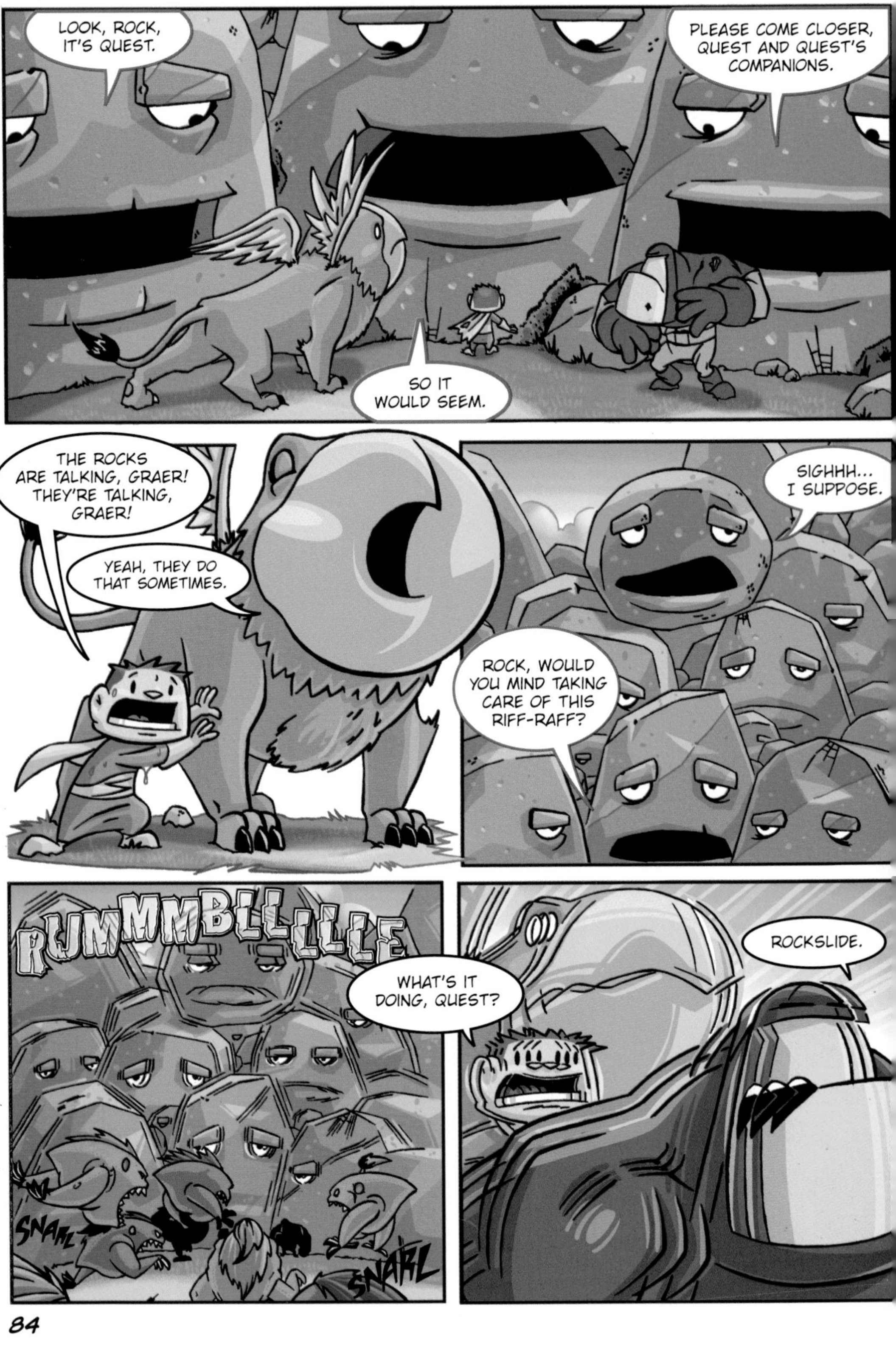
LOOK, ROCK, IT'S QUEST.
PLEASE COME CLOSER, QUEST AND QUEST'S COMPANIONS.
SO IT WOULD SEEM.
THE ROCKS ARE TALKING, GRAER! THEY'RE TALKING, GRAER!
YEAH, THEY DO THAT SOMETIMES.
SIGHHH... I SUPPOSE.
ROCK, WOULD YOU MIND TAKING CARE OF THIS RIFF-RAFF?
RUMMMBLLLLLE
WHAT'S IT DOING, QUEST?
SNARL
SNARL
ROCKSLIDE.

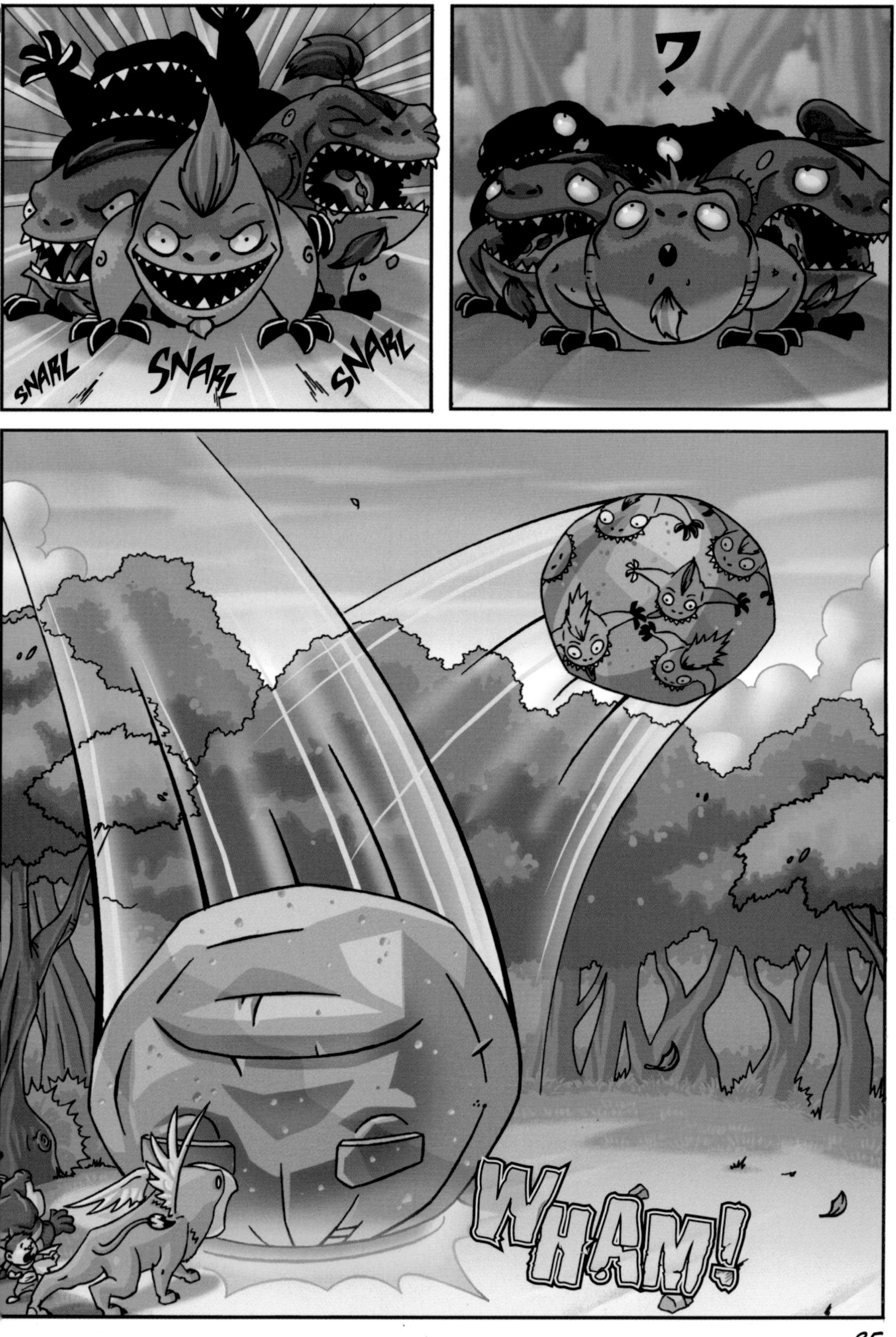
SNARL
SNARL
SNARL
?
WHAM!

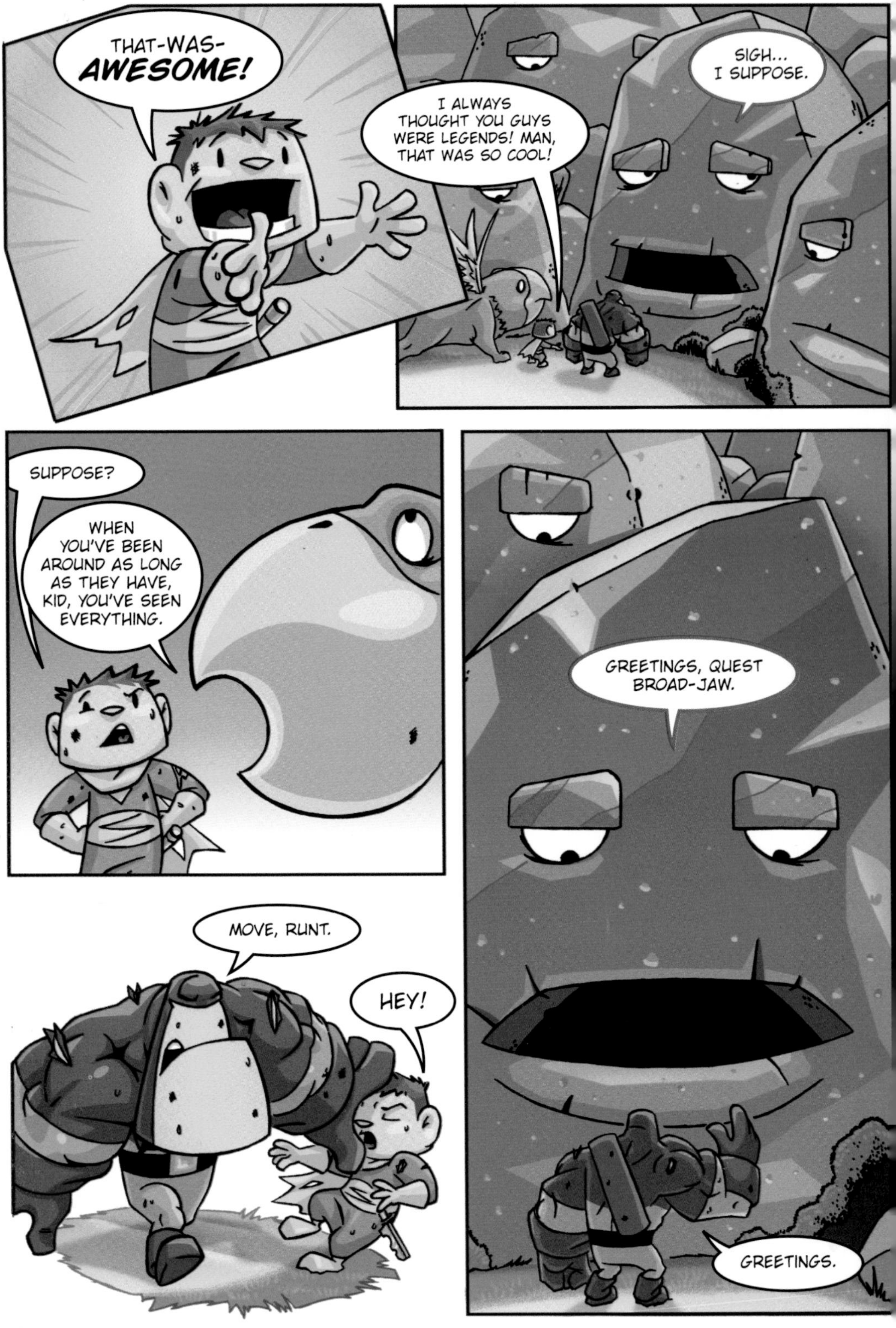
THAT-WAS-
AWESOME!
I ALWAYS THOUGHT YOU GUYS WERE LEGENDS! MAN, THAT WAS SO COOL!
SIGH... I SUPPOSE.
SUPPOSE?
WHEN YOU'VE BEEN AROUND AS LONG AS THEY HAVE, KID, YOU'VE SEEN EVERYTHING.
GREETINGS, QUEST BROAD-JAW.
GREETINGS.
MOVE, RUNT.
HEY!

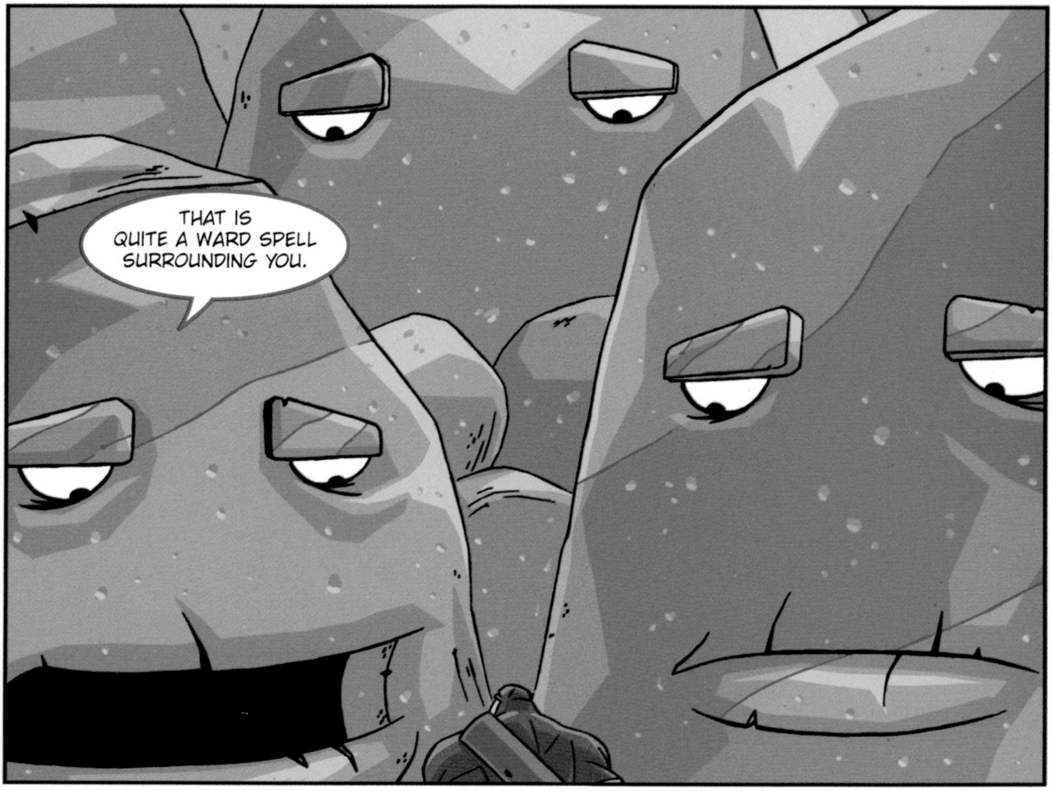
THAT IS QUITE A WARD SPELL SURROUNDING YOU.

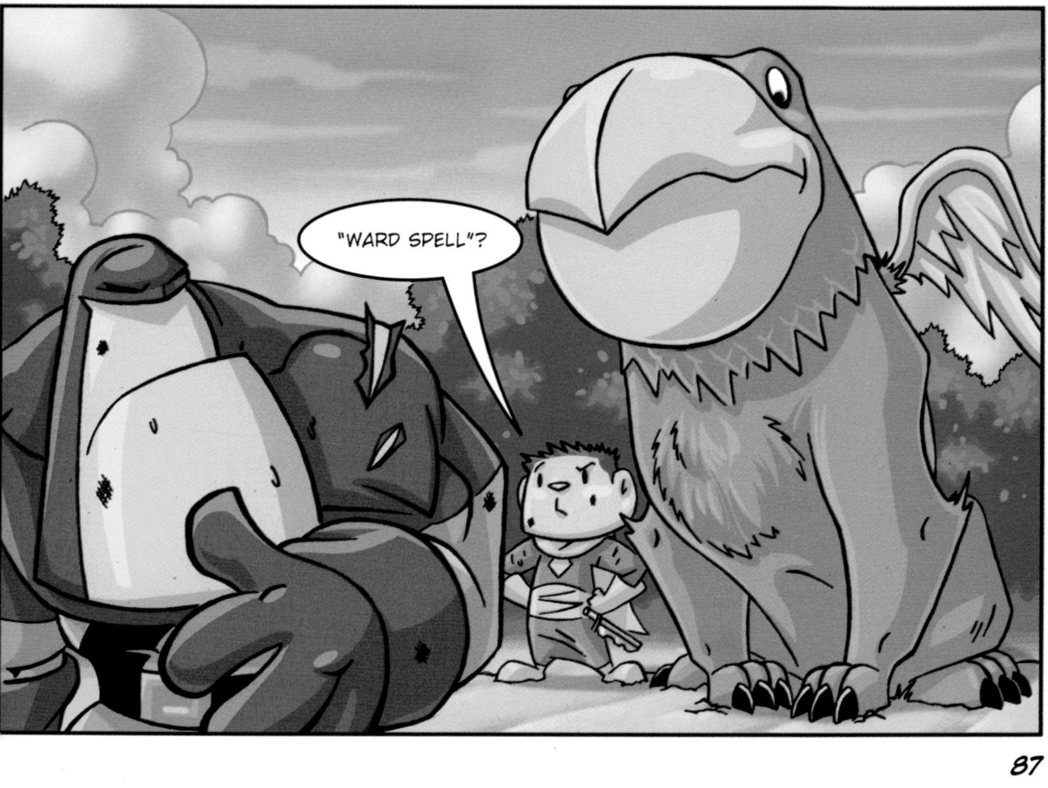
"WARD SPELL"?

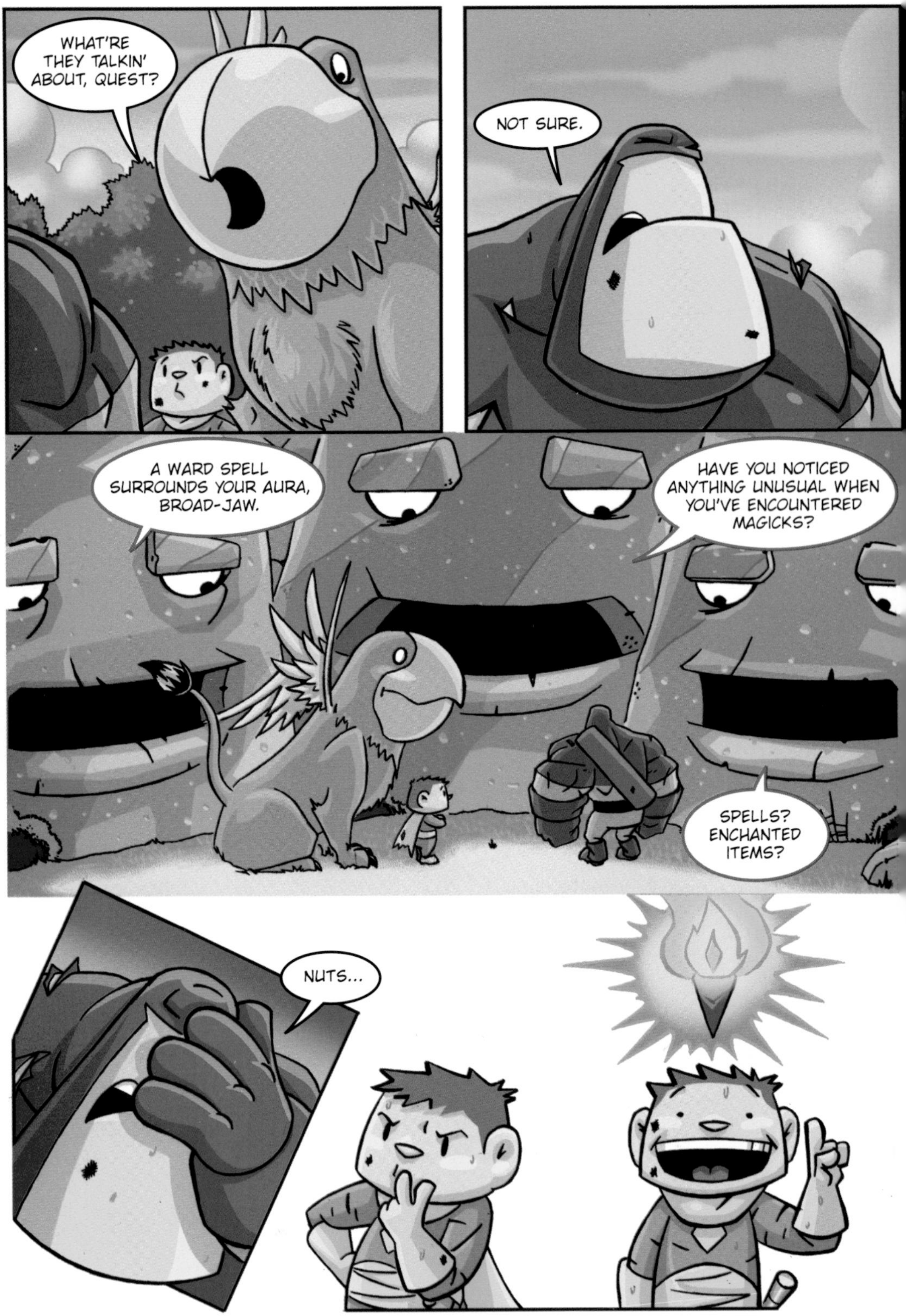

WHAT'RE THEY TALKIN' ABOUT, QUEST?
NOT SURE.
A WARD SPELL SURROUNDS YOUR AURA, BROAD-JAW.
HAVE YOU NOTICED ANYTHING UNUSUAL WHEN YOU'VE ENCOUNTERED MAGICKS?
SPELLS? ENCHANTED ITEMS?
NUTS...

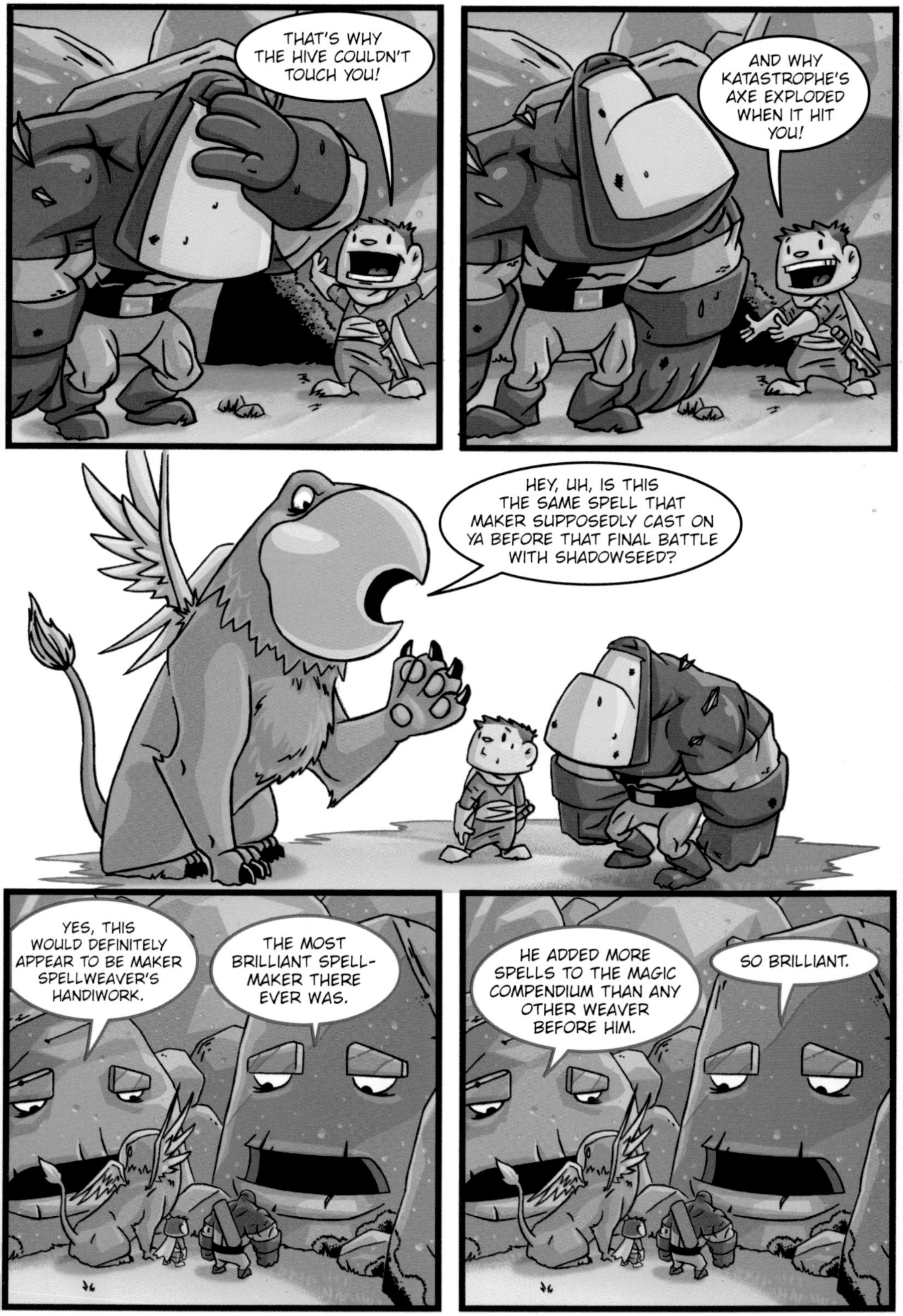
THAT'S WHY THE HIVE COULDN'T TOUCH YOU!
AND WHY KATASTROPHE'S AXE EXPLODED WHEN IT HIT YOU!
HEY, UH, IS THIS THE SAME SPELL THAT MAKER SUPPOSEDLY CAST ON YA BEFORE THAT FINAL BATTLE WITH SHADOWSEED?
YES, THIS WOULD DEFINITELY APPEAR TO BE MAKER SPELLWEAVER'S HANDIWORK.
THE MOST BRILLIANT SPELL-MAKER THERE EVER WAS.
HE ADDED MORE SPELLS TO THE MAGIC COMPENDIUM THAN ANY OTHER WEAVER BEFORE HIM.
SO BRILLIANT.

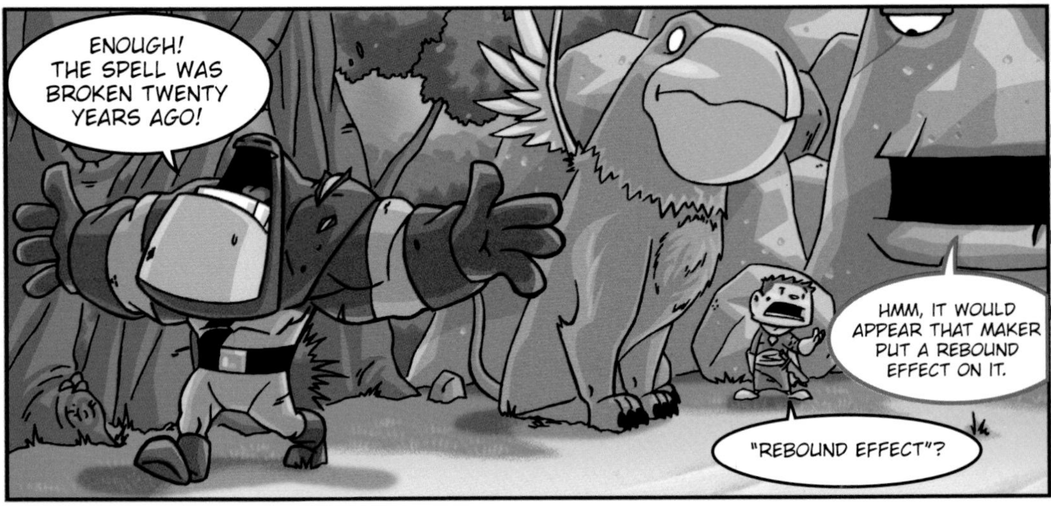
ENOUGH! THE SPELL WAS BROKEN TWENTY YEARS AGO!
HMM, IT WOULD APPEAR THAT MAKER PUT A REBOUND EFFECT ON IT.
"REBOUND EFFECT"?

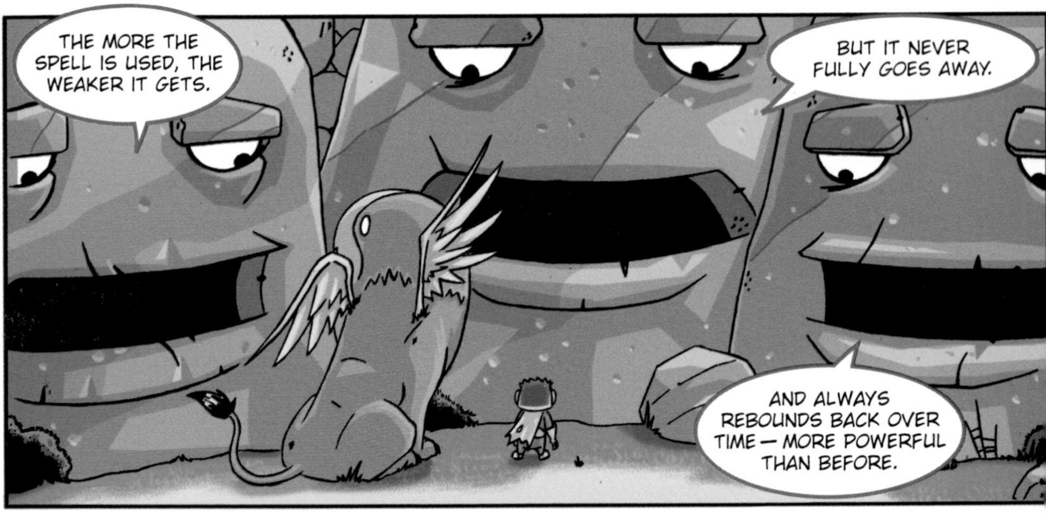
THE MORE THE SPELL IS USED, THE WEAKER IT GETS.
BUT IT NEVER FULLY GOES AWAY.
AND ALWAYS REBOUNDS BACK OVER TIME — MORE POWERFUL THAN BEFORE.

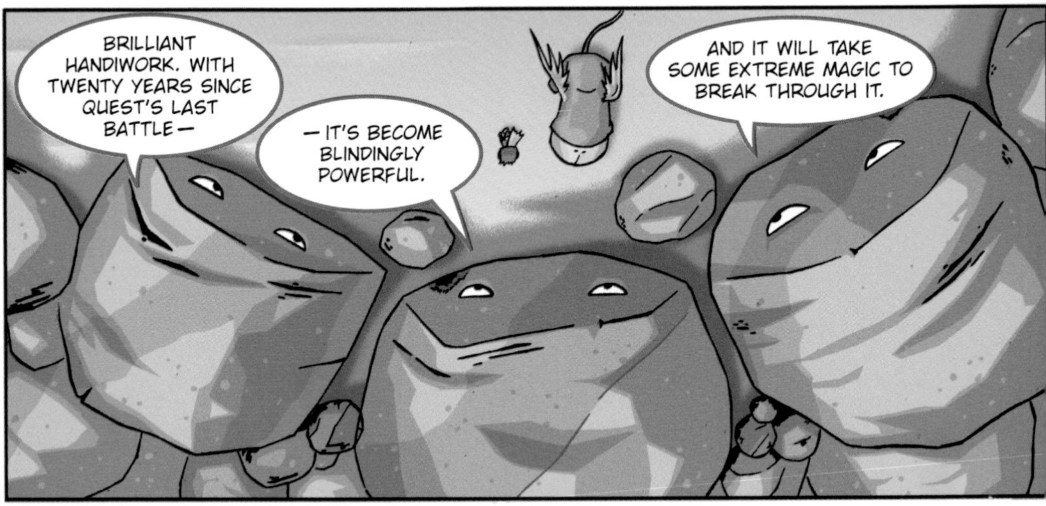
BRILLIANT HANDIWORK. WITH TWENTY YEARS SINCE QUEST'S LAST BATTLE—
—IT'S BECOME BLINDINGLY POWERFUL.
AND IT WILL TAKE SOME EXTREME MAGIC TO BREAK THROUGH IT.

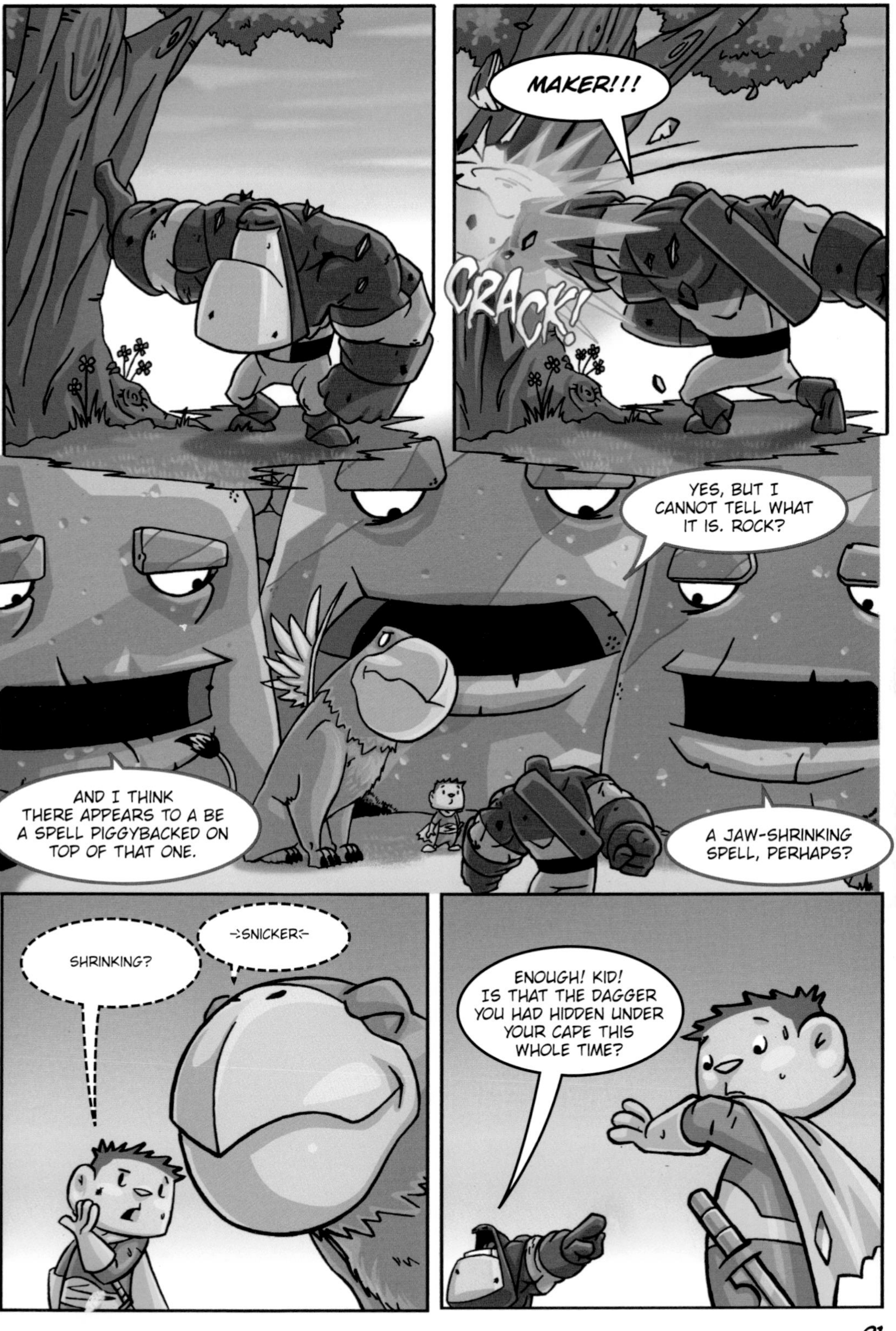
MAKER!!!
CRACK!
YES, BUT I CANNOT TELL WHAT IT IS. ROCK?
AND I THINK THERE APPEARS TO A BE A SPELL PIGGYBACKED ON TOP OF THAT ONE.
A JAW-SHRINKING SPELL, PERHAPS?
SHRINKING?
~SNICKER~
ENOUGH! KID! IS THAT THE DAGGER YOU HAD HIDDEN UNDER YOUR CAPE THIS WHOLE TIME?

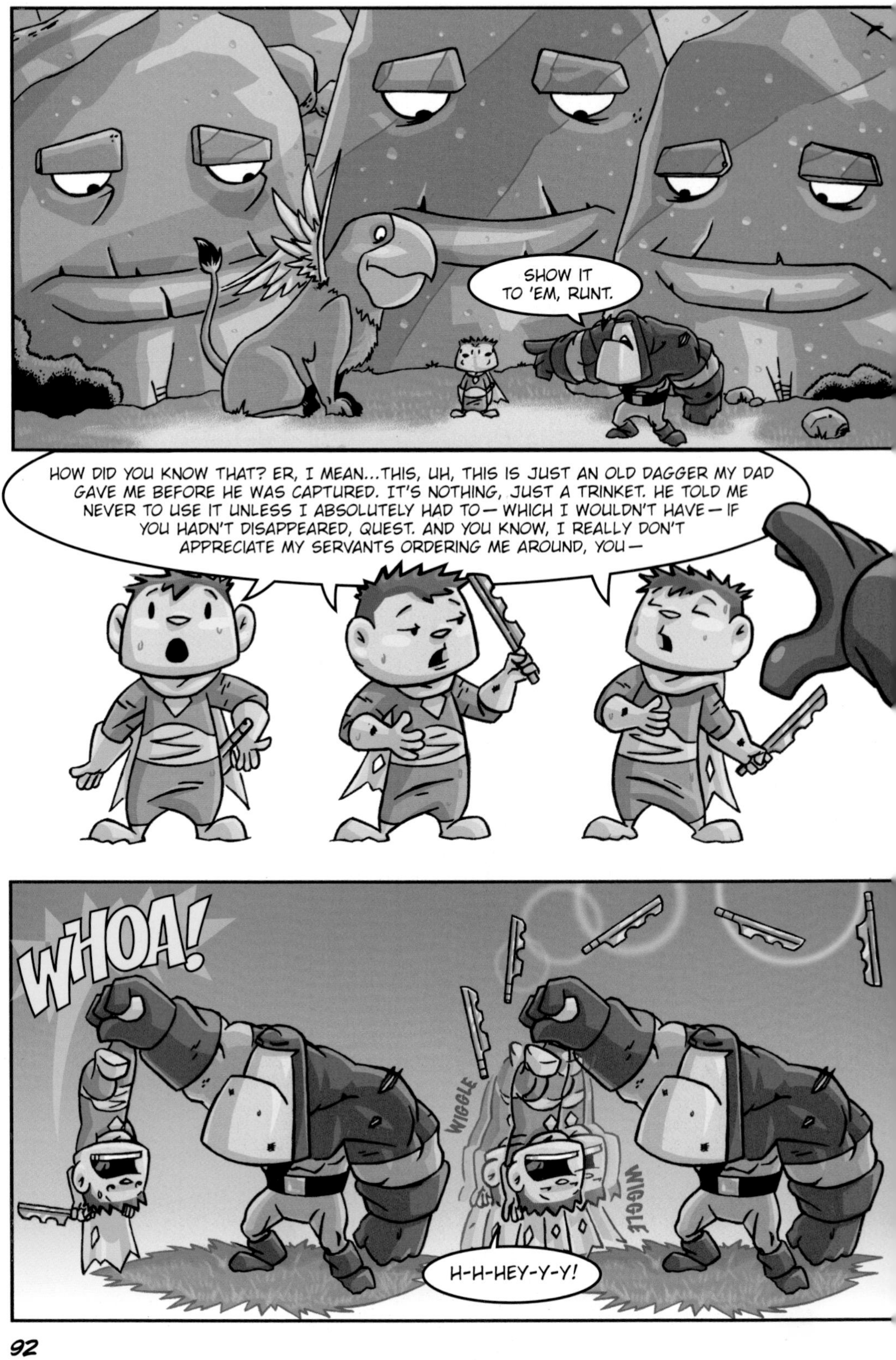
SHOW IT TO 'EM, RUNT.
HOW DID YOU KNOW THAT? ER, I MEAN...THIS, UH, THIS IS JUST AN OLD DAGGER MY DAD GAVE ME BEFORE HE WAS CAPTURED. IT'S NOTHING, JUST A TRINKET. HE TOLD ME NEVER TO USE IT UNLESS I ABSOLUTELY HAD TO— WHICH I WOULDN'T HAVE— IF YOU HADN'T DISAPPEARED, QUEST. AND YOU KNOW, I REALLY DON'T APPRECIATE MY SERVANTS ORDERING ME AROUND, YOU—
WHOA!
WIGGLE
WIGGLE
H-H-HEY-Y-Y!

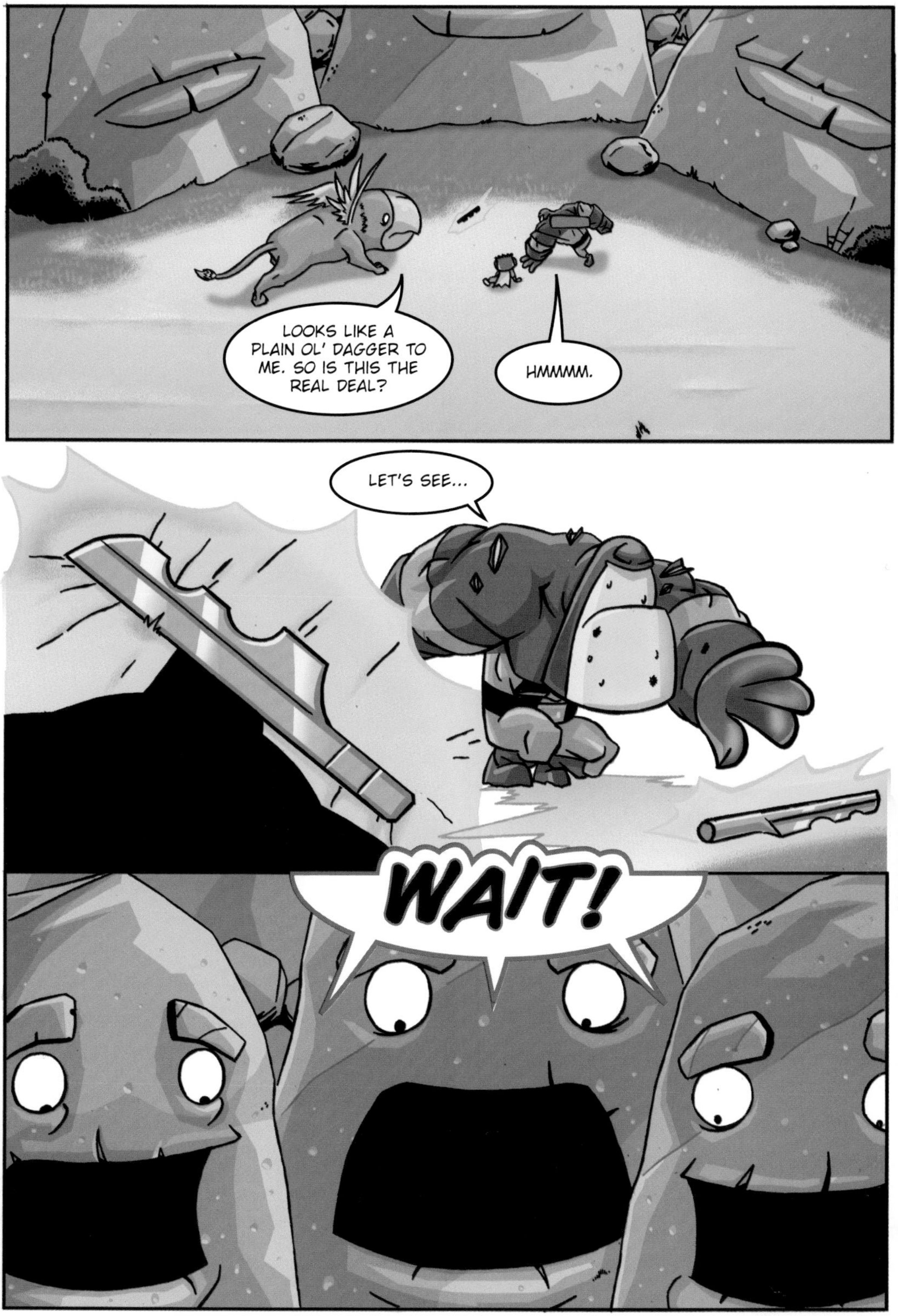
LOOKS LIKE A PLAIN OL' DAGGER TO ME. SO IS THIS THE REAL DEAL?
HMMMM.
LET'S SEE...
WAIT!

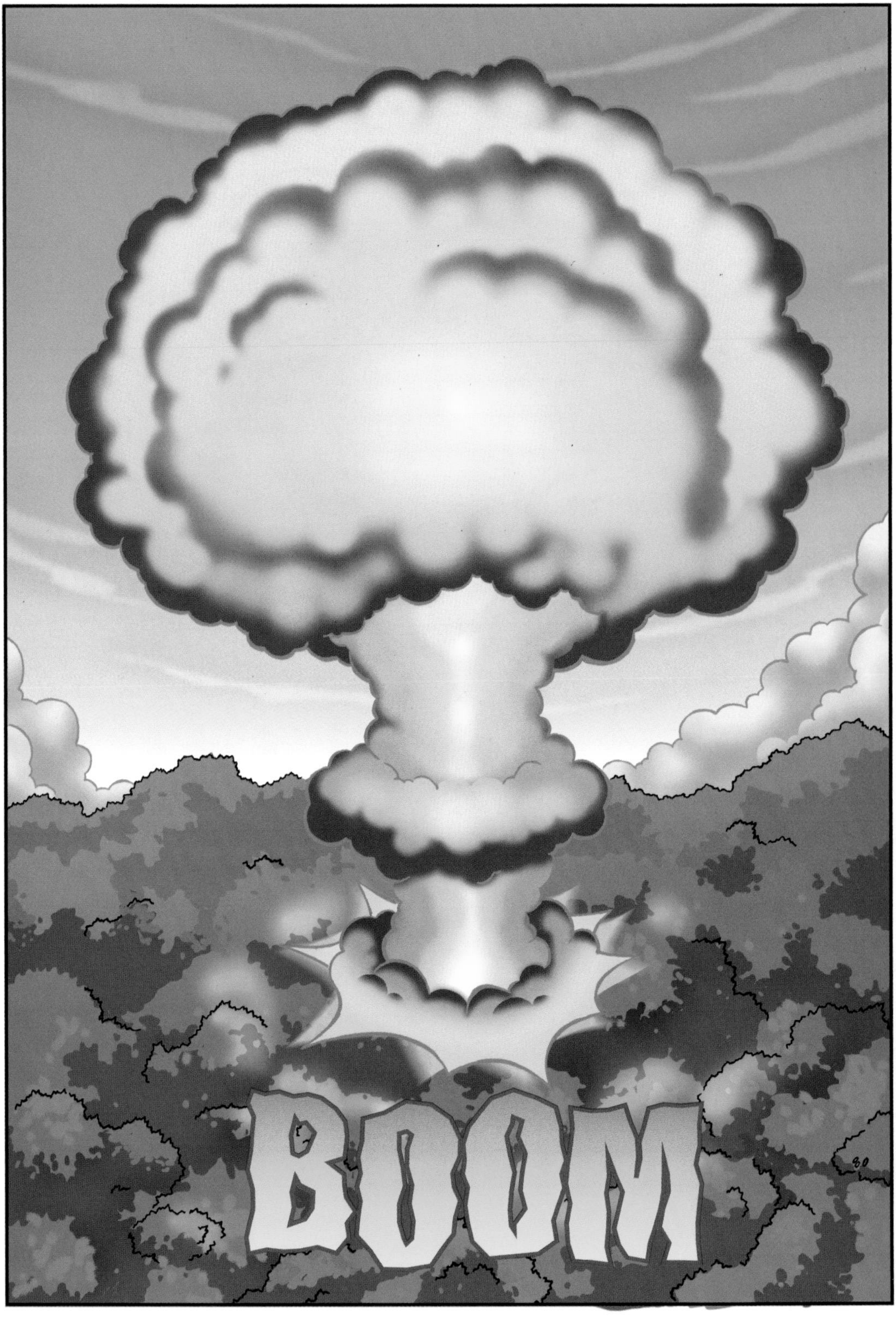
BOOM

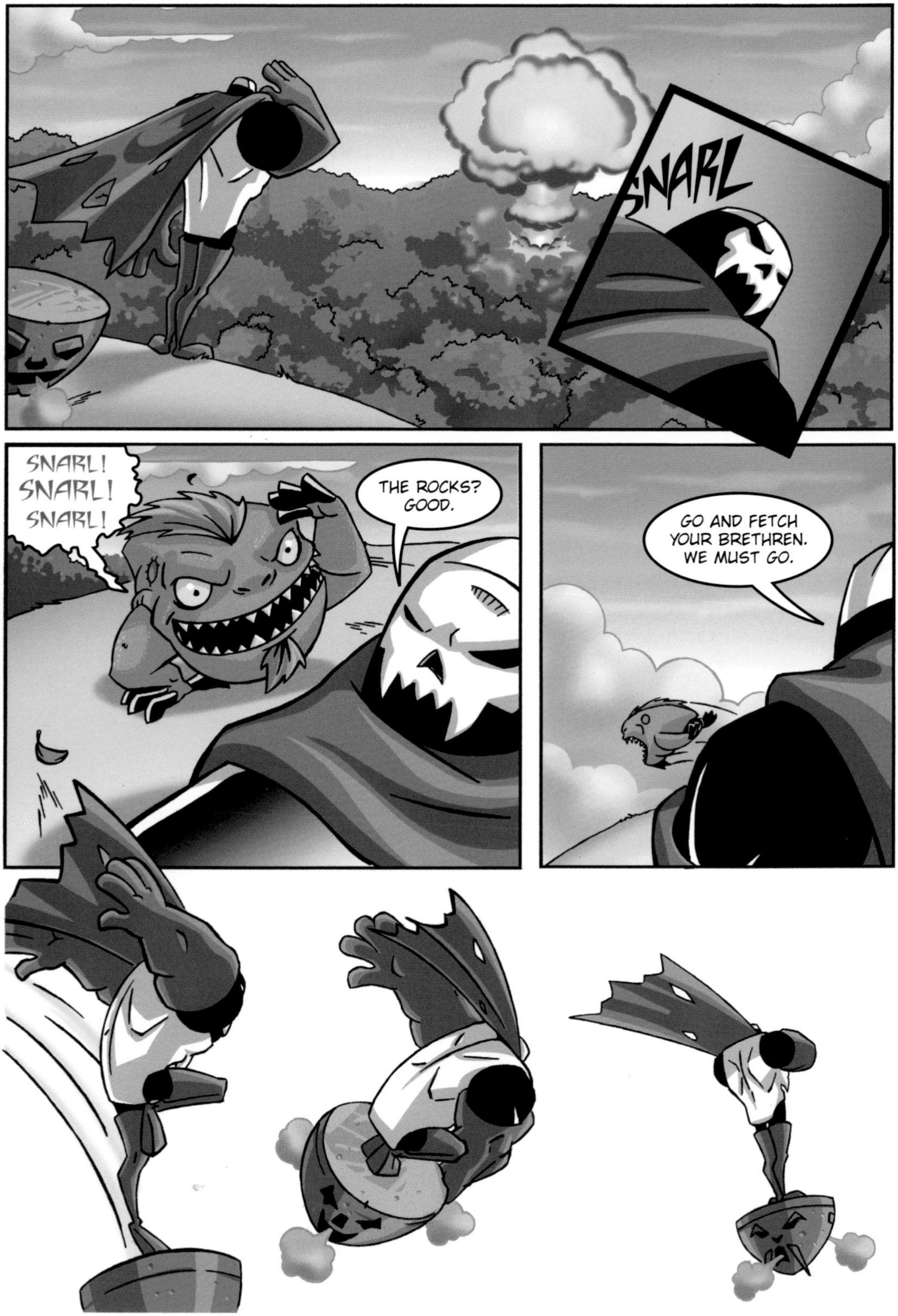
SNARL
SNARL! SNARL! SNARL!
THE ROCKS? GOOD.
GO AND FETCH YOUR BRETHREN. WE MUST GO.

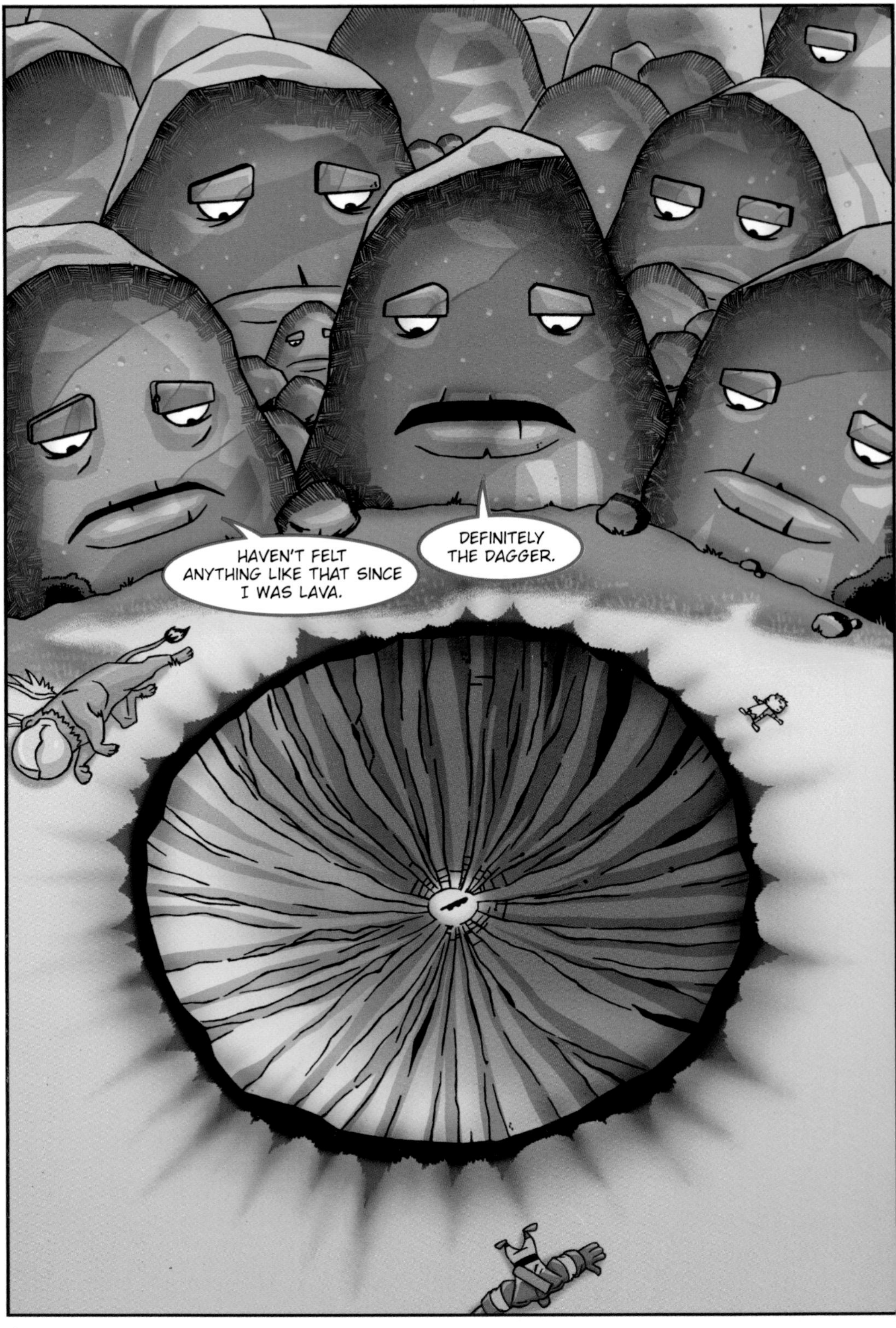
HAVEN'T FELT ANYTHING LIKE THAT SINCE I WAS LAVA.
DEFINITELY THE DAGGER.

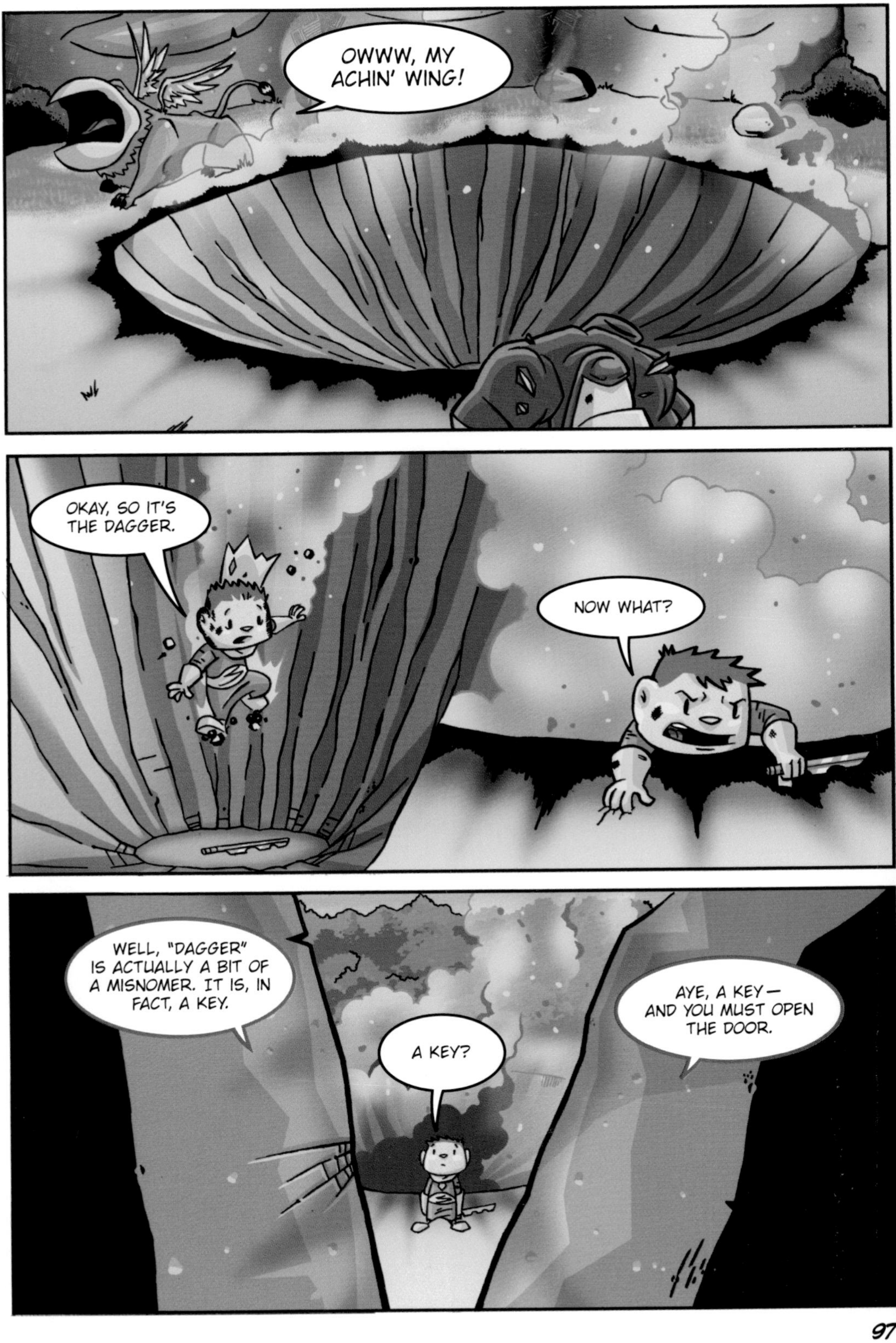
OWWW, MY ACHIN' WING!
OKAY, SO IT'S THE DAGGER.
NOW WHAT?
WELL, "DAGGER" IS ACTUALLY A BIT OF A MISNOMER. IT IS, IN FACT, A KEY.
A KEY?
AYE, A KEY— AND YOU MUST OPEN THE DOOR.

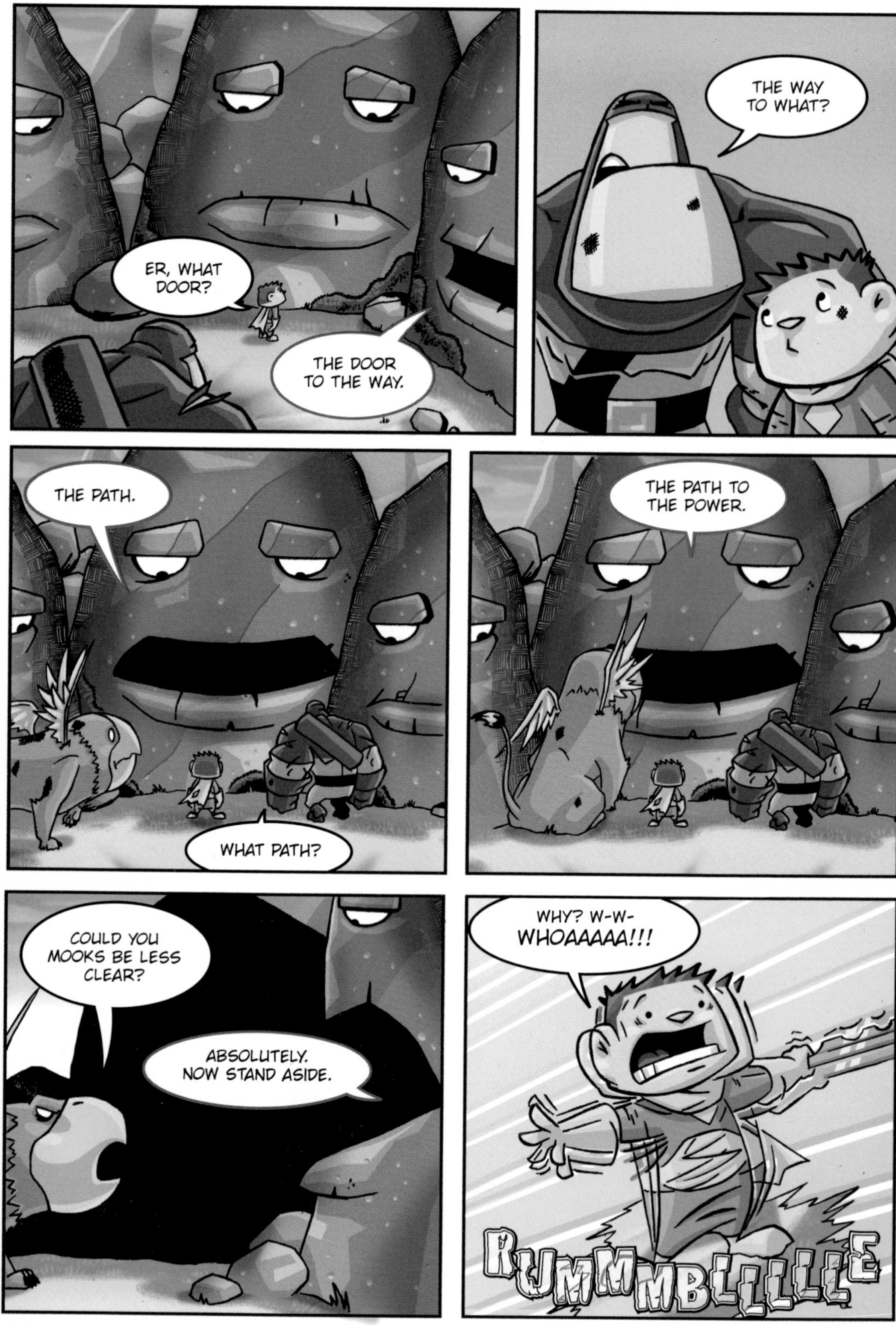
ER, WHAT DOOR?
THE DOOR TO THE WAY.
THE WAY TO WHAT?
THE PATH.
WHAT PATH?
THE PATH TO THE POWER.
COULD YOU MOOKS BE LESS CLEAR?
ABSOLUTELY. NOW STAND ASIDE.
WHY? W-W- WHOAAAAA!!!
RUMMMBLLLLLE

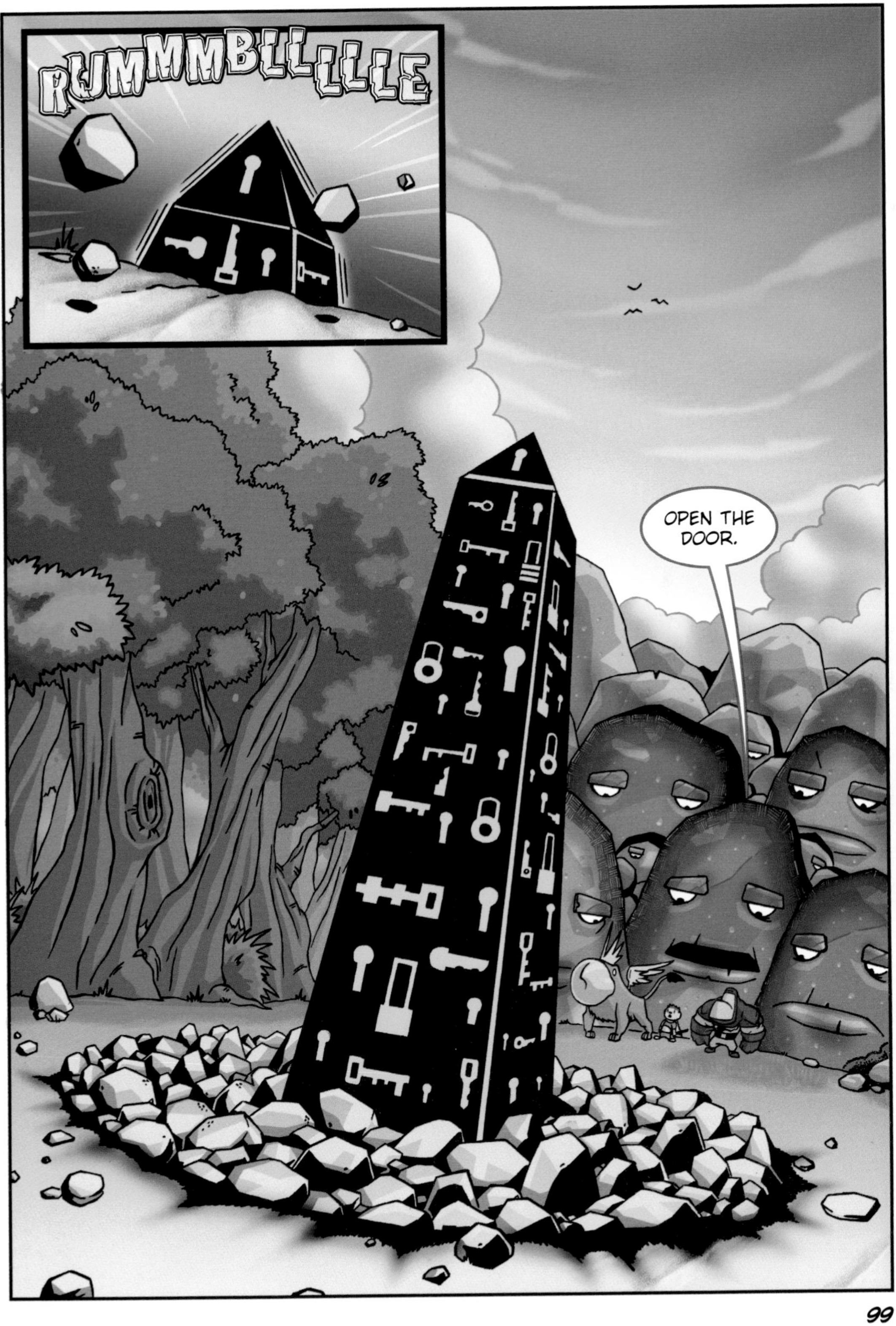
RUMMMBLLLLLE
OPEN THE DOOR.

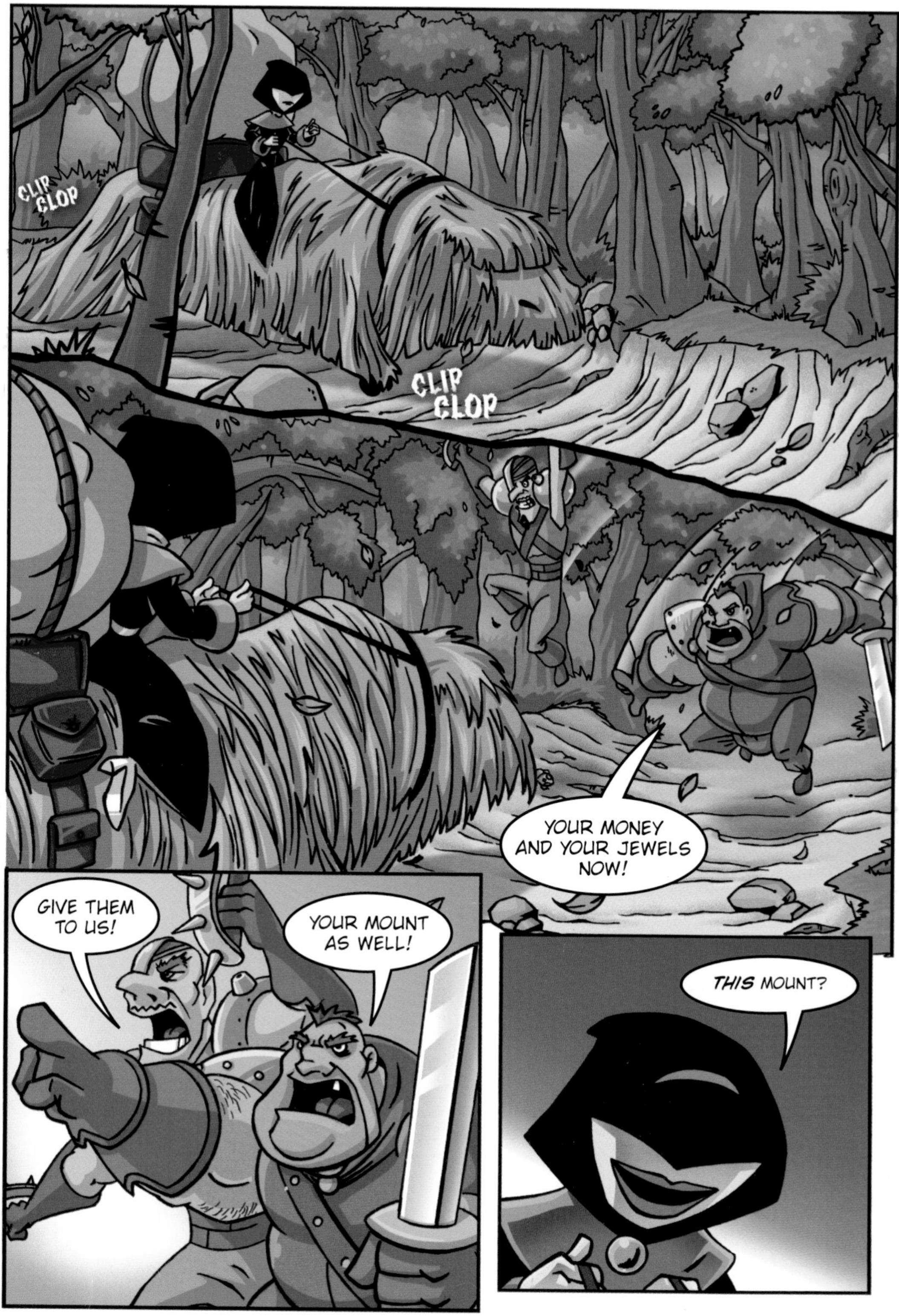
CLIP CLOP
CLIP CLOP
YOUR MONEY AND YOUR JEWELS NOW!
GIVE THEM TO US!
YOUR MOUNT AS WELL!
THIS MOUNT?

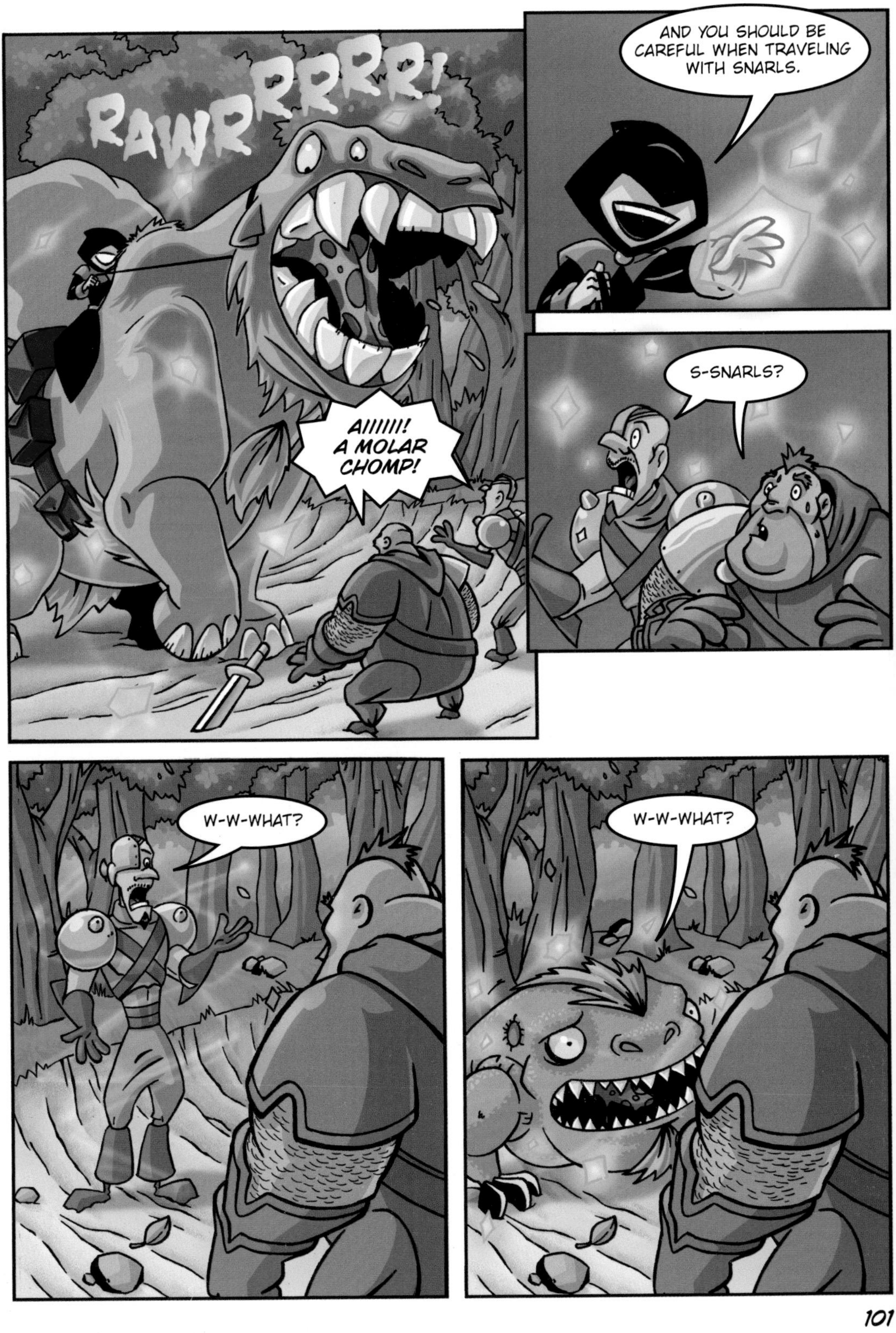
RAWRRRRR!
AIIIIII! A MOLAR CHOMP!
AND YOU SHOULD BE CAREFUL WHEN TRAVELING WITH SNARLS.
S-SNARLS?
W-W-WHAT?
W-W-WHAT?

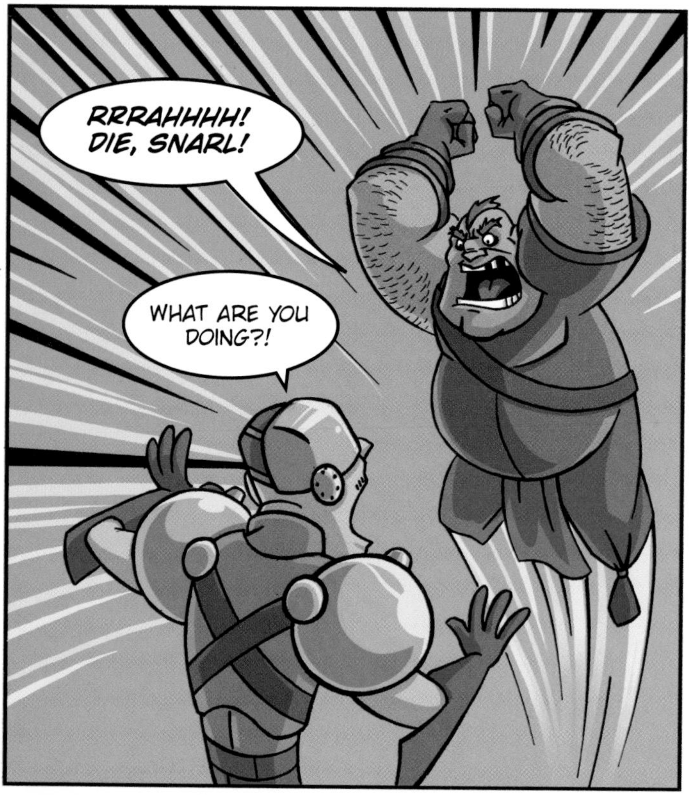
RRRAHHHH!
DIE, SNARL!
WHAT ARE YOU DOING?!

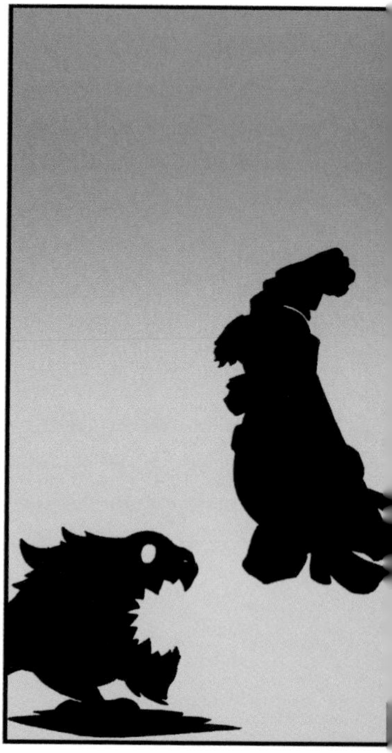

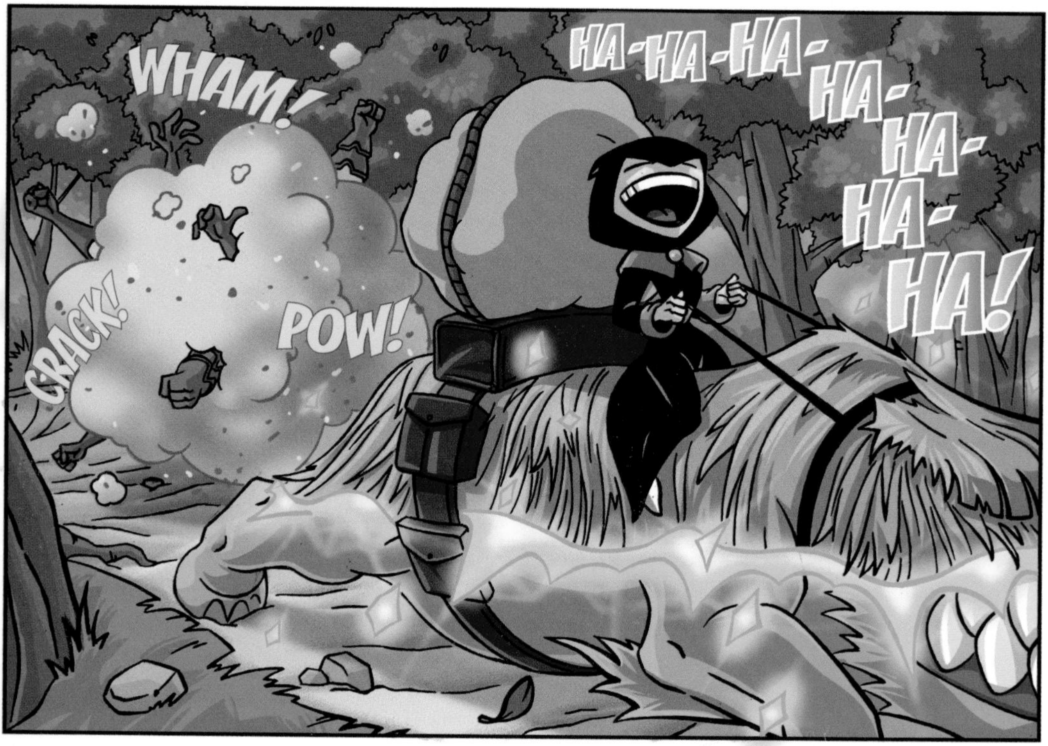
WHAM!
CRACK!
POW!
HA-HA-HA-HA-HA-HA-HA!

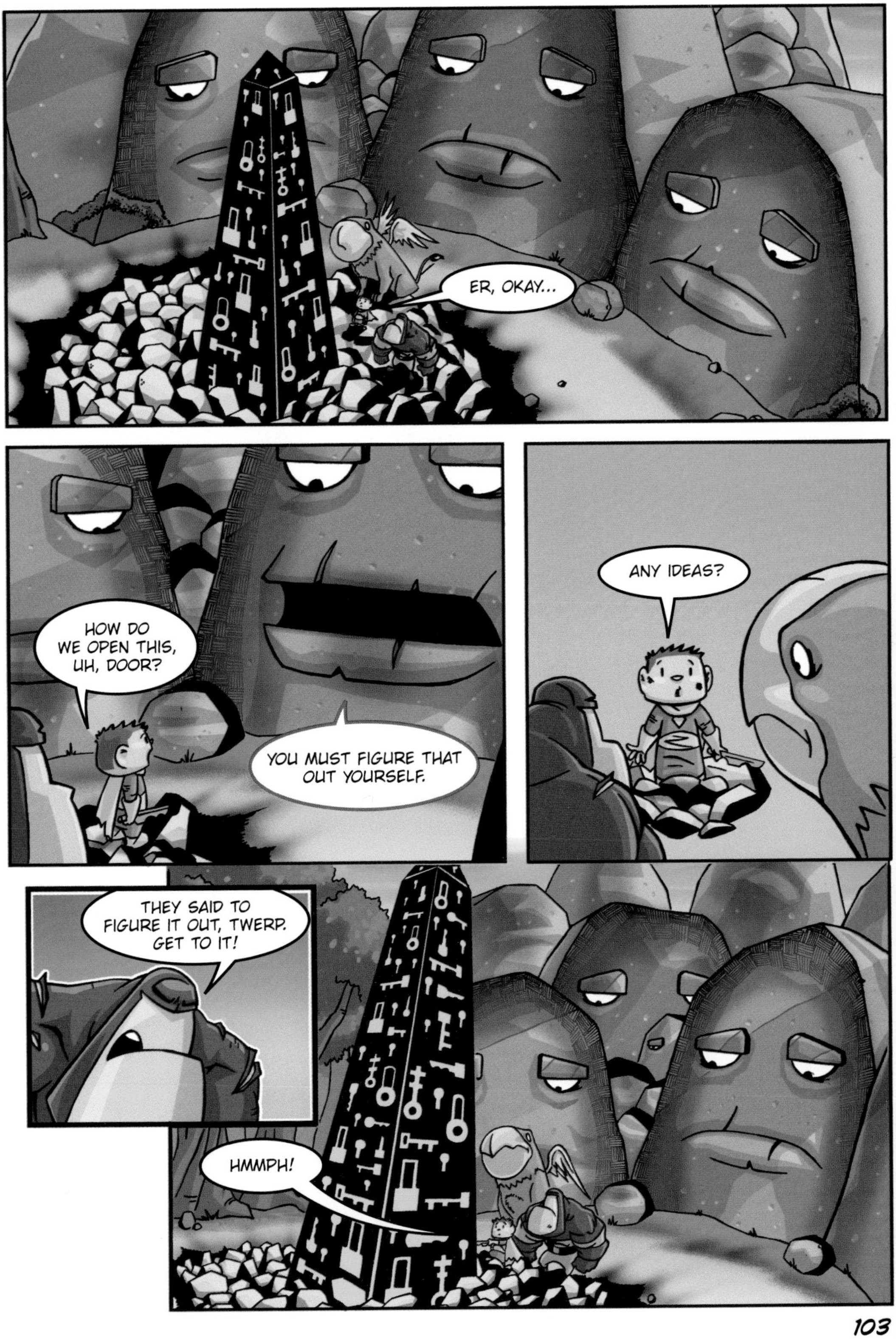
ER, OKAY...
HOW DO WE OPEN THIS, UH, DOOR?
YOU MUST FIGURE THAT OUT YOURSELF.
ANY IDEAS?
THEY SAID TO FIGURE IT OUT, TWERP. GET TO IT!
HMMPH!

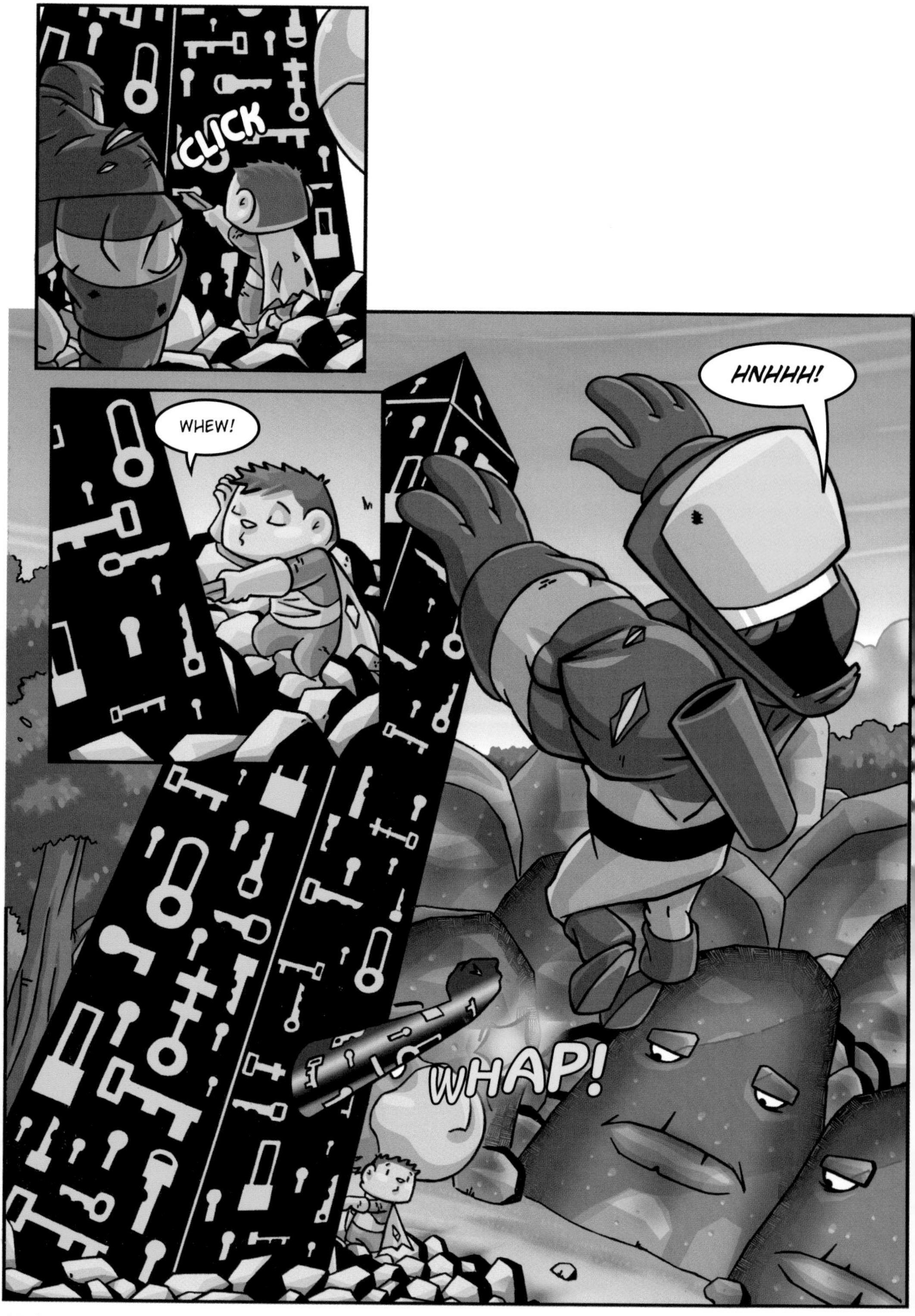
CLICK
WHEW!
HNHHH!
WHAP!

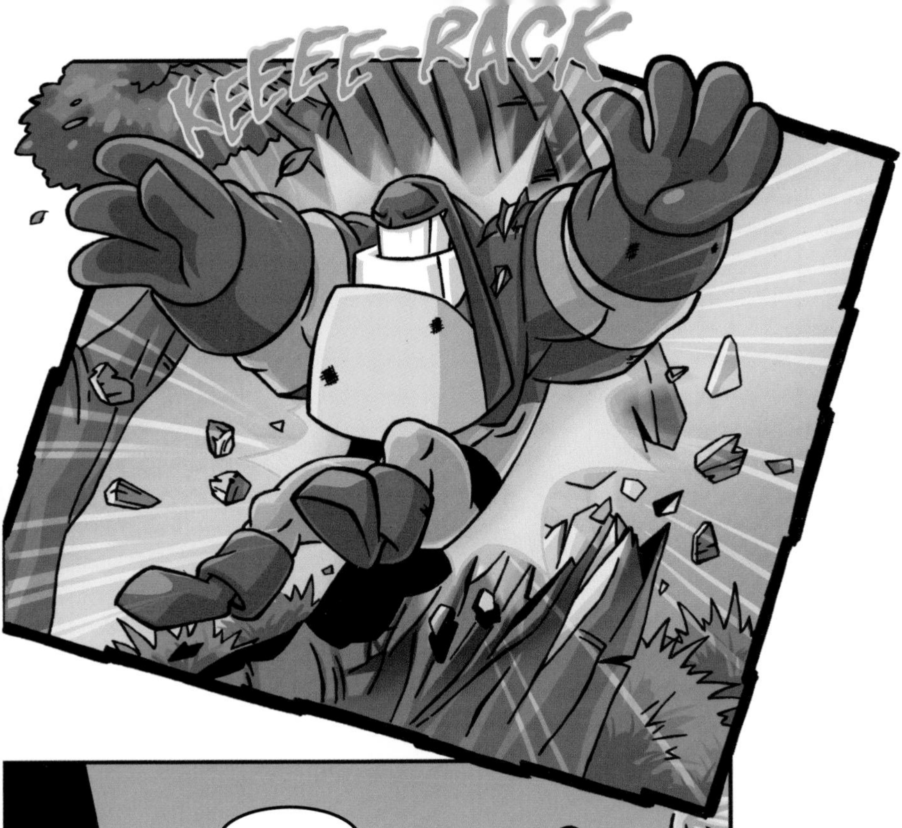
KEEEE-RACK

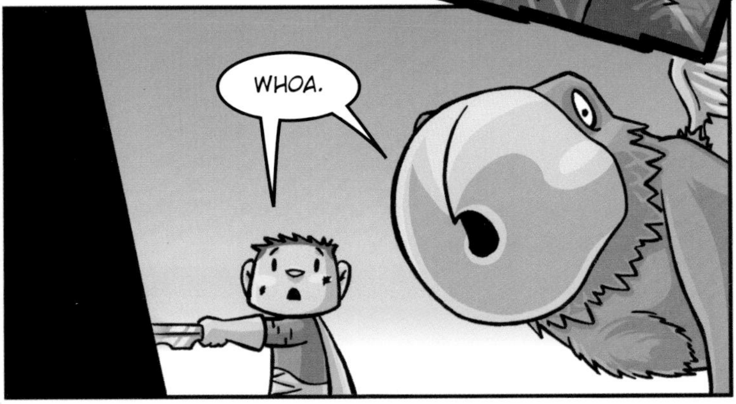
WHOA.

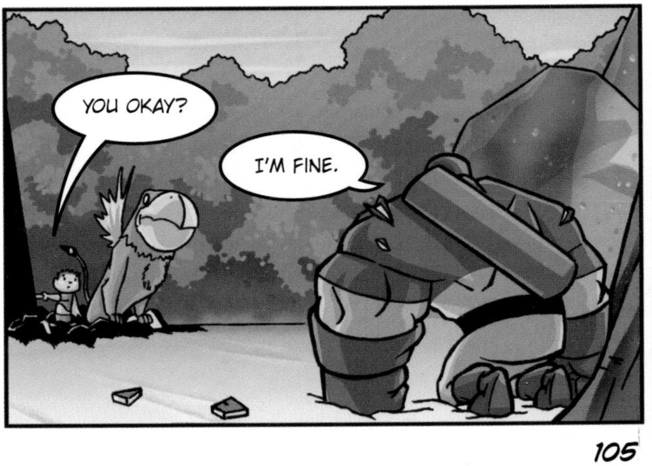
YOU OKAY?
I'M FINE.

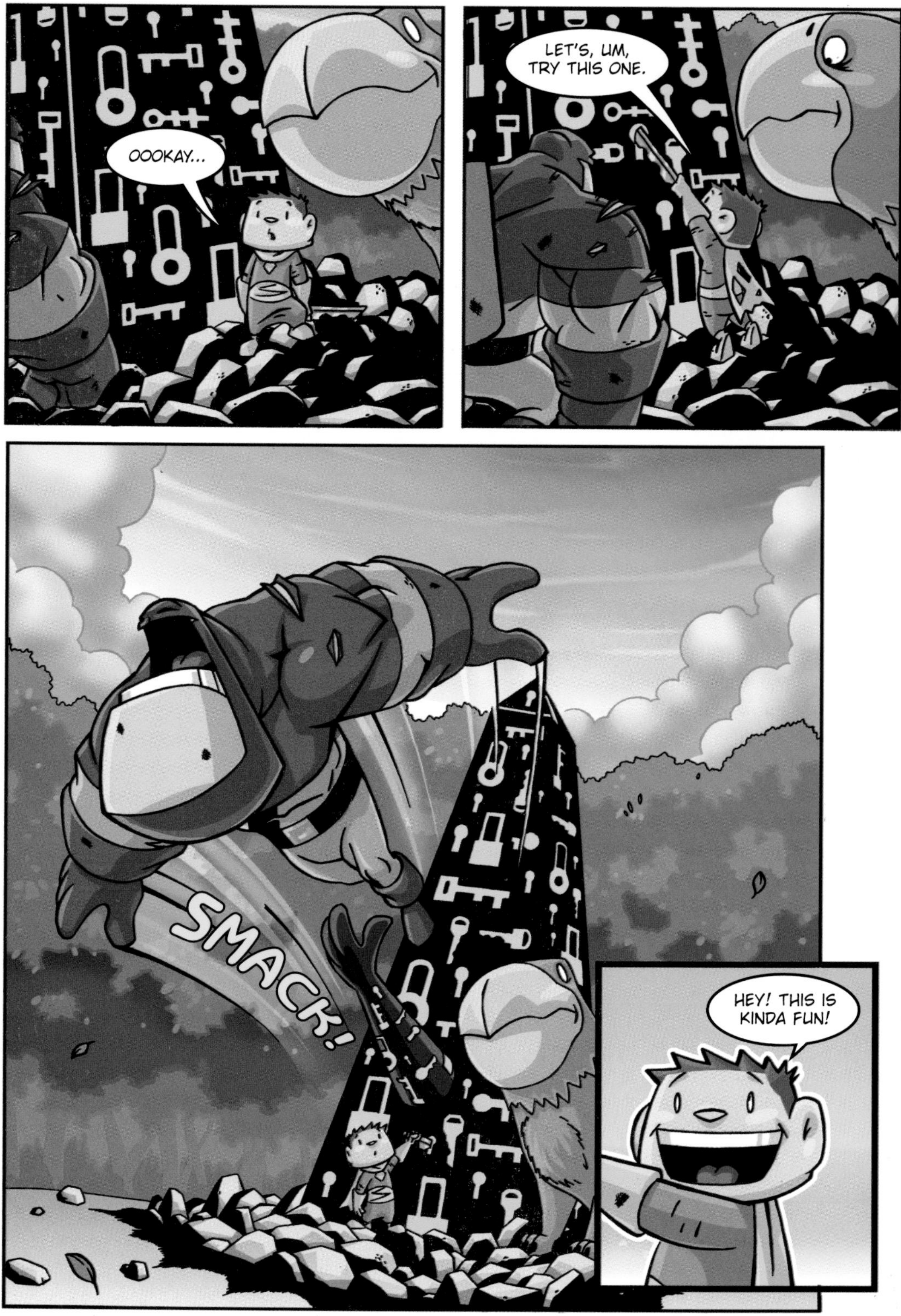
OOOKAY...
LET'S, UM, TRY THIS ONE.
SMACK!
HEY! THIS IS KINDA FUN!

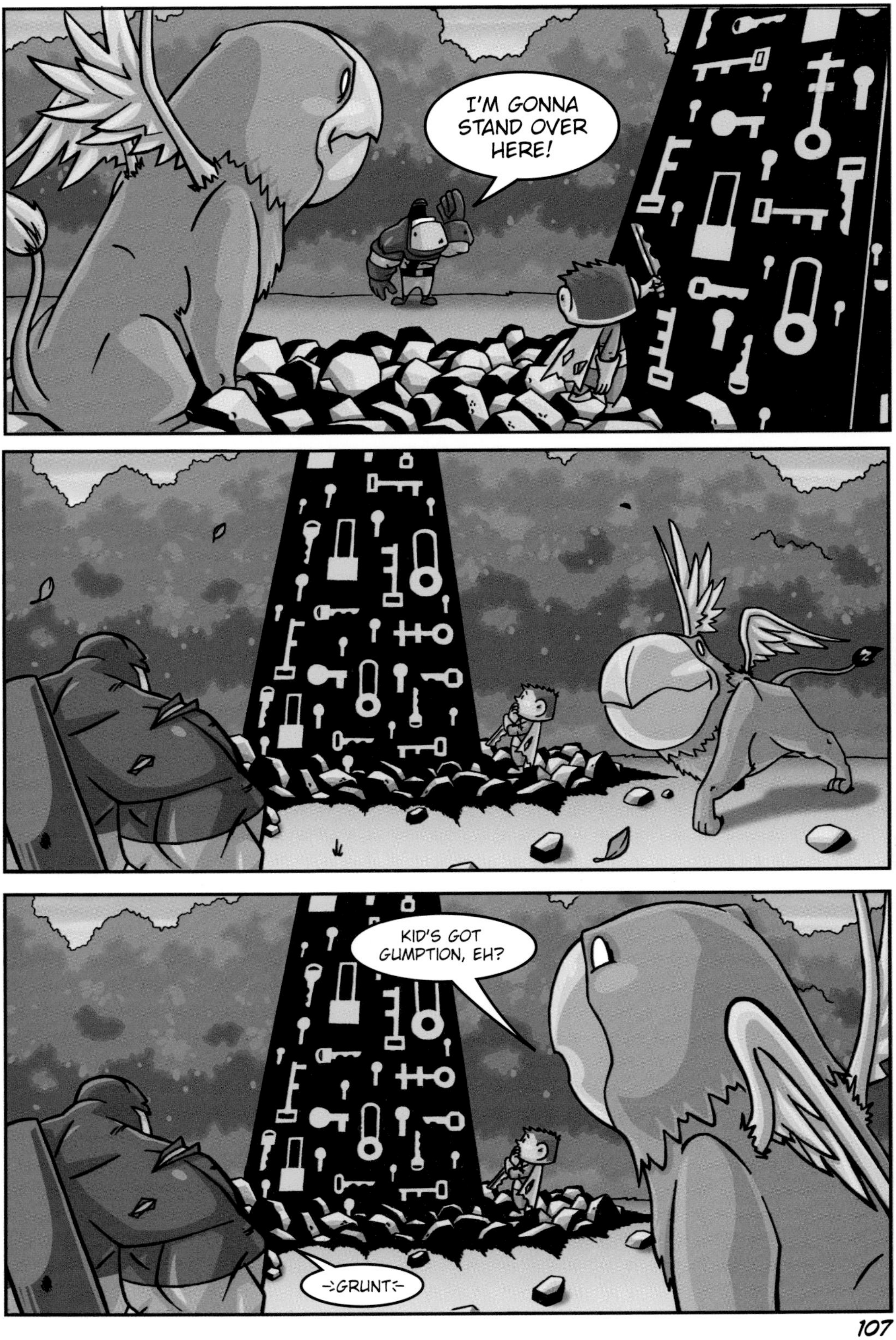
I'M GONNA STAND OVER HERE!
KID'S GOT GUMPTION, EH?
-GRUNT-

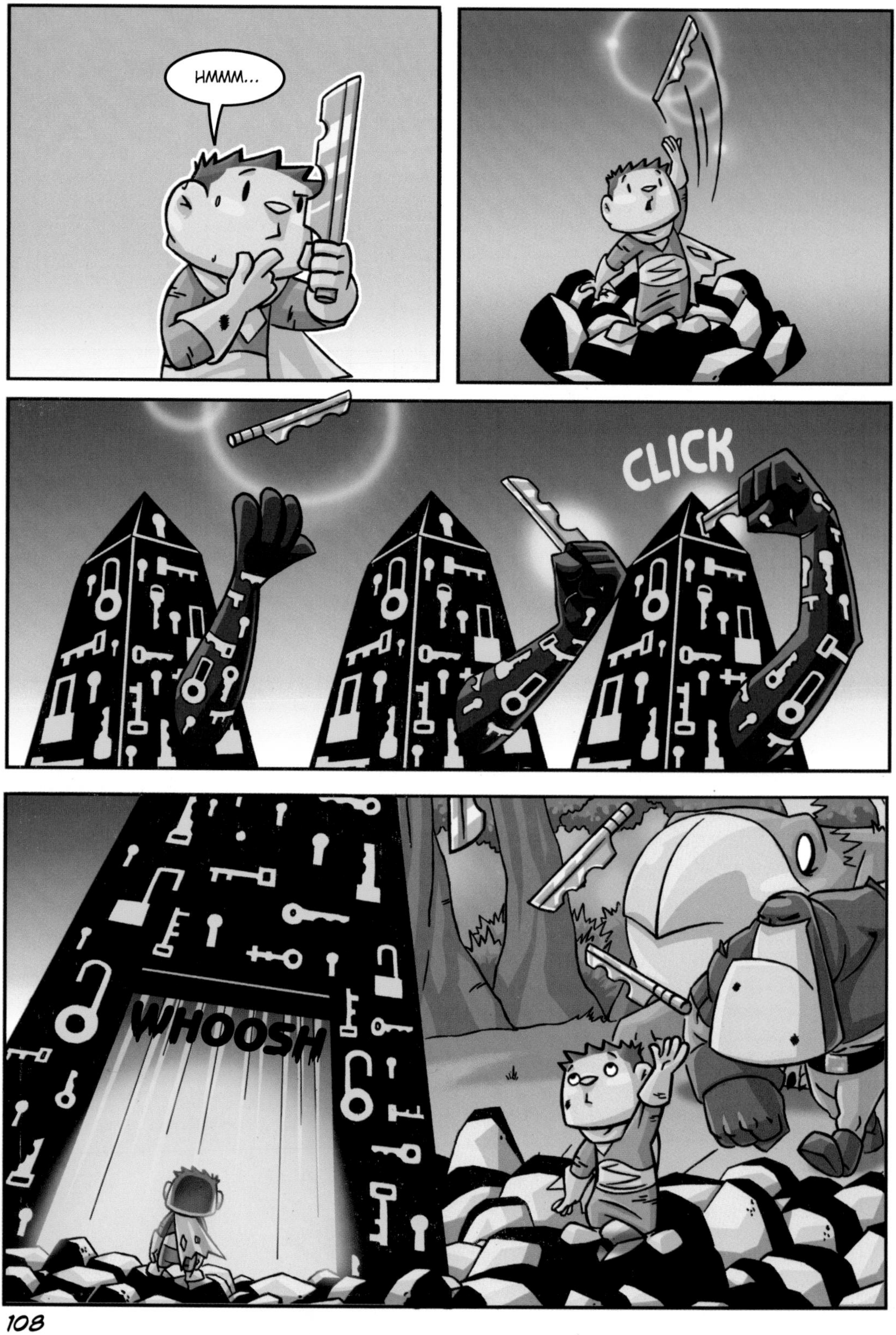
HMMM...
CLICK
WHOOSH

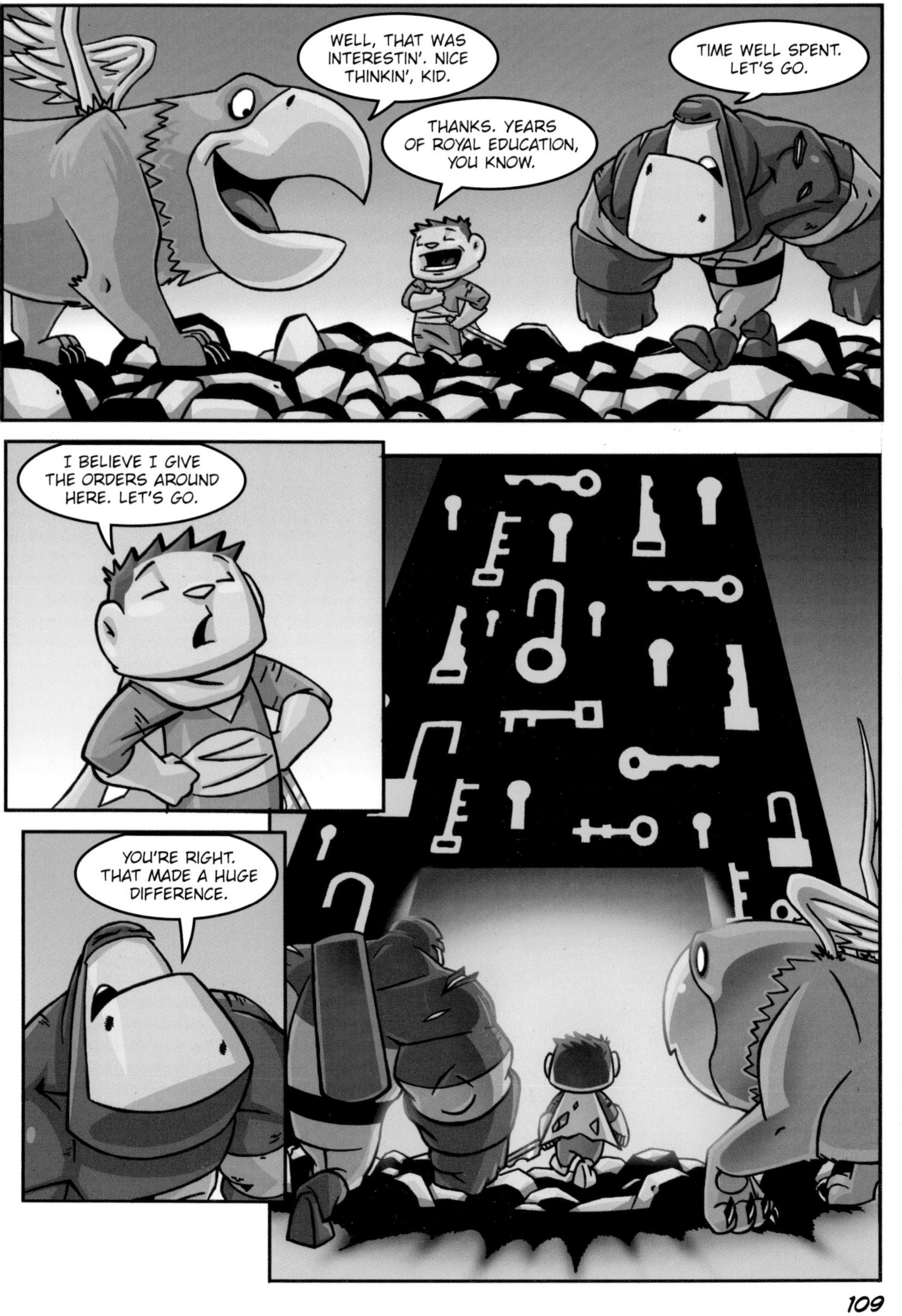
WELL, THAT WAS INTERESTIN'. NICE THINKIN', KID.
THANKS. YEARS OF ROYAL EDUCATION, YOU KNOW.
TIME WELL SPENT. LET'S GO.
I BELIEVE I GIVE THE ORDERS AROUND HERE. LET'S GO.
YOU'RE RIGHT. THAT MADE A HUGE DIFFERENCE.

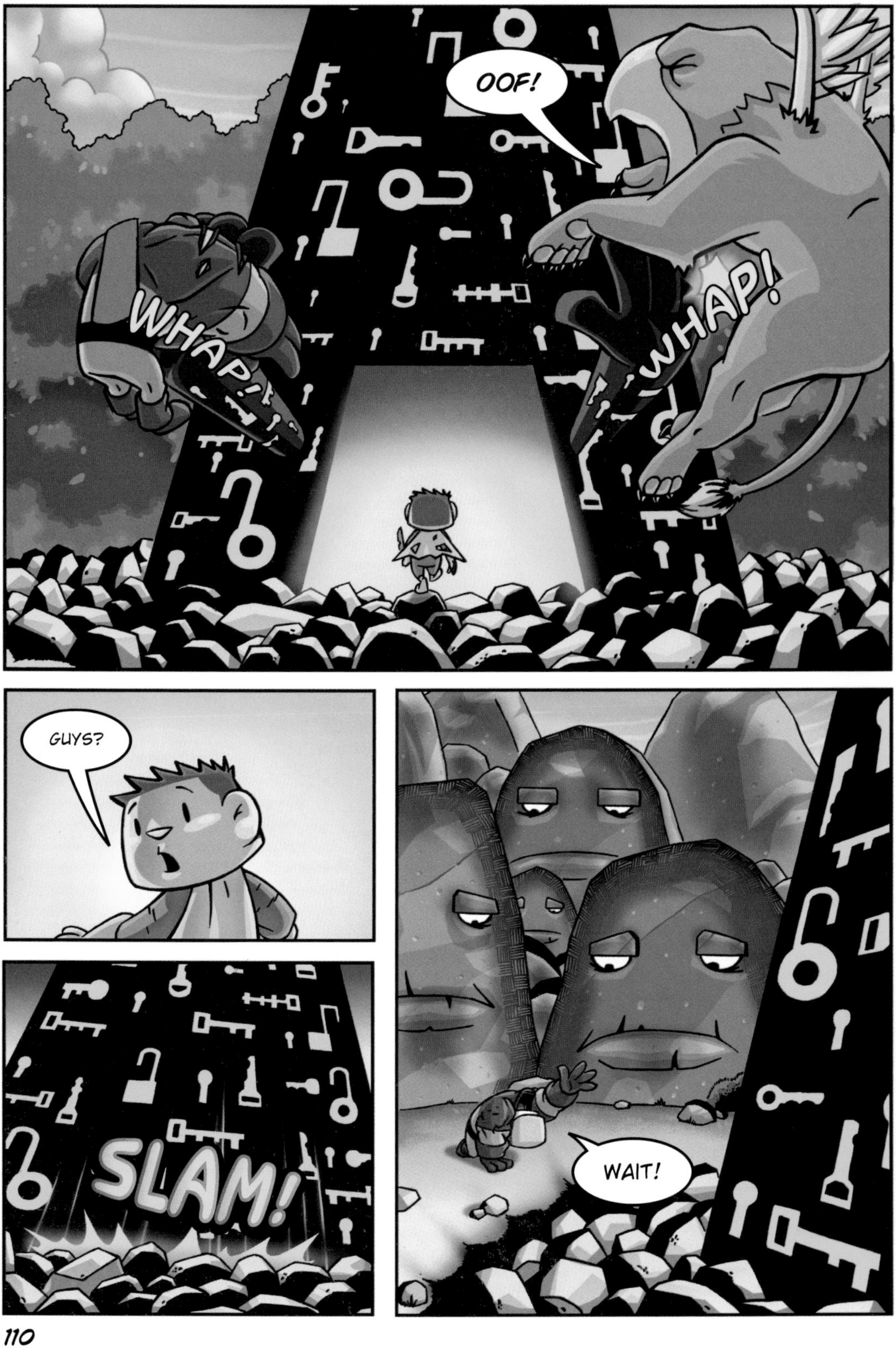
OOF!
WHAP!
WHAP!
GUYS?
SLAM!
WAIT!

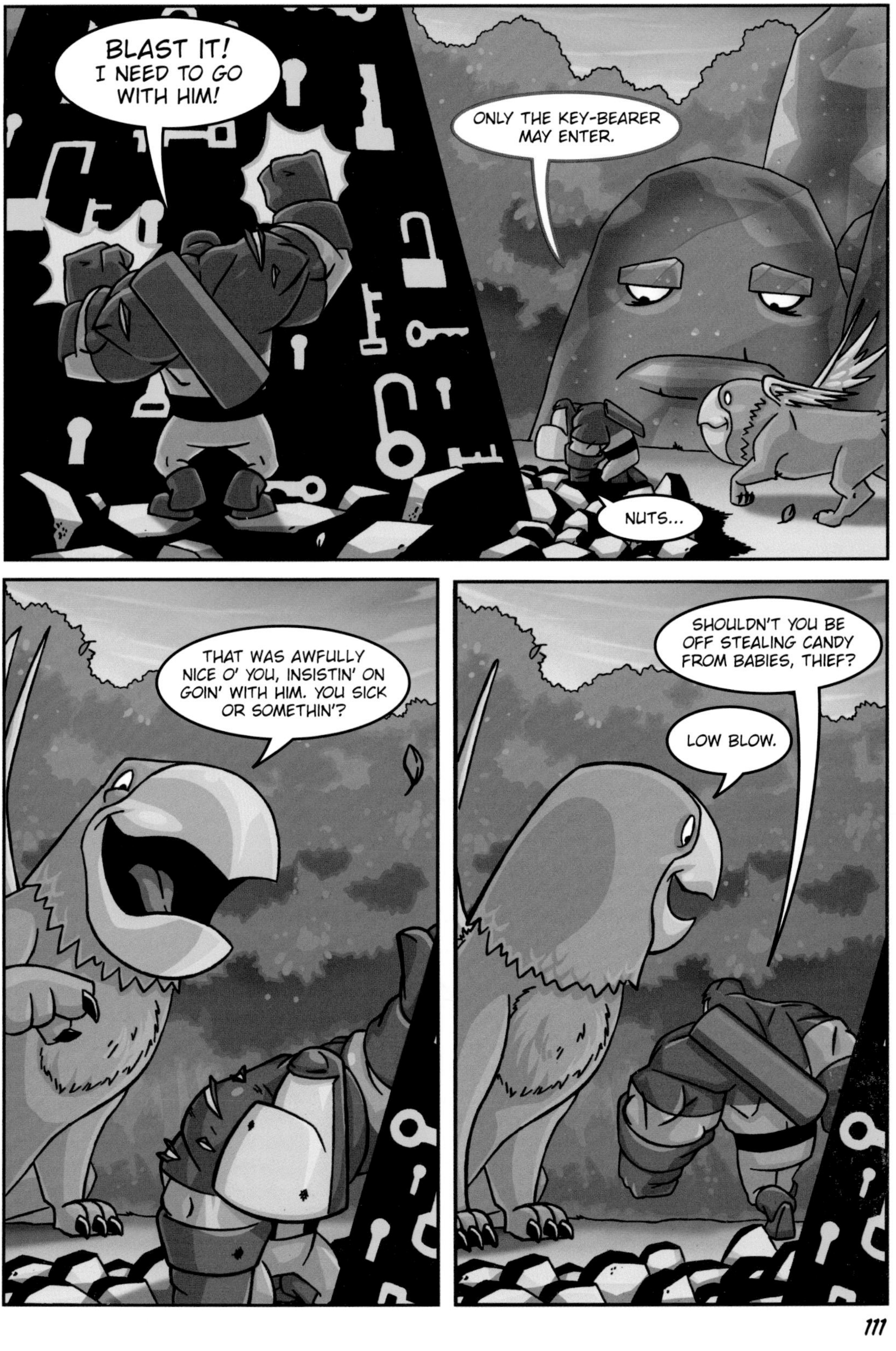
BLAST IT! I NEED TO GO WITH HIM!
ONLY THE KEY-BEARER MAY ENTER.
NUTS...
THAT WAS AWFULLY NICE O' YOU, INSISTIN' ON GOIN' WITH HIM. YOU SICK OR SOMETHIN'?
SHOULDN'T YOU BE OFF STEALING CANDY FROM BABIES, THIEF?
LOW BLOW.

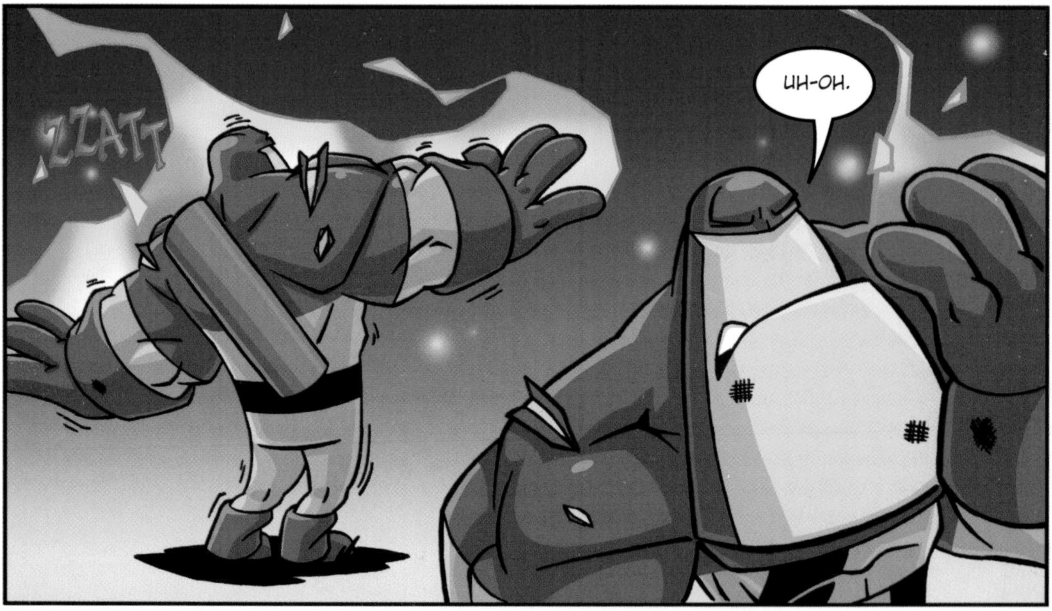
ZZATT
UH-OH.

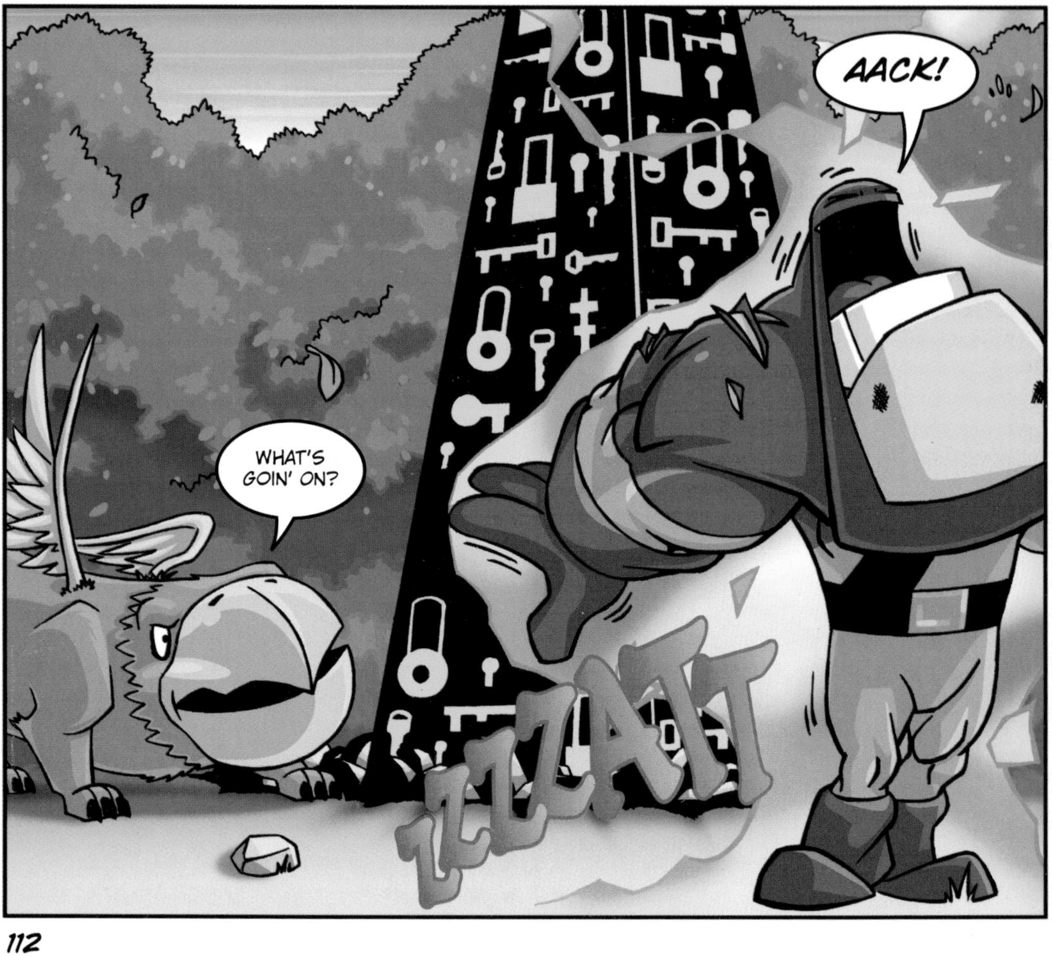
AACK!
WHAT'S GOIN' ON?
ZZZATT

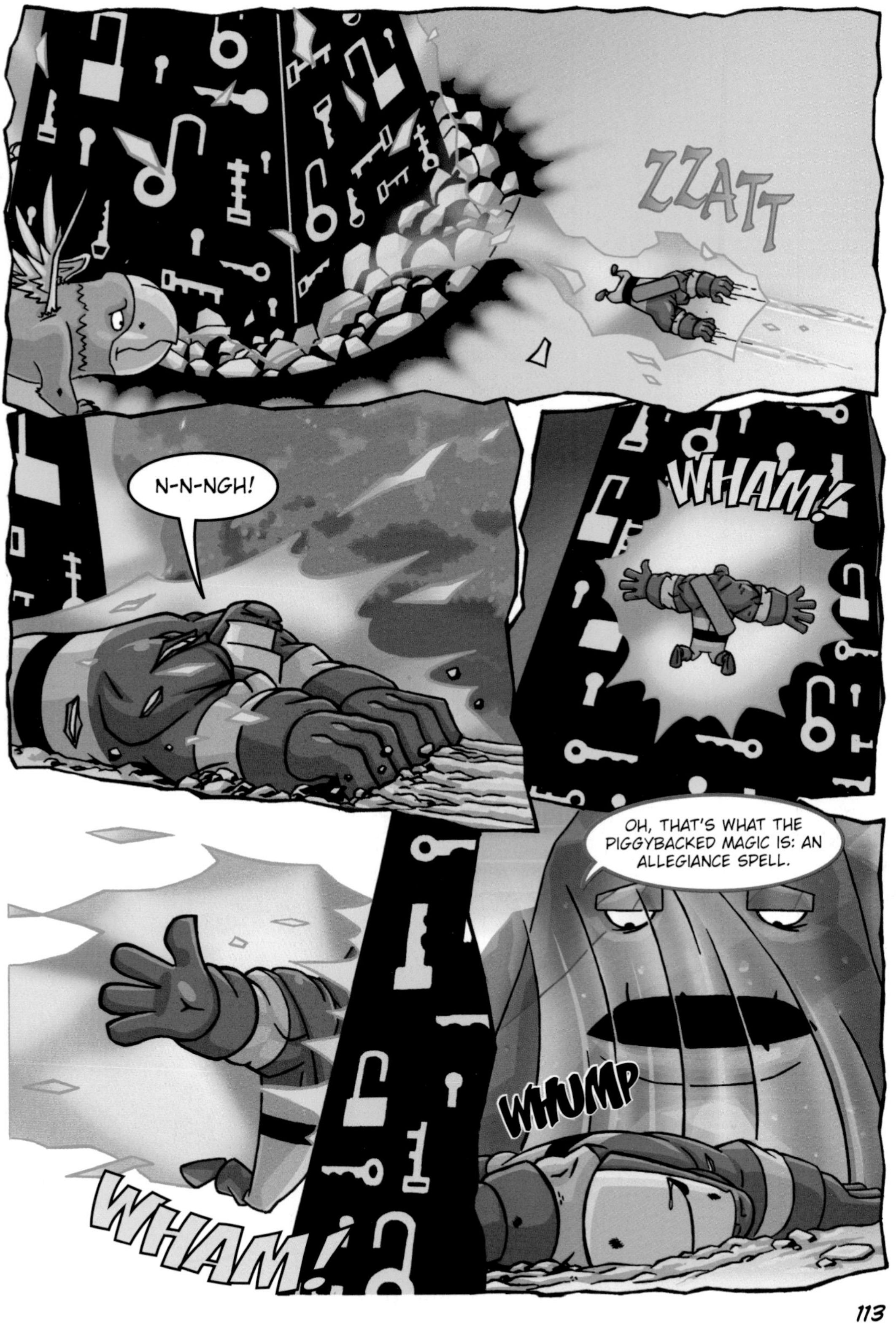

ZZATT
N-N-NGH!
WHAM!
OH, THAT'S WHAT THE PIGGYBACKED MAGIC IS: AN ALLEGIANCE SPELL.
WHUMP
WHAM!

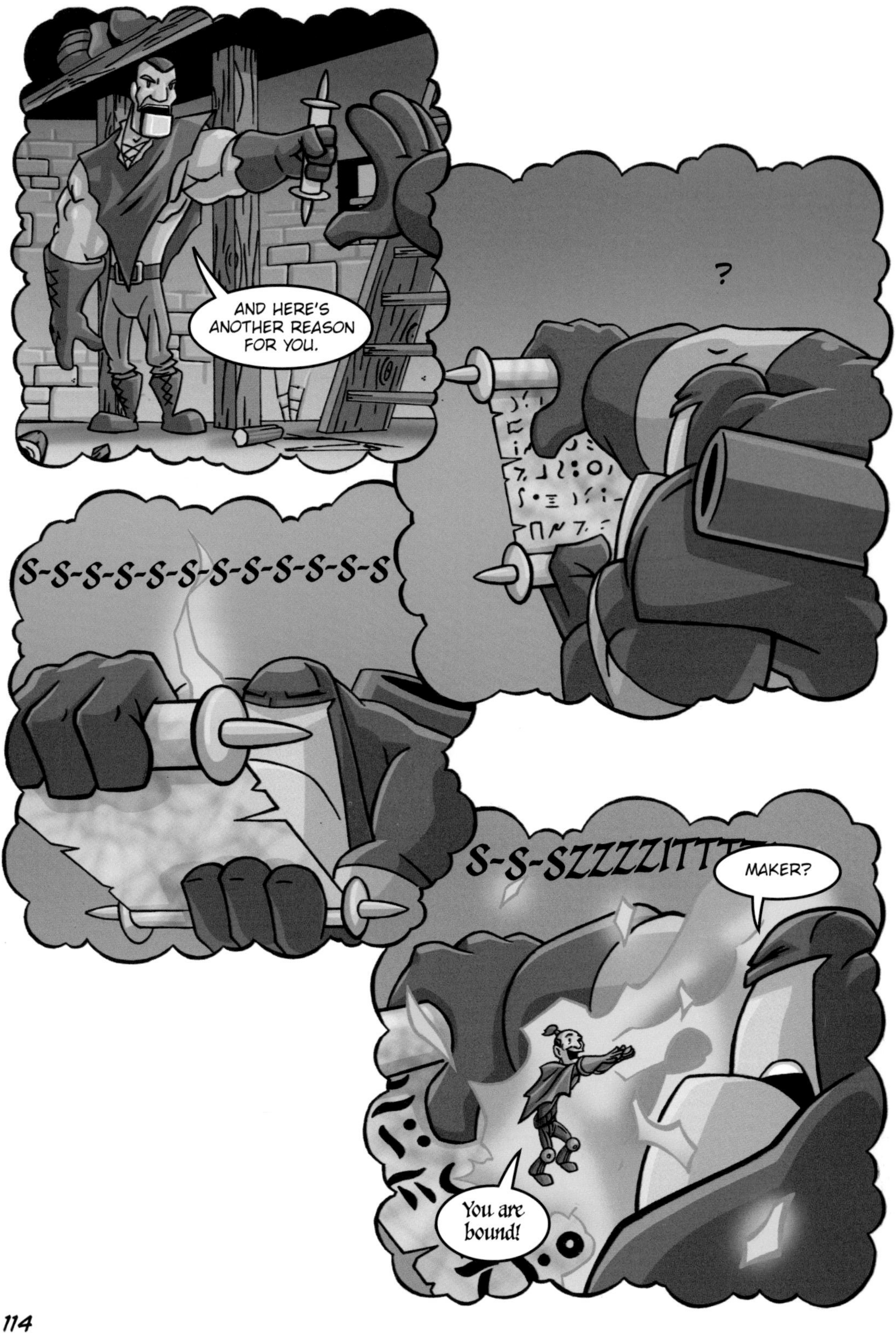
AND HERE'S ANOTHER REASON FOR YOU.
?
S-S-S-S-S-S-S-S-S-S-S-S
S-S-SZZZZITTT
MAKER?
You are bound!

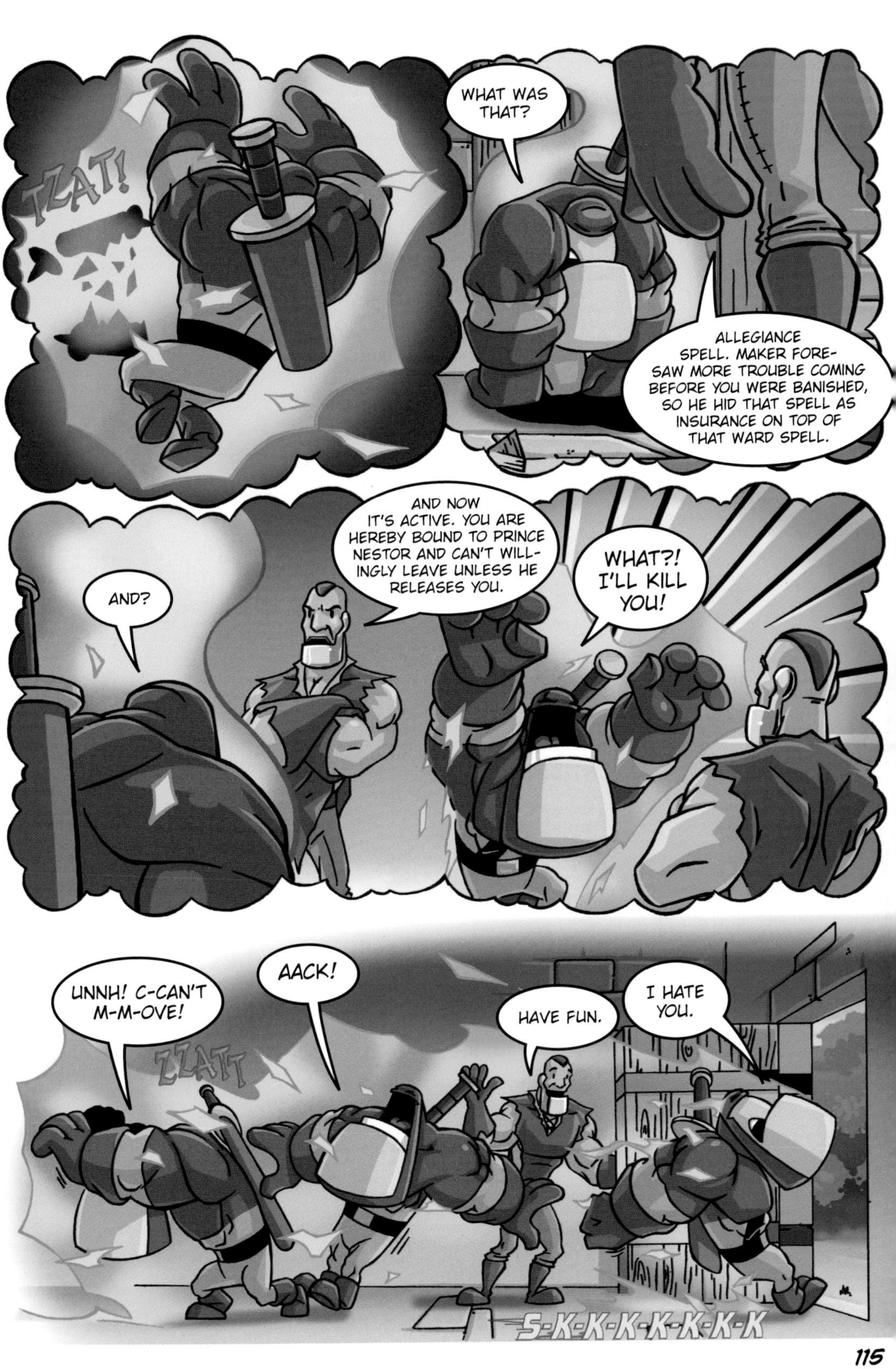
TZAT!
WHAT WAS THAT?
ALLEGIANCE SPELL. MAKER FORE-SAW MORE TROUBLE COMING BEFORE YOU WERE BANISHED, SO HE HID THAT SPELL AS INSURANCE ON TOP OF THAT WARD SPELL.
AND?
AND NOW IT'S ACTIVE. YOU ARE HEREBY BOUND TO PRINCE NESTOR AND CAN'T WILL-INGLY LEAVE UNLESS HE RELEASES YOU.
WHAT?! I'LL KILL YOU!
UNNH! C-CAN'T M-M-OVE!
AACK!
ZZATT
HAVE FUN.
I HATE YOU.
S-K-K-K-K-K-K-K

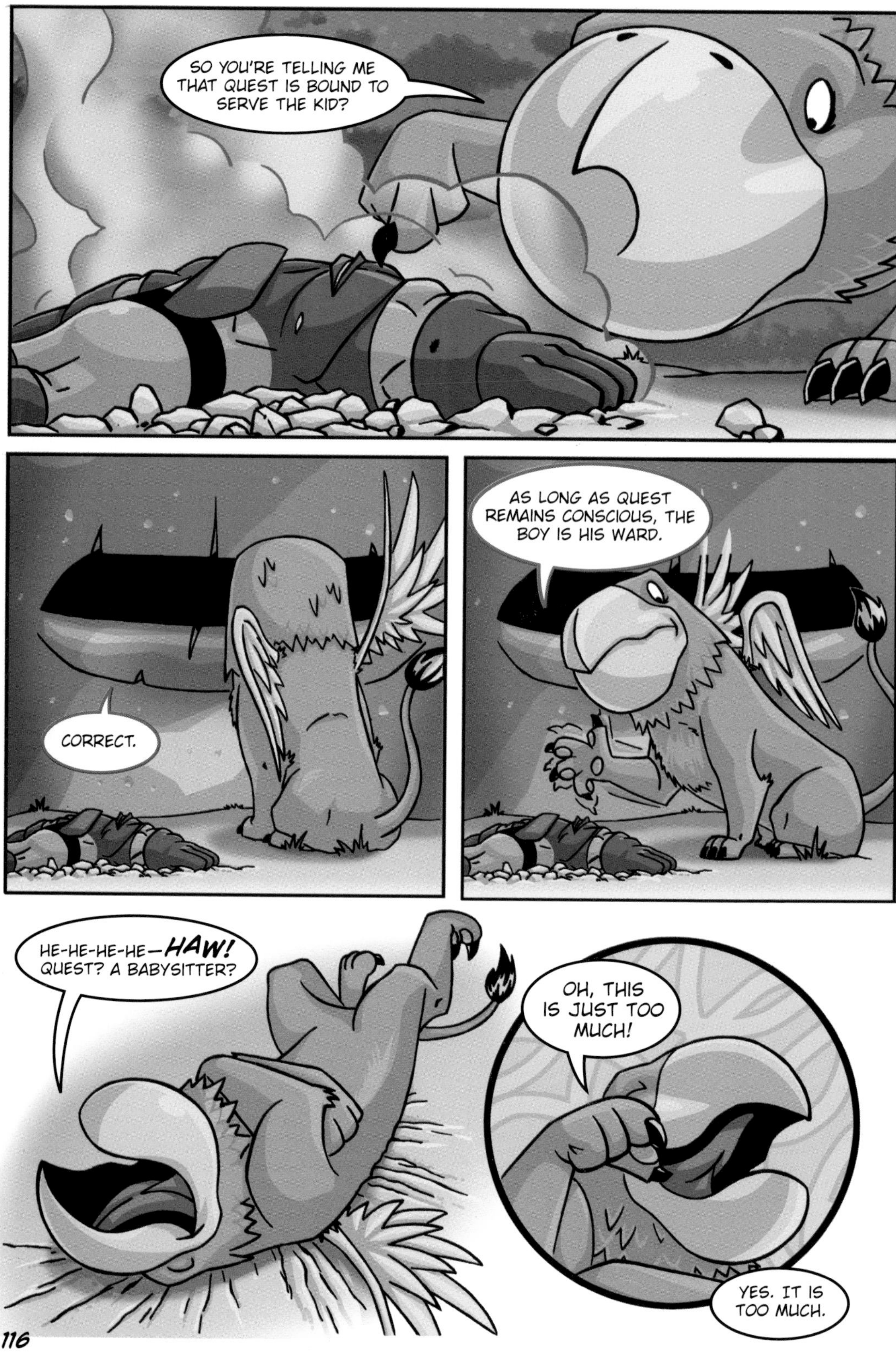
SO YOU'RE TELLING ME THAT QUEST IS BOUND TO SERVE THE KID?
CORRECT.
AS LONG AS QUEST REMAINS CONSCIOUS, THE BOY IS HIS WARD.
HE-HE-HE-HE—HAW! QUEST? A BABYSITTER?
OH, THIS IS JUST TOO MUCH!
YES. IT IS TOO MUCH.

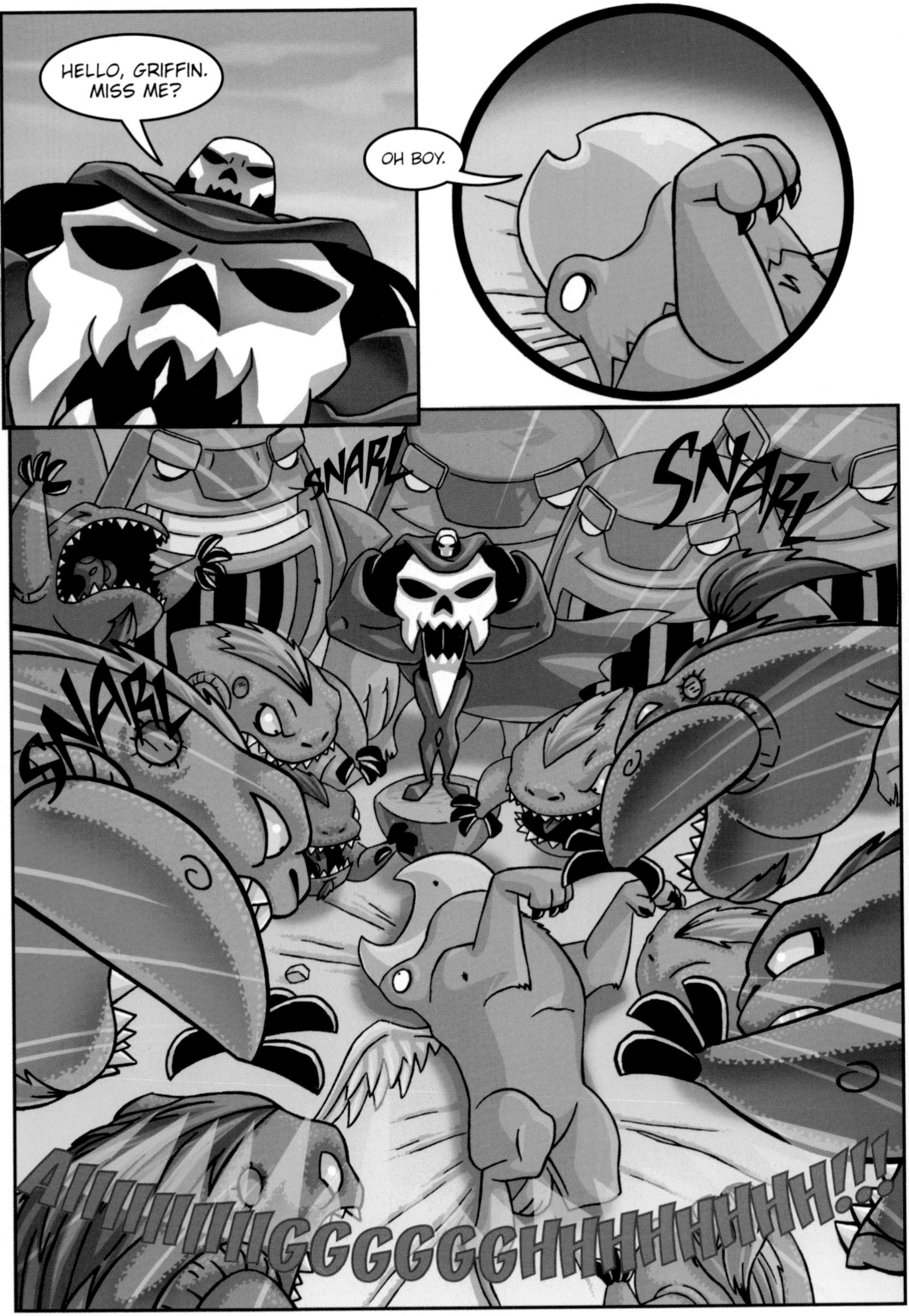
HELLO, GRIFFIN. MISS ME?
OH BOY.
SNARL
SNARL
SNARL
AIIIIIIIIGGGGGGHHHHHHHHH!!!

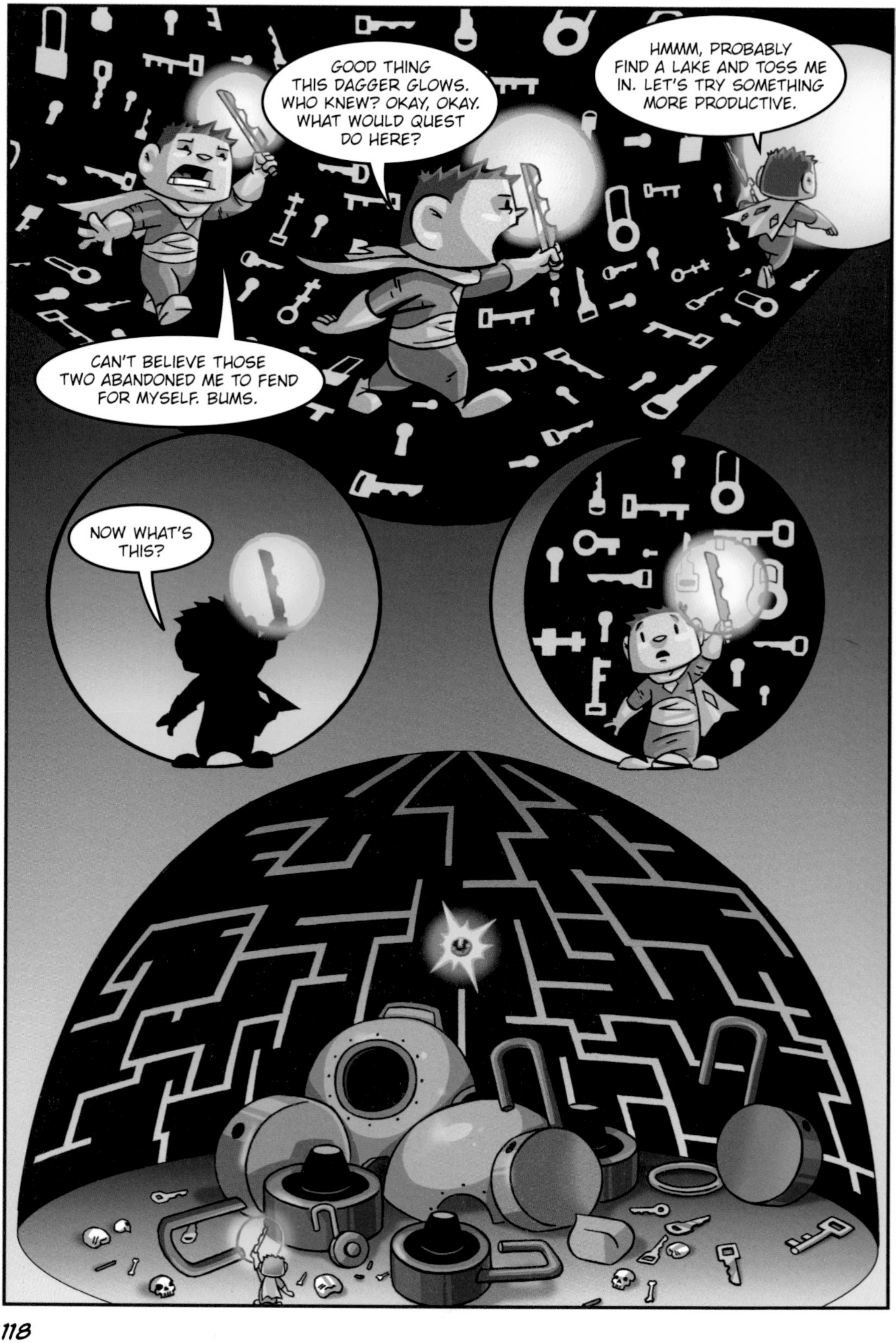
GOOD THING THIS DAGGER GLOWS. WHO KNEW? OKAY, OKAY. WHAT WOULD QUEST DO HERE?
HMMM, PROBABLY FIND A LAKE AND TOSS ME IN. LET'S TRY SOMETHING MORE PRODUCTIVE.
CAN'T BELIEVE THOSE TWO ABANDONED ME TO FEND FOR MYSELF. BUMS.
NOW WHAT'S THIS?

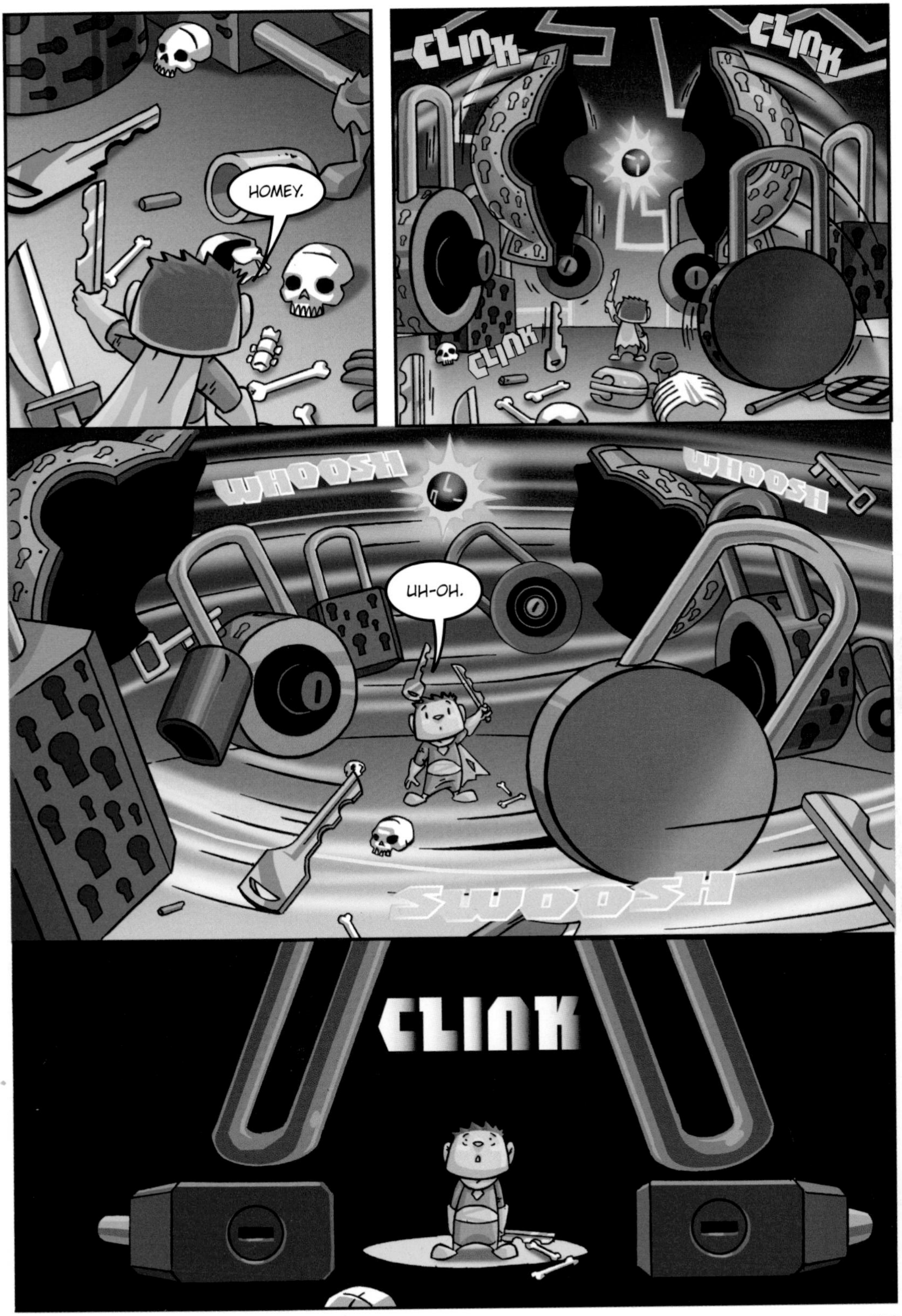
HOMEY.
CLINK
CLINK
CLINK
WHOOSH
WHOOSH
UH-OH.
SWOOSH
CLINK

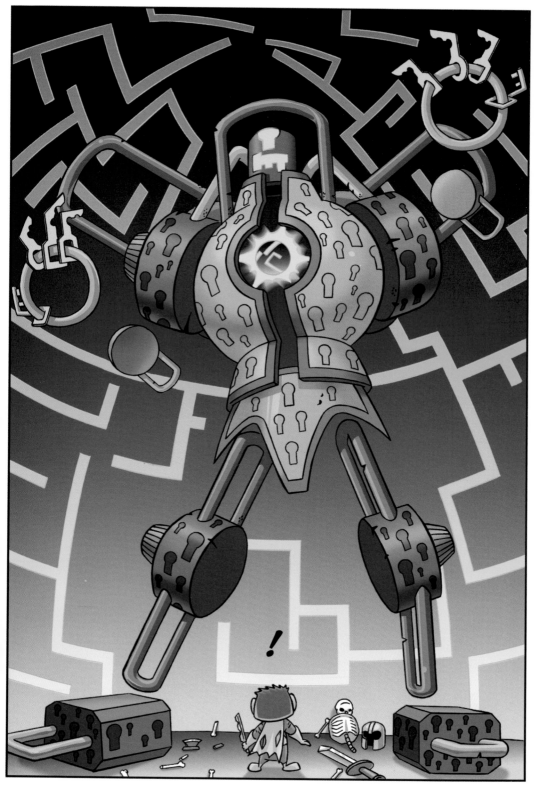

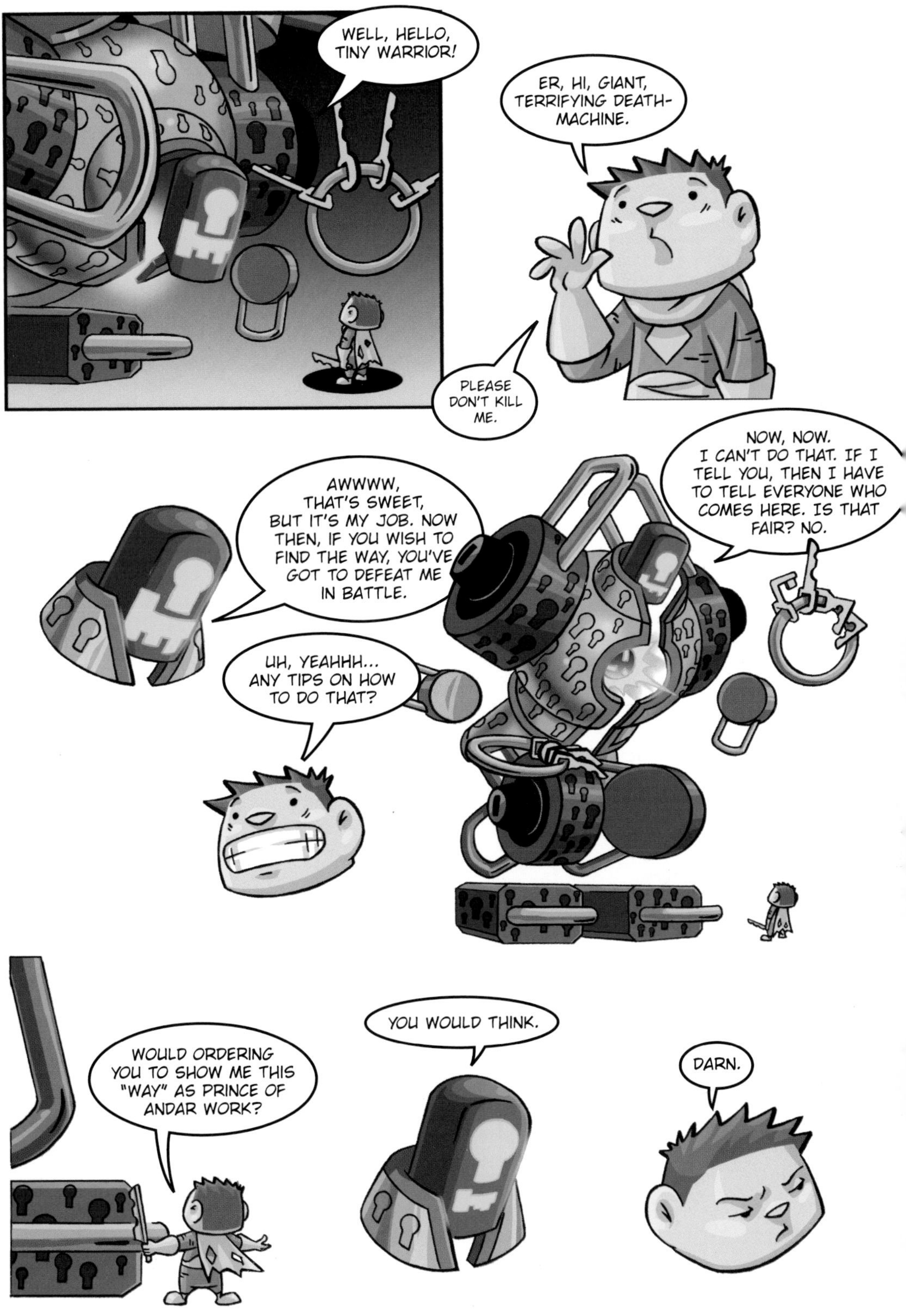
WELL, HELLO, TINY WARRIOR!
ER, HI, GIANT, TERRIFYING DEATH-MACHINE.
PLEASE DON'T KILL ME.
AWWWW, THAT'S SWEET, BUT IT'S MY JOB. NOW THEN, IF YOU WISH TO FIND THE WAY, YOU'VE GOT TO DEFEAT ME IN BATTLE.
UH, YEAHHH... ANY TIPS ON HOW TO DO THAT?
NOW, NOW. I CAN'T DO THAT. IF I TELL YOU, THEN I HAVE TO TELL EVERYONE WHO COMES HERE. IS THAT FAIR? NO.
WOULD ORDERING YOU TO SHOW ME THIS "WAY" AS PRINCE OF ANDAR WORK?
YOU WOULD THINK.
DARN.

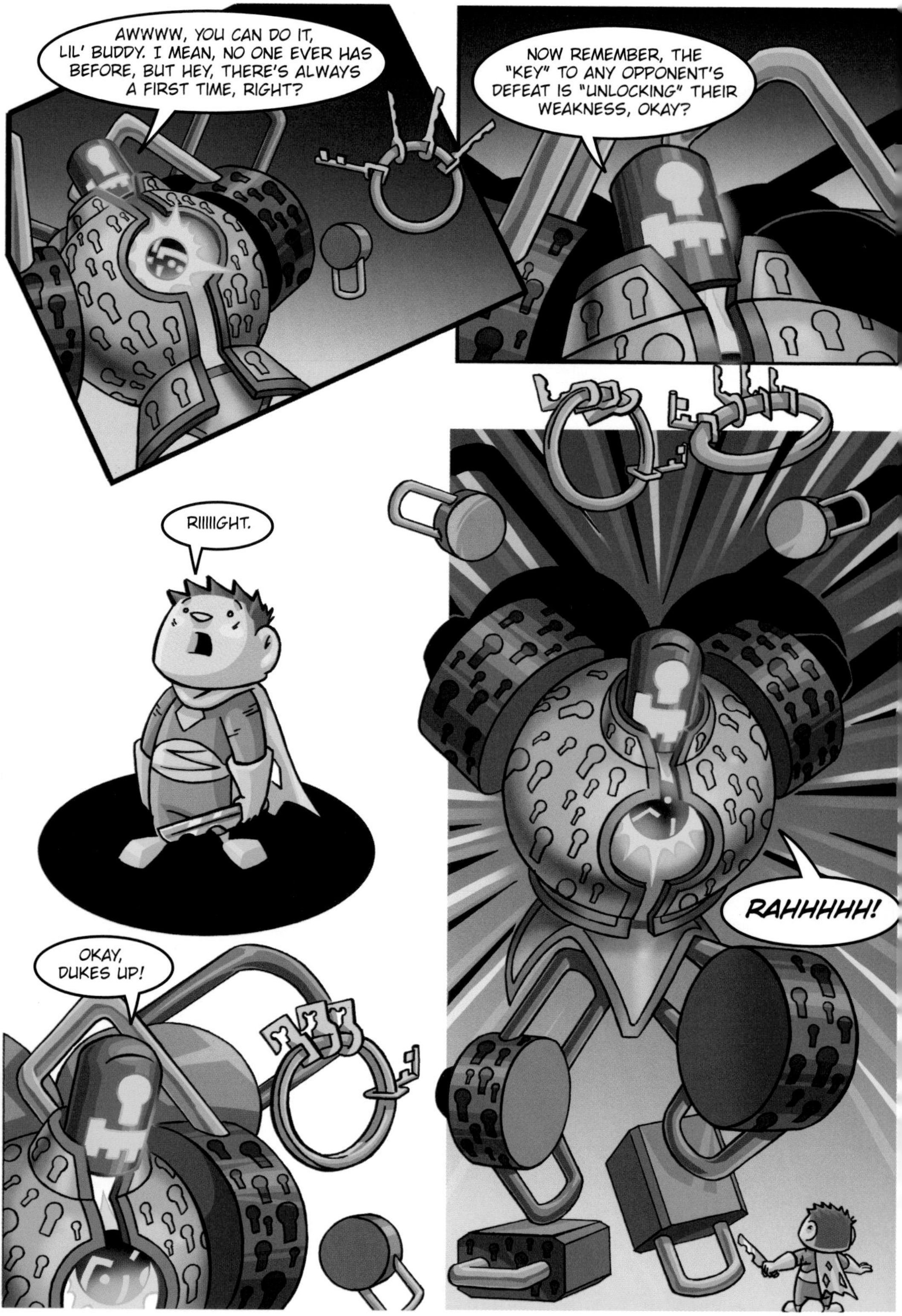
AWWWW, YOU CAN DO IT, LIL' BUDDY. I MEAN, NO ONE EVER HAS BEFORE, BUT HEY, THERE'S ALWAYS A FIRST TIME, RIGHT?
NOW REMEMBER, THE "KEY" TO ANY OPPONENT'S DEFEAT IS "UNLOCKING" THEIR WEAKNESS, OKAY?
RIIIIIGHT.
RAHHHHH!
OKAY, DUKES UP!

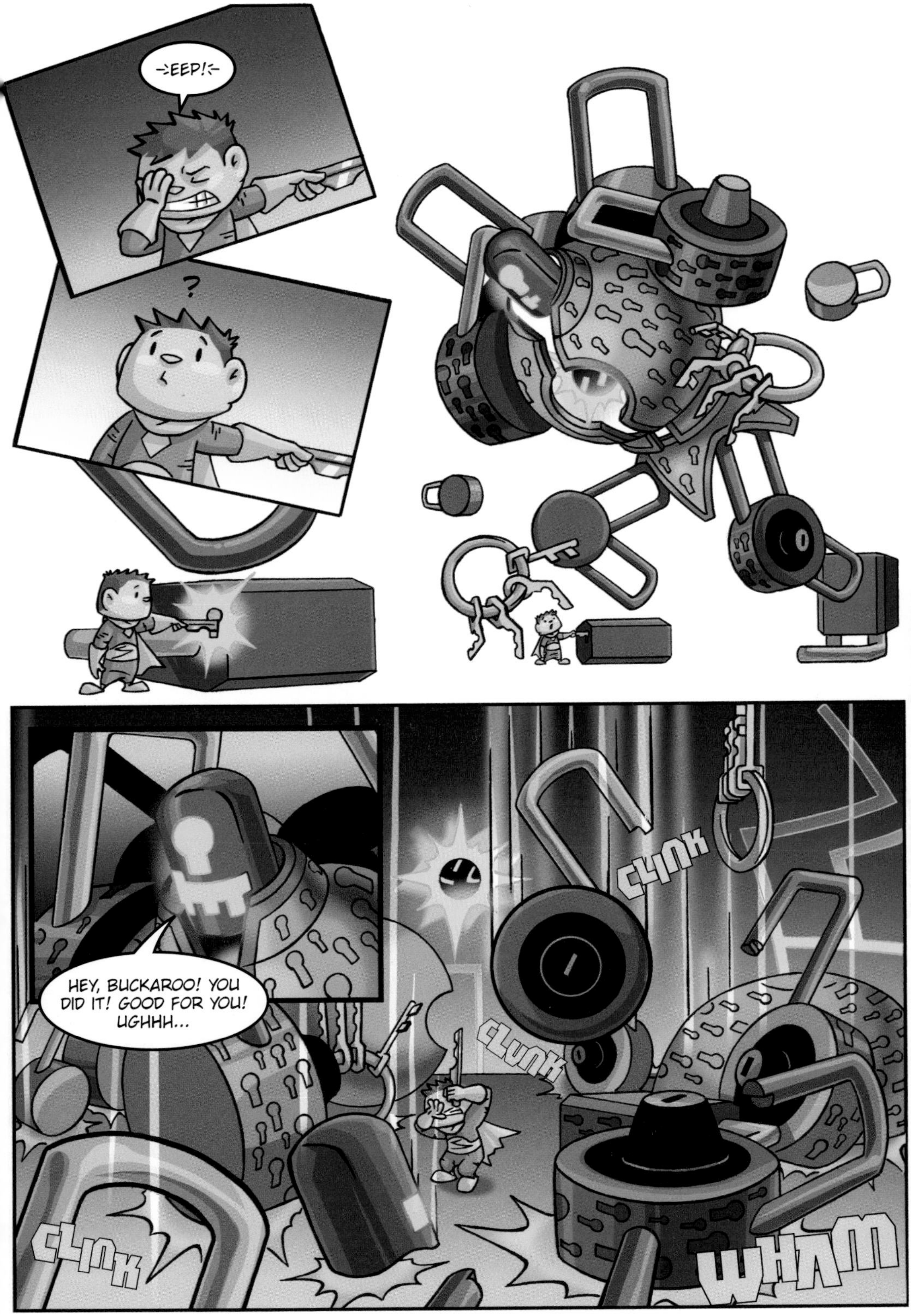
EEP!
?
HEY, BUCKAROO! YOU DID IT! GOOD FOR YOU! UGHHH...
CLINK
CLUNK
CLINK
WHAM

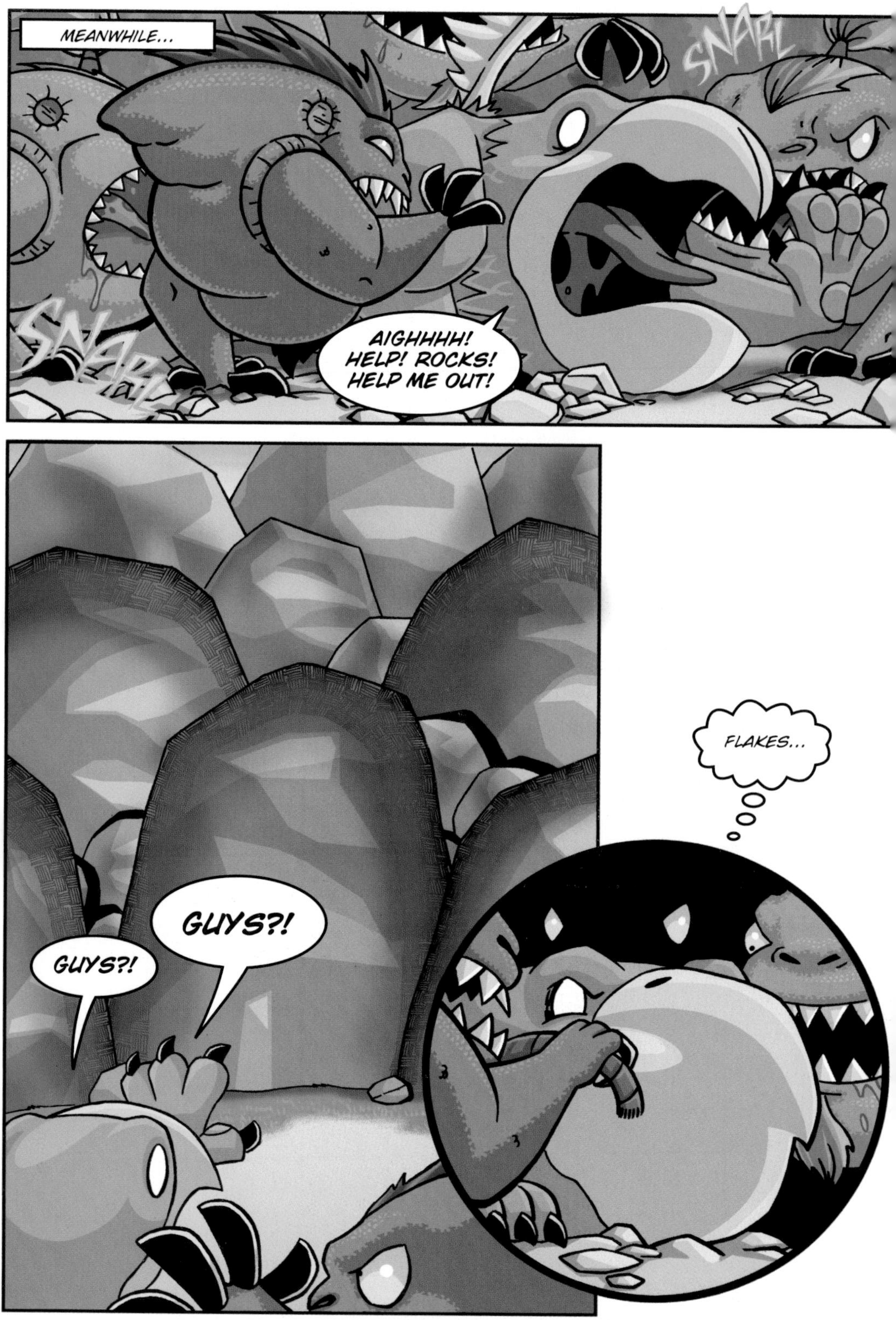

MEANWHILE...
SNARL
AIGHHHH! HELP! ROCKS! HELP ME OUT!
SNARL
FLAKES...
GUYS?!
GUYS?!

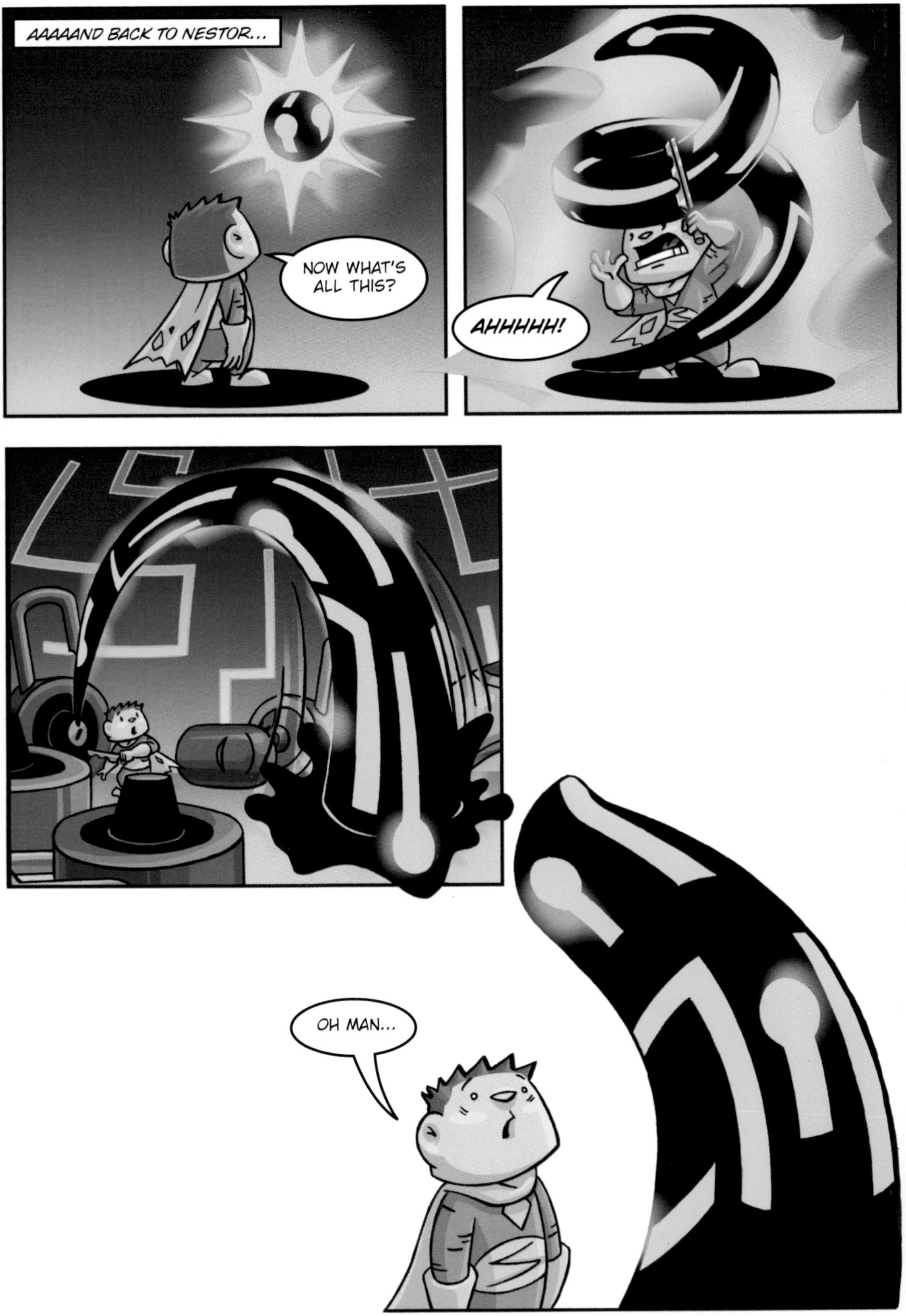
AAAAAND BACK TO NESTOR...
NOW WHAT'S ALL THIS?
AHHHHH!
OH MAN...

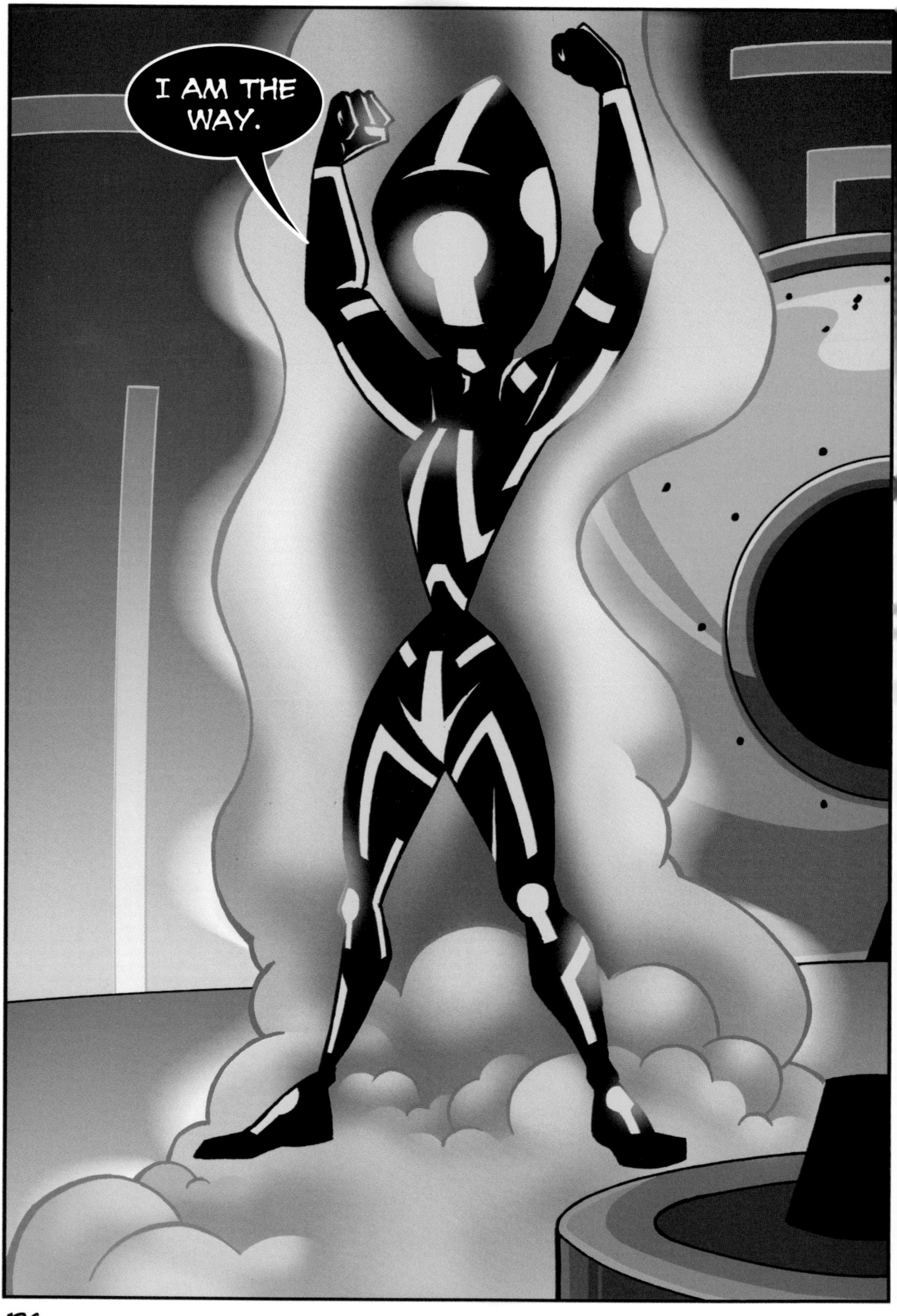
I AM THE WAY.

WHAT DO YOU MEAN, "I AM THE WAY"?

ALRIGHTY THEN. HOW DO I GET OUT OF HERE?

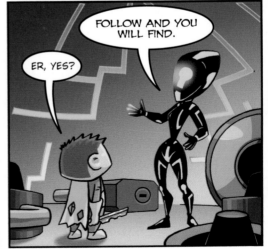
FOLLOW AND YOU WILL FIND.

ER, YES?

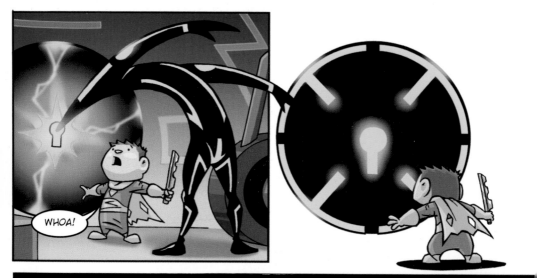

WHOA!

W-WHAT ARE YOU?

I AM THE WAY.

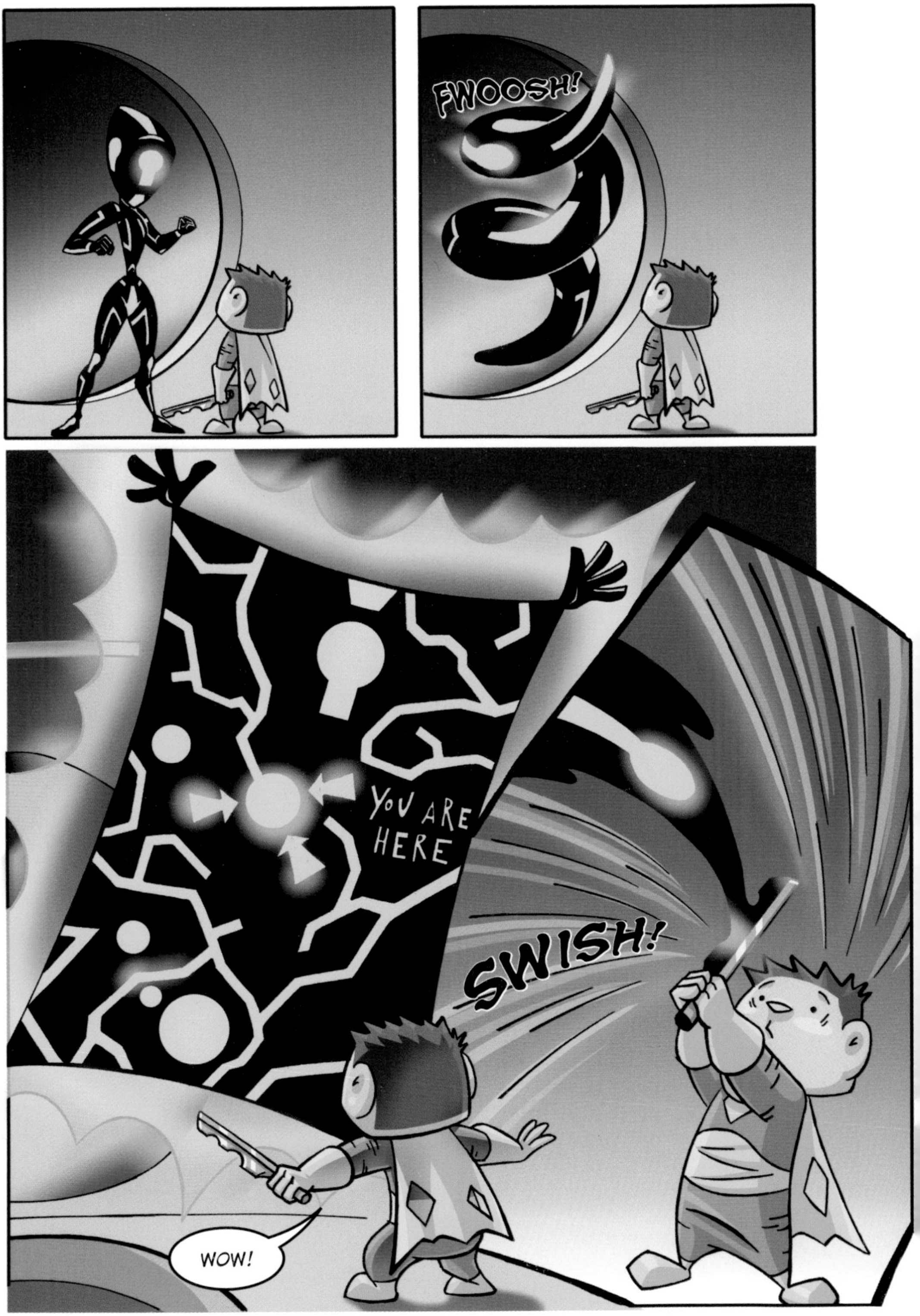
FWOOSH!
YOU ARE HERE
SWISH!
WOW!

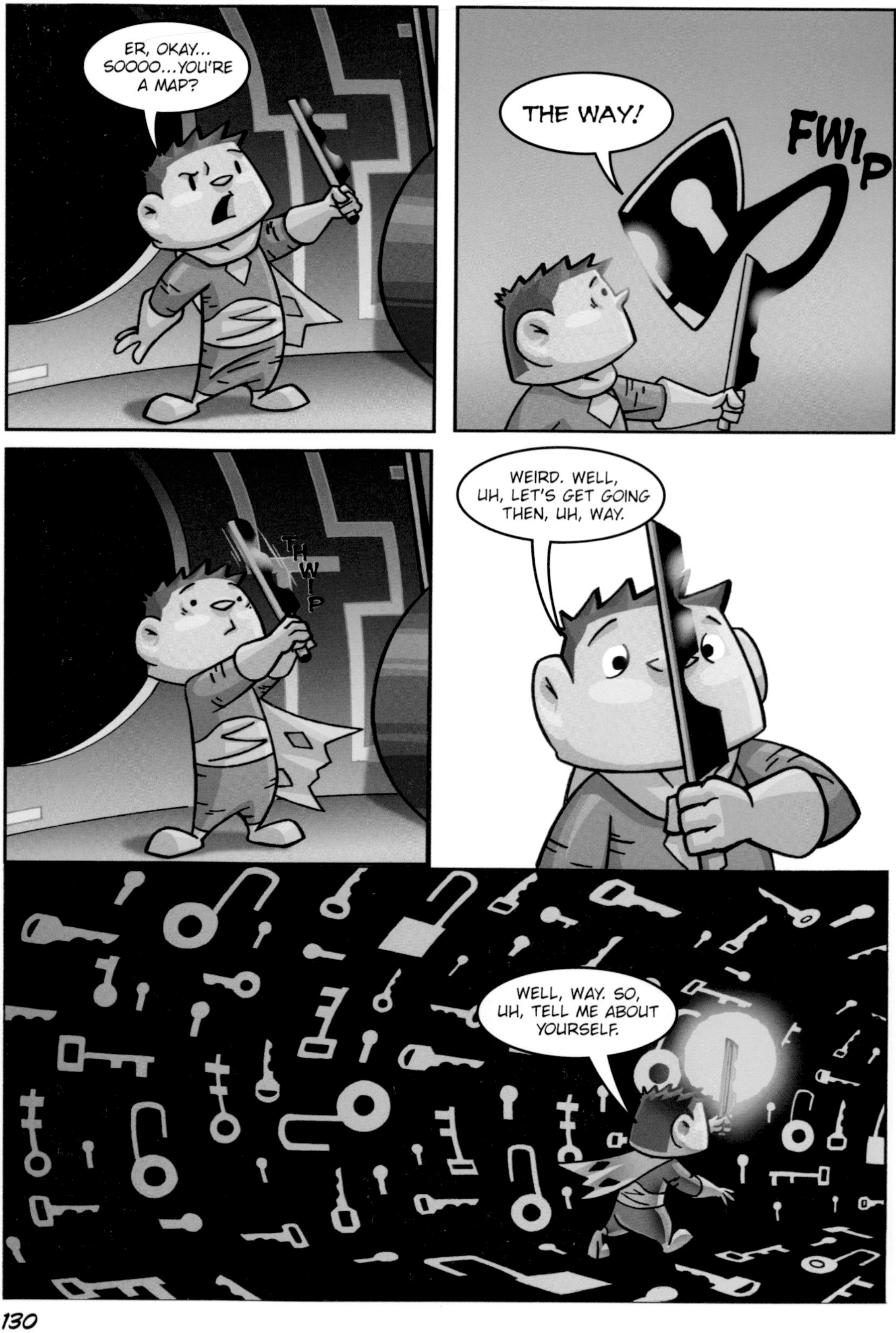
ER, OKAY... SOOOO...YOU'RE A MAP?
THE WAY!
FWIP
THWIP
WEIRD. WELL, UH, LET'S GET GOING THEN, UH, WAY.
WELL, WAY. SO, UH, TELL ME ABOUT YOURSELF.

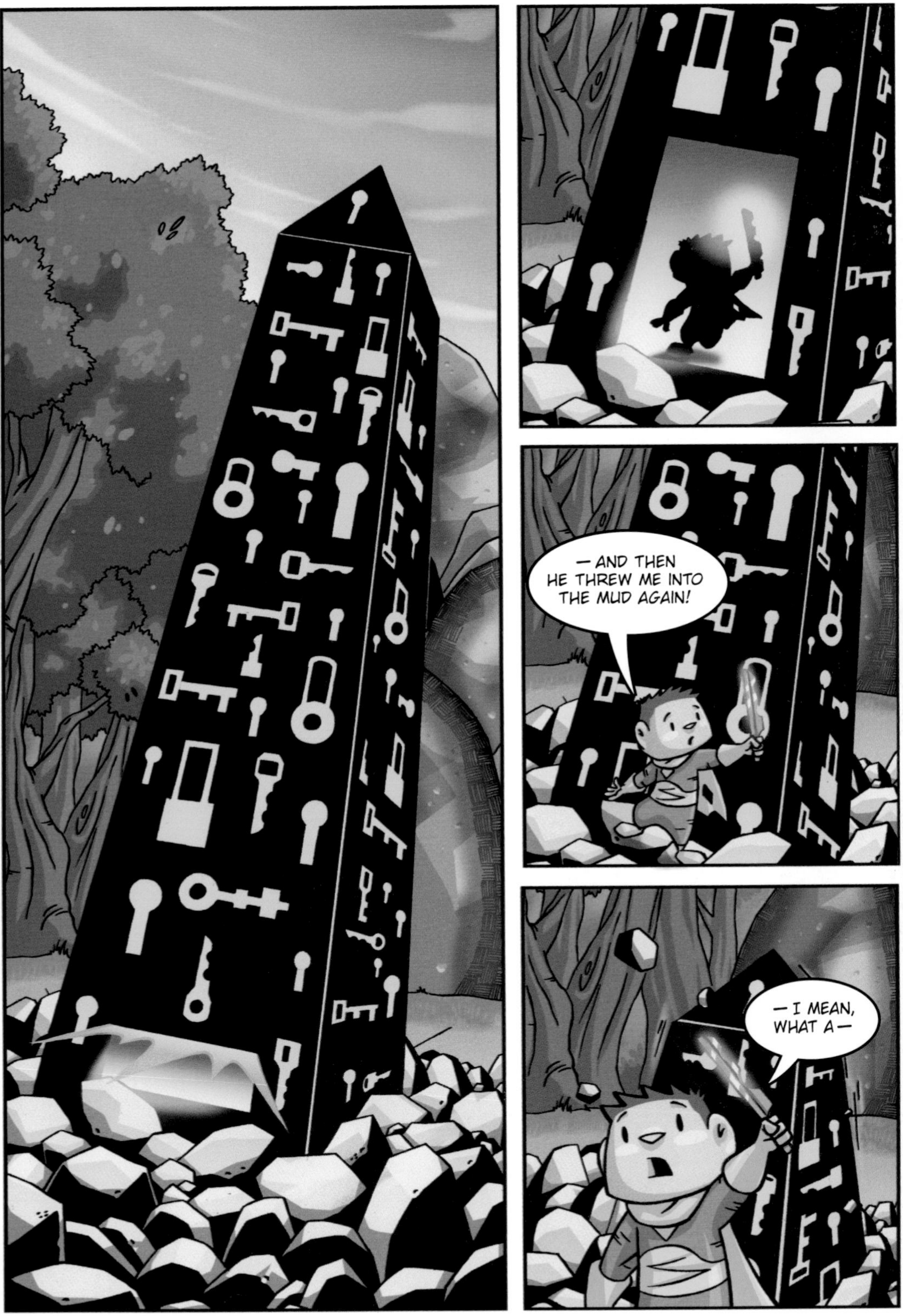
—AND THEN HE THREW ME INTO THE MUD AGAIN!
—I MEAN, WHAT A—

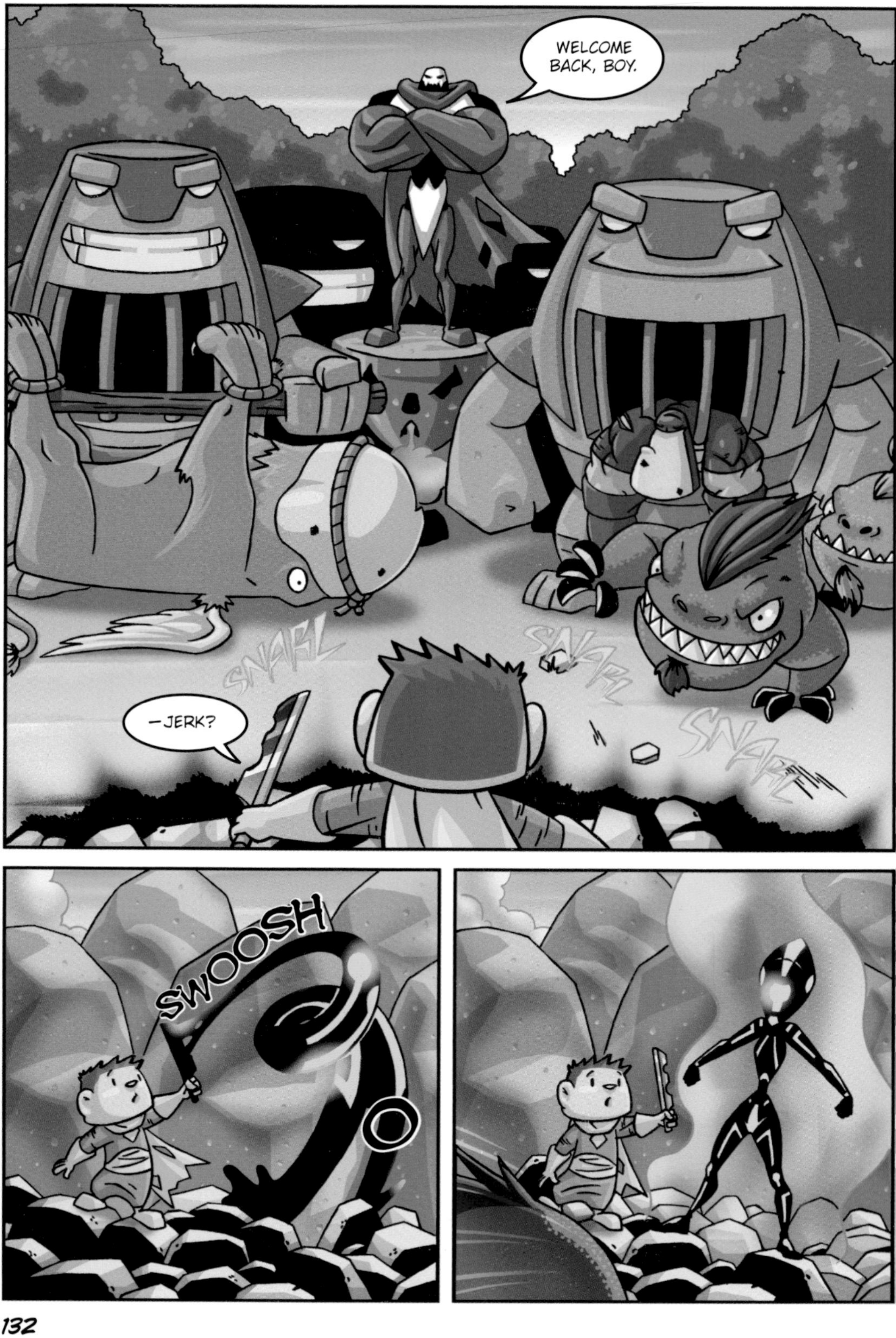
WELCOME BACK, BOY.
SNARL
SNARL
SNARL
—JERK?
SWOOSH

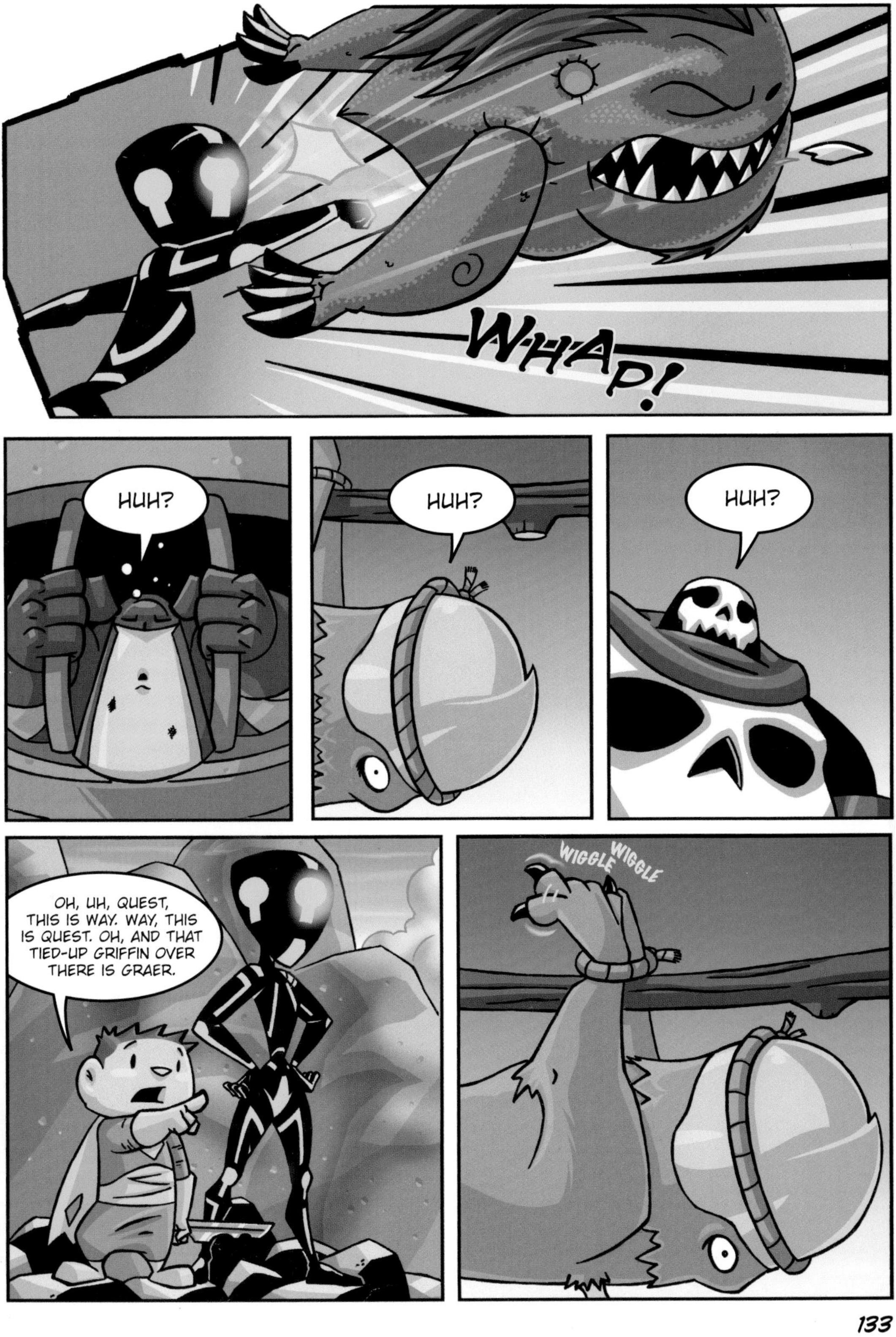
WHAP!
HUH?
HUH?
HUH?
OH, UH, QUEST, THIS IS WAY. WAY, THIS IS QUEST. OH, AND THAT TIED-UP GRIFFIN OVER THERE IS GRAER.
WIGGLE WIGGLE

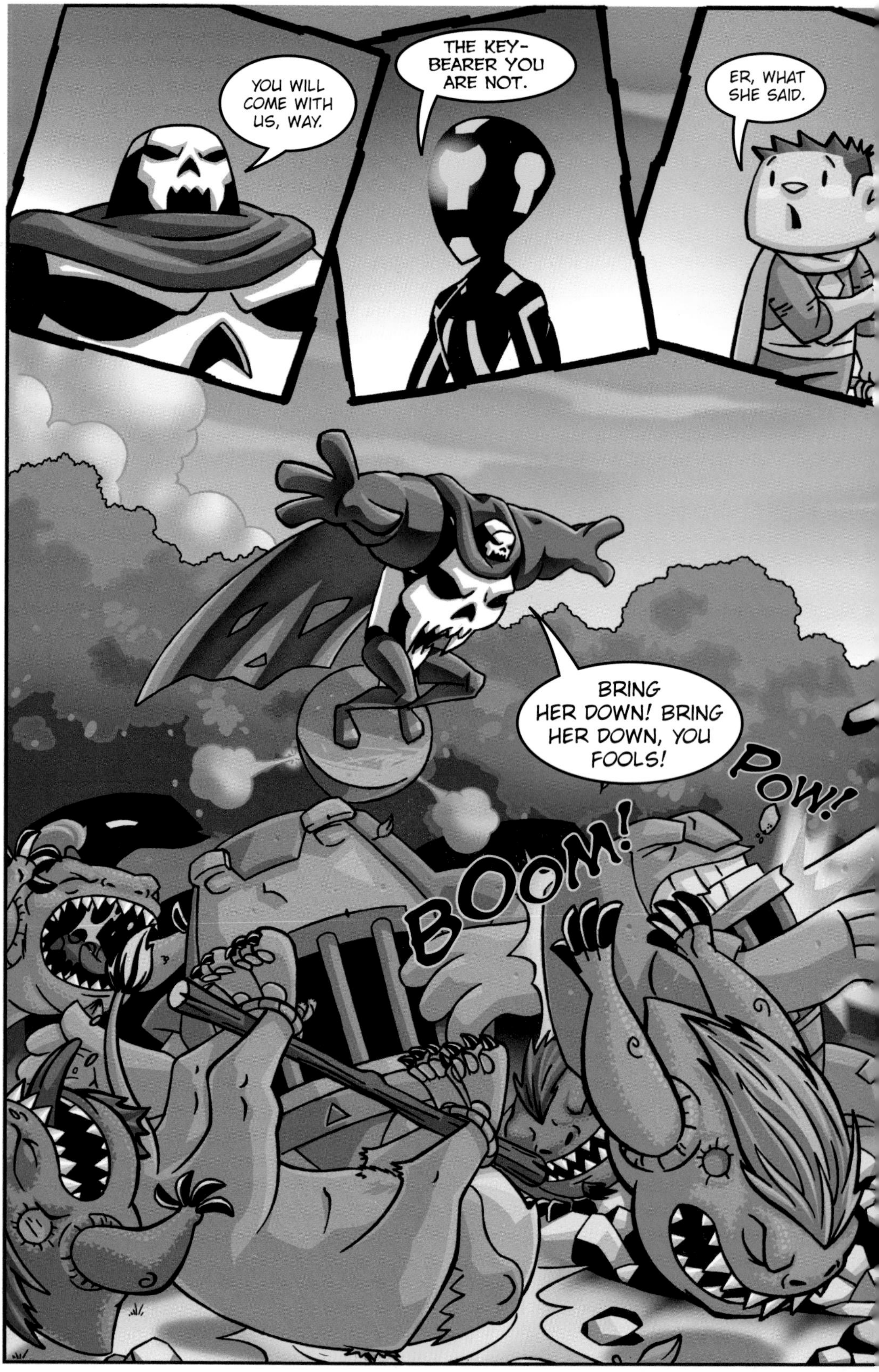
YOU WILL COME WITH US, WAY.
THE KEY-BEARER YOU ARE NOT.
ER, WHAT SHE SAID.
BRING HER DOWN! BRING HER DOWN, YOU FOOLS!
POW!
BOOM!

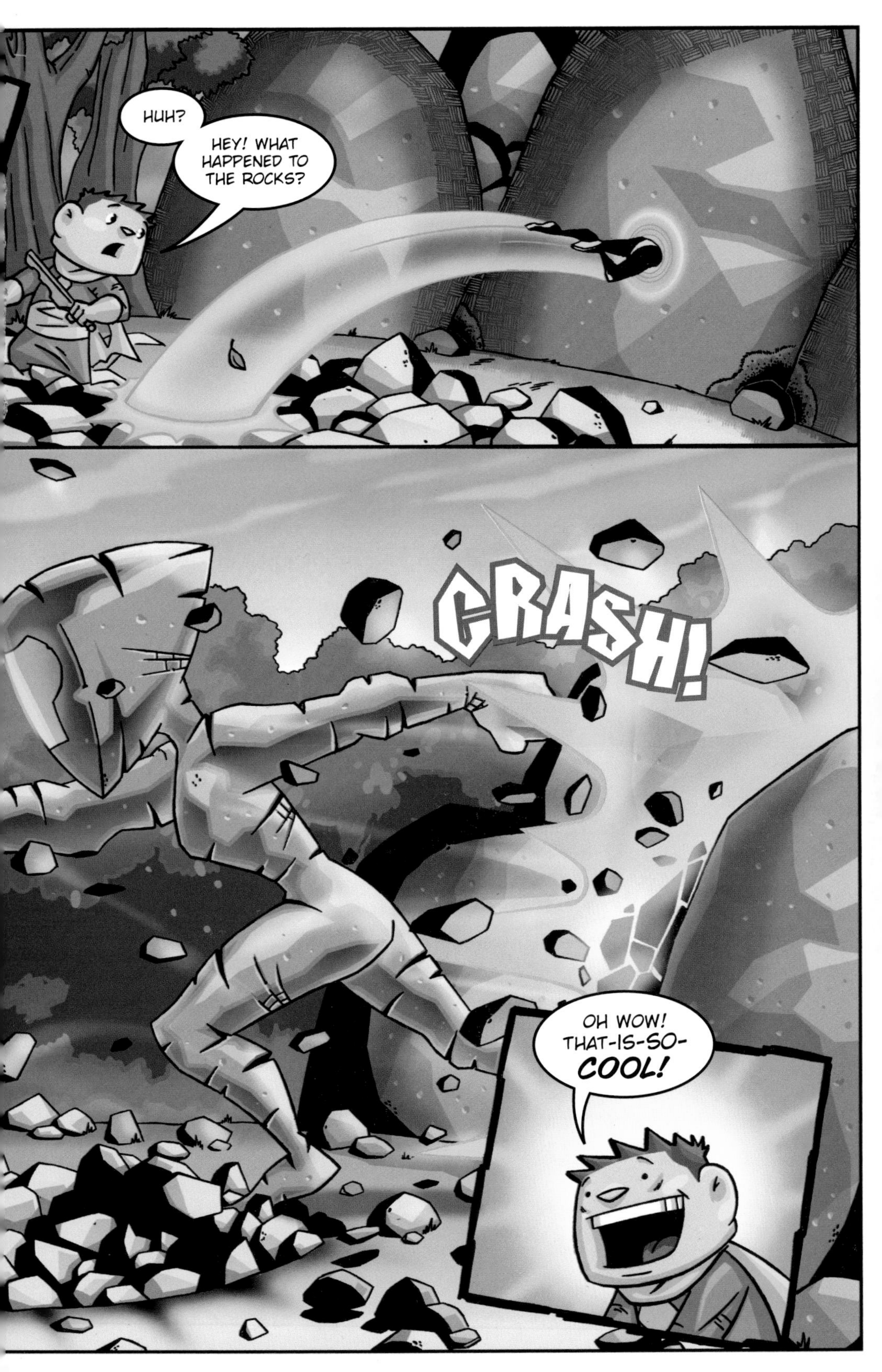
HUH?
HEY! WHAT HAPPENED TO THE ROCKS?
CRASH!
OH WOW! THAT-IS-SO-COOL!

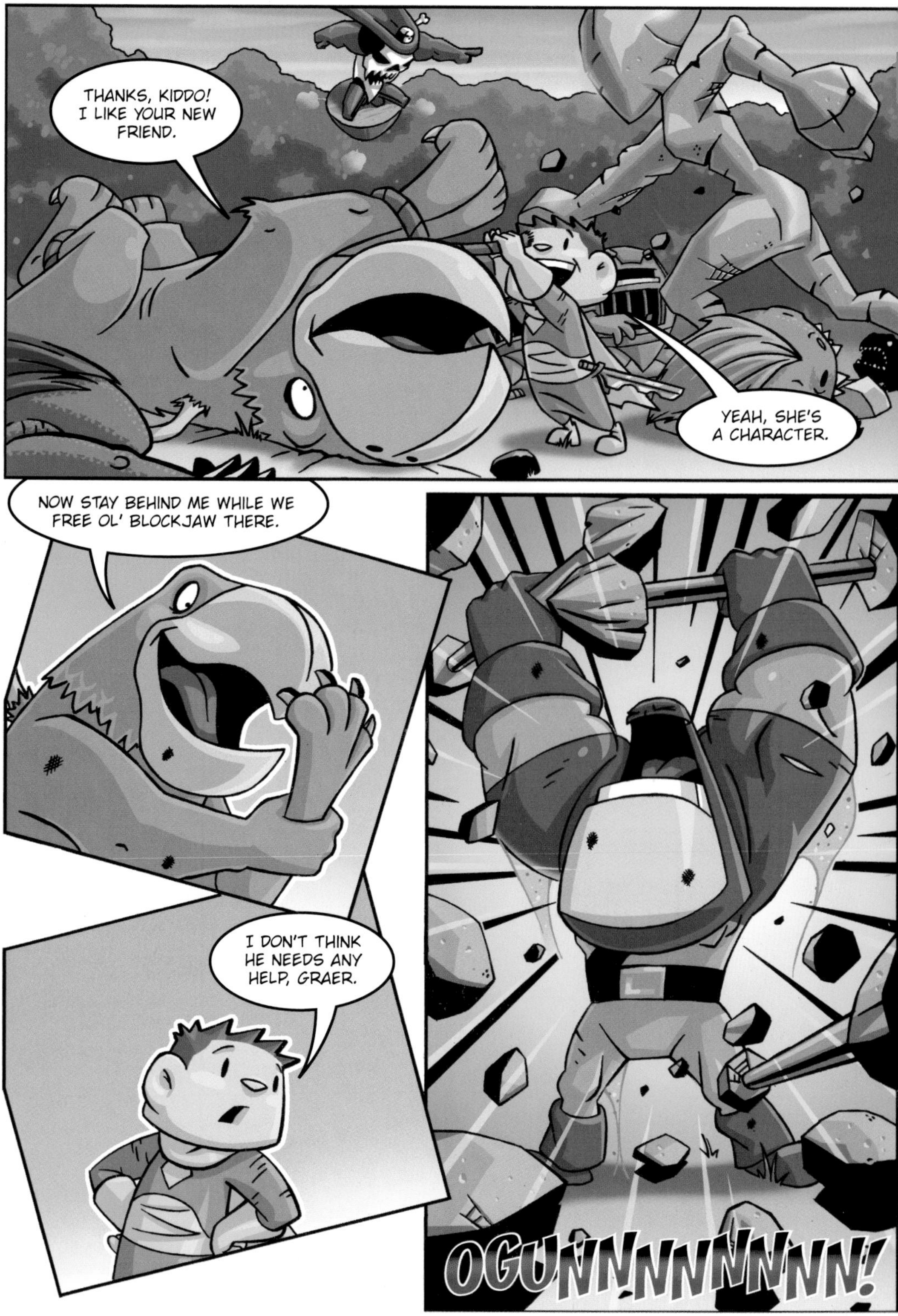
THANKS, KIDDO! I LIKE YOUR NEW FRIEND.
YEAH, SHE'S A CHARACTER.
NOW STAY BEHIND ME WHILE WE FREE OL' BLOCKJAW THERE.
I DON'T THINK HE NEEDS ANY HELP, GRAER.
OGUNNNNNNNNN!

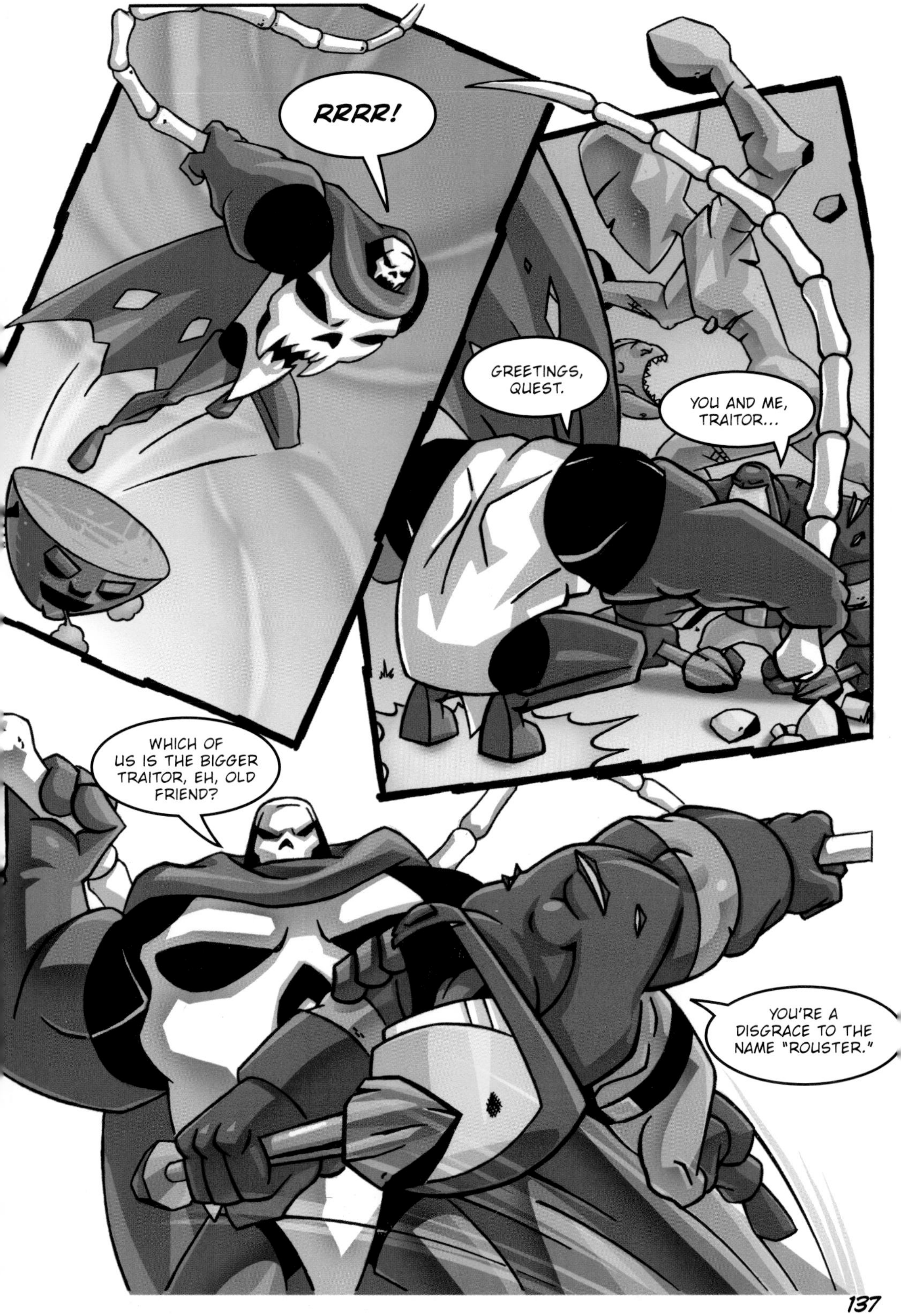
RRRR!
GREETINGS, QUEST.
YOU AND ME, TRAITOR...
WHICH OF US IS THE BIGGER TRAITOR, EH, OLD FRIEND?
YOU'RE A DISGRACE TO THE NAME "ROUSTER."

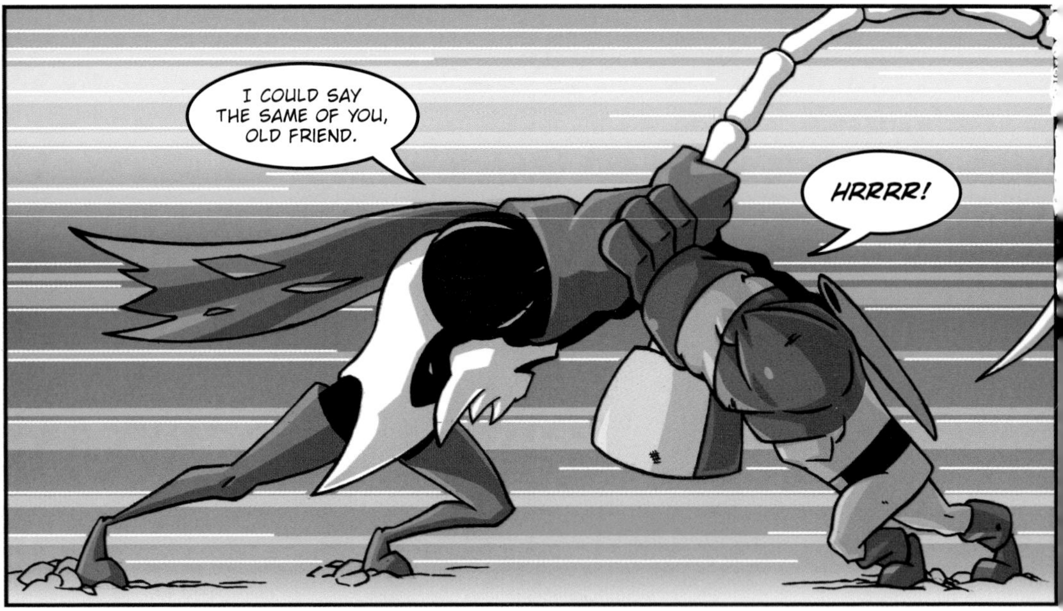
I COULD SAY THE SAME OF YOU, OLD FRIEND.
HRRRR!

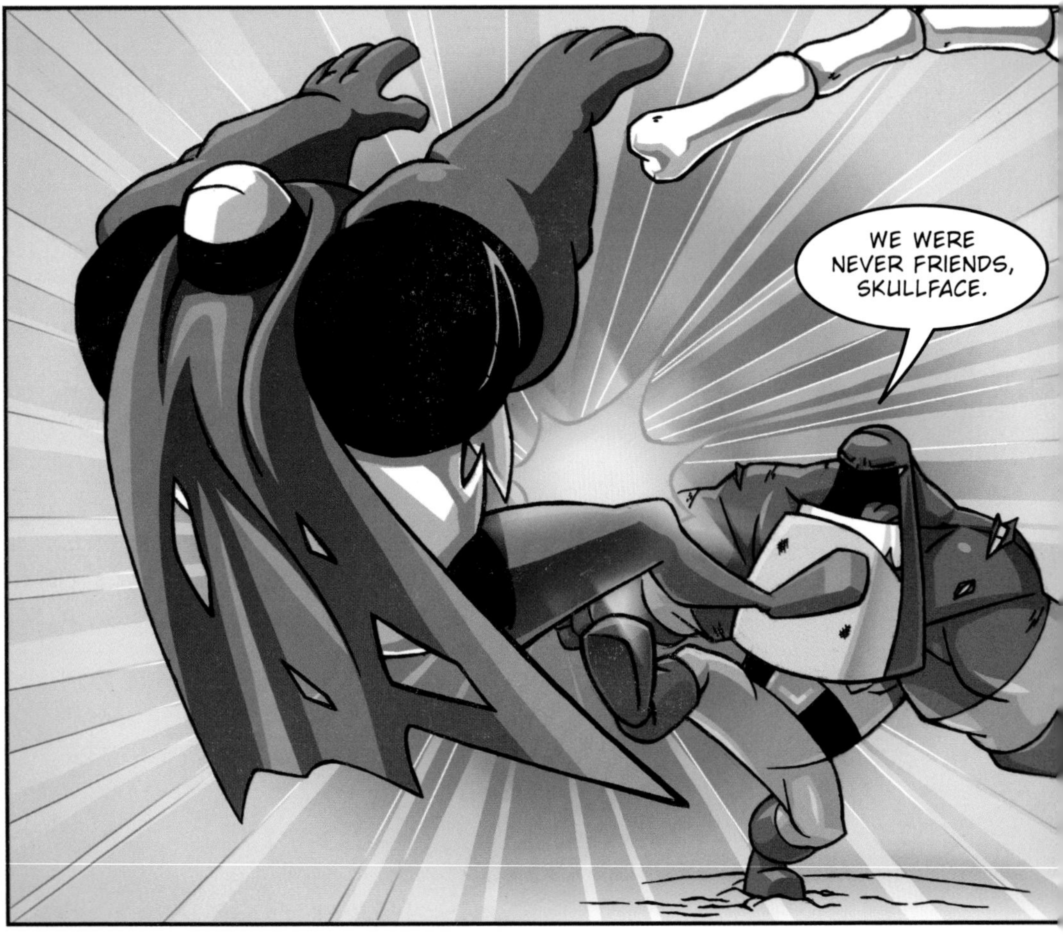
WE WERE NEVER FRIENDS, SKULLFACE.

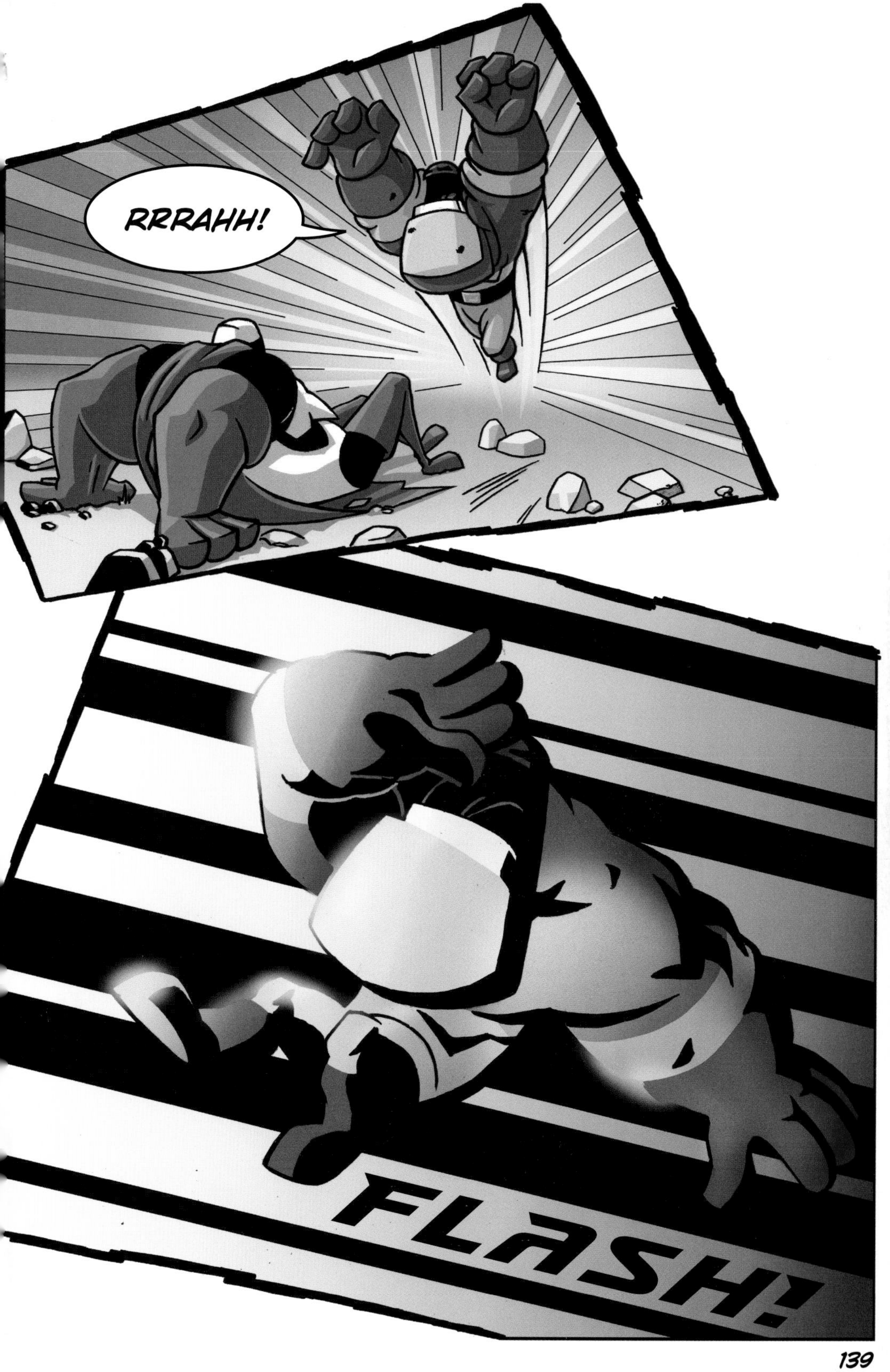
RRRAHH!
FLASH!

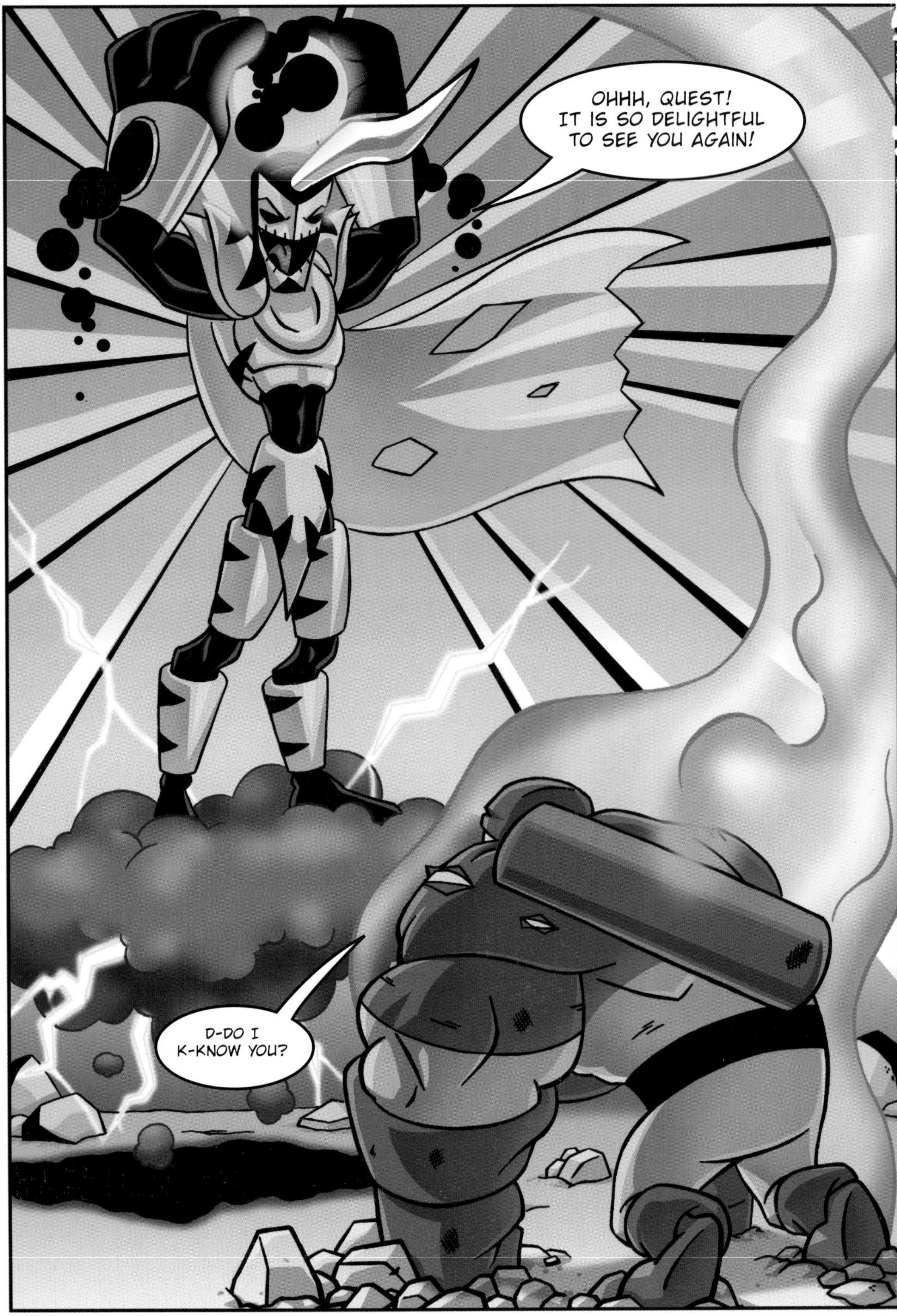
OHHH, QUEST!
IT IS SO DELIGHTFUL
TO SEE YOU AGAIN!
D-DO I
K-KNOW YOU?

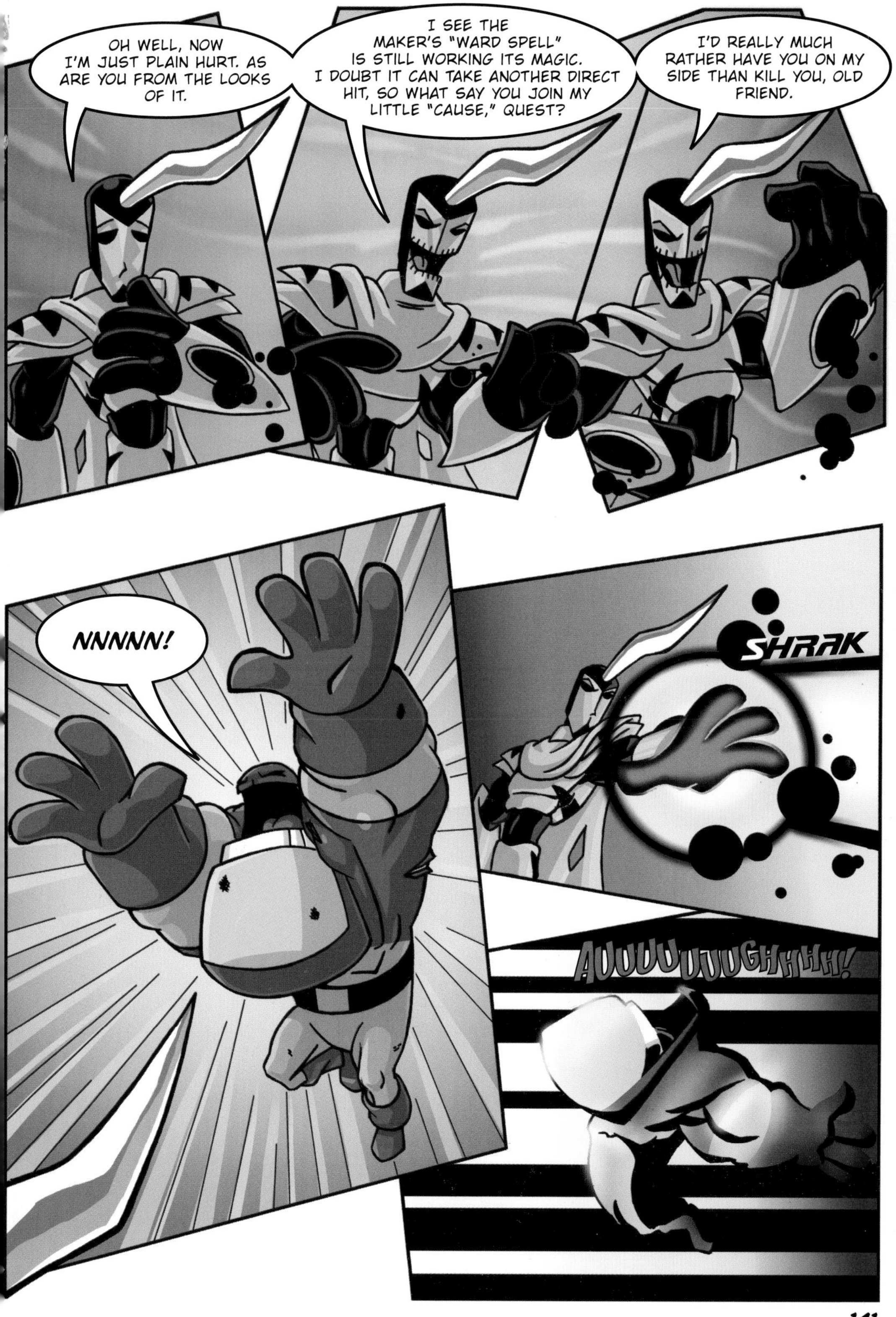
OH WELL, NOW I'M JUST PLAIN HURT. AS ARE YOU FROM THE LOOKS OF IT.
I SEE THE MAKER'S "WARD SPELL" IS STILL WORKING ITS MAGIC. I DOUBT IT CAN TAKE ANOTHER DIRECT HIT, SO WHAT SAY YOU JOIN MY LITTLE "CAUSE," QUEST?
I'D REALLY MUCH RATHER HAVE YOU ON MY SIDE THAN KILL YOU, OLD FRIEND.
NNNNN!
SHRAK
AUUUUUUUGHHHH!

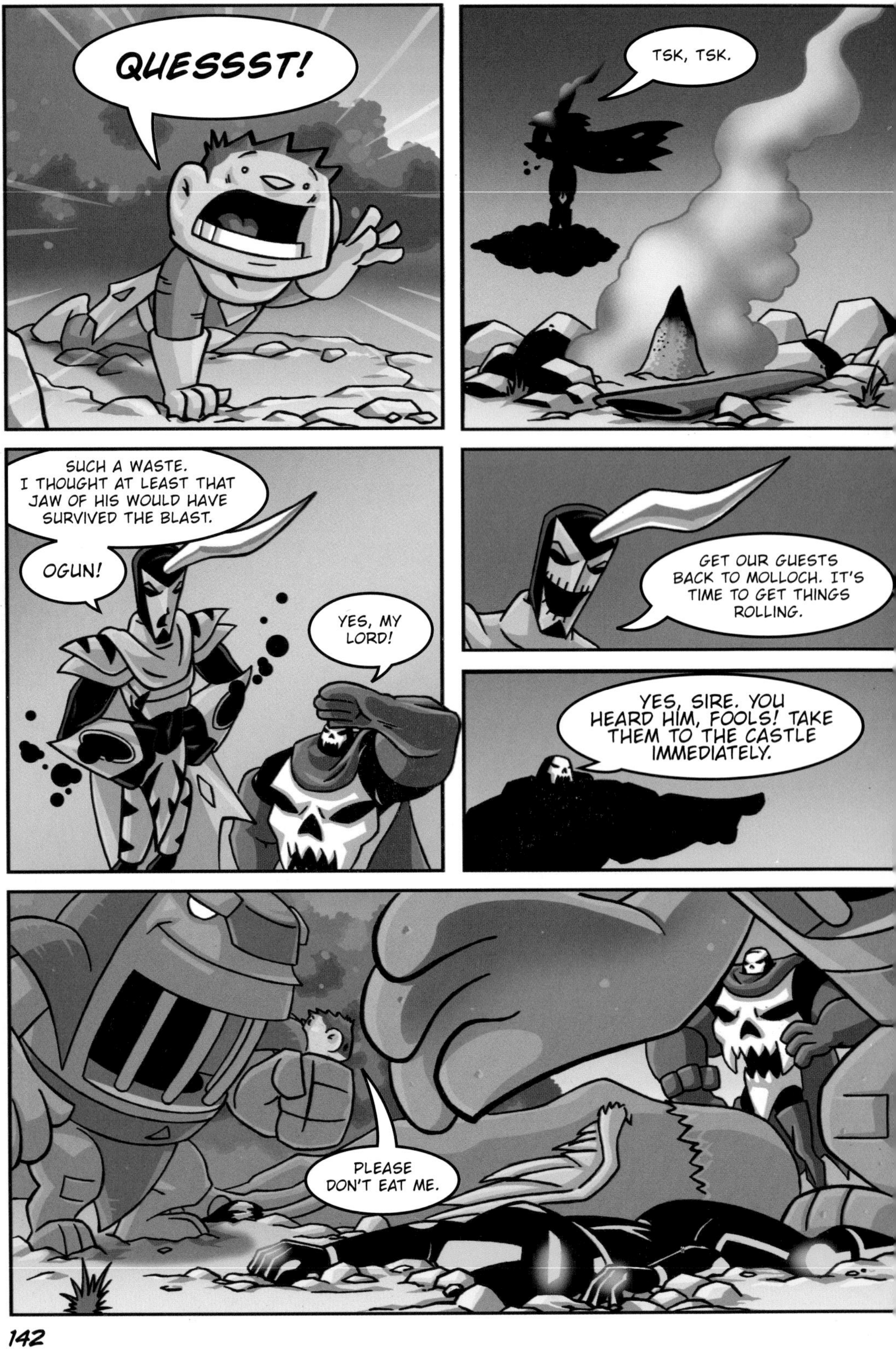
QUESSST!
TSK, TSK.
SUCH A WASTE. I THOUGHT AT LEAST THAT JAW OF HIS WOULD HAVE SURVIVED THE BLAST.
OGUN!
YES, MY LORD!
GET OUR GUESTS BACK TO MOLLOCH. IT'S TIME TO GET THINGS ROLLING.
YES, SIRE. YOU HEARD HIM, FOOLS! TAKE THEM TO THE CASTLE IMMEDIATELY.
PLEASE DON'T EAT ME.

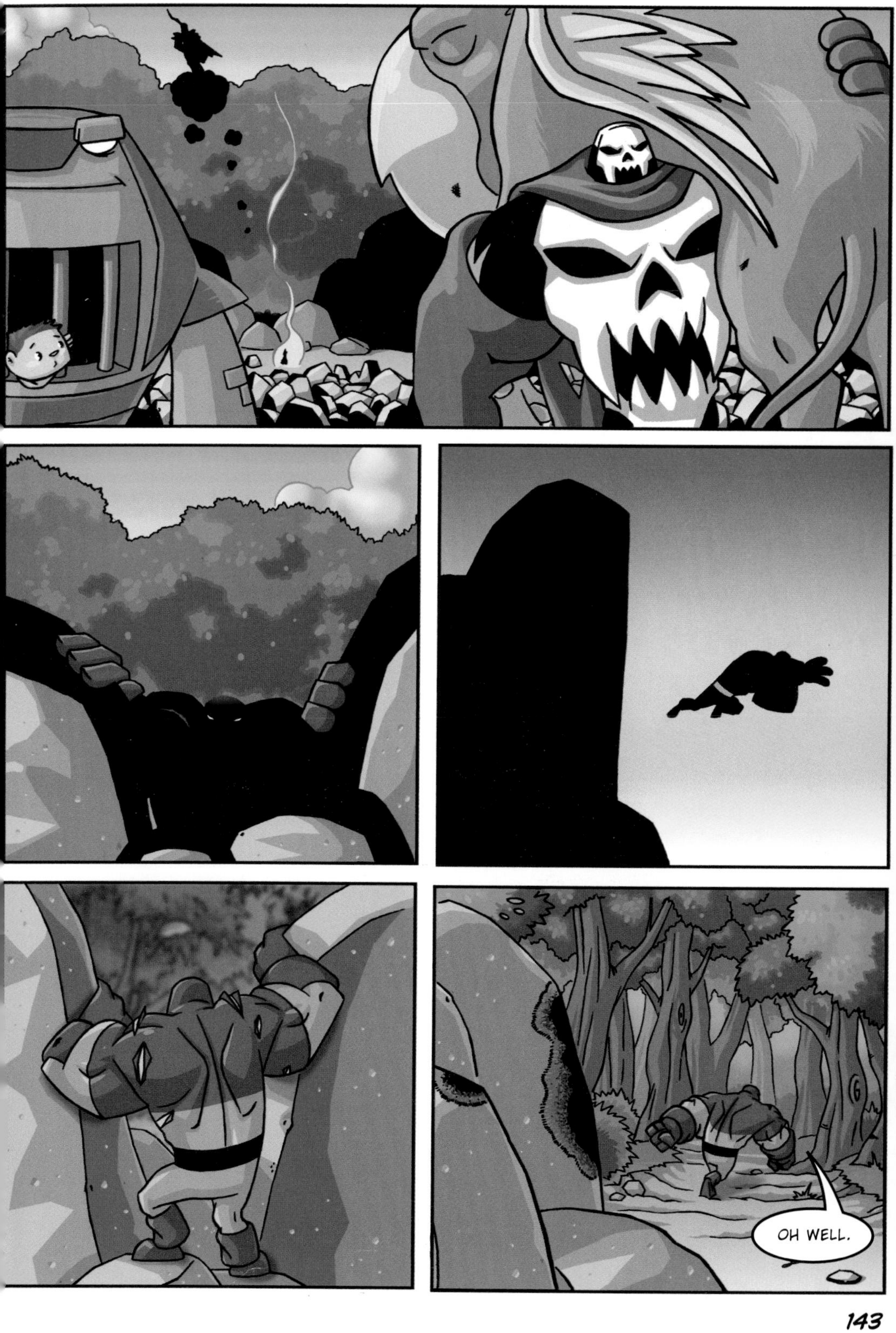
OH WELL.

JASON T. KRUSE
WRITER, ARTIST, CREATOR

SHANNON ERIC DENTON
CREATIVE CONSULTANT

YOUNG KIM
COLORIST

ABIGAIL BLACKMAN
LETTERING

YEN PRESS
HACHETTE BOOK GROUP
237 PARK AVENUE, NEW YORK, NY 10017

VISIT US ON THE WEB AT WWW.YENPRESS.COM
AND WWW.HACHETTEBOOKGROUP.COM.

YEN PRESS IS AN IMPRINT OF *HACHETTE BOOK GROUP, INC.*
THE *YEN PRESS* NAME AND LOGO ARE TRADEMARKS OF *HACHETTE BOOK GROUP, INC.*

FIRST EDITION: *DECEMBER 2008*

ISBN-13: 978-0-7595-2889-5

10 9 8 7 6 5 4 3 2 1

RRD-C

Yen Press™